GW00467821

A DAUGHTER'S PROMISE

ANN BENNETT

Andaman Press

Second Edition 2022
The moral right of the author has been asserted.

No part of this publication may be reproduced, stored in a retrieval system, or transmitted in any form or by any means without the prior permission in writing of the publisher, except in the case of brief quotations embodied in critical reviews and certain other non-commercial uses permitted by the copyright law.

This is a work of fiction. All characters and events in this publication, other than those clearly in the public domain, are fictitious and any resemblance to real persons, living or dead, is purely coincidental.

Copyright © 2019 Ann Bennett
All rights reserved.
Cover design: Coverkitchen
All Enquiries to: andamanpress@gmail.com

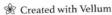 Created with Vellum

PROLOGUE

Rangoon 8th August 1988
Louise

I t was just before sunrise when Louise felt her way down the uneven staircase that led from the apartment to the street. She steadied herself with one hand against the grubby wall, her eyes straining to keep sight of Zeya's slim shoulders as he moved down the stairs ahead of her. At the bottom she waited as he fumbled with the lock on the dilapidated front door and prised it open.

The clammy heat of the Rangoon morning engulfed them as they stepped outside. Zeya paused in front of the building. Louise could just make out the gleam of his eyes in the gathering light as he turned to peer at her face.

'You quite sure you want to come?' His voice was brittle with anxiety.

'Of course. We agreed, didn't we?'

He hesitated. 'It could be dangerous.'

'I know that. You said so before,' she said quickly, her eyes searching for his in the gloom.

'I don't think you understand...'

'But you said you wanted me to come. Why change your mind now?' She stopped and stood facing him, her hands on her hips.

He looked away and hung his head, his black hair flopping over his eyes.

'You know why,' he whispered.

She touched his shoulder and moved towards him.

'It doesn't change anything about today,' she said, her voice soft, her face close to his. 'I'm coming with you. Let's go, shall we? The others will be waiting.'

Zeya held her gaze for a long moment. Then he shrugged and turned. He started to stride away from the house, his head down.

The street was silent and empty. No lights shone from the windows of the tall tenement blocks that flanked the pavements. A couple of stray dogs asleep beside a pile of rubbish, stirred and eyed them lazily as they passed. Louise stumbled on some broken paving stones as she struggled to keep up with Zeya.

They reached the end of the narrow street and emerged onto Strand Road. The stench of the Rangoon River mingled with the rank smell of drains rose to meet them. They turned and walked along past the derelict go-downs in the direction of the city centre.

Soon the crumbling white stucco façade of the Strand Hotel loomed ahead with its colonnaded entrance. Louise noticed there were lights on in some of the upstairs windows. A uniformed doorman standing between the pillars of the porch eyed them passively as they approached. A shiver went through Louise, despite the heat. Was it only a week since she'd been a guest there in that faded room on the fourth floor? It felt like a different lifetime.

Beyond the Strand they turned inland from the river, past the crumbling edifice of the old Customs House. They began to make their way up Phayre Street towards the city centre. The normally busy road was eerily traffic-free. Usually at this hour ruined buses would already be crawling along the road, packed with workers. Their absence was the first sign that this day was going to be different.

Hawkers and food sellers were setting up stalls on the wide pavements, the smoke from their fires hanging on the morning air. Despite her nerves about the day ahead, Louise felt a pang of hunger as the delicious aroma of baked roti reached her. Then for the first time, she noticed other people walking quietly and purposefully in the same direction, either singly or in small groups. She glanced at Zeya striding along beside her, dressed in his turquoise plaid longyi and crisp white shirt, his eyes fixed on the road, a frown of concentration on his face. She felt a fresh wave of uncertainty. *I don't really know him at all. I don't know any of them. What on earth am I doing here?*

She quickly banished the thought and carried on walking; past the once-grand colonial buildings now crumbling with age and neglect; bank headquarters, trading houses, the old telegraph office. These were buildings that only a few days ago she had first seen as a naïve tourist. The road had been quiet that day, but now the pavements were thronging with people all moving in the same direction.

At the junction with Merchant Street Zeya's three friends stood waiting for them, scanning the crowd with anxious eyes. Zeya paused long enough for a hasty greeting, then moved swiftly on, the three others falling into step beside them. The group made their way towards the City Hall with its Moorish arches and crenelated domes. The grey haze of the morning gradually lifted and Louise looked up to see the soft golden glow of the Sule Pagoda rising between the buildings at the end of the road.

The crowd gradually thickened as they got closer to the pagoda. They were pressed together now and Louise could feel the fine hairs on Zeya's arm brushing against hers as she walked,

his sweat mingling with her own. She glanced sideways at him
for reassurance as the bodies jostled them closer, but he seemed
unaware of her presence now. His face was taut with concentration, his focus on the march and on the day ahead. She looked
instead at the faces of his friends. The two girls, Myat Noe and
Yupar and the young man Nakaji. All young students she'd got to
know over the past few days. They were all staring in front of
them too and wore that identical tense expression. Louise could
almost feel the passion and excitement radiating from them all.

Fuelled by anger and determination, they moved forward.
Until now, the crowd had walked in dogged silence, but as they
neared the end of the road a lone voice suddenly went up;

'Daw Aye' 'Democracy,'

Immediately, Zeya and his friends joined in. *Daw Aye, Daw
Aye*, they chanted in unison and the air was filled with the words,
shouted from thousands of throats. They moved on, punching
the air, shouting the words again and again.

They soon reached the point where the road widened. On
one side was the City Hall and on the other the great Sule
Pagoda. Everyone came to a standstill where the roads converged
and the press of so many bodies meant it was impossible to move
forward. All the streets radiating out from the pagoda were
densely packed. Some people were still chanting, others held
home-made banners above their heads. Louise stood on tiptoe,
straining to see what was happening.

Someone was addressing the crowd from the pagoda. It was a
man on a podium with a microphone. Louise couldn't understand his words, but people in the crowd were chanting agree-
ment, cheering every word. She glanced at Zeya again and he was
looking back at her now with that huge endearing smile, his eyes
shining. She smiled back into his eyes and for the first time that
day she was glad she'd come.

At first she didn't hear the commotion behind her, but as she
strained her ears, listening out for any familiar words from the

speaker, she became aware of a dull rumble somewhere far behind. The mood of the crowd seemed to change. It dawned on her that what she could hear was the sound of engines.

Within seconds, people behind her were screaming. Then came the sound of gunfire. Shots ripped the air. Louise span round to look just as the first tank hove into view. The crowd was scattering in all directions as the faceless green vehicle cut a path through them. Her heart pounding, Louise started to move away. Then more shots were fired, indiscriminately, the great gun moving from side to side firing into the crowd. Fear sliced through her as two young men in front of her dropped to the ground, screaming, blood spurting from their wounds.

The tank was moving closer now and the friends had scattered. *Where the hell is Zeya?* She looked round for him in panic, but she knew she had to get out of the road. She began to run, swept along with the panicking crowd towards the nearest building; a covered market with arched entrances opening off the pavement. People ahead of her were pouring in through the archways, desperately seeking safety.

She had almost reached the shelter of the market when she heard more shots up ahead. Terror coursed through her now. Within seconds soldiers on foot had formed a line in front of the building. They were pushing people in the crowd back, stopping them entering the market. In panic she tried to turn round, but the inexorable motion of the crowd forced her forwards. Sharp elbows pushed her, bumped her in different directions. She tripped and almost fell, but somehow managed to stay upright. She was still being pushed forward.

Suddenly she was looking up into the face of a soldier. He stared down at her, a look of contempt in his black eyes, a sneer on his lips. She was close enough to smell his rank breath.

'*Kula,*' he said, and she felt his rough hand seize her arm. 'You come.'

He dragged her aside and pulled her through the crowd.

'Please! You can't do this,' but she knew her words were point-less. They were swallowed up in the clamour and chaos around her. Then he was dragging her through the crush of bodies and towards a side alley beside the market building. A line of soldiers guarded the entrance to the alley, keeping the yelling crowd at bay. The soldier pushed her roughly between two others in the line and into the space of the alley. What she saw there made her stop, terrified. A line of Burmese men stood against the wall, their hands above their heads.

'You no look. You walk on.' She felt something hard pushing between her shoulder blades. She kept her head down and stum-bled blindly on along the alley. Her eyes ran along the feet of the men who stood there. She sensed the fear radiating from them in the heat of the morning. Her heart froze as she caught sight of a pair of cheap sandals and the turquoise plaid of a longyi. She couldn't bring herself to lift her head.

'Move! No stop!' there was another prod from the gun and she stumbled forwards. An animal howl ripped from her throat as she heard the first shot.

1

Grace
Devon, July 2015

When Grace ripped open the parcel and glimpsed what was inside, she had to sit still for several minutes to recover from the shock. Finally, with trembling fingers she drew the three sheets of paper out of the huge cardboard envelope and laid them out side-by-side on the dining room table. Then she sat down in front of them, just staring at them, letting her mind flood with long suppressed memories.

She'd been humming along to a Beethoven concerto on the radio, chopping onions for supper, when the delivery driver had knocked. She'd rushed to the door wiping her hands on her apron. Now, as she sat staring at the artwork on the table in front of her, she forgot all about the frying pan simmering on the stove, about the half-peeled potatoes in the sink, the chicken defrosting on the worktop.

'Jack,' she murmured.

Jack's handiwork was visible in every brushstroke of the watercolour of the rose-covered cottage. It was there too in the pencil drawing of a busy street of shop-houses with Chinese roofs. The last piece puzzled her the most though; a roughly sketched map drawn in charcoal on grubby brown paper. From the way the paper was worn and creased she could tell it had been folded many times.

Grace groped for her reading glasses on the chain around her neck, and perching them on her nose, leaned forward and peered at the lines and shapes of the plan, trying to make out what they represented. As she looked closer she realised that some things were labelled in Jack's flowing hand in tiny letters: *guardhouse: cookhouse: sleeping huts: cemetery.* Beside a crudely drawn tree near the edge of the cemetery he'd marked a cross.

Dread washed over Grace as she made the connection. This must be something from Jack's time as a prisoner of war in Burma. It was a time she knew virtually nothing about, but that had hung over their marriage like a dark, silent cloud.

She opened the letter that had dropped out when she'd ripped the package open. She recognised the flamboyant writing instantly.

Dear Mrs Summers,

I hope you are keeping well. The gallery received these items belonging to your late husband from a Mr and Mrs Bell with whom he lodged in Oxfordshire for a few months in the early eighties. The Bells were clearing their attic with a view to selling their house and found these works in the back of a cupboard. They initially approached the gallery to have them valued, realising that some of Jack's paintings have recently changed hands for a considerable sum. However, we advised that these particular works had little value, so were asked to pass them on to you.

Do drop in and visit us next time you are up in London and if you would like to discuss the sale of any more of your husband's works we would be only too happy to help.

Yours ever,

Luke Chapman.

CLOSING HER EYES, Grace tried to cast her mind back to the early eighties. Had she ever met a Mr and Mrs Bell? Had Jack ever mentioned them? She frowned with the effort of remembering. Jack had travelled around so much during those years. A few months here, a year or two there, working on and off, getting commissions to paint from time to time; houses, portraits, horses and pets. Grace sighed, remembering the hope in his voice on the phone when he used to call her with news.

'I've got a new job, Gracie. This one's going to last, I can feel it in my bones. I'll be able to send some money for you and Louise next month, I promise.'

She vaguely remembered him working as a caretaker at a school in Oxfordshire, and getting a commission to paint a big country house for Lord someone or other. But the details were scanty. She knew it hadn't lasted long and he'd moved on to... was it to somewhere in Wales? Shropshire? Grace sighed and shook her head. It was so hard to remember.

She frowned and peered at the map again. It must be a plan of one of the prison camps in Burma that Jack had been in. There was no name, and even if there had been, it wouldn't mean anything to her.

Then, laying the map aside, Grace turned back to the sketch of the oriental street scene. She picked it up and stared at it. It wasn't in Jack's usual style. It showed a row of shop-houses on a busy street. There were food stalls and vendors on the pavement, baskets of fruit and fish on display. People in conical hats going to and fro on bicycles and rickshaws, some pushing hand carts, others carrying baskets on poles across their shoulders.

Right in the centre of the picture, beside the front door of one of the shop-houses stood a young woman. She was the only still figure in a sea of movement. Long black hair framed her slender face and she was barefoot, dressed in a plain saree and short-sleeved blouse. She was looking directly out of the picture, with a solemn face and large, soulful eyes.

Grace turned the picture over. On the back was written: *Marisa, Petaling Street, Kuala Lumpur, 1941*. Puzzled, she looked at the drawing again. She knew Jack had been stationed in Kuala Lumpur before the Japanese invaded Malaya. Perhaps he'd drawn this then? But she quickly realised he couldn't possibly have done. The paper was smooth and well preserved. It didn't look like something Jack had carried with him through the battles of the Malaya campaign and for three and a half years moving from camp to camp as a prisoner of war. He must have held this scene in his memory and drawn the picture when he was living in Oxfordshire in the early 1980s.

Who was the girl with the beautiful eyes? Was her name Marisa? A prickle of something unsettling entered her mind. Was it jealousy? There was so much about Jack's past she had no idea about. And now she'd never know. Why should it matter to her now anyway?

Grace glanced across the room at the photographs on the windowsill. Her eyes skated over the one of Jack sitting on Brighton beach in a suit, smoking a cigarette, while Louise as a toddler with her shock of white hair played beside him with a bucket and spade. Beside it stood the photo taken on their wedding day. She hadn't looked at it, not properly at least, for a long time. There she was, grinning from ear to ear, dressed in her best suit and hat, clinging to Jack's arm, while Jack, smiling broadly too, looked urbane in a grey three-piece suit. Their joy and excitement radiated from the picture. Looking at it now she could still feel that buzz herself all these years later, despite everything that had followed.

She sat for a few minutes longer, musing about Jack. She usually stopped herself remembering, trying to avoid reliving the pain. But seeing these fresh, skilfully crafted pictures had brought the old Jack back with startling clarity. She allowed her mind to wander back in time as she hadn't for a long time. She thought about the Jack she'd first met in the hospital in 1945, a stick of a man with hollow cheeks from his years of starvation and sallow skin from exposure to the tropical sun. Grace hadn't seen those things about him though; it was the energy and intelligence in his dark brooding eyes that had first drawn her to him.

She went to the sideboard and took a small black box out of the top drawer. She opened it and took out the star-shaped medal inside. She ran the silk ribbon through her fingers and stared at the embossed crown and lettering on the medal itself. Jack's Burma Star. She'd kept it hidden away all these years and just looking at it brought back a flood of different emotions.

She was jolted from her reverie by the smell of burning. She put the medal back in the drawer, and leaving the pictures and the memories she dashed back into the kitchen.

'Sod it!'

The pan was smoking. She grabbed the handle with a tea towel and took it off the stove, plunging it into the sink.

She could hear Eve's voice in her head even as she did it, 'Gran, are you quite sure you can still cope on your own? Perhaps you should think about getting some more help in the house?'

'Of course I can cope,' she muttered out loud to herself now as the pan hissed and sizzled in the washing up water. 'I'm just a bit forgetful sometimes. And it's not old age, I'll have you know. It's just me. I've always been like that.'

She checked the clock above the sink. Eve would be arriving on the train from London in less than two hours. Grace had said she would collect her in the car from the station in Totnes. She glanced around the chaotic kitchen in a mild panic. She needed to hurry up and get that pot roast in the oven before she set off.

Eve

As THE INTERCITY train sped west along the sea wall at Dawlish, Eve stared out at the breakers crashing against the stones leaving foam in their wake. The sun was going down over the shimmering horizon and the summer sky was gradually losing its light. Another half hour or so and the journey would be over.

The further Eve got away from London the more she relaxed, contentment seeping into her mind, replacing the tension of recent weeks. It had always been the same, that feeling of peace stealing over her, the blessed relief of homecoming, ever since she'd been at university and living with Grace in the holidays. Now she was looking forward to spending the coming weeks with her grandmother. And yet there was a niggling feeling preventing her from fully relishing the prospect.

What would Grace have to say about the bombshell she was about to deliver? Eve wondered if she should have broken the news on the phone. She'd thought about it each time she'd called, but in the end she hadn't had the courage. This was something she needed to tackle in person. Phone calls were always difficult with her grandmother anyway. Grace viewed the telephone as a means of transmitting essential information, not for catching up on gossip. Her voice always took on that impatient tone, indicating that she was keen to finish the call, if there was nothing important to say.

Staring out at the changing seascape, Eve couldn't help remembering the tension of the last few weeks; the mounting feeling that she was losing control of her life. She thought back to the daily battle she'd had trying to remain in control of the overcrowded classroom, the constant bullying, the rowdy behaviour, the name calling, objects thrown across the room. She'd found herself weeping in the staff loo on many occasions, having to will herself to go back in there and face up to the rest of the day.

The final conversation with the head teacher a fortnight ago played back in her mind as the train rumbled through the last tunnels cut through the red Dawlish cliffs and turned inland.

'I don't think I'm cut out for this,' she'd admitted. The final straw had been when one of the Year 6 boys had stuck chewing gum on her chair, ruining her best skirt.

'Oh, I've heard that from so many young teachers, Eve. I know it's tough. This is an inner-city school. It was never going to be easy. But you'll make it. I know you will.'

'But I'm not sure if I want to. I need to have some time away. This isn't what I came into teaching for.'

He'd done his best to persuade her to stay. All the time he was speaking, though, telling her how valuable the work was, how she'd be missing out if she left, she couldn't help thinking it was because it would be difficult for him to find a replacement. There was nothing he could say to persuade her. She'd already made up her mind.

In the end he gave up and said, 'We're really going to miss you, Eve. It might not feel like it at the moment, but you've got a real talent for this. You should seriously reconsider when you've had some time away to think about it.'

But she'd had no qualms about her decision as she'd walked away from the school on the last day of term with her plastic crate of belongings, her heart soaring with a new sense of freedom.

Now she stared out at the scenery as the train moved away from the coast and raced through a patchwork of emerald fields, dotted with white farmhouses and the odd spinney. It was partly the situation with Josh that had brought about this desire to shake up her life, she reflected. They'd stopped communicating properly years ago. Probably even before they moved to London together and rented a flat. It had seemed like a natural step at the time – they'd been dating since they met in fresher's week.

It was a sign of how distant they'd become, that when Josh announced he'd got a job in New York, Eve wasn't surprised. He hadn't even told her he was going for an interview. Neither of them discussed the future during the last month they were together. It was implicit between them that his departure would bring something that had become routine and unexciting to a natural end.

When she went to the airport to see him off, he didn't suggest she should visit him, and she didn't ask to. They kissed briefly, like old friends, and she stood and waved as he went through passport control. Walking back through the terminal to the tube station, she'd felt emotionless. She hadn't even cried, but getting back to the empty flat she'd suddenly felt that it was no longer her home; that she needed to move on.

They were rumbling through Newton Abbot now. Only a few more minutes and she'd be there. She got out her mirror and ran a comb through her glossy black hair.

As the train rattled over the river Dart and began to pull into Totnes station, Eve got down her rucksack and holdall from the shelf, picked up her small case and handbag and made her way to the end of the carriage. Peering out of the window, she scanned the platform for Grace as the train juddered to a halt. There was no sign of her grandmother.

Eve sighed, but smiled to herself all the same. Grace was almost always late for everything.

'It's because I'm an incurable optimist,' she'd once said. 'I always think things will take less far time than they do.'

Eve stood on the station forecourt and watched as other passengers were collected, got into waiting taxis or walked away from the station. It wasn't until the rush of activity produced by the train's arrival had long died down that Grace's battered Rover appeared at the entrance.

'I'm so sorry I'm late, Eve darling. Bad traffic, I'm afraid.'

Eve stowed her bags on the back seat of the car and slid in next to her grandmother in the front. When she leaned over to peck Grace on the cheek, she detected the smell of smoke, mingled with the aroma of onions.

'Have you been cooking, Gran?'

'Of course. Chicken hotpot.'

'My favourite,' said Eve, resisting the urge to ask if anything had been burnt in the process.

'Well let's get home and eat. I expect you're starving,' said Grace jamming the car into gear and accelerating away.

Grace's driving was erratic; it always had been, but each time Eve visited her it seemed to get worse. At almost ninety, Grace's eyesight was deteriorating. Eve had to make a conscious effort not to grip the dashboard whenever her grandmother drove her anywhere. She clamped her jaw shut now as Grace roared up the station ramp and pulled abruptly out into the traffic, causing a van to break and blast its horn.

On the train Eve had rehearsed the words she planned to say to Grace. She'd wanted to get them over and done with on the car journey, but now it felt safer to wait until they got home. Instead, as they crawled through the late rush hour traffic and up the hill out of the town, she chatted about anything she could think of; the weather, the train journey, Grace's neighbours. After a few minutes though, she realised Grace's answers were monosyllabic. She looked over at her grandmother who was peering at the road ahead.

'Are you alright Gran? You seem very quiet.'

'I'm fine thank you.'

'Sure?'

After a short silence, Grace said, 'Well, it's just that I had a bit of a surprise today. It's made me think.'

'Surprise?'

'Yes. The gallery in London sent me some old drawings and

paintings your grandfather did. I've never seen them before. It brought back old memories.'

Eve turned to look at her. In the darkness she could see that the old lady's eyes were glistening with tears.

'Oh Gran,' she said, squeezing her arm. 'You must show me them when we get back. I'd love to see them.'

'I think you'll find they are a bit different from the usual.'

The reply was uncharacteristically tight-lipped and Eve shot a surprised look at her grandmother. She was on the point of asking more but held back sensing that this would be venturing into dangerous waters.

They carried on in silence as darkness gathered. Grace swung off the main road and they were soon speeding through narrow lanes, the headlights lighting up high grass banks on either side. Eve concentrated on the road ahead, her right foot twitching on an imaginary brake pedal. At least it was dark and Grace should be able to see any approaching headlights in enough time to stop.

It had started to rain as Grace pulled off the lane and onto the unmade road that led to her home. The old stone Devon farmhouse came into view in the headlights, long and low and nestled into a hill for shelter from the Westerlies.

'Wretched weather,' Grace muttered. 'I wanted it to be nice for your stay.'

'I don't mind, Gran,' said Eve. 'I love the rain here. It's part of what makes it home. Proper Devon weather.'

The house felt comfortingly warm to Eve as they went inside. It was filled with the old familiar smells she remembered; polish, woodsmoke and cooking.

'I'll take my bags straight up to the bedroom, Gran.'

As she passed the dining room door she noticed the big brown envelope on the table.

'Grandad's pictures? Is it OK if I have a look?'

'Let's wait 'til after supper. I'd like to show you them properly and the food will be spoiled if we don't eat it now.'

LATER, as they sat at the kitchen table finishing their meal, Eve finally summoned her courage. She took a deep breath.

'I've decided to have a break from teaching, Gran.'

She watched her grandmother's face, waiting for her reaction. Grace put down her fork and stared at Eve.

'What do you mean? Have you left your job?'

Eve nodded. 'I had to, Gran. It was unbearable. It was making me ill.'

Grace shot her a sceptical look. Eve had known that giving up on a career would go against the grain with Grace; her strong work ethic, her own ruthless self-discipline.

'But you'd only been there a few months.'

'It was two years, Gran! It started out badly and it was just getting worse.'

Grace was silent, pursing her lips. Eve sensed she was making an effort not to blurt out exactly what she was thinking. Grace herself had never quit her nursing career from the age of eighteen until retirement and had never even had a break between jobs other than when she'd had Eve's mother.

'You know, all jobs can get tough at times,' Grace said at last. 'You should have talked to me. I'm surprised you didn't.'

'I'd made up my mind, Gran. There wasn't any point discussing it.'

'I'm very surprised, Eve. You've always been so ... so conscientious. So different from your mother.'

Eve stared down at her empty plate. She didn't want to get into that conversation. The criticisms of her mother, the barbed comments about Louise's lack of direction, her 'flightiness' as Grace often termed it.

When Eve didn't respond Grace asked, 'So what are you going to do?'

'I'm not sure yet. I've got some ideas...'

'Why don't you look for a job down here? A village school might be more your cup of tea.'

Eve took a deep breath. 'Actually Gran, I thought I'd travel for a bit. South East Asia probably. I could start out in Singapore. Visit Mum and Dad for a few days.'

'Well it would be nice for you to spend some time with them of course,' said Grace, her tone careful. 'But where else would you plan to go?'

'Well I thought I'd travel up through Malaysia and on into Thailand.'

'Oh, Evie darling,' said Grace leaning over and squeezing her hand on the table. Grace's hand felt cold and bony to the touch. 'Why can't you leave it alone?'

Eve swallowed. 'Leave what alone?' she said in a feeble voice, but she knew exactly what Grace was referring to.

'It won't do you any good, you know. It didn't when you went there before. You're never going to find what you're looking for.'

EVE STARED at the three pieces of her grandfather's work that Grace had laid out on the dining table. They were each so unique they might have been drawn by three different people.

'He was really talented wasn't he Gran?' she murmured, her eyes on the sketch of the oriental street scene. 'What a shame that he wasn't as well recognised during his lifetime.'

'I wonder if it would have made a difference,' murmured Grace. Eve glanced at her. Grace's eyes were far away. She could have been speaking to herself. Eve didn't ask what she meant but she could guess what Grace was thinking.

'I wish I'd known him,' Eve said suddenly. 'And my real father too. I sometimes lie awake at night, wondering about them both.'

To her surprise, she felt Grace's arms slip around her shoulders. Grace pulled her into a stiff embrace.

'There's no point dwelling on these things, Eve.'

'But Gran...'

'Now I know that's why you've planned your travels. To look for your real father. But you know, you have to be realistic about it.'

Eve felt a prickle of irritation.

'Of course that isn't the reason Gran,' she said. 'How could I possibly hope to even start looking? I don't even know which town he lives in, whether he's alive even.'

'Well I'm relieved you're thinking that way. When you said you were going to Thailand again I automatically assumed...'

'No. I've come to terms with all that now, Gran. It's just that...' she looked into her grandmother's eyes. It was always hard to explain her feelings to Grace.

'Go on. What were you going to say?'

'It's just that I feel drawn to the place. How could I not be? Half of me belongs there after all. Just look at me, Gran; I'm half Asian and proud of that fact. But I only know it as a tourist. I'd like to go back, on my own this time, just for a few weeks, to be able to get to know it, without all the baggage I was carrying around before.'

'Baggage? Whatever does that mean?'

'You know. When I went there with Josh.'

She meant the ill-fated trip to Thailand she and Josh had made three years ago. It had been the beginning of the end for their relationship. It had seemed a good idea at the time. She'd had the long summer holiday from school and he'd been between consulting jobs.

They'd stayed for a few days with her mother and father in Singapore at the start of the trip in their penthouse flat in Raffles place. The apartment felt crowded and the atmosphere a little tense.

One evening her father had taken Josh out for a drink at his club and Eve and her mother had stayed at home. Eve had seized the opportunity over dinner.

'Mum, you know partly why I'm going to Thailand don't you?' She'd seen her mother's shoulders tense at her words.

'I've got a fair idea Eve,' Louise had said, sipping her wine.

'Well, if you've guessed, would you please tell me at least where you met my real father? Which town? A starting point at least.'

Louise shook her head and reached for her cigarettes.

'It's painful to speak about Eve.'

'Why painful?'

'I can't tell you,' she said, fumbling with the lighter. 'I don't want to talk about it.'

'But why? Don't you think I've got a right to know?'

'Look, you've never asked before,' Louise said, the discomfort plain in her voice. 'Why now all of a sudden? Hasn't Jim been a good father to you?'

'Of course he has. It isn't that. I've just got this urge to find out about my real father. My flesh and blood. I can't get away from it, Mum. Can't you understand that?'

But Louise had stayed tight-lipped and evasive. Eve could tell she was getting irritated, by the spot of red that appeared on each cheek and the way she drew deeply on her cigarette. In the end she snapped.

'Look, Eve, if you must know, I don't want to remember it. It was just someone I met. A one-night stand to be absolutely blunt. The whole trip was a disaster. It's just a bad memory.'

With that she got up from the table and went out onto the balcony, staring out across the restless city, in a cloud of cigarette smoke, lost in thought.

Eve and Josh had left the next day on the night train to Bangkok. They'd spent three weeks backpacking around Thailand, arguing about where to stay, what to do, where to eat, when to move on. Eve's naïve hope of finding out where her father lived, tracking him down and meeting him had been cruelly dashed. She couldn't raise her spirits or summon any enthusiasm for the trip. Nor could she forgive her mother either for her silence. Not for a long time.

More recently she'd softened, though, wondering if it was partly her own fault for springing the subject out of the blue on Louise like that. Perhaps if she'd mentioned it in advance, written her a letter beforehand, maybe? Perhaps Louise would have reacted differently then?

'Don't you remember Gran? That trip was a bit of a disaster.' she said now to Grace. 'But please don't worry about that. I'm over all that now. I realised back then that I'm never going to find my real father.'

Grace patted her arm, 'I know it's hard, but I'm glad you've come to terms with it I must say.'

Eve's eyes strayed back to the table. She picked up the drawing that looked like a map and frowned, reading the labels.

Her grandmother pursed her lips. 'I've no idea why they sent that one to me,' she said. 'They should have just binned it. it's just some old sketch map.'

'This must be from Burma,' said Eve, examining the lines depicting a prison camp. 'From his time as a prisoner.'

Grace nodded and let out a sigh.

'This is why Mum went to Burma wasn't it? Before I was born? To find out about Grandad's time as a prisoner there?'

'That was part of the reason, yes. But your mother was very headstrong in those days, Eve. It all went very wrong for her out there. It very nearly ended in complete disaster.'

'Do you know what happened exactly? She's never really talked about it to me.'

Grace sat down heavily on a chair and put her head in her hands. Her shoulders drooped and she seemed to crumple. She suddenly looked every one of her eighty nine years.

'I don't remember the details,' she said in a vague voice. 'I'm

not sure I ever knew them fully. All I know is that she had to leave
Burma.'

'Did she get to see the camp where Grandad was?'

Grace shrugged and shook her head. 'I don't know, Eve. We
didn't really talk about that when she came home. I think she
wanted to spare me the details. And anyway, she had other things
on her mind by then.'

Later, as Eve lay awake in the unfamiliar quiet of the countryside, listening to the patter of summer rain on the sloping roof
above her bed, she thought about her grandfather's sketch map
of the prisoner of war camp. She pictured him, skin and bone
and dressed in rags, sketching out the rough lines with a lump of
charcoal from the camp fire, then folding the paper over and over
and slipping it into his shorts. Why had he done that? Why had
he brought it all the way back to England and kept it for years?
Eve knew very little about what had happened to the prisoners of
the Japanese during the war but she could imagine it would have
been risky to have carried something like that around right under
the noses of the guards.

She thought about the cross he'd drawn on the map beside a
tree in the graveyard, wondering what it might have represented.
It didn't look like the type of cross that might mark out a grave.

She lay back on her pillow wide awake and stared into the
darkness. But gradually the germ of an idea formed in her mind.
She sat up, wide awake, her brain suddenly alive with plans.
Perhaps she could go there, find the camp if it still existed, and
see the place for herself? It wouldn't take much organisation to
add Myanmar to her itinerary. It must be much easier to travel
there now it had opened up to the world. It had got to be less
problematic than when her mother had gone there in the eighties. She could visit the place where her grandfather had suffered,
see if the cemetery was still there. For a few minutes she let her
mind run away with the idea. She lay back on the pillow, trying to

imagine the journey, where the camp might be, what it might look like now.

But then her thoughts turned to Louise and she sighed deeply, wondering how her mother would react to the plan.

2

Louise

Rangoon, 2nd August, 1988

Louise stepped out of the front door of the Strand Hotel, crossed the porch and emerged through the portico onto the wide pavement. She stood still for a moment, squinting into the sunlight, acclimatising to the sultry air, wondering which way to turn. Cars and rickshaws rattled by on Strand Road and people dressed in longyis jostled past.

Her eye was caught by the sun setting on the wide Rangoon River opposite, casting streaks of red and orange on the shimmering surface. Voices floated up from the wharves where cargo vessels were being unloaded. Fishing boats plied to and fro on the water and a paddle steamer made its steady progress from right to left up-river.

She knew she couldn't wait where she was. It was far too public. Looking around cautiously she walked along the pavement to the far end of the building and turned into the first side street she came to. It was quieter here and she walked a few paces and stopped, stepping back into one of the alcoves in the wall of the hotel. She stood there, nerves tingling with anticipation, palms sweating, not quite sure who or what she was waiting for.

'Just wait outside your hotel at sunset. They'll come to you,' the Australian backpacker she'd met in a bar in the Khao San Road in Bangkok had assured her.

It had seemed like a good idea then as they'd sat swapping travellers' tales over beers.

'Everyone takes a bottle of whisky into Burma. You'd be mad not to. You can sell it on the black market and you'll triple your money at least,' one young German told her.

'Burmese Customs always turn a blind eye. I did it last month,' said an English girl barely out of her teens.

'We've all done it,' said another traveller.

Not to be outdone, Louise had found a liquor store near her hostel and bought the requisite bottle of Scotch.

But she'd started having misgivings as she shouldered her way through the press of passengers in the overheated arrivals hall in Rangoon airport and joined everyone else pushing and shoving their way to the front. When she finally manoeuvred herself into position in front of the desk, the immigration official flicked through her passport and eyed her, stony-faced.

'How long you stay in Burma?'

She returned his stern gaze with a steady look. Was that a trick question?

'For seven days,' she said, trying to keep her eyes steady, her heart speeding up. It wasn't possible to stay longer on a tourist visa. Did he think she didn't know that?

He stamped her passport with a thud. As she moved on towards the customs desk her stomach tightened and she began to seriously regret her decision. She could feel the whisky bottle cold and hard, pressing against her back through the webbing of her rucksack.

Oh God, why had she done this? Why did she always have to take crazy risks and run headlong into trouble?

Her palms were sweating and she could feel the heat in her cheeks as she approached the customs desk. The crowd had thinned out here. Was that a good thing? There were two customs officials behind the desk, chatting discreetly. They weren't searching bags, thank God. All she needed to do was to walk though nonchalantly like everyone else. Just follow the crowd.

She kept her eyes down as she passed the desk and had just got clear of it when one of them called out, 'Miss?'

Her heart did a somersault. This was it. There would be no trip to the Burmese interior after all. Her carefully laid plans were shattered through one silly impulsive act. She would never fulfil the promise she'd made to her dying father now. What an idiot she was.

She turned back. One of the men approached her smiling and she froze to the spot.

'Your bag is undone, Miss,' he'd said. In a second he'd fastened the buckle. She'd muttered her thanks and moved on.

She recovered her composure on the ramshackle airport bus as it crawled through the queues of traffic along the potholed roads towards the city centre. She stared out at the unfolding scenery, letting her heartbeat return to normal. The rolling green countryside gradually gave way to streets lined with once grand colonial buildings, now crumbling with neglect.

She must be careful here, she told herself. It wasn't like Thailand where Westerners were welcomed and the ambience was tolerant and relaxed. Here the Military junta was known for its brutality, the police kept an eye on tourists, and their whereabouts was carefully monitored and controlled.

Now, as she waited in the side-street beside the Strand Hotel she stared at the building opposite. Like many other monolithic structures that lined the streets of Rangoon it was built on a grand scale, with arched windows and elaborate plasterwork. But its paint was scabbing, showing the brickwork underneath and greenery grew from cracks in the plaster and sprouted from window ledges. She wondered what it might have looked like in the heyday of Empire.

As she stood waiting, it began to rain. Just like it had every day she'd spent in Bangkok. It was the rainy season after all. She knew what to expect now. What started as a few dark spots on the hot pavement soon escalated to a full-scale deluge. Huge raindrops pounded down, blown sideways by gusts of wind. Louise pressed herself against the wall, hoping that the hotel eaves would give her some protection.

She was just about to give up and rush back inside when a battered blue Chevrolet bowled round the corner of the street and drew up beside her. The back door flew open.

'Get in quickly,' hissed a young man from the back seat. She slid in beside him. This was probably crazy, but her instinct told her it would be alright.

She shut the back door and the car took off.

'We go round the block,' said the young man.

She glanced at him. He looked about her own age, dressed in jeans and a leather jacket. His hair was carefully gelled and spiked.

There were two men in the front of the car. Neither turned round or acknowledged her presence. The driver held a cigarette in one hand and steered with the other. The passenger, a slight man with short hair, stared straight ahead. The rain drummed on the roof and the wipers slewed water from side to side on the windscreen.

'What have you got?' the boy asked.

She drew the bottle of whisky out of her pack. He took it, rolled it round in his hand and held it up to the light; examining it with an expert eye.

'Good stuff,' he said with a brief smile, showing a row of even teeth stained red with betel nut.

'How much?' she asked.

'We give you thirty US,' he said. 'It's the going rate.'

'OK.'

He started rolling a cigarette. The men in the front hadn't once turned to look at her.

'You want one?' he asked.

'OK. Thanks.' She watched him get another skin from his packet and fill it with raw tobacco. He handed it to her and held a lighter to it. She took a long drag of the rough, pungent tobacco and blew a stream of smoke out of the open window. It had a real kick.

He handed her three crisp ten dollar notes and she gave him the bottle of whisky.

'We take you back now,' he said and, leaning forward, spoke to the driver in Burmese. The car stopped abruptly, reversed around a corner with a squeal of tyres, and headed back towards the Strand.

'You want a tour of the city tomorrow?' asked the boy. 'My cousin here speak English very well. He know the city. He's an excellent guide.'

He nodded in the direction of the front passenger who remained staring ahead, showing no sign of having heard.

Louise hesitated. She didn't really want a tour of the city, but she did need to find someone who would help her with her plans. Time was so precious here, and the seven days on her visa were already ticking away.

She took another drag on the cigarette, contemplating the offer.

'So what do you think about a tour?' asked the boy. 'My cousin college student. Very trustworthy.'

Then he leaned forward again and said something in Burmese to the passenger in the front who turned around and flicked a glance at Louise. She caught a glimpse of an unsmiling face, serious eyes.

'Perhaps,' she said.

'Good. So what time he come to your hotel in the morning?'

She laughed. 'Hang on a minute...'

'He'll give you very good price too,' said the boy, smiling.

The car had stopped beside the pavement where it had picked her up. They were waiting for her to get out. On an impulse she made a decision.

'OK then. I'll meet him at ten tomorrow morning in the hotel lobby.'

You won't regret it,' said the boy as she got out and slammed the door. She stood in the rain watching the car take off down the road with a squeal of bald tyres, wondering what she had let herself in for.

LOUISE TOOK the antiquated lift with its folding metal doors to her room on the fourth floor and showered in the old Victorian bathroom. The water was cold and it came out first as a trickle, then in erratic bursts. The hotel had once been a grand place, so much was obvious, but years of military rule and socialism had stripped it of its finery and glamour. Now it felt like a functional government building, with lino on the floors and scuffed grey paintwork. Still, she was glad she'd decided to stay here. It was good to see something of the old Burma and the conditions in the backpacker hostel in the Khao San road had dented her enthusiasm for hostel-living.

She put on her only good shirt; white linen, crumpled from the journey, and a cotton skirt and sandals. Then she glanced in the cracked mirror. Her face was already tanned from her few days in Thailand, her nose covered in freckles, and her long fair hair tinted golden at the ends by the sun. She sighed. If she was going down to the bar she should really apply some makeup. She dashed on some lipstick and eye liner and headed down the sweeping marble staircase.

She felt a shiver of nerves, entering the dark panelled bar with its leather chairs and atmosphere of a gentlemen's club. It smelled of cigar smoke and the accumulated alcohol fumes of decades past. A few tables were occupied by groups of American tourists. The barman didn't show any surprise at a young woman drinking alone. She ordered a gin and tonic and he nodded towards a table in the window, behind some potted palms.

'You sit down over there. I will bring your drink.'

'I'd rather sit here, if you don't mind,' she said, sliding onto a high seat in front of the bar. She knew that sitting discreetly at a table in the corner there would be no chance of meeting anyone and picking their brains about her plans.

She sipped her drink and absorbed the atmosphere. Saxophone music played on the crackling sound system and ceiling fans whirred overhead. She watched the barman polishing the counter behind the bar with its elaborate mirrors and glass shelves.

After a few minutes a European man entered the room alone and went straight up to the bar.

'Double whisky please Jaaw. God what a day!' his accent was English, Home Counties Louise guessed.

The bartender was full of smiles and banter as he poured the drink. The newcomer downed it in one and slammed his glass down on the bar.

'Fill her up again.'

Then his gaze turned to Louise.

'Hello? Can I get you a drink?' he asked, moving to sit on the stool next to her. She glanced at him. He was probably in his mid thirties, with dark hair receding at the temples. He had the air of a perennial ex-pat. He wore a linen suit which had a threadbare, lived-in look.

He held out a hand, 'I'm Jim Yates. Are you here on holiday?'

'Of course,' she said. 'And you?'

' 'Fraid I live in this God-awful hole for my sins,' he said. 'On my last couple of weeks, though. Can't say I'll be sorry to leave.'

'Really? What do you do?'

'British Embassy.'

'That sounds fascinating.'

He stared into his drink. 'Hhmm. Some might say that. I'm quitting though.'

'What are you going to do?

'Got a job in a bank in London. It won't have the cudos of the Foreign Office but far better paid. An international bank. I'll be using my languages.'

Then after a pause, 'What did you say your name was?'

'I didn't. Louise Summers.'

'So, Louise, are you here with a tour group, or on your own?'

'I'm on my own.'

'Well, I must say that's incredibly brave of you. You know things haven't exactly been smooth-running in this country for the past few months. Not the best time to visit.'

'I know. But I had to come.'

'Really? *Had* to come to Burma? That's a new one on me.'

The barman put a fresh gin and tonic down in front of Louise and a bowl of cashew nuts. She took a sip. This one was stronger than the first. Her new friend obviously had influence. She took a deep breath. If she was going to find out about how things worked around here, he was as good a person to start with as any.

'My Dad died a couple of months ago,' she said.

'I'm very sorry to hear that. But if you don't mind my asking, why would that bring you to Burma?'

'He was here during the war.'

'Oh I see. The Burma campaign? We do get a few veterans wanting to visit.'

She shook her head.

'No. He was a prisoner of war. He worked on the Thai-Burma railway.'

'Ah. We don't get many of those chaps visiting. He was on the Burmese end of the line you mean?'

She nodded.

'He said a few things about it at the end,' she said. 'He'd never really talked about it before, but it obviously had a huge effect on his life. It made me want to come here.'

Jim Yates took a swig of his whisky and eyed her carefully.

'You know that the Thai-Burma railway was only built as far as Thanbyuzayat in the south of the country don't you?'

She nodded. 'Yes I know that. My dad was in a camp there actually. In Thanbyuzayat itself.'

'And you must also know that tourists are only allowed to travel to certain places in the country. Travel for foreigners is tightly controlled. The south is completely off-limits. You do know that don't you?'

She nodded and tried to return his gaze with a steady look. Perhaps Jim Yates wasn't the best person to ask for help after all.

'I... I just wanted to come to the country. To get a feel for the place,' she said dropping her eyes. His eyes were sceptical.

He took out a packet of Silk Cut and held it out to her. She took one, thanking him.

'Like gold dust these are around here,' he muttered, lighting up. 'Can't buy them for blood nor money in Rangoon. I'm running out, though. Don't suppose you brought any into the country did you?'

'No. I've been smoking roll-ups.'

'Pity. Jaaw? Another whisky and one more G&T please.'

'Look,' he said, turning back to Louise. 'If you ask my advice you'd be better off visiting the railway in Kanchanaburi in Thailand. You know? The Bridge on the River Kwai? There are no problems there. It's all set up for tourists.'

Her heart sank further. He obviously didn't understand.

'I went there last week for a couple of days. While I was passing through Bangkok,' she said.

He smiled. 'Well there you are then. You've seen the railway.'

'I suppose so...'

Her trip to Kanchanaburi had been interesting, but it hadn't fulfilled the need to see the place where her father had been a prisoner. She'd travelled on the original Thai-Burma railway from Bangkok, in an ancient carriage with wooden seats. It creaked along through the outskirts of Bangkok and into the countryside, past paddy fields and through sections of untamed jungle.

She'd been shocked by the blatant tourism of the place itself; the crowds of tourists walking over the bridge, the nick-nacks sold at the tacky market alongside it. The one museum she'd managed to find was housed in some flimsy atap huts, made of bamboo and thatched with palm leaves; replicas of those the prisoners had lived in. She'd wandered around looking at the displays showing the appalling conditions the men had been subjected to, the illnesses they had suffered, the varying tortures the Japanese had used on those transgressing their rules. She'd visited the huge cemetery in the centre of the town, and wandered around reading the inscriptions on the gravestones, appalled by how many very young men had lost their lives.

But it had felt remote from her own father's experience, far, far away at the other end of the line in Burma. She'd had an instinctive feeling that things would have been different for prisoners there. And besides, she needed to get to Thanbyuzayat to fulfil the promise she'd made to her father.

'You need to know that there's been a hell of a lot of trouble in the country for several months now,' Jim Yates went on, blowing smoke rings in the air. 'Some people think it is far from over. It's quite a dangerous place to be at the moment.'

'Yes I knew there were some protests in March, but I thought it had all quietened down.'

He shook his head slowly.

'What you read in the Western press doesn't really give the whole picture. It hasn't quietened down. Far from it, I'm afraid. There's a lot of unrest. It feels to me as though it's building up to something big.'

'Well that's very bad news, but I don't think it will disrupt my visit.'

He looked at her sideways and took another drag on his cigarette.

'Unless you were planning to go off-piste, of course.'

Louise turned to look at him. His eyes were unfocused, the eyes of a drinker, and there were high spots of colour on his florid cheeks.

'Does anyone ever actually do that?' she asked, flicking ash in to the ashtray, trying to keep her voice casual.

'If they do, they soon get into trouble. I've had to help out a few British tourists who've succumbed to the urge to stray off the beaten track.'

'What happened to them?'

'Picked up by the Military police, roughed up and treated pretty badly. Kept in the cells until they could be deported. The worst one was a journalist who wanted to report on the dissident Karen hill tribes and tried to travel to the rebel held region in the north east. He got caught at a road block and sent back to Rangoon with an army escort. When we finally got to see him he was in a pretty bad way.'

Louise was silent, reflecting on this for a moment. Surely nothing like that could happen to her, a young female student on a personal pilgrimage?

'I was going to ask you,' she said, 'how far south is it actually possible to go?'

He laughed.

'I knew it! So you *are* planning something. As a matter of fact you can get as far as Moulmein without any problems. It's not actually forbidden to go there, just not encouraged by Tourist Burma. They like to focus on the places they're going to get big kick-backs from.'

'Moulmein? But that's not too far from Thanbyuzayat is it?'

'Around about fifty miles. But there are road blocks and check points on that road... Now don't tell me you're going to try to get to Thanbyuzyat?'

'No of course not,' she replied laughing. 'I'm not adventurous enough to try anything like that... I wouldn't mind seeing Moulmein though.'

'It's worth the trip to see the pagoda Kipling wrote about. You know? *By the old Moulmein Pagoda. Looking lazy at the sea..?* You can get down to Moulmein by train, but hardly any tourists do go down that way. You'd have to be prepared to rough it. It isn't a comfortable ride and the accommodation in Moulmein is pretty rough, even by Burmese standards.'

As soon as she could without being rude, Louise made her excuses and prepared to leave. Her companion said, 'If you're staying in Rangoon for a few days I could always show you around. I've got a couple of days' leave to use up.'

'That's very kind of you,' she said, grasping around for a suitable excuse, 'but I've already organised a tour for tomorrow.'

'Oh well, never mind. Perhaps we'll meet again in here later in the week? I'm in here most evenings about this time for a sundowner.'

'Yes, perhaps,' she said politely sliding off her stool.

'Oh, and here's my card,' he said, taking one from a thumbed pack in a rubber band and handing it to her. 'If you need anything whilst you're in Burma you can always contact me.'

3

Grace
Hammersmith Hospital, London
November 1945

'You're late, Nurse Everett,'
The ice-cool tones of the ward sister greeted Grace as she hurried through the double doors of the medical ward at seven minutes past eight that chilly Monday morning in November 1945.

Damn. This was exactly what Grace had hoped to avoid. She'd overslept, having forgotten to set her alarm the night before. It was only because her father had knocked on her door before he left for work that she'd woken at all. She'd dashed out of the house without any breakfast. The Bakerloo line train had been more cramped than usual and she'd had to stand, hanging from a ceiling strap, all the time panicking about what time she would arrive and what acerbic reprimands Matron or the ward sister might dish out.

She thought she might just have made it as she emerged from the underground into the damp fug of the West London rush hour. Weaving her way across the road through the stationery traffic to the front entrance of the hospital, her mind was on the day ahead. She had no idea that this day would change the course of her life.

The clock on the hospital tower showed five past eight.

Sod it. Her watch must be slow. She ran up the front steps, through the glass doors, her hasty footsteps echoing across the marble entrance hall. There was no time to wait for the anti-quated metal lift; she took the stairs two at a time. The fear of Matron's wounding glare fuelled her as she panted up the last few. She'd never been late for work before, but she'd seen others disciplined and humiliated for even minor transgressions.

It was her bad luck that the ward sister was there at the door waiting for her now. She stopped abruptly and felt the blood pulsing into her cheeks. Hanging her head like a guilty school-child, she was hardly able to meet the other woman's stare.

'I'm sorry, Sister,' she said, her mind grasping for a plausible excuse, bracing herself for the dressing down. 'Delays on the tube...'

'Don't let it happen again, Nurse,' was all the sister said. 'I'm glad you're finally here. A couple of girls are off with a stomach bug and two more have gone down to help out on the surgical ward. Now hurry up and get ready. Then come to my office and I'll brief you on your duties.'

Grace changed into her uniform in the chilly locker room, and emerged onto the ward smoothing down her pinafore, adjusting her starched cap, attempting to look calm and collected.

'What happened to you?' hissed her friend Nancy as she passed.

'Tube delays.'

'I bet,' giggled Nancy rolling her eyes. 'Sure you weren't out on the town last night?'

'Of course not.'

Nancy came close to Grace and whispered, 'There are a couple of new men on the ward. Came straight from Southampton by ambulance in the night. Nearly died on the ship on the way home.'

'Way home?' Grace asked, frowning. Were men *still* coming back from the war?

Inside the tiny office Sister said; 'Now I'm putting you in charge of the care of these new patients, Nurse.'

'Yes Sister. Where have they come from?'

'From the Far East apparently, on a hospital ship. Now what type of hospital that might have been one can only wonder. Several other men were taken to Southampton Hospital, but they simply didn't have room for these two. They've been prisoners of war for three and a half years. They both have fevers. One of them has had a leg amputated. The doctor will examine them later this morning. Until then please ensure they are comfortable, and that they have enough water to drink.'

'Yes Sister.'

'And Nurse Everett,' the sister was looking into her eyes, deadly serious.

'Please prepare yourself. These men are very sick.'

'Of course.'

Whatever did she mean? Grace was used to soldiers, to seeing hideous wounds and intense suffering. They'd been coming in wounded or sick in a steady stream ever since she'd started on the ward in the summer of 1944. She'd nursed them to the best of her ability; spoon-fed them if they couldn't eat, made sure they took their medicine, emptied their bedpans and washed their bodies. She'd also become adept at laughing at their bad jokes, ignoring their bawdy remarks and on occasion rebuffing their advances. Some of them had let slip fragments of information about France and the action they'd seen there. But most of them were just glad to be out of it, back in London, alive, safe and cared for.

She walked towards the side ward where Sister had told her the new men had been put. It was a room that was rarely used, away from the other patients who were mostly civilians now; old men with ulcers or chronic illnesses. Grace wondered why the newcomers had been hidden away. She'd been taught that patients recover more quickly on the main ward, seeing the nurses at their work and feeling part of the daily routines.

Pausing in the doorway, Grace took her first look at the new patients.

Good God. Her breath caught in her throat. The two men lay with their eyes closed. For a dreadful second she wondered if they were both dead. Then she realised from the gentle rasping sounds and the rise and fall of their chests that they were breathing; one slept with his mouth wide open, spit glistening on his chin.

Logic told her that they must be young men, but from their fragile appearance they could have been in the last stages of life. Their skin was sallow, their hair lank and greasy, their cheeks hollow, dark bruised patches under their eyes. One slept with his arms flung outside the blankets. Grace couldn't tear her eyes away from those arms. Bones with yellowing skin stretched over them. She'd never seen anyone alive with so little flesh on their body.

She hovered in the doorway, shocked, despite everything she'd witnessed over the past year. What must they have suffered during their captivity? Sister had told her to look after these men, but what could she do to help them? Should she fetch them something to eat? Had they been here when breakfast was served at seven? Could they even take normal food?

As she stood there dithering, her training momentarily deserting her, she became aware that someone was watching her.

The man in the far bed had woken up and was looking in her direction, his sunken brown eyes resting on her face. She felt colour rush to her cheeks. He must realise she'd been staring at him as if he were a zoo animal.

'Good morning,' she said quickly.

His eyes followed her as she moved towards his bed. Automatically she bent to tuck the blankets around him. Close up she saw that his pallid face was covered in a film of sweat.

'Where is this place?' he asked, his voice cracked and thin.

'You're in Hammersmith Hospital, in London. Didn't they tell you?'

He didn't reply. He carried on staring at her, his eyes following her every movement. She found it disconcerting; all her instincts told her to look away, but she forced herself to return his look.

'You came up this morning by ambulance,' she said, straightening up, trying to make her voice sound natural. 'They said you'd docked in Southampton. Don't you remember?'

He breathed out and closed his eyes briefly. She noticed long dark lashes against high cheekbones. Then he snapped them open again.

'Yes. HMS Homoara. I had a bout of malaria the last couple of days. I don't remember much.'

'What's your name?'

'Jack. Jack Summers.'

'I'm Nurse Everett. I suppose you don't want any food, Jack?'

He shook his head.

'I'll bring you some water, then.'

She turned to go, keen to get out of the room for a while and recover her composure alone.

'Don't go for a moment, Nurse,' she heard him say as she moved away. She turned back towards him.

'It would do you good to drink something,' she said, her professional no-nonsense voice returning.

'Just stand there for a moment. Please. I just want to look at you.'

She was about to retort in the voice she used to discourage advances from amorous patients, but when she saw the pleading in his dark eyes she held back. She sensed he wasn't flirting; it was something much deeper. She stood there for a few moments, smiling stiffly, while he simply looked back at her, his eyes full of something she couldn't fathom.

The spell was broken by a groan coming from the other man. She moved towards the far bed.

This man, who introduced himself as Ernie, was older.

'It's me leg nurse,' he said, his face pale and sweaty. 'You got any painkillers?'

'I'll fetch some aspirin. The doctor will be coming to examine you soon.

When she returned from the kitchen with a jug and some pills she gave them both water and made sure they were as comfortable as she could. As she put the jug down on the bedside cabinet beside Jack she noticed a notepad on the shelf.

'Is this yours?'

Jack's eyes registered surprise.

'Oh, someone must have brought it with me from the ship,' he said. 'It's just a few scribblings.'

'He's being modest Nurse,' the other man piped up. 'Why don't you take a look?'

'Do you mind?' she asked Jack.

He smiled. 'Go ahead.'

She flicked through the pages of the sketch book. It was full of drawings of bone thin men, like the ones in the room. The backdrop to all the pictures was the deck of a liner. Some men were standing against the rails, others sitting on the boards of the deck, in groups or alone. There were a few close-ups showing men smiling, their character clear in their faces. The drawings were careful, lifelike and precise. It struck Grace that they'd been done with real compassion for the subjects. There were a couple too of sunsets over a shimmering ocean. Even though the drawings were in pencil, in an uncanny way they seemed to convey the colour and light and movement in the scenes.

She looked up and smiled at Jack.

'They're beautiful,' she said.

'I told you so,' laughed Ernie. But Jack just carried on watching her, his brown eyes on her face, a gentle smile on his lips.

As Grace went home after her shift that evening, instead of flicking through the evening paper or a magazine as she usually did to pass time on the journey, she sat in the corner of the carriage staring out at the blank darkness of the tube tunnel thinking about those men.

Their medical notes had come with them from the ship and were hanging on clipboards at the end of the beds. Their height and weight were written down on their notes. Neither of the men weighed more than eight stone. Jack's weight was recorded as seven stone two pounds, and his height was six-foot one inch.

She'd watched the doctor examine them when he came on his rounds. Doctor Powell was portly and bombastic. He arrived flanked by a couple of medical students. He took everything in his stride and went about his rounds a larger than life presence, dishing out orders to nurses and patients alike. But when he saw these men, Grace noticed the concern on his face. He treated them with a reverential respect which she'd never seen before. He took their temperatures, listened to their chests. Afterwards he took her aside.

'These men are all suffering from malnutrition and all sorts of tropical illnesses. They both have malaria so I'm going to prescribe quinine. The man with the amputated leg will probably need another operation before long. It looks to have been a botched job.'

She nodded. 'What can I do?'

'They will need building up quickly, nurse. We must make sure they have plenty of bland food at first. They won't be able to stomach anything else. Potatoes and bread. Fresh vegetables. I'll let Matron know and she can ensure the kitchens make special preparations.'

Grace thought too about the chirpy humour Ernie had displayed all day, and how it was plain that these men cared for and looked out for each other. There seemed to be a strong bond between them. But in their eyes was something she'd never witnessed before. It was a faraway look that hinted at horror; as if they had witnessed things no human being ever should.

She was still thinking about them as she walked from the tube station through the dark suburban streets towards home.

'You're late Gracie!' her sister Joan called from the top of the stairs as Grace came through the front door. 'I've been watching from the window for you. Did you forget? We're meant to be going out for a drink with Arthur and Les tonight.'

Joan appeared on the top stair. She was all dressed up in a cornflower blue dress with a wide, pleated skirt. Her blonde hair was arranged in glossy curls and her face carefully made up.

'I'm not sure, Joan. I'm really tired,' Grace sighed hanging her coat on the stand and kicking off her shoes. 'I've had a hell of a day.'

'But you promised!' said Joan, with a sulky frown. 'You can't let Arthur down. He's expecting you to come and so are we.'

'Joan's quite right, Grace,' her mother appeared in the hallway, wiping her hands on her apron. 'You can't go letting people down. Arthur's a nice young man. You don't want to upset him. Now come and eat your supper and then you can go up and get changed.'

'They're calling for us in less than an hour so you'd better hurry up,' chimed Joan.

Grace sighed, bowing to the combined force of the pair of them and followed her mother through to the kitchen.

Everything felt different that evening as she took Arthur Bancroft's arm. They followed Joan and Les along the dark pavements towards the High Street and the lights of the Plough Inn, their breath cloudy in the lamplight. Last time they'd been out together, only two nights before in fact, they'd gone to the Paramount Ballroom in Tottenham and Grace had been in high spirits. She'd even begun to think she was falling in love with Arthur. He *was* very good looking, polite and considerate. He was charming too, and quite witty in his own way. He was everything she could have wished for. She told herself that the only thing that had stopped her falling for him was the fact that he worked for her father. In fact that was how they had met.

She'd been accompanying her father to a business function at the Savoy. Her mother had had one of her headaches and had asked her to go in her place. Grace often stepped in for her mother at short notice. She knew Mother found these occasions overwhelming. She was shy and awkward and in addition disliked the wives of the other members of the board.

'Stuck up and unfriendly,' was how she described them. She'd much prefer to stay at home and listen to the wireless and sew or play patience.

Grace was happy to go along. Dressed in her black silk evening gown, with her hair piled up and mother's pearls round her neck, she felt like a million dollars; lifetimes away from the drudgery of her everyday life. She didn't even mind the wives. They were a little intimidating it was true, in their flashy jewellery and expensive clothes. They gossiped together and blew smoke rings from cigarette holders and hardly bothered to speak to her anyway. She was happy just to sit beside her father, eating the wonderful food and soaking up the heady atmosphere of glamour and wealth.

It was when she was coming back from powdering her nose in the ladies' room that she bumped into him. He was going in the other direction and he stepped aside for her in the doorway. But as she passed he looked at her and asked an earnest voice,

'Excuse me. I hope you don't mind me asking, but are you Mrs Everett?'

Grace couldn't hide her amusement.

'Of course not! I'm her daughter. Grace Everett,' she held out her hand. His face registered relief and he pumped her hand vigorously.

'Arthur Bancroft. I work in your father's department at the bank.'

'Very nice to meet you.'

'Are you enjoying yourself?'

'Of course. What about you?'

'Well these client dos are always a bit of a strain, truth be told.'

She smiled, appreciating his honesty and looked at him more closely.

'I wonder,' he said suddenly. 'There's a band playing through there in the ballroom. I don't suppose you'd like to take a turn on the dance floor?'

She hesitated and glanced over at her father. He was deep in conversation with a portly client in a cloud of cigar smoke.

'I don't suppose Dad will miss me,' she said. 'That would be very nice.'

So they danced at the Savoy, under the chandeliers, spinning around between wealthy foreign guests, men in dinner jackets, and women dressed in silk and dripping with jewels. Arthur was an excellent dancer, holding her expertly and guiding her steps with a firm but light touch. And Grace loved to dance.

'Have you worked there long?' she asked as they moved round the dance floor.

'Only a few months. I've just come out of the army.'

'I thought you must have done. Were you abroad?'

'Yes. Northern France mainly.'

'Oh. When did you get back?'

'Just before V.E. day. We were lucky. My unit didn't see much action. Followed down behind the main D.Day landings. What about you? How did you spend the war?'

'I've been nursing for the past two years. Before that, my sister, Joan and I were evacuated to Plymouth.'

He smiled. 'Plymouth! That took its fair share of bombs.'

'Yes,' she said ruefully, 'My parents were right to send us away, though. Our street in Harrow was bombed a few times. Mum has relatives in Plymouth and she didn't want us to go to strangers. But it turned out not to be a very good choice at all.'

When the band stopped, the Master of Ceremonies announced a short interval. The lights went up and some piped music came on the sound system.

Grace looked at her partner awkwardly. In the bright light he looked younger and less assured than she'd first thought.

'I guess we'd better go back in,' he said and as they made their way back to the dining room he asked her if she'd like to go to dinner one evening.

It had gone on from there. Arthur had become a regular visitor at the Everett house over the past few months. Her mother had taken to his polite, unassuming presence immediately. Her father was happy to smoke a cigar with him after Sunday lunch and had even invited Arthur out to the golf club for a couple of rounds. Joan had been overjoyed that Grace had a sweetheart at last.

'I thought you never would. You're so *choosy*, Gracie. So high and mighty. It will be so lovely now. We can all go out together. You and Arthur and me and Leslie.'

It had all been moving in a predictable direction. Joan had been engaged to Leslie since VE day and their mother had been dropping heavy hints to Grace to follow suit.

'You don't want to be left behind by your younger sister, Grace.'

'Whatever do you mean? I'm only just twenty Mum, for goodness sake.'

'What I mean to say is it might be an idea to strike while the iron's hot. Chances like this one don't come along every day. You don't want to be left on the shelf.'

'What does that even mean? Left on the shelf. I don't need to get married. I've got my job and I could support myself.'

'Now you know I don't like that sort of talk.'

Now she walked in silence beside Arthur, mulling it all over. The pub came into view, its light casting a welcoming glow across the High Street.

As they entered the noisy bar, the hubbub of conversation and blast of steamy air enveloped them.

They found a corner table and Arthur shouldered his way to the bar for drinks. Grace sat on the bench opposite Joan and Leslie who were staring into each others' eyes. As usual Grace felt excluded from their private world. She didn't feel any envy or any awkwardness about this, though. She was genuinely pleased that Joan had found happiness with Leslie. Getting married was everything Joan had ever wanted.

Watching them now, the thought came to Grace that she'd been sleepwalking in that direction herself too. Partly through inertia, and partly because she'd thought it was expected of her and she'd had no real reason to fight against it. A shudder went through her.

Arthur returned, holding four glasses precariously. He put them on the table and said, laughing,

'Hey. You two. Give it a break won't you? There are four of us here don't forget.'

Joan giggled and Arthur sat down next to Grace, slipped his arm around her back and nuzzled her neck. She stiffened at his touch. It was almost as if she'd awoken from a long, deep sleep.

She edged away from Arthur. She needed some space to examine her thoughts.

'You're very quiet this evening, love,' he said. 'Is anything the matter?'

'I've had a bit of a day that's all,' Grace said.

'Oh Gracie don't be a bore,' said Joan. 'Arthur doesn't want to hear about all that gloomy hospital stuff, do you Arthur?'

'I don't mind. Tell us about it Grace. Tell us about your day.'

Slowly Grace shook her head. She knew she couldn't trivialise what she'd seen by talking about it in the pub. It didn't seem right for those two beaten, starved men to be the subject of idle gossip. And besides, no-one here would understand. They probably wouldn't even believe her. And they wouldn't thank her for it either. Their focus was on the future. On forgetting about the war and moving on.

'It's all right. Really. Let's talk about something else,' she said, drawing herself up and smiling a fixed smile.

The conversation moved on, and again and again Grace found her mind drifting back to Jack and the look in his eyes. She tried to stop those thoughts because she knew they were point-less. She'd vowed to herself never to get close to her patients. Part of that was professionalism and the rest of it self-preservation. So many times she'd seen patients deteriorate before her eyes and felt helpless to do anything for them. *After all, he could be dead tomorrow* she told herself taking a gulp of her drink and forcing herself to smile and join in with the others.

JACK *WAS STILL THERE* when Grace went back onto the ward the next morning looking more alive and less pallid than he had on the previous day. He was sketching when she arrived. He looked up from his work and she couldn't help noticing his eyes register when she entered the room.

'Can I look?' she asked.

'Oh. It's not finished yet, Nurse.'

'Go on, show her. Stop being modest,' Ernie insisted from the other bed.

Diffidently Jack handed her the book. This sketch was of Ernie, propped up in his bed, a broad smile on his gaunt face, displaying gaps in his teeth. The drawing had captured his expression and mood perfectly.

'It's very good indeed,' she said handing the book back.

'See I told you,' said Ernie. 'The man's got talent.'

'I'm glad to see you're both looking a lot better than yesterday,' said Grace.

'Me Missus is coming in today,' said Ernie. 'The first time I'll have seen her in almost four years.'

'That's marvellous. What time will she be here?'

'Eleven. Sister came to tell me the regiment had been in touch with her.'

'You must be delighted,' she said, turning to Jack with a smile. 'That's wonderful isn't it?

He nodded and smiled back quietly. She was about to ask if he had any family coming to visit, but something stopped her. If he didn't, he must be feeling very raw and lonely at this moment.

The ward orderly brought breakfast in on a rattling trolley. He set the trays over the beds on their extendable legs. The food didn't look appetising to Grace; two pieces of toast and jam, a boiled egg, a bowl of porridge, a stewed cup of tea. But the men received the meals with exaggerated gratitude. When the orderly left the room they both sat there staring at their plates, looks of awe on their faces. They seemed almost afraid to touch it.

'The doctor said you need to build yourselves up,' Grace

prompted gently. 'I would eat your breakfast now, before it gets cold.'

They both began to eat slowly, picking at the food, chewing each mouthful many, many times. She watched as they each finished every crumb of the toast, every morsel of the egg and both laboriously scraped the porridge bowls clean. Neither spoke as they ate. The business of eating provoked an almost trance-like expression on their faces. Grace realised that each of these men had developed a particular reverence for food, through long years of deprivation.

As they were eating Doctor Powell arrived. He beckoned Grace out onto the corridor.

'I've arranged for further surgery on Ernest Ball,' he said in a low voice. The surgeon has agreed to operate on his stump tomorrow. I don't want to leave it any longer than that, otherwise septicaemia could set in. What's his morale like?'

'He seems in good spirits today, Doctor. His wife is coming later. He's on top of the world about that.'

'Good. That's very good. He'll need to keep his spirits up. It could be touch and go.'

'Of course. I'll try to make sure he keeps positive.'

'Now, tomorrow morning, before the operation we'll need to move him down onto the surgical ward, and he'll have to stay there to recover afterwards. He shouldn't really be on this ward at all, Nurse, but Sister and I thought it best to keep the two of them together for a day or so.'

'I understand,' she said. Then after a pause she asked, 'What about the other man, Doctor? What are his chances?'

The doctor shook his head and pushed his glasses up his nose, frowning.

'Viral malaria. He's also got hepatitis and has recently suffered from diphtheria. The blood tests came through this morning. He'll go through times when he appears quite well. But the fever will keep coming back. He's very weak indeed, so I don't hold out that much hope for him I'm afraid. But we'll do our best.'

A chill went through Grace at these words and she glanced back through the doorway at Jack. He was sketching again, head down, absorbed in his work.

'He looks fine at the moment.'

'That's the nature of the illness I'm afraid. Cyclical. He's had it for several months by all accounts. If the war hadn't ended when it did, and he'd not been treated on the way home he would certainly have died.'

Grace felt shock wash through her at these words. She had to struggle to maintain her composure.

Later, Grace was bringing the medicine trolley to the side ward when a small boy with a grubby face darted out of the door, almost collided with the trolley and skidded along the passage towards the main ward.

'Jimmy!' a woman's voice came from inside the room. 'Come back here at once.'

Inside the ward a small, neat woman was sitting beside Ernie's bed. She wore a hat and coat and was dabbing her eyes with a handkerchief. Both she and Ernie were silent, meticulously avoiding each others' gaze. The child came back into the room and sidled up to his mother. He stood staring at his father with round incredulous eyes.

'So,' Ernie cleared his throat, all his earlier bonhomie gone. 'How did you say you got here Peggy?'

'By train. Dad drove us to Norwich station,' came the stiff response.

'Has he got a car now, then, your Dad?'

'No. A truck. For the farm. He bought it at the end of the war.'

'A truck! Well I never...'

The woman nodded and there was another long silence. Grace hovered in the doorway with the trolley. Ernie's wife had come early. Normally Sister had strict rules about visiting times, but her heart must have softened on this occasion. Grace was desperate to give them some privacy. There was only one thing to do. She pushed the trolley up close to Jack's bed and whisked the curtains around it, closing them off from the rest of the ward.

'Here's your quinine Mr Summers,' she said.

'Thanks for that, Nurse,' he said in a low voice. 'Ernie and Peggy need to be able to talk. It must be so difficult after such a long time apart. She had a bit of a shock when she saw him like that.'

Grace nodded. 'I'm sure.'

'He used to be so fit and powerful. Played football for the regiment, boxing champ...'

He shook his head and his eyes took on that faraway look that they had the day before, as if he had returned thousands of miles away, back to that hell-hole in the jungle, remembering whatever suffering and brutality he'd witnessed there.

'You need to take your quinine,' she said quickly, in an attempt to bring him back to the moment. At her words he blinked and his eyes came into focus.

'Of course, Nurse,' he said, and opened his mouth for her to spoon the medicine down his throat.

'By the way do I have to call you that?' he asked, swallowing. 'You introduced yourself yesterday as Nurse Everett, but surely your first name isn't actually *Nurse* is it?'

'Of course not,' Grace said laughing, but then she hesitated. Sister always discouraged the use of first names on the ward. *It doesn't do to get close to these men, girls. You need to retain a professional distance at all times.*

'Won't you tell me?' he asked. He was smiling now, teasing her, the brown skin around his eyes crinkling.

'I'm not supposed to,' she said.

'Come on. What harm could it do?'

'Hospital rules I'm afraid.'

'I'll have to guess then!'

'Oh please don't do that,' she said, exasperated. 'You'll never be able to. And I wouldn't tell you anyway. Even if you guessed right.'

He smiled. 'I bet it's a beautiful name,' he said, looking straight at her and she felt the heat creeping into her cheeks.

'Now I need to take your temperature,' she said, turning back towards the trolley to hide her confusion. As she busied herself with the equipment on the trolley, getting out the thermometer and shaking it, she realised that voices were now coming from the other side of the curtain. She smiled quietly. Ernie and Peggy seemed to be chatting more easily now.

'Would you be able to read to me, Nurse?' Jack asked suddenly as she moved towards him with the thermometer.

'I'd love to, but I don't think Matron would allow me do that,' she said, remembering how she'd been called into the office for a dressing down when she'd spent too much time reading letters to a patient who had bandages over his eyes.

'Now open wide. I need to take your temperature.'

As she removed the thermometer from his mouth a few minutes later she said.

'There's a library on the fourth floor. I'll go up and find you something. They have some detective novels in there. Raymond Chandler, Agatha Christie...'

'Anything else? I'm not too sure about crime books.'

'What sort of thing do you like?'

'Thomas Hardy,' he answered emphatically.

Grace paused, surprised. He went on.

'In one of the camps, someone had an old copy of *Far from the Madding Crowd*. It was really old and battered. But it was passed round the huts. Lots of men read it.'

'Really?' asked Grace. There was that look again. He was staring into space, seeing something way beyond Grace. But this time his eyes weren't filled with horror.

'It was like drinking from a clear spring in the middle of a desert,' he said, almost to himself. 'To read about a farm in the depths of the English countryside in that godforsaken place in the jungle...' He stopped himself, then said smiling into her eyes, 'so if the library has any other books by Thomas Hardy, I'd be very interested to read them.'

'I don't think they do, but I can check.'

'Thank you. It would help kill the time. Especially if Ernie is moving on.'

Grace hesitated, wondering again whether to ask him if he was likely to have any visitors himself, but held back. She didn't want to cause him pain and she also knew, deep down that the question would take them to a level of intimacy she shouldn't encourage.

During her lunch break she slipped up to the hospital library and scanned the dusty shelves. As she'd predicted, there was the usual mix of Readers Digest, Mills and Boon romances and detective series.

She chose a Raymond Chandler novel, *Farewell my Lovely,* and took it back down to Jack. She sensed his disappointment as she handed him the book, even though he tried to hide it.

'It will keep me company when they take Ernie away,' he smiled. 'Sister just came and told him about his op tomorrow.'

Ernie's family had now gone. He was sitting up looking chirpy, colour in his hollow cheeks for the first time.

'I'll be back up here to haunt you. Don't you worry Jack Summers,' he said.

THAT EVENING AFTER SUPPER, after they had washed the dishes, Grace's mother and Joan sat down at the kitchen table to go through a pile of wedding dress patterns. Her father went to sit beside the fire in the living room to read the evening paper, puffing at his pipe.

Grace wandered through.

'Do you mind if I get a book from your study Dad?'

He looked up and smiled. 'Of course not, Gracie. Help yourself. Lots of them are yours anyway. Didn't all your old school books end up in there when we redecorated your bedroom?'

'I think so. Thanks Dad.'

As she turned to go he said, 'I didn't think you had much time for reading any more though, what with your job, and Arthur taking up all your spare time.'

Grace looked down at the floor, a sudden wave of guilt passing through her at the mention of Arthur's name.

'What's the matter, Gracie, have I said something out of turn?'

'No. Not at all.'

He folded his paper and leant forward.

'Well what's the matter then? I know you. I know when something's wrong. Come and sit down and tell your old Pa. Is it about Arthur?'

She nodded miserably and stared into the flames.

'Well?'

'It's just that everyone expects...'

'Go on?'

'Everyone is expecting me to settle down with Arthur. And I'm not sure I'm ready for it that's all.'

Her father reached out and took her hand.

'Gracie. No one is expecting you to do anything you don't want to.'

'Mum and Joan are, I'm sure. I keep getting heavy hints.'

Her father laughed.

'I know they can get a bit carried away sometimes with this wedding lark. But you mustn't feel pressured by that.'

'Oh Dad, I know you're fond of Arthur yourself. It makes things very difficult with him working for you and everything.'

They were both silent for a moment. Shrill voices floated through from the kitchen,

'I think the ivory lace looks much nicer on that one Joan...'

'I've told you, Mummy, I want white. Ivory clashes with my hair colour. How many times do we have to go over this?'

Her father smiled conspiratorially at Grace and they both laughed.

'But seriously, Grace. You must make your own choices. In the end we all just want you to be happy.'

In the study, she ran her hand along the shelves of books that lined the whole of one wall. Her father was a methodical man and they were arranged in alphabetical order. She came to the 'Hs' and stopped. There it was. The set of three hardback Hardy novels presented to her as a school prize complete with their own presentation box. She pulled down the copy of *Tess of the D'Urbervilles*, and opened the front cover. 'To Grace Mary Everett, awarded for success in her School Certificate, 1942.' Tucking the book under her arm she went up to her room smiling to herself. Whoever read the book would be able to see her first name without being told.

4

Louise

Rangoon, August 1988

That night, as Louise lay in the saggy bed, listening to the rattle and whirr of the antiquated ceiling fan, the roar of vehicles on Strand Road and the horns of boats floating up from the river, her mind wandered back to the reason she was here. Her father, Jack. She felt that familiar sinking feeling of pain and loss whenever she thought of him.

He'd been an absent father as she'd grown up, dipping into her life now and again -each time giving her the hope of something more permanent, which never materialised. She'd tried to make up for his absence herself when she knew he was dying; throwing up her university course just before the second-year exams and going to stay in a Bed and Breakfast near where he was in hospital. She'd spent as much time by his bedside as she could. She didn't regret having done that, although it still seemed too little, too late.

'I've been a very bad father to you, Louise,' he'd said the last time she'd seen him. 'It's so good of you to be here with me. I wouldn't have blamed you if you hadn't come to see me at all, you know.'

'Don't talk like that, Dad, I'm here now aren't I?'

'I need to tell you something,' he said, straining to sit up a little and looking into her eyes.

'Go on. I'm listening,' she said.

'It's about the war.'

She looked at him in surprise. She'd never heard him speak about the war, but her mother had often alluded to it when they'd heard of some new difficulty he'd got himself into; picked up by the police for sleeping rough, admitted to an institution, out of work with no money.

'He's never got rid of his demons,' Grace would say, with that sad expression in her eyes that Louise rarely witnessed. 'He's not moved on from the war when he was a prisoner in Burma. It's very sad, but there it is.'

'Do you want to tell me about it?' she'd asked him, then. He lay back on the pillows and turned away from her, staring out of the window at the grey sky.

'Things happened to me in the war that I never came to terms with.'

'It must have been a terrible experience,' she'd said, although she was aware that she had no understanding of what he might have been through.

'Things happened in that camp. I can't describe them to you, Louise ...'

'You don't have to if it's difficult, Dad,' she said, laying her hand on his. It felt cold and bony to the touch.

'I kept a diary there. It was a risk, but I needed to write it all down. I used to bury it in the corner of the camp each evening. But when the Japs rounded us up and forced us to leave the camp one day in the middle of '43, I didn't have a chance to go and get it. It's probably still there.'

Louise's scalp began to tingle. What was he saying?

'One day... if you wanted to find out what happened, you might be able to find it.'

She looked at him with tears in her eyes and squeezed his hand.

'I'll go, Dad. I promise I'll go. Tell me where it is.'

'I buried it in a little tin box in the corner of the POW camp at Thanbyuzayat. It was behind the cook house, in the cemetery, deep in the roots of a pomelo tree. We used to go and pick the fruit up off the ground to eat we were so hungry. I buried it there.'

She hesitated. He'd turned towards her now and his eyes were suddenly eager, looking into hers, searching. He needed to know she would try to find it; she could tell that.

'I promise I'll try, Dad. But what if the tree isn't there anymore?'

'I used to have a map. You know, Louise, I kept it with me for years. I sometimes got it out and looked at it and thought about those dreadful times.'

'What happened to it?'

He shrugged and looked at her with watery eyes.

'I lost most things that mattered to me along the way. I wanted to keep it because I thought I might go back there one day. But in the end, I never had the courage... nor the money come to that,' he added with a weak smile.

'What a shame,' was all she could say.

'If you've got a pencil and paper I could try sketching it for you now.'

She fumbled in her bag and produced an old envelope and a blunt pencil. There was a magazine in the cabinet.

'Here – lean on this,' she said.

Breathing heavily, he sketched on the envelope for a few minutes, then lay back on his pillows, exhausted.

She took the envelope from between his fingers. On it he'd drawn a crude sketch-map showing a camp, with lines of buildings labelled *guardhouse: cookhouse: sleeping huts: Asian camp; Jap quarters.* There was a cemetery in one corner. Beside it was a tree, marked with a cross.

'That's where it is,' he said weakly, pointing to the cross. 'Under that tree.'

She stared at the map, trying to imagine what the place might look like on the ground. She tried to visualise how it might have been back then, filled with emaciated prisoners and their guards, and then what it might look like now. She looked into his eyes. He was watching her eagerly. She realised that although she'd known her father had been a prisoner of war, this was the first time she'd actually seen any concrete evidence. It suddenly struck her how little she actually knew him, despite the time they'd spent together these past few weeks. He was still watching her face, a question mark in his eyes.

'I'll go, Dad. I'll go to Burma and look for it.'

He sat back and a sigh escaped him. He felt for her hand again.

'Thank you, Louise.'

'Don't thank me.'

'And if you do find it, it will tell you what happened to me there. Things I've never been able to talk about. It might help to explain some things...'

THE YOUNG MAN waiting for Louise in the hotel lobby the next morning was not at all what she'd expected. In the car she'd not seen his face properly and she'd assumed that he would look similar to his cousin; dressed like a westerner, desperate to wear the latest fashions.

This boy was the antithesis of that. He was tall for a Burmese man, and very slight, as if he'd burned up all his fat with nervous energy. His hair was cut short, with a fringe that flopped over his eyes, and he wore a blue short-sleeved shirt and a traditional checked longyi. He was pacing the lobby impatiently, although Louise wasn't late for their appointment. When she approached him, he shook her hand with a firm grip and gave her an intense stare.

'Very pleased to meet you,' he said without smiling. 'My name is Zeya. We met with my cousin in the car yesterday.'

Louise smiled and told him her name.

'The sun is very hot today,' Zeya said, frowning. 'You don't have a hat? Wait one moment.' He hurried over to the desk and after a rapid exchange in Burmese came back brandishing a large black umbrella.

Taking Louise's elbow he guided her out of the front entrance and through the traffic to the other side of Strand Road. There, under the shade of the umbrella, on the bank of the river, he began to tell her all about the origins of Rangoon. It had started life as a tiny fishing village named Dagon, he explained, established by the Mon hill tribes. Later it had developed into a trading post. Gradually it became the capital of the region and an important lynchpin in the British Empire.

Sightseeing normally bored Louise, but this boy was so eloquent, so full of passion and knowledge for his subject that she was enthralled.

When he'd finished his speech by the waterside, he took her arm again and guided her skilfully across Strand Road threading between the queues of cars and motorcycles.

'I will show you along this street here next to the hotel. It is called Phayre Street. There are many important buildings from the days of the British Empire along here.'

Louise glanced at him. He'd said the words 'British Empire' with a kind of suppressed anger, but his face betrayed nothing. They walked along the uneven pavement, picking their way between the street hawkers and food stalls. The smell of spices floating on the air made her mouth water.

Phayre Street was a wide, elegant road lined with the former headquarters of huge trading companies, government departments and banks. Like the building she'd looked at the previous evening, these great monoliths were decaying. Moss grew on their walls and vegetation sprouted from the corniced plaster work.

'These buildings must have been beautiful once,' she said. From the way his face instantly clouded over she knew she'd made a mistake. He turned towards her.

'You mean beautiful when the British were here to keep us ignorant Burmese in order and make sure their precious buildings were kept pristine?'

Louise felt heat rise to her cheeks.

'I'm sorry,' she stammered, 'I didn't mean that at all. Please forgive me.'

'You are right, though,' he went on bitterly, his voice low, 'They *were* once beautiful. Our corrupt Government does nothing to maintain them. They are so busy lining their own pockets and exploiting their fellow countrymen. There is nothing left for infrastructure or heritage.'

Louise studied the pavement as she walked. The words of someone in the hostel in the Khao San road rang in her ears.

'Don't ever talk politics with a Burmese person. They're not allowed to. Anyone could be listening in. They all live in fear for their lives if they step out of line. It will only embarrass them if you bring it up.'

And yet here was this boy criticising the Military Government in one of the busiest streets in the capital, with people passing by on every side. She wondered what to say.

'Did your cousin say you are a student,' she said at last, deciding it was safest to change the subject.

He was silent for a few moments and Louise began to worry that he was so offended by her previous remark that he wasn't going to respond.

'Yes, that's true,' he said at last.

'What do you study?' Louise asked quickly, grasping onto the subject as if it were a life-line.

'Engineering. I study in the faculty of engineering. I am doing a Batchelor's in mechanical sciences.'

'That's very impressive.'

'Not really. It has taken me a very long time to get this far. We have to pay our own way in Burma you know. I have had to take two years out to get enough money to carry on. My family is very poor. There are no student grants here, unfortunately.'

'That does sound very tough,' Louise said, going silent herself.

'And what about you?' he asked. 'Are you a student also?'

It was Louise's turn to be defensive.

'I suppose so. I was studying for an English degree. But at the moment I'm taking some time out.'

He turned and stared at her.

'But why? In your country your fees are paid and your living expenses too - is that not correct? Why would you take time out?'

'My father died. I needed to be with him, so I had to miss some exams. I will have to repeat a year if I go back and I'm not sure that I want to.'

Zeya stopped walking and turned to stare at her, a puzzled frown on his face.

'I'm very sorry to hear about your father. But surely you should go back if you have the chance. Why would you not?'

She hung her head and couldn't meet his eye. How could she explain to this boy, who'd made tremendous sacrifices just to be able to attend university, how she'd squandered her own education?

'I didn't do that well actually, in the first year. I wasn't sure it was for me, to tell you the truth.'

She didn't want to tell him about her chaotic life during that year. The constant parties, the drinking, the serial relationships, the debts she'd run up. The fact that she'd hardly attended lectures or tutorials. And that other thing: the thing that was worse than the parties and the drinking. The thing that made her go hot and cold whenever it entered her mind. She felt ashamed to even think about it in his presence.

Zeya began to walk again. Quickly this time, his head bowed.

'I simply do not understand you Westerners. You have every chance in the world but you do not appreciate that.'

Louise remained silent. She understood how he felt and she was ashamed, suddenly, of the casual way she'd abandoned her studies. She'd only recently admitted to herself that in a way her father's illness had given her the perfect excuse. She'd been only too glad to have a reason to leave the place where she'd made such a fool of herself that she could hardly show her face amongst the other students.

She struggled to keep up with him in the cloying heat. Her T shirt was sticking to her body and her feet slipping in her flimsy sandals.

'Where are we going?' she asked breathlessly.

'I will show you some more important buildings from the British period. Then we can go to Sule Pagoda. It is opposite city hall, in the very centre of the city. On the way, perhaps we could drop into a tea shop if you would like that?'

'Yes. That would be interesting.'

They had already walked past several of these establishments, where people sat at tiny tables on low chairs, drinking from miniature cups, deep in conversation. She was glad she was with Zeya, despite his prickliness. She wouldn't have had the confidence to go into a tea shop alone. Perhaps there he would calm down and she could ask him about how to get to Moulmein.

They came to a cross-roads and he led her down another wide, tree-lined street. A huge, imposing building, painted red and white, with majestic turrets and a square clock-tower, loomed up in front of them.

'This is the High Court,' said Zeya. 'Designed by a British architect and built by the Victorians.'

She stared up at the building, awed by its size and elegance.

'It is a pity that British justice has disappeared from this country along with the British themselves,' Zeya said.

They walked the length of the building, then, in a side street, Zeya showed her into a busy tea-shop. Beside the entrance a shoeshine boy, who couldn't have been more than nine or ten, sat on a low stool, bent over a last, furiously polishing a man's shoe. He looked up at Zeya and the two exchanged a few words.

'He wants to know if you'd like your shoes cleaned while you're drinking tea?' Zeya asked Louise. She looked down at her sandals which consisted of series of thin leather straps.

'I'm not sure there's anything to polish... she began, but then noticing the small boy's expectant expression, she kicked them off and handed them to him.

'Of course,' she said.

'Thank you,' said Zeya. 'His parents are sick and the family needs all the money it can get.'

A group of young people at a corner table waved to Zeya as they entered the shop, and for the first time, she saw him relax. A huge smile spread across his face. She noticed that unlike his cousin, he had perfect white teeth.

'Do you mind if we sit with my friends?' he asked. 'They are students too.'

'Of course not,' she said, relieved at his change of mood.

The group made room for them and they sat at the table on tiny stools. Zeya explained that the brown tea, in a battered metal teapot in the middle of the table was free, but that spiced chai would be charged for.

She ordered some cardamom chai, because she sensed it was expected, although she would have been quite happy with simple tea. Another young boy, about the same age as the shoeshine boy brought it instantly. As Louise sipped the cloying, tan-coloured liquid, Zeya introduced the people at the table. Louise smiled and nodded as they all shook her hand.

There were three young men and two girls he introduced as Myat Noe and Yupar. Both girls were slight and had fine, delicate features. But while Yupar was pretty, with sparkling eyes and a broad smile, Myat Noe was stunningly beautiful, with high cheekbones, perfect skin and full lips. They both took Louise's hand and smiled their hellos.

'We will speak in English for our guest,' said a young man called Nakaji and the others all murmured their consent.

The conversation resumed. At first they discussed their tutors and their university courses, but soon the conversation turned to politics. In hushed tones, they began to swap stories of injustice and ill-treatment at the hands of the government.

'You know. We were all involved in the March uprising,' Zeya said, turning to Louise. 'The soldiers stormed the protesters and several people were killed the week of March 12th. One of our own friends died that day.'

'Really? But that's dreadful!' said Louise, shocked.

'It started as a peaceful protest, but it was brutally crushed. There were tanks on the streets for days, soldiers with guns. Denpa and Htut here were both in prison for several weeks.'

Louise stared at the two young men. They looked so slight, so young and vulnerable.

'I thought... I thought,' she said, lowering her voice, 'that it wasn't a good idea to speak about politics here.'

'There is no need to fear in this place,' said Myat Noe, smiling, looking earnestly at Louise, 'This tea shop owner is our friend. He knows all his customers. We are safe to speak our minds here, as long as we are discreet.'

'So perhaps you could tell me. What was the March uprising about?' Louise asked.

'It started as nothing much. Just an argument in a tea shop a bit like this one. But the argument ended in a fight. The police were called and one student was shot and killed. The protests were about police brutality, but not just that. The currency had been devalued and the economy paralysed by the Generals. The people are poor and crushed. It was a protest against the government.'

'Did it change anything?' Louise asked.

'Well General Ne Win resigned last month. He was the head of the Government for years. That's a start, although he said some threatening things about the army being prepared to shoot to kill.'

'It will not be long now, though,' said Zeya. 'Not long until our big day.'

'What does that mean?' asked Louise.

'We cannot talk about that. Not even here. But you wait. In a few days' time, the world will wake up to the fact that the Burmese people aren't giving up the fight for democracy.'

More people entered the tea shop and the conversation round the table moved on. Keen to practice their English, the students asked Louise about life in England, about her family, her home, her studies. But soon, Myat Noe got to her feet followed by Nakaji.

'We have to go,' she said. 'We have a lecture at noon. Goodbye, Louise, it was very nice to meet you.'

One by one the other students drifted back to their studies.

'Thank you for introducing me to your friends,' said Louise, smiling at Zeya. He looked relaxed now. He had lost that brooding, hunted look he'd worn when she'd first met him.

'A pleasure. They are all good people. Committed to their studies and committed to our cause too.'

'Yes. I could see that. It was an honour to meet them.'

'Would you like to go to the Sule Pagoda now? It is not far from here,' Zeya asked.

'In a moment,' she replied, pouring herself another cup of chai. She took a sip and looked at him steadily. Could she trust him? After speaking to his friends she was sure she could. She took a deep breath.

'There's something I need to ask you first,' she said.

'Really?' he looked at her with a frown.

'Yes. You see I came to Burma for a reason. I need to get to Thanbyuzayat.'

Zeya frowned. 'Thanbyuzayat? That's in the South. Foreign visitors cannot go there. It's rebel territory.'

'Yes, I know. So that's why I need help.'

'But why do you need to go there? There is nothing there. Just a small town and a war cemetery. It was the end of the Thai-Burma railway.'

'That's the reason I need to go there. My father was there you see, during the war. He asked me to go.'

'Ah. I see...' he said slowly.

Then she told him about the last conversation she'd had with her father, about the diary, about the promise she'd made to find it. When she'd finished, Zeya was silent. She looked at his face to try to gauge his reaction, but it was impossible to tell what he was thinking.

In the end, he looked at her and said, 'I can help you. I can go to the train station and buy you a ticket to Moulmein if you let me take your passport.'

'Thank you. That's very kind of you. But that's not the difficult part.'

He laughed, showing his white teeth.

'They do not speak or write English in the train station. You might find it quite tricky to explain what you want.'

'Yes, you're right. I'm sorry. But I will need help getting from Moulmein to Thanbyuzayat.'

He was silent again for a few moments. She listened to the clatter and hubbub of the tea shop, the horns and engines of the traffic on the road outside. Finally he said,

'Alright. I will help you. But it will be risky and you have to understand that. I will write you a letter to take to a friend of mine in Moulmein. You will have to pay him, but if I ask him, he will be able to drive you to Thanbyuzayat in his truck.'

She turned to him smiling with relief, at the same time her heart beating a little faster at the thought of the risks they both might be taking.

'Thank you,' she said. 'Thank you so much. That's very kind of you.'

He held up his hand as if to fend off the thanks. She stopped speaking. His expression was grave now.

'But in return I have to ask you to do something for us,' he said in a low voice, 'For our cause.'

'Of course,' she answered without hesitation. 'What is it?'

'I would like you to take some documents for me. To our friends down there.'

She nodded. That didn't sound too risky.

'At the moment they cannot travel out of the region, they have been banned from doing so by the government, for their part in the recent demonstrations. So they cannot pass road blocks. If you take them some new identity papers, they will be able to come to Rangoon. And we need them here soon, for the big day that I mentioned.'

'You mean you want me to take some false identity papers to your friends?' her nerves began to jangle at the thought.

'Yes. That is what I'm asking.'

He was looking at her steadily, seriously.

'We cannot take them ourselves as we are banned from travelling too. We cannot post them because they would be opened by the censors.'

'I see,' said Louise slowly, her scalp tingling as the implications of the bargain began to dawn on her.

'It will be a risk for you,' Zeya went on. 'If the police catch you, they will take you into custody and deport you. You would never be able to return to Burma again. You must understand that before you agree.'

'I agree,' she said instantly before she had time to think properly. She knew she had to seize the opportunity. There was so little time to organise her trip, and whoever she asked to help might have similar conditions.

'Good,' Zeya said, getting up from the stool. 'So that's settled. Now I will show you the Sule Pagoda. We can then go on to the great Shwedagon Pagoda – the pride of our city. And this evening I will bring the papers and the letter to your hotel.'

5

Grace
London, 1945

Jack took the book from Grace with trembling hands and laid it on his lap. For several minutes he didn't speak, or even look up at her. When finally he did though, she could see the emotion in his eyes.

'Thank you,' he whispered. 'This means a lot to me.'

'I'm glad you like it.'

'Where did you find it?'

'I brought it from home actually. I read it when I was at school.'

'That's very kind of you. I'll take good care of it.'

When she went in to give him his medicines later on that morning, he said, after he had swallowed the pills, 'Thank you, Grace.'

He was looking straight into her eyes. Smiling at the sound of her name she held her finger over her lips.

'Don't let Sister find out you know my name,' she said, 'or I'll be for the chop.'

'It'll be our secret,' he said.

Now that Ernie had left, and Jack was improving, Grace was asked to help the other nurses on the main ward. Each time she glanced in on Jack, though, his head was either bent over *Tess of the D'Urbervilles*, or he was busy sketching.

Sometimes he would speak about the book; 'Alec D'Urberville is a nasty piece of work don't you think?' or 'Do you think Angel is meant to be weak and vain?' and she would pause and exchange a few sentences with him about it, aware that she was lingering longer than she really should each time.

The days passed, and Jack seemed to get stronger by the hour. By the end of his first week, he had gained several pounds in weight. His skin had lost that original greasy pallor that had so frightened Grace, there was now colour in his cheeks and his eyes were brighter. He was still painfully thin, but now he could get out of bed and walk slowly around the ward with Grace holding his arm.

Ernie was recovering well from his surgery and one of the nurses on the surgical ward wheeled him up to visit Jack each day.

Grace would occasionally look in on them as they talked. When Ernie was there, Jack seemed to relax in a way he never did with anyone else. Again, she realised that whatever they'd been through together had given them a special bond that no-one else shared.

One day, as she stood in the passage watching them from the doorway, Nancy sidled up to her and whispered,

'You're sweet on that Jack Summers aren't you?'

'Of course not,' said Grace briskly, turning and starting to walk back towards the main ward, but she felt a flush creep up her cheeks.

'Oh, I think you are,' said Nancy hurrying along beside her.

'I've seen the way you two get on when you're in there. He's got a definite soft spot for you too.'

Grace shrugged. 'Don't be silly. He's no different from any of the other servicemen we've had in here.'

'Oh, I think he is different. I've seen the evidence with my own eyes.'

'Whatever do you mean?'

Nancy winked at her. 'His sketchbook. I took a quick peek myself. I was on the evening shift yesterday. He was sound asleep, bless him.'

'Nancy. You shouldn't have done that,' Grace said, shocked.

But as she went about her duties on the ward that morning, her mind kept returning to Nancy's words. Her curiosity was piqued, but she was determined not to stoop as low as Nancy had and look inside the book. Patients' effects are their own private belongings. Matron's words came back to her. They should always be respected and treated as such.

For several days, things carried on in the same routine. Jack finished *Tess of the D'Urbervilles* one day.

'What a very sad ending,' he said. 'But a brilliant book all the same. Thank you so much for lending it to me.'

'Would you like me to bring another one? I think we've got most of Hardy's books at home.'

'That would be wonderful. You're very kind.'

'It's no trouble. Which one would you like?'

He shrugged. 'Why don't you just choose one for me? I'm not sure of all the titles actually.'

The next morning, Ernie was sitting next to the bed when Grace entered the room with the book. She had chosen *The Mayor of Casterbridge*.

To her surprise Ernie was dressed in a three-piece suit, his new wooden leg protruding from the right trouser leg.

'I'm leaving today,' he told Grace with a broad grin that showed the gaps in his teeth.

'The surgeon came and told me himself this morning. They're discharging me. The operation's been a success he reckons.'

'That's marvellous news Ernie. You must be delighted. Is Peggy coming to collect you?'

He laughed. 'Her dad's coming in that truck of his all the way from Norfolk to fetch me. Should be a sight for sore eyes.'

'I'm so happy for you. We're going to miss you so much.' She glanced across at Jack who sat with his sketchbook open on his lap.

'Like a hole in the head we will,' joked Jack.

'You could give me a couple of your sketches to remember you by. What have you been drawing lately Jack?' asked Ernie.

Jack closed his sketchbook quickly.

'Oh, not much really. There's nothing to see,' he said. 'Just a few scribbles.

'Come on,' Ernie insisted. 'I've told you before there's no need to be shy. Nurse Everett knows how good you are. She said so herself on our first day don't you remember?'

With a wink at Grace, Ernie leaned forward and snatched the book from Jack's lap. He began to flick through the pages.

'Come, come and take a look, Nurse. There's one of you in here.'

'Oh, I don't know...' Grace hesitated glancing at Jack whose cheeks were pink now. He was avoiding her gaze.

'Come on. It's very good.'

She approached tentatively and looked over Ernie's shoulder. She was amazed at what she saw as he turned the pages. There were many pictures of her in amongst ones of Ernie. There was one of her standing in the corner of the room her hair lit up by the sunlight from the window. There was another of her face close up, smiling, her eyes shining, and yet another of her standing behind the trolley. In each picture she looked far more beautiful than she actually was. They were idealised, romantic images, and she couldn't help feeling flattered that Jack should picture her in that light. She could feel the heat in her own cheeks now.

'These are amazing Jack I don't know what to say,' she said, but Jack wasn't looking at her. Ernie himself looked flustered now. He closed the book abruptly.

'I said he'd got talent didn't I nurse?' he muttered.

'You were absolutely right Ernie.'

There was an awkward pause.

'Are you going to give me that one of me sitting up in bed then, Jackie boy? I reckon that would look nice framed, hanging on the wall at home. It might remind the family how lucky they all are that I came back. When the novelty's worn off that is.'

'I suppose so,' said Jack, bending forward to tear out the page.

Ernie's nurse appeared in the doorway.

'It's time to say your goodbyes Mr Ball,' she said. 'Your father-in-law is waiting downstairs.'

The nurse helped Ernie to get up and handed him his crutches.

Then he moved to Jack's bedside and leaned forward. For a moment Grace thought he was about to hug Jack. Instead the two men shook hands. Grace noticed that there were tears in both their eyes. Ernie stood up and saluted Jack, then turned and made his way towards the door. He stopped beside Grace.

'Thank you for everything, Nurse,' he said quietly, touching her arm.

'Look after this blighter here for us,' he added, nodding in Jack's direction.

'He's been to hell and back,' he muttered under his breath as he walked away.

When the tapping sound of Ernie's crutches in the corridor had finally faded, Grace turned to Jack. He was making an effort to compose himself.

'Ernie is a brave man,' she said.

Jack nodded. 'I'm going to miss him and his ridiculously cheery ways.'

'You two must have been through a lot together,' she said.

Jack didn't answer and she caught him with that pensive expression again as if he wasn't in the present at all but far away in that hell-hole in the jungle.

'Here's the book I brought for you,' she said briskly, changing the subject. '*The Mayor of Casterbridge*.' She handed it to him.

'THANK YOU,' he said coming back to the present moment and looking at her with deep gratitude. 'You're too kind.'

'When did you start drawing, Jack?' She asked gently, thinking it would be better to acknowledge what she'd seen rather than let the embarrassment grow between them.

'Oh, as a child. It was the only thing I was ever good at. I was always scribbling away at something. Mum bought me some paints and I used to sit at the kitchen table copying pictures from her magazines.'

'Did you sketch when you were in the camp?'

His face clouded over and she immediately regretted the question.

'It wasn't really that sort of place,' he said. A brooding silence came over him again and Grace sensed that he needed to be alone with his thoughts.

'I'm sorry. I didn't mean to upset you.'

But he didn't answer. He looked miles away. She stood there helplessly, regretting her impetuous tongue.

GRACE SAT opposite Arthur at their corner table in the River Restaurant at the Savoy Hotel. He smiled at her and slid his hand over hers on the table. That sinking feeling she'd had on and off all evening returned in force and she gave him a sickly smile.

She'd caught the tube into the city after work and met him on the steps of Farquhar's Bank where he and her father worked. They'd often done that on a Friday. Grace loved coming into the city in the early evening, making her way along the crowded pavements towards Bank, the buzz of the place and the frisson of excitement as city workers left their offices at the start of the weekend. It was the anonymity of the city that she relished. It made her feel free - as nowhere else did.

She got off the tube at St Paul's and took her time walking down Cheapside, enjoying the atmosphere and the fresh winter air on her face after her day on the stifling ward.

She was looking forward to being able to relax and unwind after the rigours of her week. Arthur usually took her somewhere cheap in the backstreets behind Threadneedle Street. They would have a drink in a pub followed by a simple meal. But this evening, as she approached the steps of the bank and saw him standing there in his Cashmere overcoat, impatiently scanning the rush-hour crowds for her, she knew instinctively that he had something else in mind for tonight. As she got closer she saw that he was wearing a new three-piece suit, that his hair was freshly cut and Brylcreemed, and that he must have been to the barber's for a shave in his lunch hour.

'You're looking very dapper tonight,' she said lightly, pecking his cheek, trepidation entering her heart. Her early suspicions were confirmed. He seemed different from usual. Nervous, formal, a little distant.

He put his arm around her shoulders and shepherded her through the crowds.

'Shall we go to Simpsons?' she asked.

'No, not tonight,' he replied. 'I've got a surprise for you.'

'Really? Where are we going?'

'Wait and see,' he said. 'I think you'll like it.'

He hailed the taxi and ushered her into the back seat.

She didn't hear what he said to the driver, but from the direction the cab took, she soon realised that they were travelling towards the West End.

'Where are we going?' she asked again.

'That's my surprise,' he said. 'Wait and see.'

'Is it somewhere posh?' she asked. 'You should have told me to dress up.'

He turned towards her and for the first time looked her in the eye.

'You don't need to dress up, Gracie,' he said, his expression serious with a trace of longing in his eyes. 'You always look classy, whatever you wear.'

The taxi edged along the Embankment now and she stared out at the River Thames, at the lights of the boats and buildings dancing on the water, she realised with sudden panic that this evening she was going to have to face up to some unpalatable truths she'd been ducking for some time.

As they drew up at the riverside entrance at the Savoy, he took her hand and said, 'Our special place, Gracie. Remember?'

'Of course,' she said, getting out of the taxi and waiting as he paid the driver, wishing she was a million miles away.

Now as she watched Arthur across the table, she knew the dreaded question was coming. It had only been a matter of time, she'd known that for a while. She felt trapped; trapped by her own complacency, her selfishness and weakness. She knew that the time had come to get out of that trap, but that it wasn't her who was going to be hurt. And that made her feel guilty too.

As she sat opposite him waiting for the food to arrive, her thoughts came together. She wondered why she had sleepwalked into this situation. Did she care so little for her own status, her own personal preferences that she had allowed herself to be swept along by this arrangement that would dictate her future happiness and the course of the rest of her life? The thought of it now made her catch her breath. It was as if she'd wandered to the edge of a precipice and woken up just in time to realise that she was about to plunge over the edge.

It came to her that her conversations with Jack had awakened another side of her, someone interested in exploring life, seeking new experiences, living life to the full. The spectre of life with Arthur now looked dull and set. It felt like atrophying, as her mother had done. She knew she couldn't do it.

The meal was almost over. The waiter had brought liqueurs and chocolates. Conversation hadn't flowed as it normally did between them. To Grace it felt like a combination of being over-awed by the surroundings, and the knowledge that the end of the meal would bring the awkward conversation.

Arthur cleared his throat and said, 'Gracie, you must have an idea why I brought you here tonight.'.

'I'm not sure Arthur,' she began.

'I want to marry you,' he was leaning forward and looking into her eyes now. 'You must have realised I was going to ask. I've been wanting to for a while now.'

Grace shook her head, searching for words.

'I've got great prospects at Farquhar's you know. I'm headed for promotion in a few months' time. We could afford to live somewhere very nice. Near your parents if you like. Near Joan and Les too.'

She tried to maintain her smile while he spoke, but all the while she was wondering when he was going to tell her how much she meant to him, how much he loved her, but those words didn't come.

'I could provide well for you, you know. You wouldn't have to work. You wouldn't have to do anything you didn't want to. We could have a couple of kids...'

'But I love my work Arthur,' she broke in. 'I wouldn't want to give that up even if I got married.'

He stared at her, then readjusted his expression.

'Well that's fine. If you love your job perhaps you could keep your hand in...you might change your mind in time.'

She swallowed, but still she couldn't bring herself to respond to his question.

'You know Gracie, I've been wanting to ask you from the start. When I first spotted you in the ballroom that night with your father, in that black dress. You looked so... I'm not sure of the right word...spirited, I think it is. I just wanted to make you mine.'

He fumbled in his pocket and at last brought out a tiny box. He handed it to her.

'Will you marry me Gracie Everett?'

The ring was diamond, delicate and beautiful. She found her hands shaking as she took it from him.

'Arthur,' she began, and her voice was choking. 'I'm so flattered that you asked. You're a lovely man ...but the truth is, I don't think I can marry you. I'm so sorry.'

'Why ever not?' he asked, his voice registering genuine surprise.

'I'm not ready to marry anyone yet. I'm sorry if I led you to think otherwise.'

'But Joan is getting married, and you're two years older than her.'

'But I'm not Joan, Arthur. It's all she's wanted for a long time. I'm not that settled or grown up even. I'm too independent.'

She handed back the ring box and he took it, returning it to his pocket. He looked bewildered. She watched his face anxiously. He sat staring down at the linen tablecloth for a few minutes, his shoulders slumped.

'I'm so sorry Arthur. We've had a nice time together these past few months. You're such a good person. Far too good for me.'

He didn't answer, or even look at her. She was aware of the bustle of the waiters, the low hum of conversations from other tables. When he finally looked up, he had recovered his composure.

'I have to admit that this is a shock Gracie. I thought you loved me. But I must have misjudged the situation. I thought we were good companions.'

'We were. We are. It's just that it's never been too serious between us has it?'

He drew himself up and signalled to the waiter for the bill. She could tell from his expression that he'd already come to terms with the situation and that in his mind he was planning out a new version of his future without her. She began to relax and breathe again.

'You're a lovely girl, Grace,' he said, taking her arm as they walked out onto the street. 'You'll make some other lucky bloke a wonderful wife one day.'

They got into a waiting taxi. As it swung out of the drive and turned west along the river, he turned to her.

'I've got to ask you this Grace,' he said. 'Is there someone else?'

'No Arthur,' she said squeezing his hand. 'Of course not.'

'You sure?' he asked, looking at her closely. There was a flicker of hurt pride in his eyes now that she could tell he was doing his best to hide.

'Quite sure.'

Once again Grace stared out at the river as the taxi sped west, wondering if she'd been quite honest with him, or with herself.

6

Louise
Rangoon, August 1988

L ouise was waiting in the lobby of the Strand Hotel. Her nerves were on edge and she kept glancing at her watch. Zeya had said he would meet her there at seven o' clock, and it was already ten past. He hadn't struck her as someone who would be late without good reason and she was beginning to worry. Had he been stopped and searched?

She thought back to their earlier visit to the Sule Pagoda, a temple in the middle of a busy roundabout, right in the centre of Rangoon. They had taken off their shoes and walked up a flight of steps to the marble tiled platform. The huge golden stupa was surrounded by prayer halls and shrines. Zeya had explained the history of the sacred place; that it contained a relic - a hair of the Buddha - and was over two thousand years old. He also pointed to the layout of the busy streets below and told her that the

British had made the temple the focal point of the city when they were planning it.

Louise was charmed by the colour and the vibrant buzz of the place; by the throngs of people worshipping at the many shrines, bringing flowers and lighting candles. As they walked around the stupa on the hexagonal walkway that bordered it, she asked Zeya about his family.

'My mother was a teacher,' he said. 'But she is ill at the moment and cannot work. My father was a teacher too, but he... he no longer lives with us. It is very hard for my mother.'

'I'm sorry to hear that,' Louise said. 'Are you able to see your father?'

Zeya shook his head.

'Unfortunately, no. I saw him once or twice at the beginning, but things have tightened up recently, and I haven't seen him for over three years.'

'Oh... where does he live?' she asked.

'He is in prison.'

He said it with an air of finality, putting to an end to further questions on the matter.

They fell silent as they walked, breathing in the heady smell of incense and candles, listening to the chanting of monks and the low clang of the prayer bells. Louise began to understand why Zeya was so intense, so passionate about the pro-democracy campaign.

Now, she sat on one of the teak benches among the potted palms in the hotel lobby and watched a party of tourists being checked in at the reception desk. The middle-aged Americans looked hot and exhausted after their long journey, and a little shell-shocked after their first encounter with Burmese traffic. The tour guide was growing impatient with the receptionist over the allocation of rooms.

Across the hall, she noticed the debonair figure of Jim Yates enter through the front door and head swiftly towards the bar.

She snatched up a magazine and buried her face in it, worried he would notice her and want to chat.

At last Zeya appeared in the doorway. He hesitated momentarily on the threshold as he looked around for her. Sighing with relief she got up from her seat and hurried over to him. She noticed an anxious look in his eyes.

'I am sorry I'm late,' he said, 'I had to take a quiet route through the back streets. I didn't want to risk being searched.'

'I was worried about that too. I'm glad you got here safely,' she said.

'Is there somewhere private we can go? I'd prefer not to give you the papers here in the lobby.'

Louise hesitated, remembering the state she'd left her room in that morning; the bed was unmade and she'd emptied the contents of her back-pack onto the floor while searching for her sandals. She felt a flush creep up her cheeks as she recalled the half-drunk coca-cola bottles beside the bed, the overflowing ashtray. This neat, meticulous young man would probably be offended by her slovenly habits, but there was no choice; she'd have to swallow her pride and put up with his disapproval.

They avoided each others' eyes and were silent as they rattled up to the fourth floor in the ancient lift. Louise could almost feel the tension radiating from Zeya. When they reached her room, he stood behind her, tapping his foot while she fumbled with the stiff lock. As she opened the door she was preparing to apologise for the state of the room, but when she switched on the light, she saw that the room had been transformed. The bed was made and her clothes folded neatly and placed in little piles on the chest of drawers. All rubbish and debris had been removed and the ash trays emptied. Of course! The maid would have been in to clean. It was a long time since she'd stayed in a hotel with room service.

'Please sit down,' Louise said and Zeya took a seat in one of the low wooden chairs upholstered in brown faux leather. She sat down opposite him.

From a cloth shoulder bag Zeya produced two brown envelopes. One large and one small.

'This one is the letter to my friend. The address is on the front.' He handed her the small letter.

She stared at the Burmese script on the envelope- all tiny circles, squiggles and loops to her eyes.

'I can't read this,' she said, laughing.

'It's all right. I will write it down in English for you in a moment.'

'Now here is your train ticket to Moulmein. It was expensive I'm afraid. I had to bribe the man in the ticket office. I don't have authority to travel there myself.'

'How much was it?'

'Fifteen dollars,' he said, a note of apology in his voice.

'That's no problem.'

'The train leaves early tomorrow morning from the station. It goes at seven o'clock but you must be there at least half an hour beforehand to ensure you get the right seat. I've booked you second class, I'm afraid. First class was completely full. I'm sorry, but it won't be second class as you know it in your country.'

'I don't mind about that. Really.'

'And here are the documents for you to take to my friend in Moulmein. There is no need for you to look inside the envelope. The less you know about it the better.'

'It's all right. I won't open it,' she assured him.

'It's good that you are going to Moulmein though,' he said, 'if you hadn't been, my friends would have had great difficulty coming up to Rangoon for the 8th August.'

'8th August? Is that your big day?'

He nodded and leaned forward.

'A big march is planned,' he whispered, his eyes intense. 'A peaceful protest. People from all over the country are coming to march in Rangoon on the City Hall. The Generals will be very surprised at the strength of feeling against them.'

'That's next week. It's the last day on my visa.'

'So, I hope you will be able to join us on the march when you return from the south.'

'Of course,' she said, taking the large envelope from him.

'Is there somewhere you can conceal that in your luggage?' he asked with an anxious frown.

'I only have this backpack,' she said, pointing to the battered orange pack that the maid had tactfully placed on the luggage rack at the end of the bed.

'It is very unlikely that you will be searched as you travel. The soldiers tend to ignore foreigners, but if you had an inside compartment or something similar it would perhaps be safer.'

She took the backpack up with trembling hands. What was she letting herself in for? She ran her hand around inside the pack. There was a thin cotton lining inside the outer canvas.

'I might be able to sew it into the lining.'

Zeya rewarded her with one of his rare smiles. It transformed his face.

'If you have paper, I will write down the name and address of my friend. Again, you should conceal those away while you are travelling.'

There was a 'Strand Hotel' notepad on the table under the window. He scribbled on it and handed her the page.

'My friend, Thuza, will drive you to Thanbyuzayat if you give him this letter. He will probably charge you a few dollars. It will be risky for him. As I said, foreigners are not allowed south of Moulmein. The area is in control of the rebels.'

'Thank you for organising this, Zeya. It means a lot to me,' she said.

'It is no trouble,' he said, moving towards the door.

'Good luck,' he said. 'And I hope to see you again on the eighth.'

'How will I find you?' she asked.

'Here is my card. Come to my apartment at six in the morning.'

'That seems very early for a march.'

'It's the most auspicious time. We will begin our march at eight minutes past eight on the eighth day of the eighth month of the year eighty eight.'

She smiled. 'I see.' She was about to ask him if he thought it would make any difference, but she could tell from his eyes that he would be insulted by such a question.

'Goodbye. And good luck.'

And with that he was gone. Louise stood staring at the envelopes and the train ticket, conflicting emotions running through her; excitement, mingled with apprehension at the thought of what the next day would bring.

It was still dark as she walked through the streets of Rangoon towards the station the next morning. The city was waking up slowly; people were setting up shops and food stalls on the pavements, sweeping rubbish away, dusting down tables. There was little traffic about. The air was as damp and sultry as it was during the daytime and Louise soon found her back was wet with sweat beneath the backpack.

From some angles, from crossroads and glimpsed through the ends of streets, she caught sight of the shining golden light from the floodlit Schwedagon Pagoda that dominated the city from its vantage point on Singuttara Hill.

In one quiet street Louise slowed down to watch a line of monks in maroon robes proceed slowly along the pavement. As they walked they chanted, and each monk held out a small, round alms bowl. People emerged from their houses, or waited for the monks to approach, and slipped morsels of food into the bowls.

Light was beginning to creep into the sky as Louise arrived at the station, a huge white building with golden, tiered roofs like a pagoda. Inside the cavernous hall, people rushed to and fro, hawkers peddled their wares, and porters hurried for trains with luggage balanced on their heads. Louise stood for a moment, dazed, unsure where to go for the right train. As Zeya had warned her, here there were no signs in English.

She approached a man in uniform.

'You want tourist train. Platform 2, to Mandalay,' he said as she got close, barely glancing in her direction.

'I'm travelling to Moulmein.'

He peered at her frowning and snatched her ticket.

'Moulmein? Moulmein? OK. Platform 4. You go platform 4.'

The train standing on platform 4 was covered in dust, but underneath the layers it was just possible to see that it was painted brown and cream. Louise managed to find the right carriage and clambered on board. Inside the bare, unlit compartment were rows of wooden slatted seats. It was already almost full.

She stowed her pack on the narrow luggage rack and squeezed down on a bench next to an old woman who had a large wicker basket lodged between her knees. Inside were three white chickens. Louise wondered how it would feel after ten hours of sitting in this proximity to the rest of the passengers in the full heat of the day. The small fans on the ceiling looked as though they'd been out of order for a long time. There was no glass in the windows, just metal bars, many of them bent and buckled.

The train juddered out of the station with a long blast of the horn at about seven fifteen. It rumbled past a goods' yard and then out through the centre of town past disused warehouses and crumbling factories. It rattled through Rangoon's run-down suburbs, past rickety wooden homes with bare earth grounds where children played and pigs and dogs rooted in the rubbish.

Then gradually the buildings thinned out and they left the city behind. Flat rice paddies stretched for miles on either side of the track, intersected by waterways and red earth roads.

As the train gathered pace, it began to bounce erratically. There seemed to be no springs or shock absorbers, and the carriages jolted and bumped violently against each other. The passengers were jostled and thrown together. Louise found that the only way to stay on the seat was to cling onto it with both hands. The other passengers looked resigned, used to travelling in such discomfort. She knew she must adopt the same attitude. It was useless to complain. She stared out of the window at the rolling scenery and thought about her father.

She'd often wondered how he and her mother had ever got together; they seemed such different people.

Louise had seen him so seldom when she was growing up that she'd preserved the details of every moment they'd spent together carefully in the deepest recesses of her memory. Those moments were like precious jewels that she sometimes brought out to examine and to cherish.

He'd travelled the country as an itinerant artist, getting work painting portraits of children, pets and horses, and sometimes of country houses. His earnings were sporadic and Louise knew that he rarely paid her mother anything for her keep.

He wrote regularly to Grace, though, and Grace would read the letters out loud. Louise would listen breathlessly, hanging on every word. Jack would describe the places he'd been; the countryside, the villages and towns, the people he'd met, where he'd stayed, the paintings he'd been working on. His letters were long and colourful, and Louise wouldn't be content with a single reading. She would beg her mother to read them over and over again until the next one arrived.

Louise would live for the time when her mother would read out the words; 'I have found some new lodgings now, Gracie, and

I'd like to have Louise over to stay for a few days, with your permission.'

That happened for the first time when Louise was about four years old. Her mother was working nights at the hospital, so had reluctantly agreed to Louise going to stay with her father in London for the week. Louise could still recall the excitement of packing her little weekend case, and her mother taking her on the train from Portsmouth to Waterloo Station, then taking the tube to King's Cross.

Her father was living on the top floor of a once grand house in a square of faded Georgian residences between King's Cross and Farringdon. All the way there on the train, her mother had lectured her about how she must behave during the forthcoming week.

'Now please don't let your father take you into any pubs, Louise.'

'Make sure he doesn't try to get you to do anything dangerous.'

'You must eat proper food while you're there. I don't want you getting sick.'

'Make sure you don't stay up late. You need your sleep.'

Her head was ringing with instructions by the time they entered the square and made their way across the patchy grass in the central gardens to number fifty on the opposite side. She could feel her mother's tension in the way her footsteps speeded up, and how she stared straight ahead of her and gripped Louise's hand.

Louise could still recall the smell of that old house; a mixture of town gas, damp, and old cooking smells. She was breathless with excitement as they went in through the faded red door and climbed the endless threadbare stairs to the top floor, gripping the grimy bannister.

He was there waiting at the door to his studio on the upper landing. His face was creased and tired, and his hair was greying at the temples, but he was smiling. Louise dashed up the last few steps and threw herself into his arms. He picked her up and spun her around. As he put her down, she caught sight of her mother's stony face.

'Come on inside,' Jack said motioning them into the flat.

She noticed how Grace glanced around the huge, untidy room, disapproval radiating from her. The walls were painted navy blue and the floorboards bare apart from a couple of rag rugs. At one end of the room was an easel, on it a half-finished oil painting of a nude woman. Palettes and discarded tubes of paint littered the floor around it. At the other end was an old-fashioned butler sink, with a camping hob balanced on the draining board. A Calor gas cylinder with a whistle kettle sat underneath that. The sink area was a mass of dirty dishes, and a low table in the centre of the room was covered in overflowing ash trays and empty beer bottles.

'Where do you sleep, Jack?' Grace asked.

He indicated a square sofa under the window. 'It folds down into a bed. Very comfortable, actually.'

'What about Louise?'

'That's all covered. Don't worry.'

He showed them a small room next door, hardly bigger than a cupboard, where he'd made a wooden child's bed to fit into an alcove in front of the window. Louise's heart leapt when she saw it. He'd built a little ladder for her to climb up into it.

And better still, leaning up against the bed was a child's scooter.

'Is that for me?' she asked in wonder.

'Of course. I got it at a jumble sale and painted it up.'

It was pale pink and he'd painted flowers on the wheel hubs and handlebars.

'That looks dangerous,' said her mother.

'Don't worry, Grace. We'll be careful.'

When her mother had left the house and they'd watched

from the window as she crossed the square and headed back towards the station, he said,

'Hungry?'

Louise nodded.

'Come on then. Let's nip along to the Queen's Head before closing time. They do rather nice cheese and pickle sandwiches down there.'

Her eyes widened and she was about to tell him that pubs were off -limits, when he said, 'You can take the scooter if you like. I'll run along next to you.'

All these years later she could still feel the excitement of scooting furiously along the pavement on the pink machine, that fresh spring day in 1969, the wind in her hair, the front wheel bumping over the gaps between the paving stones. Every few seconds she would glance at her father, as he jogged along beside her, his white shirt billowing out behind him, his dark hair flying everywhere. As he caught her eye he laughed, and she laughed with him, laughter of pure joy and abandon.

The Queen's Head was a spit and sawdust pub, filled with smoke and alcohol fumes. All she could see as she entered was the backs of a row of men standing at the bar with pints. The tiled floor had a dip in front of the bar from centuries of people standing there to order. Her father sat her down at a corner table then went to fetch the drinks and sandwiches.

They were in the pub for a long time and two of Jack's friends joined them after a while. They had pint after pint while Louise sipped pink Corona through a straw. Louise saw that it was growing dark outside. She began to feel bored and hot, her eyes smarting with the smoke.

Much later they all went back to her father's studio. This time he didn't run along beside her. Instead he walked unsteadily and his face was flushed. In fact all three of the men looked the same. When they got home they rolled cigarettes and Jack produced a huge tin of beer, a 'Party Seven.' He cleared the coffee table, poured beer out into three china mugs and the men began to play cards.

He beckoned to Louise to come and sit on his lap. She knew it was past her bed time, but he didn't seem to bother about that. It felt wonderful to be allowed to sit up with him and not be packed off to bed like at home. Eventually her eyes drooped and she fell asleep against his chest.

The next morning, she awoke in the tiny room and at first she wondered where she was. From her bed next to the window she could see out into a yard between the rear wings of the house and the next door one. There were pigeons roosting on the windowsills, their droppings staining the walls. She couldn't see the ground, and pressing her face to the window and looking down made her feel dizzy. Then she heard her father moving about in the next room, boiling the kettle, washing up, and the sounds filled her with warmth and a sense of well-being.

In a few minutes he appeared in the doorway,

'Do you want some tea and a fry up?' he asked. 'I thought we'd go up to Primrose Hill after breakfast. We can try out the scooter on the slopes up there.'

THE TRAIN HAD STOPPED in a village station. Hawkers approached the windows, pushing food and drinks through the bars, haranguing the passengers to buy their wares. A few of them climbed on to the train and walked through the carriages, shouting for custom, carrying their produce on their heads. Louise bought a triangle of watermelon from a young girl and bit into the sweet, juicy fruit to quench her thirst.

As the train began to pull out of the station, it suddenly came to a shuddering stop, and people who weren't sitting down were thrown forwards. There was a commotion at the front of the train near the engine and the passengers leaned out to see what was going on. Louise managed to squeeze in between two women and get her head out of the window. Her heart stopped at what she saw. Four policemen with truncheons and rifles were climbing onto the train.

Her fellow passengers sat back on their seats, murmuring to each other. The atmosphere in the carriage had changed dramatically. No one was chattering or playing music anymore.

Louise's heart began to hammer against her ribs. She thought about the forged identity papers inside her back pack. She'd spent a long time after Zeya had left her the previous evening with the hotel sewing kit, unpicking the seams of the lining and sewing it up again with the papers inside. She'd thought it looked pretty good at the time, but she realised now that if anyone seriously suspected her of concealing anything, it wouldn't be difficult to spot where it was. Her mind raced with possibilities. Should she jump off the train and disappear into the village? But she quickly realised she had no idea where they were and probably nobody spoke English here.

The train began to jerk forward and move slowly out of the station. The policemen must be working their way through the carriages, searching people, checking their identity papers and travel documents. She glanced out of the window and a desperate thought occurred to her. Should she rip the papers out of the lining and throw them out of the window? But it would be impossible to do that without someone seeing her.

After a few minutes, the policemen appeared in the doorway of the carriage. Louise tried control her breath as she watched them checking the papers of everyone on board. They got closer and closer. Then one of them happened to glance up. He shouted something to his colleague and pointed over at her. They both came towards her and as they drew near she felt her mouth go dry and her face flood with heat.

7

Grace
London, 1945

The Monday after Arthur's proposal, Grace walked into the hospital with a spring in her step. She felt free for the first time in years; physically lighter too, as if an actual weight had been removed from her shoulders.

It was a sunny winter's day. One of those days when the air feels sparkling fresh and everything in the world looks clean and bright. She couldn't help smiling at the beauty all around her.

Sister called her into her office at the start of her shift.

'It's about Jack Summers,' she said. 'He had a visitor over the weekend.'

'Oh really?' asked Grace, curious, a prickle of alarm. 'May I ask who that was?'

'It was his mother.'

'Oh. He's never spoken about his mother, nor any family member for that matter.'

'Well, his mother lives a long way away. It's not been easy for her to get here. I took her aside as she was leaving and asked her about the possibility of him coming home to live with her. But it appears that Jack hadn't lived with her for some years before the war. She made it quite clear that it isn't an option. It's a most unusual situation I must say.'

'Does he have any other family?' asked Grace.

Sister shook her head. 'No. None as far as I'm aware. I'm a little concerned because in normal circumstances he would be discharged from here in the not too distant future. He's improved remarkably quickly. He won't need full-time care for much longer and we could do with freeing up the bed.'

'Of course, Sister,' Grace said, her spirits sinking.

Grace hadn't thought ahead to the time when Jack would leave the ward, but now the prospect loomed, panic swept through her. She wondered why Sister was telling her this. Had she noticed the bond that was growing between Grace and Jack? Was this her way of warning her that he would soon be just a memory?

'I'm going to get in touch with his regiment about placing him in a convalescent home. That might be the best solution all round. They'll be able to help him get a job and find his feet in the outside world.'

'Would you like me to tell him about it?'

'Not for the moment. Let's see what they say. But in the meantime, Nurse Everett, it would be a good idea to encourage him to get up and move about. He seemed a little withdrawn after his mother had left. I don't want him to lose hope and have a relapse.'

'Of course. Whatever I can do to help.'

'There are some warm clothes in the storeroom and some fresh air might do the trick. You could try getting him walking around in the hospital gardens.'

Grace hesitated on the threshold of Jack's room. He wasn't sketching or reading today, but sitting upright in his bed, his face turned towards the window. The bottom panes were made of white obscured glass, so all he must have been able to see was the milky blue sky, the odd wispy cloud.

As she stood watching him he must have sensed her presence. He turned towards her. Grace was shocked to see his face. It was pale and full of pain. His eyes had that sunken look that had so frightened her on that first day. When he saw her in the doorway, though, his expression changed. He gave her a smile that lit up his whole face.

'You look different today,' he said as she walked into the room.

She paused. 'Really? How so?'

'Like the cat that got the cream.'

'I don't know what you mean,' she said, turning away so he wouldn't see her confusion.

But he seemed reluctant when she suggested a walk in the gardens.

'I'm not sure. I haven't been outside since the deck on the ship home,' he said.

'All the more reason to get some fresh air now. It's been almost three weeks.'

'But it's winter, Grace,' he said laughing. 'I've only got pyjamas and a dressing gown.'

'Don't worry about that. Wait here and I'll find you something warm to wear.'

Grace held his arm as they walked through the double doors and along the marble corridor. He was wearing some woollen trousers, an old jumper and an overcoat. The shoes she had found were a little too big, so he shuffled slightly as he walked.

In the lift they were both silent, staring at the floor. Grace was suddenly aware of his proximity, of his breathing and of the warmth of his body. She stepped out and pulled the metal doors aside for him.

It was odd to see Jack anywhere other than on the ward. It was almost as if they belonged there together, as if the ward was their anchor point. Leaving it felt like stepping out of invisible boundaries and into the unknown.

He said with a sideways look, 'I hope you don't mind my saying, Grace, but you do look a bit frightening in that black cape.'

'Well thank you!' she said, laughing, her tension evaporating. 'I'm not sure who designed the uniform, but we have to wear it.'

'I thought you were the Caped Crusader, when you came into the room just now with it on.'

She laughed, relieved that his mood had lifted.

As they stepped out through the back doors of the hospital into the bright morning, he stopped and took a few lungfuls of air.

'No London smog today,' he said. 'It's so cool and fresh. I'd almost forgotten.'

She took his arm and they walked away from the building, along one of the flagstone paths towards the rose garden.

After walking for a while, they sat down on a bench together.

'This is a beautiful garden,' Jack said. 'So well planned. Wild but tamed at the same time. I'd love to sketch it one day.'

'We should have brought your sketch book out with us.'

'Maybe tomorrow,' he said.

'Why not?'

Then she asked after a pause.

'How did you get so good at it, Jack?'

He smiled shyly. 'I don't know that I am that good. I've always done it though. Like I said. Since childhood.'

'Have you ever thought about taking it up professionally?'

He laughed, a short ironic laugh.

'Are you joking? You have to be rich to do that, Grace. And I'm not rich.'

His voice had taken on a sudden bitter edge and she glanced at him. The bitterness seemed to be mingled with incredulity at her naivety. The easy mood between them was broken.

She wasn't sure how to respond. Why was it with him that she often got the feeling that she'd said the wrong thing? Was he poking fun at her? Was it so obvious that she came from a comfortable middle-class home?

Her mind wandered to her upbringing and how it must have differed from his life. No real tragedies had ever befallen her immediate family, although they had all lived with the effects of the Blitz and lost friends, neighbours and acquaintances during the war. Grace's father had been too old to go to war, but he had served briefly in the navy at the end of the Great War. Luckily for him and for them all he'd had a bad bout of flu and had to be sent back to hospital in Britain. While he was there the war had ended.

How blessed they'd all been, she realised, reminding herself that despite that, she had witnessed tragedy first hand every day on the wards.

'Penny for them,' Jack's voice broke into her thoughts. He was looking at her, smiling again, all traces of bitterness gone.

'I was just thinking about my family. How lucky we've been really. Compared to lots of people I mean.'

He was silent.

'I hear you had a visitor at the weekend,' Grace said at last.

'Oh yes. My mother. I don't think she'll be coming again.'

'That's a shame.'

'She lives up north you see.'

'Sister mentioned she had a long journey. I thought you were a Londoner though.'

'I am. So is she really. My dad ran off when I was tiny. I hardly remember him. We lived with my gran and grandad in Hackney. Grandad was a blacksmith. My mum worked in a clothes factory. We were very poor for years. Then one year my grandparents took us on a holiday to Great Yarmouth and my mum met my stepdad. He's from Sheffield. A steel worker. She went to live up north with him and I stayed with my gran. I never got on with Frank, my stepdad. They've got two daughters now.'

'How sad. How old were you when she left?'

'About ten I suppose.'

Grace frowned, trying to imagine a situation like that. Jack's world was so different from her own.

'Where will you go when you're well enough to leave hospital?' she asked tentatively.

'I don't know yet,' he replied. 'I haven't got anywhere to go at the moment. Like I said, Mum's got another family now up north. I might go and visit, but they won't want me to stay very long and I won't want to either. There isn't room for one thing.'

Grace thought about how pleased and chipper Ernie had looked in his three-piece suit, waiting to be collected by his father-in-law, to go home to a loving family who would care for him. Her heart twisted with pity for Jack. How unthinkable, to have lived through and survived such a dreadful ordeal, and to come home to be so alone in the world.

'I've thought about going down to Portsmouth and finding work there,' he said suddenly. 'My Grandad used to take me down on the train to Southsea sometimes for a day out. We'd walk to the end of the pier and look out at the Solent. You can see across to the Isle of Wight from there. I used to love that place. Especially when it was stormy. The colour of the sea and the sky... You know I often think about that feeling, standing at the end of the pier with the waves crashing underneath you and the wind in your ears. I'd like to paint it every evening for a month, just to capture the changes.'

'It sounds wonderful,' she said. 'I don't think I've ever been down to Southsea.'

'Tell me about your world, Grace,' he said after a pause, turning to look at her. 'You come in to the hospital every day, like a guardian angel. You're ready to give everything to care for us men with our gruesome complaints. It can't be an easy job. You sound as though you don't need to do it for the money. And you do it so well, so generously. Why do you?'

She shrugged. 'I suppose I need to be doing something. Something of my own. My father works in a bank. He wanted me to go and be a secretary there when I left school, but I wasn't going to do that. I wanted to do something to help. With the war on.'

'Did they mind?'

'At first they did, but they soon got used to it. When they realised I was serious. They don't talk about it much, though, I think they would prefer I did something in an office. Or get married of course.'

The words were out before she'd thought about them and once again she found her cheeks colouring. She leaned forward and dropped her head so he wouldn't see her embarrassment.

'Do you have any plans to do that?' she could see sense that he was smiling, teasing her.

'No,' she muttered, her heart pounding. She was desperately trying to think of a different subject but nothing came to mind. In the end she said. 'My sister is about to get married though. Everyone's very happy about that.'

Jack didn't reply and they both sat there in awkward silence, listening to the buses rumble along the Acton road.

'What did you do before the war, Jack?'

'Oh this and that. I left school without my school certificate. I worked in a bookies' for a while. Trained as a draftsman in a building company but we all got laid off in the depression. I did a few labouring jobs on building sites. Nothing seemed to work out very well. Then I joined up when war broke out. Just to have some money coming in. If I'd known....'

She thought about her father and mother again. So comfortable in their cossetted middle-class world. What would they think if they ever met Jack, about his background? His lack of prospects. Then she stopped herself and felt her cheeks burn with guilt at the audacity of her own thoughts, as if he could read them on her face. Wasn't she racing ahead of herself rather?

'You know. I meant what I said,' Jack said then. 'About you being an angel, Grace,' he said. 'I don't know how I'd have survived without you.'

'Oh, nonsense,' she heard herself saying, even as she said it, regretting how stiff and off-putting her words must sound to him. 'You would have pulled through. You're strong and young.'

'I don't mean physically. You must know what I mean.'

Grace felt her cheeks flaming. She couldn't look at him. She fixed her eyes on the rosebush opposite watching the thorny branches stir in the breeze.

'I'm falling in love with you, Grace,' he said. 'You must have realised.'

'Don't,' she said, too embarrassed to look at his face, her heart racing, confusing emotions flooding her mind. 'You mustn't. I mean...I mean you can't mean that.'

'But I do mean it. Seeing you each day, our chats, our conversations about books... about everything...You know I was beginning to think you might be feeling that way too. Was I wrong?'

Grace felt trapped, caught, like a fly under a pin. Was it so obvious? She lifted her eyes to the windows of the hospital that looked out over the garden, row upon row of them. She suddenly felt exposed.

'Look,' she said awkwardly. 'We shouldn't be talking like this. Not here. I'm on duty. I don't know what to say.'

He didn't reply. The weather was changing. Clouds obscured the sun and the air had turned damp. A shiver went through her.

'Shall we go in?' she said getting up, still not looking at him. 'You don't want to get chilled.'

8

Grace
London, 1945

'I don't know what's wrong with you, Grace Everett,' snapped her mother as they sat down to supper that evening. 'Why ever didn't you say something about the situation with you and Arthur? It was very embarrassing for your father at work today.'

'It's fine, Eileen. Leave the girl alone,' said her father, tucking into his stew and dumplings.

'What's happened?' Joan was wide eyed with curiosity, her fork of boiled potatoes halfway to her mouth.

'She's only gone and ditched the poor man, Joanie,' said their mother. 'I have no idea why. And not to say anything to us either! I just can't understand your behaviour Grace. You get odder by the day.'

'Grace!' Joan's knife and fork clattered down on her plate. 'How can you have done that? And why ever didn't you tell me at the weekend? I am your sister for goodness' sake. I thought it was strange when you didn't want to come dancing on Saturday night.'

'Have you quite finished?' said Grace. 'If you must know, I didn't say anything because I knew this was how you would react. I couldn't face it to be honest. Who I choose to go out with is up to me. And I'm fed up with you two organising my life for me.'

'Don't speak to me like that, Grace!' her mother said. 'Edward. Tell her she mustn't speak to me like that!'

'Grace,' said her father in his mild way, clearly reluctant to intervene. He put his knife and fork down. 'There's no need to be rude to your mother.'

'I'm sorry, Dad. But it's none of anyone's business except mine.'

'Well isn't it young lady?' her mother said, eyes snapping. 'While you live under this roof you can at least be civil to the rest of the family. And I really can't understand what's wrong with you. Arthur is a very good catch. You won't find anyone with better prospects. But of course, Miss High and Mighty thinks she's above finding someone decent and settling down to a normal life like other people.'

'I've had enough of this,' said Grace, pushing back her chair and shoving her half- eaten dinner away.

'Where are you going? Where's she going? Edward, stop her.'

'Let her go Eileen.'

She made for the door, her mother and sister staring at her round-eyed, her father settling back to his meal with a heavy sigh.

She slammed out of the dining room, and without stopping to put her coat on, went straight out of the front door. She paused on the front path in the pool of light cast from the dining room window. There was a lump in her throat and for a moment she thought she might cry, but it quickly passed and instead anger took over.

Leaving the front garden, she turned left towards the common. She had no desire to go towards the High Street or the station where she might meet people she knew. She needed to be alone. She walked for a long time, trying to master her anger, to calm down and understand her own feelings. She knew it wasn't just her mother's words and Joan's intervention that had annoyed her so. She was already in turmoil herself, and they had just tipped her over.

She thought about Jack and wondered why she had rebuffed him this morning when he'd spoken of his feelings. Was she afraid of what would happen if she told him she thought about him all the time? That although she'd convinced herself that she'd finished with Arthur for different reasons, the absolute truth was that knowing Jack had opened her mind to her own life, and the trap she'd been walking into? It was all so confusing. He was her patient and she knew she shouldn't have let herself be drawn in like this, and she knew instinctively that her family would think she was making a dreadful mistake if she allowed herself to get involved with Jack.

The further she walked and the more she went over their conversation in her mind, the more wretched she felt. She couldn't get the image of Jack's crestfallen face out of her mind, and his words, 'I think I'm falling in love with you, Grace. You must know that.' How could she have not responded to his honesty? Her heart twisted with pity as she thought about his emaciated body, the wheals she'd seen on his back from the beatings he must have received in that dreadful camp, how she'd witnessed him pouring with sweat through the night during a fever and how he'd fought to recover. How throughout his weeks in her care he'd not uttered a word of complaint or even mentioned the pain he must have been in.

As she came to the crest of the hill it started to rain. She stopped and stared out over the sprawling suburbs, the lines of dotted lights strung along the grid of streets like strings of fairy lights. She realised then that she had no choice. She needed to tell Jack how she felt about him. She needed to face it whatever the consequences at work. Mother and Joan would have to accept the situation. Once they met Jack they would surely get to like him and to understand.

As she turned to go home, the rain started to fall more heavily. She quickened her pace but she realised that she must have walked over two miles from home. Soon her hair was plastered to her head, her cardigan was wet through and the rain was seeping through to her skin, trickling inside her collar and down her neck. Her face was wet and raindrops blurred her vision. She was shivering now, her teeth chattering, but that didn't matter to Grace. Her mind was clear and she knew what she needed to do. Pulling her sodden cardigan more tightly around her, she started to run.

IN THE NIGHT Grace woke suddenly. Her body was covered in sweat, but she was shivering too. She must have pushed the bedclothes off in her sleep and her nightdress was clinging to her. Her head was aching and her cheeks and neck felt swollen and painful. Each time she tried to swallow it felt as though barbed wire was lodged in her throat. She managed to haul herself out of bed and went through to the bathroom where she forced down some aspirins, then returned to bed, falling into a restless, delirious sleep.

She was awoken by the alarm at six o'clock. Her body ached and the pain in her throat hadn't subsided. Automatically she sat up and put her legs out of the bed, but immediately was overcome with dizziness and fell back on the pillow.

Her father stuck his head around the door at seven fifteen.

'Not getting up, love? You'll be late again.' He came closer. 'Gracie love? Are you alright? You look dreadful.'

For three days and four nights Grace sweated it out. Her mother sat beside her bed and mopped her brow with a flannel. She brought home-made chicken or vegetable soup twice a day and spooned it into Grace's mouth. Joan came and sat beside her too, held her hand and read her stories from Woman's Realm and Reader's Digest. Neither Mother nor Joan mentioned the argument from the other day, or said what they surely must be thinking. 'If only you hadn't gone out in the cold and wet without a coat...'

When the fever was at its height, Grace slipped into near delirium. Her mind kept returning to Jack. She was beside him toiling in the jungle, being beaten by a guard until his back bled, lying in a bamboo hut fighting for his life. Her own back and shoulders ached in sympathy with his, her head seemed to pound with the oppressive heat of the jungle. Grace's own confusion seemed to meld with Jack's, and she couldn't tell where his fever ended and her own began. In her dazed state it felt as though she herself was there in that stifling hut with him, her belly taut with hunger, sweat pouring from her skin, the heat of fever radiating from it.

Jack's disembodied face swum before her a thousand times. She tried to raise her hand to touch it, but it was always just out of reach. 'I love you Grace,' he kept repeating over and over, and though she opened her mouth to reply, no words would come and she ended up gasping and choking.

When she awoke on the fourth day, her head was no longer pounding. When she opened her eyes she knew instantly that she had turned the corner. Joan appeared in the doorway with a cup of tea.

'How's the patient this morning?'

'Much better,' said Grace sitting up. 'What's the time? I think I'm well enough to go into work.'

'Don't be silly. It's nine-thirty anyway. Too late. You'll have to wait until tomorrow.'

Joan set the cup down beside the bed and sat next to Grace.

'Look Gracie, I'm sorry about the other night,' Joan said. 'I shouldn't have said anything about you and Arthur. You're quite right. It's none of my business. I was disappointed about it. But I was being selfish.'

Grace took her hand. 'Forget it, Joan.'

'Mother's been worried sick about you.'

'I know.'

'But you know what she's like. She probably won't say anything. She finds it hard to back down or say anything about her feelings.'

Grace put her fingers on her sister's lips.

'Shhh. That's enough. Let's forget all about it.'

Joan brightened. 'Thank you, Grace. You're a brick.'

She got up and moved towards the door. Then she stopped and turned back.

'Oh, by the way, do you know someone called Jack?'

Grace's heart began to beat faster. Odd fleeting memories of her delirious dreams came into her mind.

'Why?'

'You said something like' Jack', or maybe it was black, something like that. You said it a few times.'

'I have no idea,' said Grace. Joan was frowning at her, a curious look creeping into her eyes now. 'Are you quite sure?'

'Yes. I can hardly remember anything. It's all a blur. I could have been saying anything.'

'If you say so,' said Joan, with a mischievous smile, leaving the room.

9

Grace
London, 1945

The next morning Grace took the tube with the rush hour workers, strap hanging and tapping her foot, impatient to arrive. She was earlier than usual, striding through the double doors onto the ward at ten to eight. She changed hurriedly, running a comb through her hair and reapplying lipstick in the locker room mirror. Then, glancing across at the office, seeing through the window that Sister was busily writing, her back to the window, made her way straight to Jack's side room.

She couldn't wait to speak to him. He'd not been out of her thoughts since she'd woken up the morning before. All that day, she'd been planning what to say to him to make up for the clumsy way she'd responded to his honesty in the rose garden.

She pushed open the door to the side ward and stood there in

the doorway, her heart hammering, her face flushed with anticipation.

The room was empty. Both beds had been stripped and the
cupboards stood open. Her hand flew to her mouth. Had they
moved Jack on to the main ward? Then a shiver went right
through her. Was there another reason he wasn't there? Had he
had a drastic relapse of his fever? She remembered the doctor's
words. 'It will come back ... It will be touch and go.'

Swallowing her fear, she walked quickly to the office. Sister
looked up from her paperwork.

'What can I do for you, Nurse? I hope you've recovered from
your flu. Your father sounded very worried when he telephoned.'

'I'm fine now, thank you, Sister. I was just wondering what's
happened to Mr Summers.'

'Oh yes. A vacancy came up in a convalescent home. He left
on Wednesday. I mentioned I was going to speak to his regiment,
didn't I?'

'Yes.'

'Well it all happened more quickly than expected. Don't
worry, we're expecting two new patients from the intensive care
ward this morning, so you're still going to be kept very busy. In
fact, could you begin making the beds up please? They will be
arriving before lunchtime if the porters can get their act together.'

'Of course, Sister.'

Grace hovered on the doorstep, on the point of asking where
the convalescent home was, but the way Sister turned back to her
papers in a pointed, dismissive way told her firmly that the
conversation was closed. She knew it wasn't something she had a
right to ask anyway.

With a heavy sigh, she collected the sheets from the linen
cupboard and took them back to the side room. As she made up
the beds she couldn't help thinking back over all the conversations she'd had with Jack in this room and how between these
four walls their friendship had developed and blossomed. She

pictured his face when she'd brought him the Hardy books, how she'd sat beside the bed as they had discussed them. Then a thought occurred to her. Had he taken the books with him? She knelt down and fumbled in the cupboard. The books were there at the back of the shelf.

She pulled them out and flicked through them both, half expecting a note to drop out. How could he simply have left without contacting her? Panic swept through her. He must have left thinking she'd rebuffed his feelings. He must think that she had no feelings for him at all. Perhaps it had even been a deliberate act to go without leaving a message for her? Maybe he just wanted to leave it all behind and forget about her? She slammed the cupboard door in frustration She would never get the opportunity now to tell him how much she cared for him.

She carried on with her tasks, whisking the crisp white sheets over the beds so they were smooth and flat, with perfect hospital corners. As she left the room, she turned back to look at the two empty beds as a last gesture, picturing Jack and Ernie in them the first time she'd seen them.

For the rest of the morning she went about her duties on the main ward with a heavy heart. She tried her best to smile as she spooned out medicines, emptied bedpans and washed the patients' bodies. She brought them food, took their temperatures, and tried to be as cheerful and positive as she could. But all the time she was thinking about Jack, trying to suppress the anger she felt with herself and the feeling of emptiness at the thought that she would probably never see him again. She couldn't even confide her misery to Nancy, who had been put on an evening shift that week.

The two new patients arrived before lunch and were settled into the beds on the side ward by the hospital porters. One man was recovering from pneumonia and the other had emphysema. Grace did her best to make them comfortable, but neither was well enough to speak. It was strange, tending to these two men where only days before she'd been chatting to Jack. It felt firmly as if that chapter had closed.

At the end of the day, she changed back into her own clothes in the empty locker room and made her way out of the hospital into the dark of the early evening. The whole world seemed to have taken on a new aspect since she'd hurried through the streets in the morning, full of hope. Everywhere looked dull and squalid in the dank winter air.

Nearing the tube station, she caught sight of Nancy emerging from the station in the direction of the hospital. She was virtually running, her face flustered, her scarf flying behind her.

'Nancy!'

'Grace!' Nancy skidded to a halt. 'Good to see you. Are you better?'

Grace nodded. 'Yes thanks. How are you?'

'I'm late. Can't stop now.' Nancy made as if to hurry on, then she turned back.

'Oh, I nearly forgot. I've got this for you,' she said fumbling in her bag and producing a small envelope. 'Lover boy left it with me. It's for you. I don't think he wanted to risk Sister opening it.'

She shoved the envelope into Grace's hands. Grace stared at the writing.

'Miss Grace Everett,' was written in artistic scrawl. She clutched it, her heart lifting.

'Thanks Nancy!' she said, but Nancy was already on her way, blowing a kiss behind her.

There was a small café beside the tube station. Grace wandered towards it. She couldn't wait until she was home to open the letter, and she didn't want to read it on the tube, with the possibility of nosey fellow passengers peering over her shoulder.

She ordered a mug of tea and sat at a corner table. Then, with shaking hands pulled the envelope open. Inside were two sheets of thick paper that must have come from Jack's sketch book.

Dearest Grace,

By the time you read this I will have left the ward. I hope you have recovered from your flu. I just wanted to thank you for how you looked after me these past weeks. It is due to your efforts and your wonderful presence that I've recovered at all. Seeing your face each morning and our daily conversations have sustained me and given me a reason to live. But I know now that you were only doing your duty and you would have done the same for any patient in your care.

I am writing to say how sorry I was to have spoken out of turn in the rose garden the other day. I should never have put you in that position. It was an affront to your professionalism, and I apologise. I mistook the moment, and read too much into your kindness, which was wrong of me.

I hope you will forgive me and forget what happened. I didn't mean to cause you any discomfort.

Yours
Jack Summers.

INSIDE THE LETTER he'd folded one of his sketches of Grace. She unfolded it and stared at it, remembering Jack's embarrassment when Ernie had shown her the book. It was the one of her standing in front of the window smiling, her hair lit up by the sun.

She turned the letter over. There was no address for the convalescent home, no indication of where he was going. She sat for a long time staring at his words, overcome with a feeling of helplessness. She was no nearer being able to speak to him and in a way his letter made things worse. It was clear now that he would put all thoughts of her out of his head and make an effort to move on with his life.

She put the letter and sketch back in the envelope, paid for her tea and left the shop.

10

Louise
Burma, August 1988

As the two policemen made their way slowly down the carriage, Louise swallowed hard, preparing what she would say in response to the questions they were no doubt about to ask her. She was simply travelling to Moulmein to see the pagodas. She'd heard it was a beautiful place. She was studying English and had read the Kipling poem, *The Road to Mandalay*, that had immortalised it.

With an effort she managed a nonchalant smile and looked up in readiness as the two policemen approached. But they pushed past her and went straight towards a group of young men sitting two rows down from her. They started firing questions at them, shouting, pointing at them. One of the policemen slapped one man around the face. The other policeman drew his gun. There were gasps and screams from people in the carriage and the three young men put their hands up. There was a tense silence for a few moments that seemed to last a lifetime. Would he shoot?

But no shots rang out from his gun. Instead he motioned for the young men to get to their feet. Then the two policemen prodded and shoved them out of the carriage with their rifles and truncheons. The door to the next carriage was slammed shut, but through the filthy window Louise could see the policemen punching and hitting the young men. Her mouth was dry with fear. She could feel no relief that it wasn't her they'd picked on. Her heart went out to those three innocent looking boys. They looked to be about her own age.

Soon the train ground and shuddered to a halt at another remote village station. There was further shouting and commotion as the policemen pushed the three boys off the train and jumped off after them. Then the train pulled out of the station. Glancing out of the carriage, Louise could see the three men on their knees, their hands in the air, being harangued and slapped by the two policemen.

As the train gathered pace and put distance between itself and the ugly scene, the atmosphere in the carriage gradually returned to normal. People began to whisper amongst themselves and then, as they gained confidence, to talk more loudly. Vendors pushed their way through the aisles again shouting for custom. After half an hour or so, it was as if the incident had never happened.

The train was moving quickly now and the interminable bouncing and jolting had started again. They passed dusty villages of wooden huts on stilts thatched with palm leaves, surrounded by plantations of ragged banana trees. Village children stood by the track waving to the passengers. Then they rattled on past smooth rivers where buffaloes wallowed and children bathed naked. The flat plain with rice paddies soon gave way to jungle covered hills, where golden temples nestled on hilltops amongst the vegetation.

Sitting back on the wooden seat, letting the dusty air cool her face, Louise thought back again to that first visit to her father's place in London.

He owned a battered car; an ancient Ford Popular which had to be started with an old-fashioned engine crank. That first morning, he stowed the scooter in the boot, cranked the engine into a stuttering start and drove Louise up through Camden Town to Primrose Hill. On the journey she stared out at the streets, amazed by how busy everywhere was, at how many strangers there were walking the pavements. London felt a terrifying place, but the presence of her father in the driving seat next to her took that fear away.

They took the scooter to the top of the hill in the park in Primrose Hill. Her father pointed out all the landmarks dotted around the city that could be seen from that vantage point. Then they took turns to ride the scooter down the hill. She could still feel the thrill of the wind in her hair, the ground rushing along beneath her.

The first time she went down the hill she was a little nervous, and kept putting her foot to the ground to slow her down. Her mother's words kept repeating in the back of her mind, 'Don't let him make you do anything dangerous.'

But she soon forgot what her mother had said and gave herself over to the pleasure of the moment. On her final descent an Alsatian dog came bounding up to her and she turned the handlebars sharply to avoid him. She lurched sideways onto the ground, grazing the skin off her hands and knees and banging her head. Her father was with her in seconds, gathering her up, holding her to him, wiping her face with a handkerchief that smelled of tobacco.

'I'm so sorry Louise. That was a crazy thing to do. Are you alright?'

She nodded and tried to suppress her tears but could already feel a huge bruise forming on her head.

'Let's get you to a hospital.'

He drove her as quickly as the old car would go to a huge Victorian hospital in Holloway. He ran with her through echoing corridors to the Accident and Emergency ward. They had to wait a long time in a waiting room that smelled of disinfectant. Louise sat on her father's lap and he read her stories from a children's book he'd found on a coffee table amongst the magazines. Despite the pain in her head and the stinging from her palms and knees, she relished the pleasure of those moments. The doctor checked her over and dressed her wounds. Then he sent them away with a stern word to her father to take care of her and to watch for symptoms of concussion.

As they left the hospital, her father gave her a wry smile and said, 'I shouldn't have been so reckless, Louise. Probably best not to tell Mum about your little accident. Keep it between you and me, OK?'

Now the train was pulling into the small town of Martaban. Although it was the railhead of the main railway from Rangoon, it appeared a small and unassuming place. The single main street was a series of low-rise buildings and bamboo huts with a few concrete buildings near the railway station.

Louise got her backpack down and followed the tide of other passengers along a rough track down to the jetty where an ungainly looking passenger ferry was moored up. She looked around nervously in case there were any policemen here, but there was no sign of them and the little town seemed quiet and peaceful.

At the boat jetty, the passengers from the train were joined by crowds of other people carrying boxes and bags, some with sacks on their heads, making a living from transporting goods across the water. A gaggle of small boys moved amongst the crowd, haranguing people to buy food and drinks. Everyone jostled on board the ferry and Louise made for the upper deck.

The sun had started to go down and she wanted to be able to

see the crossing over the Salween River to Moulmein. She could already glimpse the town across the wide expanse of water, its famous pagodas topping a series of long wooded hills. She stood at the rail on the upper deck as the ferry edged away from the jetty, feeling a little easier now that they were so far away from the unpleasant scene earlier. She wondered what had happened to the boys who'd been taken by the police. She thought about Zeya, of his brooding, anxious face and his big, beautiful smile - all the more precious because it was so rare. She thought of his friends and how precarious their lives must be. That could have been any one of them, pleading for his life there on that remote station platform.

As the ferry chugged across the wide estuary, the sky was milky pink and the hills of Moulmein became a darkening smudge on the horizon. The sun, like a fiercely burning torch, began to dip behind the land to the west, staining the water with streaks of yellow and red. Within a few fleeting moments it had dropped beneath the hills and by the time they reached the jetty at Moulmein, the sky was completely dark.

There were no other tourists on the boat and as it docked Louise began to worry that it might be difficult to find somewhere to stay. Zeya had told her that there were a couple of basic hotels on the waterfront, but he'd been very vague. She realised she would have to wait until the next day to find his friend, Thuza.

To her relief there were a couple of rickshaw men waiting at the top of the ferry ramp. The one she approached spoke no English, but he did understand the word 'hotel.' He pedalled her through the quiet, dark streets leaving the crowds from the ferry far behind. All she could hear were the tyres on the road, the rickshaw man's occasional grunts of effort, and cicadas drilling in the trees. She had the sense that this was a pleasant airy town, far more relaxed than Rangoon. She caught a hint of sea salt on the air.

The rickshaw driver dropped her at the Government Guest

House, a run-down colonial bungalow on the waterfront. She pushed open the warped front door and stepped into a reception area which was lit by a single bulb. The whine of mosquitoes was the only sound in the echoing lobby. The old man behind the desk wore a grey uniform, shiny with age. He looked up from the newspaper he was reading and removed his glasses. His face registered genuine astonishment that a guest had arrived.

He finally agreed that she could have a room, then spent a long time painstakingly copying down the details from her passport. Louise waited patiently, answering all his questions politely. She had no wish to draw attention to herself by being impatient. Once the formalities were completed, the old man beckoned her to follow him as he shuffled along a dimly lit corridor.

Her room was bare and functional with a greying mosquito net hanging over the bed and an ancient ceiling fan turning slowly. As Louise sat down on the bed and eased off her sandals, she realised she'd hardly eaten all day. She wondered if there was anywhere to eat nearby. If only she'd had the presence of mind to ask the rickshaw man to wait so he could take her to a cafe, but after the disturbing events of the day, she couldn't face any further difficulties. Ignoring her rumbling stomach she simply got undressed, crawled under the mosquito net and closed her eyes.

But sleep eluded her. Her mind went back again to her visits to her father's flat in King's Cross.

Her mother hadn't noticed the bruise on her head after her first visit; luckily it had faded by the end of the week and her fringe covered it. Her days had resumed their normal humdrum routine once she was at home. She remembered wishing that life could be like her visit to her father all the time; outings in the old car to different parts of London, daily trips to the pub, and late nights listening to the lively conversation and the card games.

But she had to wait another year before she saw him again. When she arrived at the flat that second time, she noticed that her father was thinner than before and his face more lined and gaunt. On the first evening she discovered that he drank more beer and whisky than he had the previous year.

He no longer had his car.

'The old girl died on me I'm afraid, Louise,' he said, pulling a sad face. 'And I can't afford another one. Don't look so disappointed! In London it doesn't matter at all. We can go everywhere by bus and tube. It will be an adventure.'

It was an adventure. They travelled on the top front seat of red buses all over the capital. Each day they took a bus to a different landmark. He showed her the Tower of London, Tower Bridge, Oxford Street and the Houses of Parliament. They walked hand in hand through Hyde Park one day, and another day got off the bus at St James' Park and walked up to the railings of Buckingham Palace and peered through.

One day when it was warm and sunny he took her to Hampstead Heath to bathe in the public ponds. It felt odd swimming in the murky water; she was worried that there might be eels or frogs under the surface, but her father looked as though he was enjoying it so much that she didn't want to disappoint him.

That was the day she noticed the scars on his back. Several great wheals stretching diagonally from shoulder to waist; white against his pale skin. He noticed her looking at them when they were drying themselves.

'How did you get those, Dad?' she asked, a little shamefaced that he'd caught her staring.

'Oh, those. Those are just my old war wounds.'

'I didn't know you were in a war,' she said, shocked.

He laughed. 'It's a long time ago. And anyway, I didn't get those fighting.'

'How did you get them?'

'It was when I was a prisoner in Burma. I got them in the prison camp.'

'How?' she asked open mouthed.

'Oh, I disobeyed the rules and I was punished.'

Her eyes filled with tears at the thought of him being so badly beaten that the scars were there so many years later.

'Hey it's nothing to worry about,' he said, kneeling down and putting his arms around her. 'It's a long time ago now. The man who did it to me was punished himself after the war. Now come on. Shall we get an ice cream? There's a Mr Whippy van over there.'

He didn't speak about it again, but that night she lay awake in the little bed under the window imagining her father being whipped so badly that his back was cut to ribbons. She couldn't picture the man who did it, his face was blank in her mind, but he had strong arms and she could see him wielding a long leather whip and bringing it down hard as her father cried out. The thought of it filled her with pain and terror.

IN THE MORNING, after a sparse breakfast of boiled eggs, hard bread and bitter coffee, Louise went out onto the road with her back pack. She hadn't realised the previous night, but the Government Guest house was right on the waterfront. Motorcycles and cars passed constantly, with the occasional rickshaw. She waved one down and showed the man the address that Zeya had written in Burmese on the card.

The man nodded and set off along the wide, tree lined boulevard which bordered the estuary. Louise stared out across the smooth, flat expanse of water to the low-lying hills opposite, enjoying the fresh sea air and the relaxed atmosphere of Moulmein. At the end of the road was a jetty, where people were loading cargo onto a boat from lorries lined up along the road. Then they passed a vast covered market where the stalls spilled out onto the road. It was busy here, people selling all manner of goods, from carpets and fabrics to colourful fruit laid out in baskets. People pushed loads to and fro on barrows, and others stood bargaining with stall holders.

Beyond the market the rickshaw man turned into a dusty side street and they cycled past a line of crumbling colonial mansions, all set in overgrown grounds behind high walls. At the end of the road he stopped beside a gate and indicated that they had reached their destination. She asked him to wait for her by the gate.

She crossed the front yard of the old house. Some children playing under a tree on the bare earth looked up and stared at her. Suddenly she felt apprehensive. Would this person be as willing to help as Zeya had assumed? Before she could reach the front door, a young man appeared from inside the house and strolled across the yard towards her.

'Do you speak English?' she asked.

He nodded, but he was eyeing her with suspicion.

'Are you Thuza?'

This time he nodded. 'Yes I am. Who are you?'

'I have a message from your friend Zeya in Rangoon,' she said, and the young man took her arm and ushered her onto the porch. He was frowning anxiously now, his eyes fearful.

'You must not speak so loudly,' he whispered, glancing nervously back at the rickshaw man. 'We don't know who is listening.'

'I'm sorry,' she said lowering her voice. 'I have a letter from him and some papers.'

Glancing around again the young man said, 'It would be better if you came inside.'

She followed him into the house. They crossed a hallway where a rotting wooden staircase rose to the first floor. A group of women sat on the lower steps gossiping but when Louise entered they stopped talking and stared at her. She got the impression that this old house was home to several families.

He showed her into a high room with corniced ceilings. It was sparsely furnished but obviously served as living room, bedroom and kitchen for a family. An old woman lay asleep on a charpoy bed in the corner.

'Do you have scissors?' Louise asked. He rummaged in a drawer and handed her a large pair that looked blunt and dirty. She cut the seams she had sewn in the rucksack and drew out the envelopes.

'This is a letter from Zeya, and some papers.'

He opened the letter first and scanned it quickly. Then he opened the other envelope and drew out the papers. His eyebrows shot up and he let out a low whistle.

'These are good. Very good. No one in Moulmein can produce such authentic looking papers. We've had a lot of problems with people in our group being discovered with forgeries. Many of them have been arrested. Some of them have disappeared completely.'

He slipped them under a heavy chest and turned back to Louise.

'Zeya says that you want to go to Thanbyuzayat. I am to take you there.' He paused. 'That will be difficult.'

'Can you do it?' she waited for his response, holding her breath.

'I will have to think of a way to hide you so you don't get discovered at a road block. We can take the back routes but we won't be able to avoid them completely.'

'Do you think it's possible?' she repeated, her stomach churning at the thought of the danger she might be putting herself and this stranger in. An image of the young men being beaten by police on that remote station platform returned to her mind.

'I'll have to think of a way. Zeya has put his trust in me and you have taken a big risk to bring these papers. I must fulfil my part of the bargain.'

'That's very good of you,' Louise said, watching his face as he thought for a moment.

'It's not just about the journey though. When you get there you won't be able to go about normally. Foreigners are not allowed in Thanbyuzayat. It will be very difficult for you.'

The old woman began stirring on the bed in the corner of the room.

'You must go now. Come back here at nine o'clock this evening. It will be easier to travel after dark. Don't check out of your hotel though. The police track the movements of foreigners. If they know you've gone they will want to know where to.'

'OK. But they might realise I'm not there.'

'I can only give you twenty-four hours I'm afraid. I have to come back here to prepare to go to Rangoon for the 8th. They might not notice you're gone for such a short time. If they see you leaving, say you are going to see the sunset at the temple and that you might be late back.'

'OK. I might just do that anyway while I'm here.'

Thuza smiled. 'You should do. It is unforgettable.'

'I'll tell him I won't be wanting any breakfast in the morning.'

'That's good! You're getting the idea.'

11

Eve

London, 2015

Eve settled into her window seat as the jumbo jet gathered pace down the runway at Heathrow. It was a familiar feeling; she'd taken this flight many times since her mother and Jim had gone out to live in Singapore when she started university.

The start of a long journey always made her nerves tingle with excitement, but today that feeling was tainted with sadness. It had been hard saying goodbye to Grace that morning at Totnes station. As Eve had boarded the train and pulled the window down to wave to her grandmother, it had hit her how old and frail Grace looked. She'd felt a sudden surge of guilt at leaving her alone.

'I'll phone you as soon as I get there. And I'll write very soon,' Eve had called as the train pulled out of the station. She carried on waving as it carried her away from Grace, until Grace was just a tiny speck alone on the platform.

During the weeks she'd stayed with Grace, Eve had managed to persuade her grandmother to give her blessing to Eve's visit to Myanmar, and the camp Jack had depicted on his sketch map. It hadn't been easy, but Eve had persisted. She wouldn't have wanted to go against Grace's wishes.

The fact was, since the seed of the idea had first occurred to her, lying in bed that first night she'd arrived at Grace's house back in July, it had taken root and grown like a rampant tropical plant. Over the days and weeks that followed, it had developed into something of an obsession. She'd pored over Jack's sketch-map of the camp and spent long hours on her laptop, researching internet sites about the history of the Thai-Burma railway.

She found that there was a great deal of information about the Thai end of the railway, but not so much about the Myanmar side. She quickly discovered that a museum was being built in Thanbyuzayat at the site of the old camp. That increased her determination to go there. She was sure the people at the museum would be interested in Jack's sketch map of the camp.

She'd had to tread carefully around Grace's feelings at first though, knowing that Jack's wartime experience was something Grace was very sensitive about. She'd first broached the subject a few days into her visit. Grace had been reluctant to talk about it then, changing the subject each time it was introduced.

And when Eve pushed the idea as gently as she could, Grace had been scathing and dismissive at first.

'What on earth do you want to go *there* for Eve? It's all in the past. Your grandfather's long gone. There's nothing to be gained by digging it all up now.'

'I'd like to understand something about him,' Eve had tried to explain. 'I've heard so many stories about him. I'd be so interested to find out about what happened to him during the war.'

As the days wore on, they'd gradually rekindled the closeness that they'd had when Eve used to spend her holidays from university in Devon with Grace. They fell into their old routines. They would drive to Dartmouth, eat lunch at the Craved Angel and stroll along the front, taking in the boats to-ing and fro-ing in the harbour. They walked arm in arm beside the river Dart at Totnes and ate fish and chips on the pier in Torquay on a windy day. They even drove up onto Dartmoor in Grace's old Rover, and though Grace could no longer walk on the moorland paths she loved, they did manage a few halting steps from the car towards Hay Tor, letting the wind blow in their hair while they stared in awe across the expanse of the bleak and rugged moor.

On other days, when Grace was tired, they would stay at home and Eve would cook and clean the house for her while Grace rested. Sometimes Eve would work in Grace's huge unruly garden, pruning and weeding, or mowing the lawn, while Grace pottered around or sat in a deck chair reading.

As the days passed, Grace had started to speak to Eve about her marriage to Jack. It seemed to Eve that the shock of seeing those paintings had prompted Grace to look back over the past. She'd seen a different side to Grace then – a vulnerability that Grace had always taken care to hide before. And as Grace opened up about the past, she came round to agreeing to Eve visiting Myanmar.

'It's not something I would ever want to do myself,' she'd said grudgingly. 'I could never understand Louise wanting to go there all those years back. But the war is a very long time ago. You didn't live through it. I suppose going there might help someone of your generation come to terms with it all.'

And as the summer passed, in dribs and drabs, Grace began to tell Eve about her marriage to Jack.

'So you see, Eve,' she'd said a few days before Eve was due to leave for Singapore, as they sat over their morning coffee, 'There was always this invisible barrier between me and Jack. It came from his time during the war. It destroyed him and it ruined our marriage. I tried so hard to get him to talk to me about it, but he never would. It was as if he'd shut something monstrous away in a dark cupboard, hoping it would go away. But it never would go away, it just grew and grew and got more malevolent as time went on. It ate him up from within. I could see it, even if he refused to admit it to himself.'

'How very sad, Gran,' Eve said, reaching out for Grace's hand on the table. Grace gripped it with her bony fingers and sat silent for a while.

'But I'm wondering now if there wasn't something else as well,' Grace mused, when she'd recovered her composure. 'I've been wondering about it ever since those drawings arrived out of the blue.'

'What is it, Gran?'

'It sounds silly, I know. But it's that drawing of the Indian girl. She was so beautiful. Jack seemed to have drawn her with such love. But the odd thing was, Jack must have sketched it decades later. He must have held that exact scene in his mind for all those years. Perhaps it was someone he loved before the war? I must have seemed a very poor substitute for her if it was.'

'Oh Gran. Surely not? He would have said something about someone who meant that much to him.'

Grace shook her head. 'Not Jack. He was a closed book in so many ways. As I said, there were so very many things he kept locked deep inside.'

The cabin crew were making their way up the aisle with the drinks trolley now. Eve could see from the flight path indicator on her screen that the plane was making its way over Europe. She ordered a gin and tonic and stared out of the window at the darkening sky. She recalled Grace's strange request at the end of that conversation.

'Perhaps you could go there on your journey, Eve? To that street in Kuala Lumpur. Petaling Street. You could take Jack's picture along. See if anyone recognises the girl?'

'I *could* go there, of course Gran.' Eve had said tentatively. 'But it's such a long time ago. Surely no-one will remember the girl now? We don't even know if she lived there, or her full name even.'

'Someone might. If you're passing through. Could you try for me?'

Eve had tried to convince Grace that she mustn't hold out any hope of finding out any information about the girl in the picture in Kuala Lumpur. And now, as she chewed her way through the meal of tough chicken curry and potatoes in its foil container, she thought again about how sad it was that her grandmother was clutching at straws like that. And how sad too that she could feel jealousy towards a mysterious girl in a drawing, who was probably long gone, even though Jack himself had been dead for twenty-seven years.

With a sigh, Eve settled down to read her guidebook about Myanmar for the rest of the flight.

As she made her way through Changi airport at Singapore, she called up Louise on her mobile phone.

'My flight has just landed, Mum. I'm coming through customs now. I'll get the train into the city. Will you meet me at Raffles Place MRT station, or shall I just come up to the apartment by myself?'

'There's no need,' came Louise's voice as Eve made her way out through the sliding glass doors into the arrivals lounge.

'I'm here! I've come to meet you.'

Eve scanned the rows of faces of taxi drivers crowding the barriers, waving and holding up signs for arriving passengers. Then she caught sight of Louise at the end of the row, jumping up and down and waving. She ran towards her mother and they hugged.

'You're looking very well,' Louise said after a few minutes, holding Eve at arms' length. 'Considering you've just spent thirteen hours crammed into a tin tube eating that rubbish that passes for airline food.'

'Oh Mum. Honestly. It wasn't that bad... You're looking pretty good yourself.'

But even as she said this, she noticed that her mother looked subtly different from the last time Eve had visited. Her face was thinner and her hair greying at the roots.

'Have you been on a diet, Mum?'

'Not really, no,' Louise said, quickly taking the luggage trolley from Eve and beginning to walk. 'Come on Ahmed's waiting with the car. He couldn't find a parking space so he's driving around.'

'Thank you for coming to meet me,' said Eve as she settled beside Louise on the back seat of Jim's Mercedes and the car crawled through the endless traffic between rows of glass skyscrapers.

'I wouldn't have minded getting the train, you know.'

'Nonsense. You must be exhausted. And I was so looking forward to seeing you. You must tell me all about everything now you're here. About Josh, about your job, about Mum. We couldn't really talk on the phone.'

So, as the car inched its way through the traffic on the freeway, Eve told Louise about how she and Josh had drifted apart, about how her job had become unbearable in the last few months and how she couldn't stand it anymore. But all the time she was talking, she was thinking of ways of telling her mother about her planned trip to Myanmar. How would Louise react?

The apartment hadn't changed much since she'd last visited. Spacious, pristine and modern, with floor to ceiling windows and those stunning views of the harbour and out across the shimmering ocean.

Eve took her luggage into the guest room. She took a quick shower and put on fresh clothes. When she came out Louise was emerging from the kitchen with a tray of tea things. She slid the glass doors open and went out onto the large balcony.

'Come on, Eve. Let's have tea out here and look at the view. That's something I never tire of.'

They sat down in basket chairs at the coffee table, surrounded by the luxuriant plants that Louise spent a lot of time tending. Louise leaned back in her chair and lit a cigarette.

'You're still smoking, Mum. You said you'd give up.'

Louise shrugged. 'I will one day. I can't seem to find the will at the moment.'

'What's wrong?'

'Nothing really,' she blew a smoke ring into the sultry air and watched it rise. 'Nothing could be wrong could it? Look at the place we live in here.' She gestured around her, but there seemed to Eve to be a trace of bitterness in her tone.

'There is something. I can tell.'

'Everything's fine,' Louise said briskly. 'Now, come on. Tell me all about your plans for the next few months. You haven't said how long you're staying here or where you're planning to go.'

Eve took a sip of tea. It was jasmine tea that Louise had always made. She smiled at the familiar taste, the taste of her childhood. She didn't feel ready to tell Louise about her plans to go to Thanbyuzayat, but at the same time there was no point putting it off or lying. She took a deep breath and looked her mother in the eye.

'I thought I'd go to Myanmar,' she said, a catch in her voice despite her attempts to sound normal.

Louise frowned and sat forward to peer into her eyes, 'Myanmar? Why on earth do you want to go there? It's a pretty dangerous country, you know.'

'Not any more, Mum. People go there for holidays all the time.'

Louise shuddered.

'You know what happened to me there don't you?'

'Well not really, no. You've never actually told me.'

'Well I'm telling you now. It wasn't a pleasant experience. I got caught up in some sort of demonstration and arrested. If it hadn't been for... for Jim, God knows what would have happened to me.'

Eve stared at her mother with renewed admiration, surprised by Louise's courage. A new picture was forming in her mind of a young Louise. A Louise very different from the prickly, difficult, anxious woman she'd become.

'I had no idea you'd been through all that,' she said.

Louise laughed, again with that edge of bitterness.

'You didn't know me then, Eve. I had guts in those days. Not sure where *they* disappeared to down the years.'

Eve stared at her, trying to imagine a younger version of her mother in the middle of a seething crowd holding banners and chanting slogans.

'Things have settled down there now, Mum. Nothing like that will happen to me.'

'That's what they say. But you still need to be careful. It's still run by the military government after all. Why not go to Vietnam instead? Or Cambodia?'

'Well I got interested in what happened to Grandad during the war while I was staying at Gran's. She got sent some pictures, you see... That started me thinking about it.'

'Pictures?'

'Yes. Pictures by Grandad that turned up in an old cupboard somewhere he'd once stayed. The gallery sent them. I've got them in my case. Shall I fetch them?'

'Of course. But let's go inside. They might spoil in the humidity out here.'

Eve brought the drawings into the open-plan kitchen and laid them out on the glass table-top.

'Well, one's a sketch, and one's a map actually. There was another one – a painting of an English country cottage, but I haven't brought that one.'

Louise leaned forward, her hands on the table, her head bent down, staring down at the map. She was still for a long time, then when she raised her head she said slowly,

'This is extraordinary, Eve. He gave me one just like this when he was dying. He said he'd lost the original. But I suppose this must be it.'

She pored over it again, frowning, lost in thought.

'Why did he draw a map?' asked Eve. 'I've been wondering about it all these weeks. He's marked something out. A cross. Look. There.' She put her finger on the place on the map.

Louise turned to her, with a faraway smile. 'You know I can't get over this. The one he drew for me was exactly the same. After everything he'd been through. And even though he was dying and it was over forty years later. He must have remembered that prison camp exactly as it was.'

'So? Why did he give it to you? Did he want you to go there?'

Louise nodded. 'He told me he'd buried a diary in an old tin. In that spot where he put the cross. That's why he wanted me to go there. He said that if I read the diary, it would explain a lot about him. Why he never recovered from what happened to him there. He made me promise...'

A chill ran through Eve, 'So did you go there? To the camp? Did you find the diary, Mum?'

Louise fell silent and looked down at her hands. Then she drew deeply on her cigarette, got up from her seat and crossed the room to the window, staring out at the twilight. The sky was now violet, shot through with streaks of orange and red. Eve watched her mother closely, beginning to wonder if she'd heard her question at all. As she watched, Louise's shoulders stiffened, and a shudder seemed to run through her whole body. Then Louise shook her head, as if to rid herself of something; a painful memory perhaps. Eve held her breath and after a while Louise turned back towards her and began to speak again, in a low voice, almost as if speaking to herself.

'You know, when I told Jim where I wanted to go, he said that it was impossible. That the territory was out of bounds to foreigners.' Eve could hear the pent-up tears in her mother's voice as she spoke.

'So you didn't go?' she asked. 'You just dropped it?'

Louise screwed up her face and tears filled her eyes now. Eve jumped up and crossed the room. She put her arms around her mother and held her close. She felt Louise's body shake with sobs as Louise gave into the tears and let them fall.

'Please don't upset yourself, Mum,' Eve said, trying desperately to think of something to say to calm her down. In the end it came to her: 'You know I could go there and see what I could find...'

Louise pulled herself upright and wiped her eyes on the back of her hand.

'Let's talk about it later, shall we?' she said, her voice a little steadier now.

'Of course, whatever you want.'

Louise stubbed out her cigarette and wiped her eyes. After a pause she said, 'And what about this other picture? What's this one?'

She picked up the street scene and held it up to the light. 'Wow! It's very good isn't it? A completely different style to most of Dad's pictures. I wonder who this girl is?'

'Gran wondered that too. I know this sounds odd, but she wants me to go there to see if I can find anything out about her.'

'Really? That doesn't sound like Mum... Is she OK do you think?'

Eve shrugged. 'I'm not sure. She seems to have got it into her head that Grandad was in love with this woman. It is really strange. But I agreed to try at least. She was very insistent.'

'How very odd of her. I hope she's alright.'

'She seemed a bit wistful. She talked a lot about the past and about Grandad.'

'Poor old Mum.'

After a pause Eve asked, 'What time are you expecting Dad home?'

'Around seven, I think. The usual time.'

'How is he?'

'Oh, the same as ever.' Louise said briskly as she crossed to the sink and began washing the tea cups. 'Busy at work as usual. I hardly see him.'

But Jim was back well before seven. He burst into the apartment filling the place with his energy and his ebullient presence.

'Hey! Eve! My little angel,' he said, dropping his briefcase and picking Eve up, swirling her around in a circle. It's what he used to do when she was tiny.

'Hey, steady on, Dad. I'm not a kid anymore,' Eve said laughing when he put her down.

'I can't help it. It's so good to see you!' he said. 'Now let me get rid of this suit. Why don't we go out tonight to celebrate? Louise? What do you think? You haven't started cooking dinner have you?'

They both turned to look at Louise who was hanging back, standing alone in the kitchen. Eve was struck by her expression. She was staring at them, her lips pressed together angrily and there were spots of colour in her cheeks.

'Are you OK, Mum?'

'Of course.'

'So, what do you think for tonight then Lou?' asked Jim. 'Why don't we try that new steak place. The one that's just opened in Marina Bay.'

Louise gave him a pointed look, and after a pause said, 'Oh I don't think Eve will want to eat steak, will you Eve? Something more local on your first night back in Singapore, surely?'

'I really don't mind,' Eve shrugged, sensing tension in the air between her mother and Jim, and desperately wanting to dispel it. It was that old familiar feeling from her childhood. Her mother acting prickly, Jim full of bonhomie, trying to jolly Louise along with humour and his irrepressible energy. Eve had always felt for her father in these situations. Why did Louise have to be so sulky and difficult? Why did she have to spoil things with her sudden mood changes, create an atmosphere with her attitude? A wave of impatience passed through Eve. But as she always had, she held her words back.

'It doesn't matter where we go,' she said. 'You choose, Mum. It's just good to be here and to see you both.'

'Alright then. How about Cantonese? Let's go to Hua Ting shall we? I'll phone and see if they've got a table.'

Eve exchanged glances with her father as Louise went through to the living room to make the call. Jim shrugged and raised his eyebrows conspiratorially.

Later, as they sat around the table in the sumptuous atmosphere of the Cantonese restaurant, Jim ordered Champagne and raised a glass.

'Here's to you Eve. And to your travels and to the future.'

'Eve's planning to go to Myanmar,' said Louise, as she took a sip of Champagne.

'Really?' Jim asked, putting his glass down. His eyes were on Louise as he went on. 'That'll be interesting, Eve. You know that's where your mother and I met. I was posted in Rangoon, sorry Yangon now, for more than three years in the eighties.'

'Yes, I know,' said Eve. 'Have you got any old photos or books? I'd love to see them before I set off.'

'I'm not sure. I might have some but maybe not here. They probably went into storage when we moved from England.'

'What a shame!'

'Eve's thinking of going to Thanbyuzayat to see where Dad was a prisoner,' Louise said suddenly.

Jim took a sip of his Champagne. 'Really? Well things will certainly have changed a lot since I was there.'

His eyes were on Louise's face. 'What do you think about it, darling?'

'Well, it's not up to me, is it? Eve's a grown up now. If she wants to go there, it's her decision.'

'Of course. I just wondered...'

'But actually, since you ask, I think it's a great idea. Eve brought a map that Dad drew when he was in the camp. She's going to take it to the museum in Thanbyuzayat and see what she can find out.'

'That sounds fascinating Eve,' said Jim, but Eve could tell from his voice that the idea worried him. Perhaps it was the memory of what had happened to her mother there, and the turbulent state of the country at that time.

'It does sound fascinating doesn't it? said Louise, putting down her glass and dabbing her mouth with a napkin. When she looked up, Eve saw that she was smiling, her eyes were at last full of genuine pleasure for the first time that evening.

'In fact,' Louise went on, 'Since you told me your plans this afternoon, I've been thinking about it a lot.'

She leaned forward and said to Eve, 'Please say no if this sounds too much of a drag, Eve, but If you'd like some company on your travels, I'd love to come along with you.'

12

Grace
London, 1945

The train steamed through the South Western suburbs of London and out towards Surrey. Grace stared out of the dusty window, through the clouds of steam from the engine, at row upon row of neat houses, their gardens full of regimented bean canes and raised vegetable plots. It was just after the rush hour and the train was almost empty, going against the flow of commuters coming into the city.

There was one other woman sitting in the corner of the second-class compartment. Dressed in a suit and hat, she clutched her handbag to her, her eyes occasionally darting over to steal a look at Grace. Grace avoided her gaze. She wanted to be alone with her thoughts.

She hadn't told anyone where she was going. Not even Nancy, and especially not Joan, who hadn't stopped asking her questions about who she'd been talking about in her delirious state during her illness.

As far as her parents were concerned it was a normal working day. She didn't mention the fact that she'd taken the day off work. She felt a little guilty as she set off for Harrow station at the normal time. She wasn't used to deceiving them, but there was no way she could tell them where she was going without prompting a lot of awkward questions. Instead of changing trains at Oxford Circus as she normally did, she'd carried on the Bakerloo line to Waterloo station and boarded a train bound for Guildford.

It was a fortnight since she'd returned to work after her illness. It had taken her all that time to find out where Jack had been sent. For the first few days, she'd gone through the motions of the hospital routines, her spirits at a low ebb, forcing herself to put on a cheerful front for the sake of her patients. All the time though, she was going over and over her regrets about Jack, torturing herself with thoughts of what she could have said to him, how she could have handled the situation differently.

On the fifth day, Nancy and she were working the same shift. As they emptied bedpans in the sluice room, Nancy had asked her about the letter.

'I just knew he was sweet on you from the beginning. Didn't I tell you?' Nancy said when Grace told her the gist of it. Then she added, 'I hope you're going to write back.'

Grace shook her head miserably. 'I can't. He didn't leave an address or even say which town the place is in.'

Nancy didn't hesitate. 'Well that's easy. Why don't you look in the files in Sister's office? You could sneak in there when she goes off duty. There's bound to be a note of it there.'

'Oh, I couldn't do that, Nancy,' said Grace, scandalised. 'I'd get the sack if anyone found out.'

'I could do it for you.'

'Don't be silly. You mustn't do that.'

Nancy shrugged. 'As you like, Miss Goodie Two Shoes. There must be a way, though.'

The breakthrough came a few days later, when Grace was accompanying one of the patients to the rear entrance of the hospital to wait for an ambulance. He was being transferred to another hospital for an operation.

Grace knew Sam, the elderly man on the transportation desk. He was always ready with a joke and a witty comment for the nurses. Grace exchanged a few words with him as usual, then, on an impulse she asked whether he kept the records of people going to convalescent homes.

He grinned up at her, 'Maybe we do. Who wants to know?'

'*I* want to know, Sam. It's someone from our ward. He left while I was off sick. I'd like to send him a get-well card.'

Sam eyed her with amusement. 'Pull the other one. Get close to the fella did you? I've heard it all before.'

She didn't reply but could feel her cheeks burning. Sam sighed.

'Go on then. I'll have a look. Name? Date of discharge?'

'Jack Summers. Three Wednesdays ago.'

He consulted his ledger, running his fingers down the columns, flipping back and forth through the pages. Grace held her breath.

'Ah. Here we are. He went to Great Down House in Seale. Surrey that is. Near Guildford I reckon. They took him in army transportation, not an ambulance, on account of him being military and all.'

She'd thought about writing to Jack at Great Down House, but in her impatience, she couldn't wait the three or four days it would take for letters to go back and forth between them. Besides, she didn't want to take the risk of him not replying to her. It seemed far better to seize the moment and make the journey to see him in person.

At Guildford station she got off the train and took a taxi to the village of Seale. It cost her half a crown, but on a quick scan of the bus timetables in front of the station, she gathered that Great Down House was some miles from the nearest bus route.

The taxi took her out of the town, labouring up the long hill onto the Hog's Back. She watched the countryside roll past, forests giving way to heathland. Her whole body was tingling with a mixture of nerves and excitement at the thought of seeing Jack. She'd felt bold and optimistic as she'd made her preparations and left home this morning, now she wondered what headstrong madness had prompted her to do this.

Great Down House was an imposing red-brick gothic building, sprawling along the ridge with a commanding view of the windswept heathland of the North Downs. Grace bit her lip as the taxi swept past twin gatehouses and up a gravel drive through parkland. The driver stopped at the bottom of a long flight of steps that led up to the house.

'Shall I wait for you here, love?' he asked switching off the engine.

'I'm not sure how long I'll be.'

'If you're going to be anything less than an hour I might as well wait. You won't find another taxi for miles around here, and business is slow at this time. I've got me flask and paper to keep me company.'

She walked up the long flight of steps that led to the house, her heart pounding. What if Jack didn't want to see her at all? He could be watching her even now from any one of those dozens of blank windows, preparing his excuses.

Inside the chilly front hall she rang a bell on a desk and waited. She recognised the familiar smells and sounds of a medical establishment, but this was quite different from the bustling hospital she was used to. It had the gentile atmosphere of a country house hotel.

Finally, a brisk woman appeared.

'It's not visiting time yet, I'm afraid, Miss. You can wait here until eleven if you like. Who have you come to see?'

'Jack Summers.'

The woman smiled for the first time. 'Oh, well, you're out of luck I'm afraid. Mr Summers discharged himself two days ago.'

Grace stared at her.

'Are you sure?' she asked at last.

'Of course, my dear.'

'Do you know where he's gone?'

'Now, that I *don't* know. He walked into the village to take the bus to Guildford. He said something about looking for work in Portsmouth, but I can't be sure.'

'So, you don't have an address for him then?'

'No. As I said.'

'Oh.' Grace stood there feeling foolish, wondering what to do. The woman stood there looking at her, poised, waiting for her to leave.

Grace turned to go, the force of this disappointment beginning to descend on her. She felt as if she spoke her voice would wobble and she might cry. As she reached the door, the woman said in a grudging voice,

'You might try his regiment, I suppose. I know he needed to be in touch with them for the rest of his back pay and discharge money.'

'Thank you. I'll try.'

She walked back to the taxi in a daze. Of all the permutations her anxious mind had dreamed up on her way here, she hadn't considered this one. She'd been so sure that Jack would be there, that she would be able to speak to him, to tell him how she felt about him. Even if he'd changed his mind about the way he felt, at least she would have tried.

'You were quick, love,' the taxi driver remarked in a chirpy voice, folding his newspaper, as she got back into the back of the cab. She didn't volunteer an explanation, simply asked him to take her back to the station.

The next train to London wasn't for another forty-five minutes. She went into the station café on the platform and ordered a tea. She sat at a high counter staring out of the window across the platforms. Occasionally a train arrived, disgorged passengers and moved on. Other trains rumbled through without stopping, creating a blast of smoke and steam as they went.

On the platform opposite a sign was painted, '*Portsmouth End*' with an arrow pointing along the platform. Each time Grace looked up from her tea she caught sight of it. It seemed to beckon her.

Suddenly she knew what she must do. She drained her tea, went to the ticket office and bought a return ticket to Portsmouth and Southsea. She had to run across the bridge to catch the train which was pulling in from London as she came back onto the platform.

It was mid-afternoon when the train rolled into Southsea. She couldn't remember ever having been here before, but the image of what the seafront would look like was clear in her mind from the description Jack had given her in the rose garden. She could remember every word of that conversation.

Pulling her coat tightly around her, she wandered down the pier and stared out at the thick grey line marking the landmass of the Isle of Wight across the choppy waters of the Solent. There were the great round Napoleonic forts, standing guard at the mouth of the harbour, but the leaden skies made the place look very different from the scene Jack had described.

Grace wandered back down the pier and bought a ham sandwich from a kiosk. It was blustery now and bitterly cold. She found a booth to sit in and eat, sheltered from the rain. What a fool she was to have come here on a whim. It would have been far better to write to the regiment as the woman had suggested.

She decided to wait until dark. Sunset could only be an hour or so away. That way, if Jack was going to come here today, he would already have done. She bought a magazine and killed time by sitting in yet another café on the seafront as the light of the late winter afternoon faded quickly. She watched the light dim on the shimmering water, occasional glimpses of clear sky through the clouds as the sun made a late showing. Lights came on along the pier and seafront.

'We're about to close up, love,' the woman behind the counter said. Grace glanced at her watch. It was five o' clock.

She left the café and wandered up the pier one more time. She walked all the way to the end and leaned over the bars to watch the waves crashing and foaming against the stanchions, gulls soaring and crying plaintively overhead.

Then she turned round and began to walk back to the station. As she made her way towards the sea front, she caught sight of a tall figure making its way onto the pier at the far end. Her heart leapt. She knew instantly that lanky shape, still thin from his wartime ordeal, clothes slightly too big for him. She would recognise the ambling stride anywhere. As he got closer she could see that he was carrying a sketchbook.

'Jack,' she called out in relief, breaking into a run.

13

Eve

Singapore, 2015

Eve and Louise sat side by side staring out of the window as the express train powered across the narrow causeway between Singapore and Johor in Malaysia. It was a sparkling, clear morning. The sun glittered on the expanse of flat, still water which shimmered blue under a vast sky.

'I'm glad you persuaded me to take the train,' said Louise, smiling.

'You *did* take a bit of persuading, but it wouldn't be a proper journey otherwise,' said Eve.

'You're right,' laughed Louise, squeezing Eve's hand. 'The trouble is, I've got so used to business class travel with Jim over the years. VIP lounges, five-star hotels. Spoilt, I suppose. I'd forgotten how much fun it is this way.'

'Do you think he'll be alright?' Eve asked after a pause.

'Who, Jim?' asked Louise, the smile gone. She slid her hand

away from Eve's and turned once again towards the window.

'Yes,' ventured Eve. 'He seemed a bit down when we said goodbye.'

'He'll be fine,' huffed Louise, her eyes studying the horizon. 'He's perfectly capable of looking after himself.'

'I know that. I just mean...'

Eve stopped herself. She wanted to ask her mother straight-up what was wrong between the two of them. The atmosphere in the apartment had been electric with tension. Her mother had hardly spoken to her father at all, and when she did it was mainly to criticise him, or to contradict something he'd said. Jim was clearly making huge attempts to bridge the divide. He brought Louise flowers one evening, which she received with raised eyebrows and silence.

Not now, Eve told herself. *I'll have to wait until later, until the moment is right.*

The train rolled into Johor Station and they gathered their bags to disembark for passport control.

A few hours later, after a journey through palm oil planta-tions, stretches of untamed jungle, past small towns with their ubiquitous low buildings with rusting roofs, and remote villages, with tethered animals and wooden houses they finally arrived in Kuala Lumpur Sentral Station.

'It's a shame they don't use the old Colonial station anymore,' said Louise as they walked out through the gleaming modern concourse. 'That really *is* beautiful. All Moorish domes and full of atmosphere.'

Eve smiled at her. 'I expect a lot has changed here since your backpacking days, Mum.'

'Including me! It feels odd to be carrying a rucksack again. Especially at my age.'

'It suits you,' said Eve. Looking across at Louise, she felt a sudden rush of warmth for her mother. She realised that in a matter of hours, released from the confines of the apartment, the boredom and dissatisfaction of her daily life, Louise looked as though she had shed ten years. She had tied her hair back in a pony tail, and wore no makeup. She looked slim and young in jeans and T shirt. To a casual observer, they could be friends, backpacking round Asia together, not mother and daughter.

They emerged from the concourse onto the taxi rank.

'We didn't decide on a hotel,' said Eve. Louise shrugged.

'Jim and I stayed at the Hilton last time we came to KL. Let's go somewhere completely different, shall we?'

'We can ask the taxi driver to recommend somewhere.'

The Number 1 Cathay Hotel had once been one of Kuala Lumpur's best-known buildings, or so the old Chinese man on the desk told them as they checked in. Now, its façade with pillared veranda was crumbling. And like all the former shop-houses on Alor Bintang, it was decaying sedately, forsaken by big business for the shimmering office blocks of the financial district that loomed a few streets away.

Eve took in the shabby lobby with its mosaic marble floor, army of ceiling fans and wrought iron staircase that wound gently upwards, exuding the atmosphere of old Colonial days.

'This takes me back,' said Louise, looking around approvingly. 'Just the sort of place I'd been hoping to find.'

They exchanged incredulous glances when the Chinese man told them the price of a room. Eve asked him to repeat it. Less than ten pounds for a large room with an en-suite bathroom.

'Sounds too good to be true,' said Louise.

An aged porter hovering beside the desk insisted on hoisting both their rucksacks onto his bent back. He stooped ahead of them with the key to their room. They followed him up the winding stairs to the second floor. As promised, the room was cavernous with a high celling, nicotine coloured walls and heavy dark brown furniture.

As soon as the old man had shuffled off with a tip of ten ringitts clamped in his fist, Eve wandered around the room, checking it out properly. The shuttered window overlooked a busy road behind the hotel. Not so different from London, Eve thought, pushing back the shutters and peering down at the lines of stationery traffic that quivered in the haze of heat and pollution. The ceiling fan whirred and clicked away, muffling the sound of hooting horns

The plumbing in the bathroom was Victorian, the old bath and cistern rusting, and the place looked as though it hadn't been painted since Malaysia became independent. Eve glanced at her mother who was already sitting on one of the sagging beds studying her face in a small mirror. Was she really up for this?

But Louise showed no signs of being daunted, or even mildly disappointed.

'Shall we have a quick shower and go there then?' she asked, putting her mirror away.

'Go where?'

'To Petaling Street of course,' replied Louise, swinging her legs off the bed. 'The place in Dad's drawing? It's the reason we decided to stop off here after all, isn't it?'

'Are you sure? I thought we might do that tomorrow morning. It's nearly dark now.'

'There's no time like the present,' said Louise.

An hour or so later they were wandering between thronging market stalls along Petaling Street in Chinatown. It was late evening and quite dark now, but the street was lit with red Chinese lanterns. The warren of smaller streets their taxi had nosed its way through to get here were still ablaze with light and buzzing with activity. Delicious aromas of Chinese spices rose from food stalls and restaurants that spilled out onto the street. The whole scene was a constant sea of colour, movement and clamour.

Eve peered at the buildings that lined the street, itself covered by a blue glass roof. The buildings were mainly shops, hotels or restaurants, their fronts obscured with gaudy neon signs. A few of them looked as though they could have dated from before the war, but many more of them were modern.

In one hand Eve clutched a plastic wallet that contained her grandfather's picture. They walked the length of the street, nudging their way through the crowded alley between the stalls which overflowed with cheap jewellery, fake designer handbags, T shirts, DVDs, ornaments, watches and trainers. At the end, the stalls thinned out and the domed glass ceiling came to an end. As they stepped out from under the roof it started raining; a sudden tropical downpour, huge drops that hammered down, soaking them to the skin in seconds.

'I don't think we're going to find it,' Eve said. She had to shout above the noise of the rain.

'Let's go back under cover,' said Louise.

They wandered back between the stalls. The din was even greater now, with the rain thundering down on the glass roof. Stallholders called out to them, peddling their wares. They stopped at several stalls this time and Eve showed the picture around.

'Do you recognise these buildings? This woman?' she asked.

It was greeted with polite interest, but bemusement.

'They're all too young to remember,' sighed Louise at last. 'Shall we go into one of these restaurants? I'm starving.'

They chose a simple place, set back from the road, less busy than the rest. They found a quiet table in the corner.

An old waiter shuffled up with the menu.

They ordered nasi goreng and lager and sat in silence for a while, watching the to-ing and fro-ing on the street outside.

'It's not going to be easy to find anyone who remembers the girl in the picture,' said Eve.

'No. But we didn't really expect it to be did we?'

'At least I'll be able to tell Gran that we've tried.'

The food arrived and they ate in silence. Eve's mind wandered to Jim, sitting down to a solitary meal in the apartment. Again she thought about how crestfallen he'd appeared when they had said goodbye.

'I wonder what Dad's doing. Perhaps we should call,' she said.

Louise put her chopsticks down and frowned at Eve.

'Do you think we could just have a few minutes now and again without talking about Jim?'

'I'm sorry,' said Eve.

'Look,' she went on, after an awkward silence, 'I wish you'd tell me what's wrong between you two. There's obviously something. If you're going to get annoyed every time his name is mentioned, I think you should tell me why.'

Louise pushed her food away and lit a cigarette.

'There's nothing wrong.'

'Oh, come on! You could have cut the atmosphere with a knife in the apartment. You were in such a mood all the time. Dad couldn't do anything right.'

Louise shot her a look. 'Just drop it please. I don't want to talk about it.'

'So, there is something then? Come on Mum, surely you can tell me?'

Louise was silent for a while. She was looking at Eve. From the frown on her face, Eve could tell that Louise was struggling to make a decision whether or not to confide in her.

'Oh, I don't know.' Louise said at last, blowing the smoke out in rings. 'I've got to thinking lately. About how I've wasted my life, you know. I haven't really achieved anything at all.'

'Well, you had *me*! That's got to be an achievement,' Eve quipped, trying to lift the mood.

'I even made a mess of that didn't I?' Louise said, leaning forward and looking into her eyes. 'Coming out here to live at a time when you probably could have done with me staying around in England?'

'You shouldn't be so hard on yourself, Mum. It made perfect sense for you to come out here to be with Dad when he got the job in Singapore. I was off to university. Gran was around. I often came out to see you during the holidays. We discussed it all at the time and it worked out fine.'

'I've just been a trailing wife all these years, Eve. Fitting in little jobs here and there. Being around for Dad when he came home from work. Fat lot of good it did me.'

'Why do you say that?'

Louise drew on her cigarette and stared out at the teeming street. She was still for a long time, her face turned away from Eve's. She turned back and opened her mouth to say something, but at the same time the old waiter loomed at the table.

'All finish? Food good?' he asked, taking the plates.

'That was delicious, thank you,' said Louise, 'I don't think we have room for more. But perhaps we can ask you whether you recognise this picture?'

He put the plates down again and took the picture. He looked at it, frowning, concentrating for several minutes. Then he handed it back.

'This is Petaling Street. I remember from when I was a boy. These buildings not here anymore though. They were pulled down. After independence.'

He pointed vaguely across the road. 'They were where the Orchid Hotel is now. Nothing left from that time.'

'And the girl? Do you recognise her?'

He held the picture up close to his eyes and examined it again. Eve looked up at him, holding her breath, hoping, but finally he shook his head.

'I was only a young boy. She is a pretty lady though.'

He put the picture back on the table and took the plates up again.

'What a shame,' said Louise as he retreated towards the kitchen. 'I thought we were on to something there for a moment.'

She stubbed out her cigarette and stood up. 'Shall we go then? I'm suddenly exhausted.' She took her bag and hurried over to the desk to pay. Eve followed, with a sigh, realising that the moment had passed for her mother to confide in her.

They took another taxi back to the hotel and Louise was silent during the journey, staring out through the streaming rain at the drenched city. Eve decided not to ask again, at least not for the time being. She didn't want to put a strain on their relationship, especially now. They had several weeks of travelling ahead of them. She wanted to persuade Louise to open up about her own trip to Burma in 1988. That would never be possible if she kept asking unwelcome questions about what was going on with her father. Even so, it troubled her that Louise and Jim were at loggerheads.

They had agreed that whatever happened they would only spend one night in Kuala Lumpur. They were both keen to press on with their journey to Myanmar.

The next day, they checked out of the hotel after breakfast and stood around in the high-ceilinged lobby under the whirring fans. The old man behind the desk was full of smiles. They'd left a large tip at breakfast.

'We've got a couple of hours before our train to Bangkok,' Louise said to him, 'Could we leave our bags here if we go out for a while?'

'Of course. Of course. Please do,' he said, opening a hatch in the counter and beckoning them to bring their bags through. 'There are many wonderful things to see in Kuala Lumpur. Petronas Towers, Jamek Mosque, Little India. Would you like me to call taxi?'

'Perhaps. We haven't quite decided what to do yet.' Louise turned to Eve. 'Do you think we should go back to Petaling Street?' she asked. 'It might look different in the daylight.'

Eve shook her head. 'I didn't expect to find anything really. I only agreed to go there for Gran's sake. If the building's not there anymore it's not likely anyone will remember anything more than the waiter in the restaurant.'

Eve looked down at her grandfather's sketch. 'It's a shame though. Gran would have been so pleased if we'd been able to find anything.'

'Perhaps I can help?' asked the old man peering over the counter. 'May I take a look please?'

Eve handed him the sketch. 'What are you looking for?' he asked.

'My grandfather was in KL during the war and he sketched this scene. We're trying to find out anything we can about it, and about the girl in the centre.'

Like the stallholders the previous evening, the old man stared at it gravely for several minutes, then he shook his head.

'These buildings are no longer there,' he said. 'I remember them from before the war.'

'And the girl?' Eve asked, her voice full of hope. 'Do you remember her? Or anyone like her?'

The old man smiled. 'Of course. There were many like her. Many faces passing through. Kuala Lumpur was overcrowded during the early days of the war. Many people came in from the countryside for work. Some were fleeing the fighting.' He peered down at the picture again.

'But I think this woman might have come from the city. Just from the way she is dressed. And many people left too, during the occupation. They were taken away by the Japanese for work.'

'What do you mean? Taken by the Japanese?'

'Many local people were taken away to work on the railway in Burma in 1942 and 43. They were offered good wages, good conditions. Those were very poor people, glad of any offer of work.'

He shook his head sadly, and was silent for a few seconds, his eyes far away, brimming with memories.

'But they were treated very badly,' he said finally. 'Many of them starved or died of disease. Most of them didn't come back. Many, many thousand in fact.'

14

Grace

London, 1945

Jack took her into his arms and held her close for a long time. Neither of them said anything. All the imagined conversations Grace had gone over in her frenzied mind on the way down from London melted away. She felt his warmth enveloping her body, driving out the chill she'd felt all day. His lips were on her hair. When she finally looked up at him they kissed quite naturally, as if it wasn't the first time.

'I got your letter,' she said as they moved apart. 'I just wanted to tell you that I'm sorry. I didn't mean...' she struggled for the right words. 'What I meant to say is, I was wrong to treat you the way I did. In the rose garden that day.'

'You don't need to explain,' he said. 'I understand. It's enough that you came today. But how on earth did you know I'd be here?'

'I didn't know for sure. I went to the convalescent home near Guildford first.'

As she spoke, they turned and began to walk back towards the seafront. Jack put his arms around her shoulders.

'They told me there that you might have gone to Portsmouth. I suddenly remembered what you said about watching the dusk from Southsea Pier. How you wanted to capture it every day for a month to observe how it changes...'

He stopped and stared at her, putting his hands on her shoulders and observing her at arms' length.

'That's incredible, Grace. That you came all the way down here on the off-chance. I was even thinking about not coming to the pier today, the weather's been so bad.'

'I would have contacted your regiment and found out where you were if you hadn't come.'

'But this way was far more spontaneous! You are an amazing person.'

They walked on in silence, contemplating the serendipity that had brought them together. Reaching the seafront, Jack guided her across the road, through the darkened Pleasure Gardens, around the boating lake and across Southsea Common towards the lights of a pub on the other side.

'Did you find a job?' she asked.

'Yes. I started at the beginning of the week. I've got a job in the dockyard. Carpentry. It's not much but I've managed to rent a room in a boarding house around the corner from here. I'm working an early shift. It means I'll have time to paint in the evenings.'

They reached the pub, the Castle Arms, and went inside. The clammy air enveloped them as they entered and it was a relief to be out of the bitter wind. The pub was a cavernous Victorian monstrosity, with ornate polished fittings and high ceilings. The lighting was dim and people turned to look as they entered. It was still early and there were a few customers at the bar. Jack bought a pint of beer and a dry Martini for Grace and they found a corner table beside the window.

'I can't tell you how happy it's made me to see you,' he said, his dark eyes on her face.

'I couldn't believe that you went without leaving an address! I had to find you. I couldn't let it rest, Jack.'

'I didn't mean to upset you,' he said at last. 'But I needed to protect myself.'

'Protect yourself? From me?'

'I've had enough loss in my life... It's hard to explain.'

'I'm so sorry Jack. You mean losing your family?'

He shook his head. 'No. Not that. Others, during the war.'

His face was suddenly so full of pain that Grace's heart went out to him. She put her hand over his on the table.

'Can you tell me about it, Jack?'

He shook his head, looking down, so she couldn't see his eyes.

'It might help,' she prompted gently.

He was silent for several minutes. Grace couldn't see his eyes; they were screwed shut now, his long lashes resting against his cheeks. He was holding his body rigid, still, away from her. He didn't appear to be breathing. Finally, he seemed to shake off whatever vice was gripping him and with a shudder his eyes snapped open.

'Let's not talk about that now,' he said with a brisk smile that she could tell was forced. 'Let's talk about you, Grace. Tell me your news. What have you been doing these past few weeks?'

So, she told him how she'd thought about nothing but him since she'd returned to work and found out he'd left the ward. How she couldn't rest until she'd found him, how she'd tortured herself with the thought that she might never be able to explain to him that it wasn't that she had no feelings for him, she'd just felt too awkward and clumsy to express them.

All the time she was speaking he was listening intently, smiling occasionally, and as she spoke she could see that he was relaxing, that he had spoken the truth. She had nothing to fear. He was genuinely overjoyed to see her.

The time melted away. He told her about his job at the docks; how he was learning the trade from a master craftsman, about the other men, some of them ex-servicemen like himself. 'They're a tough bunch, but they're friendly enough.'

He told her about the lodging house. How it was run by a fierce old woman, who wouldn't tolerate drinking, smoking or women on the premises. He said he'd joined the lending library and had borrowed a copy of *The Return of the Native*. Grace admitted she hadn't read that book, so he told her a bit about the story.

'I've been missing our chats,' he said. 'It's not been the same reading a book without being able to talk to you about it. There's no-one in the docks or in my boarding house who would be interested.'

'We've got it at home. I'll start reading it as soon as I get home,' she said. 'I can write to you if you like. Tell you my first impressions.'

'Would you? That would really cheer up my days. And when we meet again we can catch up properly, discuss it. You know, like we used to in the hospital?'

'Of course.'

She glanced at her watch.

'Goodness, it's seven o'clock. I need to get going to the station. It takes at least two hours to get to London, then I've got to get home from Waterloo.'

His face fell, and she noticed that look of despair creep back into his eyes.

'Do you have to?' he asked.

'I'm afraid so,' she said. 'I have to work tomorrow. My parents don't even know I took the day off. They'll start to worry soon. I'll need to telephone them from the station and say I'm on my way.'

'Of course,' he said, recovering his composure. 'I'll walk you to the station. Are you hungry? There's a chippy on the way.'

They bought chips from a shop on the seafront and ate them

quickly sitting on a damp bench overlooking the water. Then they walked to the station, their arms entwined. Jack waited at a discreet distance while she telephoned home. She told her mother she'd had to work late. She was surprised how easily the lies tripped off her tongue.

The London train was already in, letting off steam and chuntering like a living beast.

Jack walked her along the platform to an empty carriage.

'Well, here it is,' she said, feeling awkward now at the moment of parting.

'When can we meet again?' he asked.

'I can come down next Saturday if you like?'

'Yes. Please. Please do. I don't work at the weekends.'

'And I'll write if there's time before that. Tell me your address.'

She fumbled in her bag, finding her pocket diary as a blast of the horn came from the engine and the guard shouted at passengers to board. She scribbled down the address as he spoke.

'Goodbye then, Jack.'

They kissed again, this time self-consciously under the stark lights of the railway station, but it was a kiss full of longing and promise. They were both already anticipating the empty moments after the parting.

For three months Grace kept her liaisons with Jack secret from her family. She managed trips down to Southsea once every ten days or so to see him, and on his days off he would come up to London. They would meet on the steps of Waterloo station, go to the cinema, holding hands in the back row, or walk in Hyde Park or along the banks of the Thames, deep in conversation. Parting was always the most difficult part.

She couldn't quite explain, even to herself, why it was impossible for her to tell her family about the relationship. She berated herself continually. If she loved Jack, which she knew she did, why was she so fearful of their reaction to him?

She tried to understand this in herself, lying awake in bed, watching the pattern of the trees dancing on the ceiling in the light of the streetlamps. Was it his social standing, his lack of education and prospects? These things meant nothing to Grace herself, but she knew they would to her mother. After all, Mother had set her heart on Arthur for a son-in-law, or someone out of the same mould.

She knew her father would come round. He was ultimately reasonable, and she knew he wanted his daughters' happiness, but Mother would take a lot of convincing. For the time being Grace wanted to avoid the discussion. She wanted to keep Jack a secret until she was sure she could handle the inevitable confrontation. And that meant keeping it all secret from Joan too because she knew that Joan wouldn't be able to keep anything from her mother.

But Joan's wedding was fast approaching. Grace was to be the only bridesmaid and had to submit to dress fittings and endless discussions of styles and colours. She was vehemently opposed to all her mother's attempts to get her to wear something frilly and flouncy, choosing instead, a pale blue silk material in a simple style with a straight skirt and scoop neck.

'It's a shame you haven't got anyone to bring as your guest,' Joan said the week before the wedding, as they got dressed in the back room of the dressmaker's house after their final fitting. 'Are you sure there's really no-one you could bring? You've been disappearing off a lot lately.'

'I've had to work some extra shifts, that's all,' said Grace, buttoning her dress, avoiding her sister's eyes.

'Are you absolutely sure about that? You've been very secretive about your comings and goings.'

Grace glanced at her, wondering. Perhaps now *was* the time to introduce Jack to the family. They had at least got used to the fact that she wasn't going out with Arthur any more. Everyone would be busy and preoccupied on the day of the wedding, which might make it easier to introduce him that day than bringing him to the house.

BUT JACK WAS reluctant when she broached the subject the next time they met.

'I don't think it's possible, Grace. I'm afraid I don't have anything to wear,' was his first objection.

'Perhaps you could hire something?' she asked tentatively.

He turned and stared at her. 'I don't have that sort of money, Grace. You know that.'

She felt guilty then, the yawning gap in their circumstances opening up between them again. She wanted to suggest she could help him pay for it, but she knew he would find that humiliating. They were sitting in a café near Waterloo station, having a cup of tea before he caught his train home. They'd been to see an afternoon movie in Leicester square and had walked together arm in arm through the streets and across the river to the station. She'd wanted to broach the subject as they walked, but her courage had failed her.

'I'm sorry Jack. But I'd really like you to meet my family, and it would be a good opportunity,' she said now.

'Are you sure? You wouldn't be ashamed of me?'

'Don't say that. How could I possibly be ashamed of you? I love you. You know that.'

'I'd only let you down. I'm not very good at small-talk.'

'It doesn't matter. Please, Jack? For me?'

So, he agreed, but after she'd waved him goodbye on the platform, she started on her homeward journey with trepidation. There was no choice but to tell her parents about Jack now. How would they react? Coming face to face with the reality of her two worlds colliding made her head spin with anxiety.

But she needn't have worried. Her mother was so preoccupied with last-minute wedding arrangements that she didn't subject Grace to her usual level of forensic questioning. In fact, she hardly asked anything about Jack or his circumstances. Hearing that he had served in the army during the war was enough to satisfy her.

'I don't know why you haven't told us about him before, Grace. It's really very odd of you.'

'Probably something to do with what happened about Arthur,' Grace replied, knowing this would stop any further discussion. 'I just wanted to keep it to myself for a while. That's all.'

Her father hardly commented. Looking up from his paper, he said mildly, 'Well, I'm glad you're bringing him to the wedding. And I'm sure he's a wonderful chap if you've chosen him.'

Joan was overjoyed. 'I just knew it! Why didn't you tell me? Well never mind. I hope you'll be bringing him out with me and Leslie when we're back from Brighton?'

Grace smiled, but didn't respond. She couldn't imagine Jack being happy to make up a foursome for outings to the pub or dance halls as Arthur had done.

On the day of the wedding, Grace was tingling with nervous energy. As she followed her sister down the aisle of St Mary's Church, carrying a bouquet and Joan's heavy lace train, she couldn't prevent her eyes scanning the crowded pews for a glimpse of Jack. He'd said he would make his way to the church alone, but she still wasn't certain he would be there. Her heart leapt when she caught sight of him standing head and shoulders above two elderly women. She caught his eye as she passed. He looked so well turned out in a grey suit and tie, her heart swelled with pride. He smiled at her and from the look in his eye, she knew it was going to be alright.

At the reception at the Harrow Hotel she introduced Jack to family and friends. He was on his best behaviour, with a polite word for everyone he met. But occasionally when she glanced over at him, she could see that although on the surface he appeared relaxed, he was perspiring with the effort of the occasion, and although he smiled, there was pent up tension behind his eyes.

She watched anxiously at how her mother reacted when she introduced them. To her relief her mother seemed to be quite taken with him, laughing at his polite jokes, responding to his understated flattery with pleasure. Her father offered him a cigar and Grace watched them go outside onto the terrace to smoke.

'He seems to be making quite an impression, your Jack,' said Joan, coming up beside Grace. Grace turned to look at her sister. How beautiful she looked in her white lace gown, her face alight with happiness and excitement. Grace put her arms around her.

'It's your day, Joanie darling. No-one's making an impression like you and Les.'

After Joan and Les had left in a taxi and the guests began to drift away, she found Jack smoking alone on the terrace. He was staring out into the dark garden, that brooding, faraway look in his eyes.

She sat down beside him. 'That wasn't so bad was it?' she asked.

He smiled, flicking ash away.

'No. Of course it wasn't. Your family seem very nice.'

'Would you like to come back to the house afterwards? Mother and Father will be leaving soon.'

'If it's all the same to you I need to get off to the station. It's a long way back to Portsmouth.'

'Of course,' she said, with a flicker of disappointment.

'I'll go now then. I needn't go back in. I'll go straight out this way to the drive.'

She stood up with him.

'Aren't you going to come in and say goodbye to my parents?' She didn't want him to leave. Not like this. Why this sudden change in his mood when things had apparently been going so well.

He shook his head. He was still staring out at the night, dragging on his cigarette, not looking at her.

'Look Jack,' she said, moving towards him, putting her hand on his shoulder. 'I know it's been a strain for you today. I do appreciate your coming here you know.'

He turned to look at her. She was shocked at his expression. There was that old look she'd come to dread and which she couldn't erase, even with all the love she felt for him. It was that look of pain and anguish, as if he'd stared into hell itself and the memory was stamped on his mind.

'Please don't patronise me, Grace,' he said, suddenly, shrugging off her hand and stepping off the veranda onto the lawn.

'Oh Jack, I didn't mean...' she called, but he was gone, striding across the lawn towards the hotel entrance without a backward glance. Grace stood at the rail, watching him go, tears smarting her eyes.

15

Grace
London, 1946

G race didn't see Jack again for over a fortnight. She lived through those days in a state of anguish. Although it pained her, she decided to sit tight and wait a while before contacting him, even though her heart was telling her to jump on the train down to Portsmouth at the first opportunity.

The house seemed empty and lifeless without Joan, and without the distraction of the wedding preparations. Mealtimes were forlorn, stilted affairs.

'When are you seeing your young man again?' asked her mother a couple of days after the wedding. 'It was a shame he had to leave so early. I don't think I even got to say goodbye to him.'

'I'm sorry, Mum, he had to rush for his train. He didn't have time to say goodbye properly. He did send his apologies, though,' she lied, wondering why she felt the need to justify his behaviour like this.

'You didn't say what he does for a living down in Portsmouth, Grace.'

Grace put her knife and fork down and looked her mother full in the face.

'He works in the docks actually,' she said. 'He's training to be a carpenter.'

Her mother's eyes widened.

'Grace! Are you quite sure?' her voice was scandalised. 'He looked to be quite an educated person.'

'Of course I'm sure, Mum. I do know him. And he is an educated person. He's intelligent and well read. And he's a brilliant artist too.'

Her mother's eyes narrowed. 'Ah, so now I understand. *That's* why you kept him quiet all those months.'

'Not at all! Why should his work be anything to be ashamed of?'

'Don't be silly, Grace. You know just what I mean. He's not quite like us is he? Working in that environment? Let's face it. He's from a different world. He doesn't have the same values.'

'Not like us? Wasn't your mother a housemaid and your father a groom, Mother? You don't have any right to condemn what he does for a living.'

Her mother drew herself up and said in a prickly voice.

'My parents encouraged me to move up in the world. And I hope I've brought *you* up to have aspirations for yourself Grace. Not to go backwards as you seem hell bent on doing.'

'I do have aspirations. And they don't include the sort of petty snobbery that you display.'

Her father looked up from his paper. 'Now, now Grace,' he said mildly. 'Don't be rude to your mother.'

Her mother's attitude made her all the more desperate to see Jack. Each day she checked the post for a letter, but none came.

She had been hoping he would write and apologise for the way he'd walked off at the wedding, but after a few days she realised that wasn't going to happen. She got her pen and paper out to write to him several times. She started several letters, but ended up tearing them up. Her pride wouldn't let her beg.

On her day off she decided to take action. She took an afternoon train from Waterloo to Southsea, remembering all the times she'd taken it over the past few months. Those journeys had been made in the knowledge that she would be spending the day with Jack, planning what to say to him, anticipating seeing him waiting for her at the end of the platform, seeing the look on his face when he saw her. This time was different. She wasn't sure that she would see him at all, and if she did, she wasn't sure how he would react.

It was five o' clock when the train rolled into Southsea. She knew where she would go first. She didn't want to risk going to his boarding house – she knew the men weren't allowed to take women there and she didn't want to embarrass him by going to the door.

Instead, she went straight to the pier and walked the wooden boards right to the end. It was deserted, like the first time she'd been here. The weather was warm today, there was a smell and a sense of spring on the salty breeze. She leaned on the rail and stared out across the Solent. Today, the Isle of Wight was a clear green strip between a dark blue sea and paler blue sky. She stood there for a long time, taking in the beauty, the changing sky, the constant movement of the clouds and of the water.

She didn't hear footsteps behind her, but she felt the touch of a hand on her shoulder.

'Grace.'

Her heart leapt and she turned to look at him. He stood there, in a battered overcoat. He seemed even thinner than before. His face was haggard, his eyes full of emotion, but he wasn't smiling.

'Why ever did you come?' he said in an anguished voice. 'I

thought you would give me up as a bad job, the way I behaved at the wedding.'

'I needed to see you. I've been so miserable.'

He stood staring at her, not making any move to touch her.

'I'm no good for you Grace. That's why I went like that.'

'What do you mean?' she asked, alarmed.

'When I saw you amongst all those decent, polite people at the reception, I felt a fraud being with you. You belong amongst them. You deserve a comfortable, happy life. I suddenly knew I could never make you happy.'

'That's not true Jack. How can you think you don't make me happy? Think of all the good times we've had together.'

He turned away and put both hands on the rail and stared out to sea.

'I'm better off alone. That way I won't hurt anyone but myself,' he muttered.

'Jack, why are you talking like this? Please... look at me.'

'There are things you don't know about me, Grace. Things that happened during the war. I can't speak about them, but they've touched me deep inside. That will always be between us.'

She put her arms around him then, but he was still rigid, not looking at her.

'What things? Please Jack. You can talk to me. I'll try to understand. Please.'

'No. You'd never understand. No one who wasn't there would.'

She paused, her mind searching frantically for the right response. In the end she said;

'You don't have to tell me if you don't want to. I won't ever ask you again if it hurts you. Please.'

She was aware that she was begging now, but the thought of losing him, and for this reason, filled her with panic.

She felt the muscles in his arms relax. He straightened up, and turned and looked at her face now. She was relieved to see the look of terror and desperation had gone.

He kissed her then, with a fierce passion she'd not known before.

'I missed you so much,' he murmured as they pulled apart.

'I couldn't go on without seeing you,' she said.

They went to sit in one of the booths on the pier, and they talked for a long time, while the sun set and the pier lights went on. Then, for the first time, they walked down onto the beach. The tide was out and Jack spread his coat out on the sand. They sat and watched the lights of the cargo ships and liners going to and fro from Southampton, and the Isle of Wight ferries paddling past.

'I need to go soon,' said Grace at last. 'I'll need to get the next train.'

He kissed her then, and for the first time she decided not to suppress her desire as she usually did, the words of her mother ringing in her ears; 'Save yourself for your wedding night, my girl.'

She lay down on the sand and he lay down with her and kissed her again, and moved on top of her, she was pulling him closer, moving with him, drawing him in, becoming one with him, and there on the beach, under the stars, they made love for the first time.

16

Louise
Moulmein, Burma
August 1988

Louise left the guesthouse in the late afternoon. She'd decided not to draw attention to herself by taking her backpack. Instead she took a few belongings for the night in a shoulder bag. As planned, when she went past the desk she told the old man that she was going to see the sunset from the pagoda, and that she wouldn't want breakfast in the morning. He stared at her from behind his thick glasses for a few seconds, nodded briefly and then turned back to his newspaper.

She took a rickshaw to where the covered steps started to rise to the pagoda and walked up between market stalls and hawkers. There were dozens of flights of stairs. Wild monkeys sat on the railings contemplating the passers-by with mournful eyes. Sometimes they jumped on someone who was carrying food, shrieking. By the time Louise reached the top she was breathing heavily and her T shirt was drenched in sweat.

The pagoda took her breath away. She stood staring up at it; a huge golden stupa surrounded by a marble platform filled with smaller, ornate ones. The chanting of monks could be heard from the prayer halls and the smell of incense filled the air. People knelt in front of shrines, laying flowers and gifts. Afterwards they sat cross-legged, meditating in silence as the light faded from the sky.

Louise went to the edge of the platform and looked out over the town towards the Salween river. The low buildings were interspersed with lush greenery and palm trees. The sun was going down over the river and from where she stood she could see dozens of flat islands, grey in the pink estuary like clouds in a stormy sky. It was beautiful. She wondered if her father had been here and stood in this place during the war.

She sat down on one of the marble benches and let her mind drift back to her father. She thought back to the time when she had realised that he was vulnerable. It was the last time she had visited the flat in King's Cross. She must have been ten years old. This time he seemed troubled. He would sleep late into the mornings and would start drinking whisky with his breakfast. This time he hadn't organised any trips out for them apart from evenings in the Queen's Head.

'Shall we go out today, Dad?' Louise asked on the third day.

He stroked her hair. 'I don't really feel like it today, precious. Can't we just stay at home? How about doing some painting with me?'

He gave her one of his old shirts to wear over her clothes and set up a small easel next to his own. He helped her sketch out the shape of a house beside a lake. Then he showed her how to mix the paints on the palette. She loved the oily smell and the greasy texture of them. At last he came alive, if only for a while, and she caught a glimpse of his old self as he chatted and laughed with her that morning. Louise was proud of the picture she painted that day. It still hung on her bedroom wall in her mother's house.

But the next day he slept in until lunch time. Louise tried to shake him awake, but he just grunted and turned over. She made a pot of tea at the makeshift kitchen in the corner of the room and took him a mug, careful not to spill any. He raised himself on his elbows.

'Thank you. That's really sweet of you,' he said smiling.

'Are you ill?' she asked.

'Not ill,' he said. 'Just out of sorts I suppose.'

'Out of sorts? What does that mean?'

'Oh, I don't know. Just feeling a bit down. Nothing seems to be going right at the moment.'

She stared at him awkwardly, not knowing what to say.

Later that day two large men in shiny suits came to the door and thrust a piece of paper into Jack's hand.

'What's this?' Louise heard him ask.

'Eviction notice. You need to clear out of here. If you're not out by nine tomorrow morning we'll come and make sure you go ourselves.'

'But you can't do that. I've got my little girl staying. Where can I go?'

'You should have thought of that when you stopped paying your rent.'

'I didn't have any work for a time. I've got some money now. I can pay part of it. Here...' he went to a tin beside his bed and took out some crumpled notes.

'It's not enough. If you can't pay all the arrears right now you're out. We've got a court order.'

When they'd gone he sat on the bed, his head in his hands. Louise crept close to him and put her arms around his shoulders. They were shaking gently and she realised with a shock that he was crying.

'I'm sorry Louise. I've let you down badly,' he said. 'I'm such a failure. Everything I touch seems to turn to rubbish.'

'Where shall we go?' she asked.

'We'll find a B&B. There are lots around King's Cross. And when I've saved up a bit more money, I'll be able to rent another flat.'

The Bed and Breakfast place he found was dirty. The tiny room had two saggy beds and a stained chest of drawers and looked out over the Euston Road. The passing buses and lorries rattled the window panes. There was a communal bathroom along the passage that was always smelly. Other guests in the house were a noisy, drunken lot. They seemed to come and go at all times of the day and night, banging doors, shouting.

Louise watched her father. He seemed to sink lower by the day and he was drinking even more. In the evenings he would drink whisky and drift into oblivion, leaving Louise to put herself to bed. This and the Bed and Breakfast place frightened her, and for the first time since she'd been with him she wanted to go home.

He phoned her mother to let her know where to collect Louise from, and when she came there was a fearful argument. Louise had never heard her mother swear before, but Grace didn't hold back.

'How can you bring her to this filthy shithole? It's no place for a child. The people staying here look like druggies or prostitutes or both. I shouldn't have trusted you, Jack. You're so irresponsible.'

'I'm sorry Grace. I've been down on my luck lately.'

'Down on your luck? You've been drinking. I can smell it on you. The whole place stinks of it and there are empty whisky bottles in the bin. You can't fool me Jack Summers.'

Her mother fumed all the way home on the train but she didn't mention the matter again. The letters stopped coming but the following summer in the lead up to the holidays Louise asked,

'Am I going to stay with Dad again this year?'

'No. You're not going there again. He can't be trusted to look after you. You can stay with Granny instead.'

She'd had to wait two years before she saw him again and by that time he'd moved out of London and was living in a converted barn on a farm in rural Buckinghamshire. His paintings had become popular for a time and he had plenty of work. Staying with him away from London hadn't got the same air of adventure and excitement, though. They would go for country walks and frequent the village pub. Although Louise still relished the time she spent with her father, she missed the buzz of the city that she associated with him.

Grace
London, 1946

GRACE AND JACK were married on a raw, grey day in November 1946. The red brick Register Office on the Fulham Road, with its functional lino corridors and disinfectant smells, reminded Grace of her ward on the hospital. But that didn't bother her. She was marrying Jack that day and nothing could knock her off her cloud.

On the back seat of the taxi on the way there, her father squeezed her hand and said,

'I'll always be here for you, Gracie, whatever happens. You know that, don't you?'

'Yes Dad,' she said, squeezing his in return.

She knew what he was referring to, but she didn't want to spoil the day by discussing it just then.

It had been six weeks since she'd written to Jack to tell him that she thought she was pregnant. She hadn't been able to bring herself to tell her mother, or even Joan, who was full of her own plans for starting a family. Having a baby out of wedlock was so outside their experience, Grace simply couldn't begin to imagine how they might react.

Jack had written back by return, his letter overflowing with love and enthusiasm.

'I want to marry you Grace, if you'll have me. Come on down to Portsmouth to see me as soon as you can.'

He'd met her at the station at Southsea and they'd walked arm in arm to the end of the pier where he'd gone down on one knee, looked up into her eyes and said, 'Will you marry me, Grace Everett?'

He'd given her a silver ring with a tiny diamond and her heart swelled with love and gratitude, tinged with a touch of guilt. He must have spent all his savings on it.

They'd spent a blissful day walking arm in arm beside the sea, planning their future. When she'd returned home, she'd plucked up the courage to tell her mother that she was getting married.

'To that Jack Summers?' her mother had said straight away. Then she'd frowned. 'But why so quick?' her face had clouded with suspicion and she stared pointedly at Grace's waistline. 'You're not expecting are you?'

Grace had coloured but kept her eyes steady. 'Of course not, Mother.'

She couldn't admit it then. Not in that atmosphere of blame and hostility. She'd wait until after the wedding. Everything would fall into place then, she was sure of it. How could Mother not come round to accepting Jack, even if he didn't have the sort of job she approved of, once she realised how genuine and loving he was? How could she not appreciate him once she got to know him properly?

As Grace stepped out of the taxi in the forecourt of the Register Office, wearing her best suit that she'd let out at the seams, and pillbox hat trimmed with feathers, there was an awkward little crowd waiting in the icy drizzle. Her mother was there with Joan and Les, Sister and Nancy, a handful of Grace's friends from the hospital, and a scattering of relatives. And there was Ernie, leaning on his crutches supported by Peggy, standing a little apart from the rest of the party.

It wasn't until she was halfway across the forecourt and almost at the steps of the building that Grace caught sight of another guest. A small, worn-down little woman wearing a battered cloche hat standing well away from the others. Grace paused momentarily, wondering who it might be and then she realised. It must be Jack's mother!

After the ceremony when everyone was standing on the steps for photographs, Jack introduced them. His mother looked pale and dreadfully ill at ease. She wore a plain blue coat and scuffed shoes. She flashed Grace a nervous smile and handed a tiny jewellery box to her.

'You might want this. It's a memento from his childhood. I've kept it all these years 'specially for this day.'

Grace murmured her thanks.

'Couldn't Frank come?' Jack asked.

His mother shook her head. Grace observed a slight drawing up of the woman. Was it defensiveness?

'He couldn't get time off, Jack. I'm sure you understand...' the mother's voice faded and she looked away.

'Who's looking after Betty and Kath?'

'A neighbour's keeping an eye. But they don't really need looking after any more, Jack,' his mother said with a hesitant smile, 'They're sixteen and fourteen now. Don't you remember?'

Grace felt for Jack. That expression that she'd come to dread clouded his face again. She knew what he was thinking. That he'd lost three and a half years of his life in captivity. Everything had changed back home and the world he'd come back to wasn't the one he'd left. It was hard for him to take it all in. For a moment he looked bewildered.

But he'd regained his poise by the time they set off to the nearby hotel for the reception. He kissed Grace in the back of the taxi.

'Everything's going to be alright, Gracie,' he said. 'What's in the little box?'

She opened the box his mother had given her, removed the cotton wool padding expecting there to be precious stones or a piece of jewellery inside, but instead there were a lot of tiny white objects, some of them flecked with dried blood.

'They're teeth!' she said in surprise, closing the lid of the box.

'Good God. My baby teeth,' Jack said shaking his head. 'I had a feeling I recognised the box. I don't know why she gave them to you. I'm so sorry Grace.'

'Don't be silly,' she said, 'It's not your fault, and I'm sure she meant well.'

She kissed him again, but the unsettling feeling she'd had seeing those tiny white baby teeth lingered with her for the rest of the day.

The hotel was the only building still standing between two bombsites that had been cleared, but for great piles of rubble dotted about on the surrounding wasteland. Grace had refused her father's offer of a big reception like Joan's.

They ate in a gloomy dining room with the light outside fading fast. The food was plain and traditional. When the meal was over Jack cleared his throat and stood up to give his speech. Grace found herself suddenly nervous for him. Far more nervous than if she'd had to deliver a speech herself.

The room fell silent, watching Jack, waiting for him to begin. Grace twisted the napkin in her lap, willing him to speak. The seconds ticked by, and Jack stood there, motionless, his face pale. For a while Grace was afraid that he might crumble and run out of the room. But when he finally spoke, his voice was barely more than a whisper, shaking with emotion.

'I'd like to thank you all for coming today,' he said. 'This is the proudest and happiest day of my life. I'm humbled that Grace agreed to marry me.'

There was a long pause before he went on, 'When I met her I was ready to die, and I nearly did die. But knowing Grace gave me a reason to live....'

Again, Jack fell silent. People looked down at their plates or rustled their napkins. From where Grace was sitting she couldn't see Jack's face, but she could sense that he was struggling to maintain his composure. Finally, he said in a rush...

'And I'd like to thank Mr and Mrs Everett for this wonderful spread and for welcoming me into their family.'

He sat down quickly, breathing heavily. During the embarrassed applause, Grace caught her mother's eye. Her mother gave a quick shake of her head and the expression in her face quite clearly said, 'You could have done far better for yourself, my girl.'

Her father got to his feet and gave a diplomatic, polished speech full of praise and generosity. When he'd finished Grace went up to him and he took her in his arms.

'Thank you, Dad,' she said, fighting to hold back the tears.

Grace and Jack spent two nights in a cheap B&B on the Isle of Wight and then went back to begin their married life in the tiny flat in Southsea that Jack had recently rented.

The week after the wedding, Grace started a new job at Portsmouth General hospital. Sister and Matron from the Hammersmith had given her excellent references, but it felt odd moving away from everything and everyone she knew and starting afresh in a new place amongst new people. The work and the routines were unfamiliar and she struggled to settle down. It was difficult to make friends amongst the other nurses, especially as she was anxious to hide her condition for as long as she possibly could. She knew though, that she was on borrowed time and that going out to work as the mother of a baby was virtually unheard of. But she and Jack needed the money badly, so she worked as many shifts as she could during those early weeks.

One day the ward sister called her into the office.

'Please sit down. Now I've heard a rumour that you're expecting a baby, Nurse Summers. Is that right?'

Grace looked across the desk at the older woman. Sister was one of those middle-aged nurses who'd devoted her whole life to her profession. Grace was sure she wouldn't understand her own predicament. After all, Sister wasn't even married herself, let alone a mother. Grace had to think quickly. She was on the point of denying it, but she realised that would be pointless. She knew that nothing would escape Sister's shrewd gaze for long.

'Yes. It is true,' she said finally, trying to sound as normal as she could.

The Sister's expression didn't change.

'You know you shouldn't really be working here in your condition. You need to be fully fit to be able to carry out your duties on the ward properly. And in any case, this sort of work isn't good for an expectant mother. You should be resting as much as possible.'

'I feel fine, Sister. I hope you haven't got any complaints about my work.'

'On the contrary Nurse Summers, your work shows great promise. Nevertheless, it's hospital policy that you shouldn't be working on the wards, I'm afraid.'

Grace sensed panic rising inside her. She felt powerless. She wanted to get up and shout at Sister, but she stifled that impulse. She bit her lip to maintain her calm and threw herself on the other woman's mercy.

'I don't know what we'd do without my job. We need the money you see...'

She felt a lump rising in her throat, but with an effort of will stopped herself from bursting into tears.

To her surprise Sister's expression softened and she said, 'Well, I don't suppose it would do any harm for you to carry on for a month or two, Nurse. Until you are unable to hide your condition any longer. It wouldn't be seemly to carry on then. This *is* a ward full of men after all.'

'Thank you, Sister. I won't let you down.'

But a month or so later the dilemma was solved for her.

As Grace was getting up one morning she felt sudden, crippling cramps in her lower abdomen. Jack had already left for work and she was running late herself. She carried on getting ready, trying to ignore the pain, but it increased minute by minute until she was forced to lie down, doubled up on the bed. It was then that she realised that she was bleeding profusely, the blood already oozing down her legs and staining her skirt. She wrapped herself in towels and lay down on the bed alone.

'I'm so sorry, Jack,' she sobbed into the silence.

Grace
Portsmouth, 1947

FOR MONTHS AFTER THE MISCARRIAGE, Grace felt numb inside, detached from the world. It was almost as if she was going through life in a dream, making no impression on her surroundings or on people around her.

The loss of the baby had hit Jack hard. He retreated into himself. Grace could feel his pain, overlaying her own. But she sensed that there was something much deeper for Jack. Unfathomably deep.

She felt isolated and very alone. Although she wrote home dutifully each week with her news, her mother rarely wrote back and Grace got the impression that she was gradually being eased out of her mother's orbit. Joan wrote erratically, with news of the latest purchase she had made for her kitchen, or of the jam she'd made for the Women's Institute coffee morning or with gossip from the neighbourhood.

Once, her father made the journey down from London by train on Grace's day off. He took her to lunch in the Grand Hotel.

'Is everything quite alright, Gracie?' he asked as they waited for their soup to arrive.

'Of course, Father. Why wouldn't it be?'

'You look rather thin, that's all. And not very well if you don't mind me saying so.'

'Everything's fine. You don't need to worry,' she said, but she couldn't meet his eye, afraid that if she did her defences would come down.

'Look, if you're finding it hard to make ends meet, you can always ask you know. It could be an arrangement between you and me. Your mother wouldn't need to know a thing about it.'

'No Father,' she said fiercely, 'Jack and I can manage. I wouldn't dream of it.'

~

'I SO WANTED THAT BABY, GRACE,' Jack admitted one night, as they lay in bed, watching headlights of passing buses on the ceiling. 'To try to make up for things.'

'Things? What do you mean, try to make up for things?'

He ignored her question and went on, staring at the ceiling, as if speaking to himself. There was an intensity in his words.

'I would have loved and protected that baby Grace. So that nothing in the world could hurt it. So that it would grow up loved and cared for and free of pain.'

'I know, Jack,' she said. 'I wanted that too. Everyone wants that for their children.'

She glanced at him and at that moment pain was etched on

his face and he was staring into emptiness, as if he was witnessing something truly terrible.

'Are you alright Jack?' she asked, propping herself up onto her elbow, but he didn't reply.

She lay back down beside him, trying to find words that wouldn't upset him more. Perhaps this was her opportunity to ask him? A door into his past that might help him speak to her about what he'd witnessed, and about his troubles. What had happened, back there deep in the jungle in Burma to fill him with such terror and pain still. Grace was burning to help him.

'It wasn't your fault you know, Jack,' she said finally. 'Whatever happened when you were a prisoner Jack, it wasn't your responsibility,' she said. 'You must stop blaming yourself.'

He turned on her then, his eyes suspicious, accusing.

'What do you know about it?'

She shrunk back, alarmed at the vehemence of his speech.

'Nothing Jack. Nothing at all. I just know that you are troubled by something. I'd like to help you, but you won't talk to me about it. You shut me out.'

'No one who wasn't there could ever understand,' he muttered.

'We can have another baby, Jack. It's my fault. I was working too hard. Getting too tired. I should have listened to Sister and to my own body.'

He didn't reply, and they lay there silently, until Grace knew from the rhythm of his breathing that he had fallen asleep.

But in the night she awoke suddenly. Jack was moving restlessly, thrashing around in his sleep. He was moaning too, and at one point he cried out, a word she'd never heard before. It was a word in a foreign language or was it a name?

The words were indistinct and meant nothing to Grace. But he said them again and again. It sounded like 'Cash...win.' What did it mean?

In the morning they hardly spoke when they got up for work.

It was as if they were both consciously avoiding any reference to their discussion the night before. Grace couldn't bring herself to ask Jack about the words she'd heard him say in the night. She never did manage to ask him, even though she would hear them again and again in the years to come.

17

Louise
Moulmein, Burma
August 1988

When Louise arrived back at Thuza's house just before nine o' clock that evening, there was a small truck parked up in the drive. Thuza came out of the house with another man. This man looked older than Thuza. He was short and wiry.

'This is Mo Chit,' said Thuza. 'He will drive us down to Thanbyuzayat. He is taking a cargo of fruit down to the market there.'

He shone a torch at the back of the truck and for the first time Louise noticed that it was piled high with huge green prickly fruit.

'You can hide in amongst the fruit. It will be uncomfortable and smelly, but it's the best chance of getting you there without being seen.'

Louise went up to the truck, reached out a hand and touched the fruit. It was covered in sharp spines. A pungent smell was rising from it; a mixture of bad eggs, onions, and rotting vegetables. She couldn't help pulling a face.

'It smells really bad. What is it?'

Thuza and Mo Chit exchanged smiles.

'Don't you know? They're durian fruits. They smell so strong that they're banned in lots of public places. Some people love them though. They can be a real delicacy.'

She stared at him.

'I've got to travel in there? Are you serious?'

Thuza's smile vanished. He took a step closer to her.

'Perfectly serious,' he said quietly, his tone suddenly changing. 'We're taking big risks driving you down there. Think what that means for us. Surely you can put up with a few hours discomfort to avoid trouble? We chose durian fruit because the police won't want to go near it at the road blocks.'

She saw the determination in his eyes and was reminded of the boys on the train and of how people here could take nothing for granted. She felt a stab of guilt. She had no right to put her own comfort before their safety.

'I'm sorry,' she said. 'You're right. It's a good idea.'

His face relaxed.

'Come on inside the house,' he said. 'You need to change into some different clothes. I've thought of a way of disguising you while you're there.'

Inside the dimly lit front hall stood a young woman. Two small children clung to her saree. She was slender and delicate-looking, darker skinned than most Burmese people. There was an anxious look in her large brown eyes.

'This is Neema. She lives here in the house. She doesn't speak English, but she will lend you some clothes and show you how to dress like her.'

He said something to the young woman who smiled shyly and beckoned to Louise to follow her upstairs. Louise followed behind the two children who still held on to their mother's legs. They kept staring back at her. Their eyes wide with curiosity.

Neema showed Louise into one of the upstairs rooms. It was small and cluttered with furniture and possessions. She said something to the children and they went to play on a mat in the corner. Then Neema produced some clothes from a chest and motioned to Louise to take off her shorts and T shirt. Louise obeyed, feeling a little self-conscious. Neema then showed her how to tie the blue checked longyi securely round her waist, to slip the embroidered blouse on, and to cover her hair with a long pink scarf. Finally, she motioned to Louise to sit on the floor. Then from a china bowl, she smeared thanaka bark onto Louise's cheeks. It felt cool and soothing against her hot skin. When Neema had finished she handed Louise a mirror.

Louise peered at herself. With her brown eyes and tanned face, her hair covered and her cheeks smeared with traditional Burmese face paint she could perhaps pass as roughly authentic, as long as no-one looked too closely.

'Thank you,' she said and Neema beamed into her eyes. As she got to her feet she noticed Thuza standing at the door.

'Good,' he said simply.

Then he said something to Neema who went behind a screen and emerged with some papers. She handed them to Louise. Louise stared at them. They were written in Burmese script, but there was an official stamp at the top and a photograph of Neema. They must be Neema's identity papers. She turned to Thuza.

'Why is she doing this?'

He shrugged. 'We have shown her kindness, letting her live here. She is a Muslim. There aren't many of her kind left around here. They descend from Indians who were brought here by the

British to work in the docks when Moulmein was a thriving teak port.

'Many of them have been persecuted but in our community, we have always protected her from harm. Her husband died recently, and we now let her live here rent free with her children. She is repaying our kindness.'

Louise nodded her thanks and goodbyes to Neema, who smiled and bowed her head.

As they went out to the yard, Thuza said, 'The disguise isn't fool-proof. If you're stopped and questioned, you'll just have to remain silent and hold the veil across your face. Pretend you are too afraid to speak. Neema would be in grave danger if the authorities discover she's given you her papers.'

'Of course. I understand,' Louise said, but she felt sick with nerves as she approached the back of the truck.

Mo Chit had cleared a path through the durians. Louise clambered over the tailgate, and pushed through the fruit to the middle of the truck. She found a space on the floor in the centre and tried to sit down.

'Here. Sit on this, then it won't be so painful,' Thuza said, handing her a cushion.

'How long will it take to get there?' she asked, settling herself onto the cushion as best she could.

'Two to three hours. We're not going to take the main road, so you might find it a bit bumpy I'm afraid. There will probably be just one road block after about an hour and a half. It shouldn't be too much of a problem. The police there will normally take a bribe.'

She sat on the cushion while Mo Chit and Thuza piled the durian fruits back around her. Soon she was completely surrounded by them. The prickles dug into her skin and the weight of the surrounding fruit pressed down on her. The foul smell caught the back of her throat.

Then she felt the truck starting up and the sudden motion as it rumbled out of the yard. As they moved away from the house, Louise felt the vibrations of the wheels on the rough surface, of every bump and pothole in the road. She wondered how she would survive the journey without succumbing to motion sickness, assisted by the gut-churning stench of the durians.

She gritted her teeth as the truck made its way along the dusty lane. It was not long before it was moving along the main highway though and she could feel it begin to pick up speed. She could see nothing beyond the odd glow of lights from other vehicles. After a few minutes on the smoother highway, the truck turned off onto another bumpy road. This time there was no letup. The ruts and potholes continued, interspersed with hills and sharp turns. All she could hear was the roar of the engine and the whine of the Burmese pop music the two men were listening to in the cab.

She tried to get comfortable by pressing her back and shoulders against the wall of fruit behind her. Then closing her eyes, she relaxed into a sort of reverie.

She needed to think about something else in order to get through this. Again her thoughts returned to her father. She wondered if maybe it was a way of coping with her loss, but also, perhaps, preparing herself for what she might find out at Thanbyuzayat.

After he'd left London, her father had never lasted very long in any one place. Louise could never work out whether that was because he liked to move on or because his circumstances forced him to. He lived in the cottage in Buckinghamshire for less than a year. He'd written to say that he was touring Gloucestershire and Wiltshire, finding work doing paintings of country houses, horses and pets.

She didn't hear from him for several months after that, but in June her mother sat her down and told her once again that she wouldn't be visiting him that summer.

'Why not?' Louise asked, disappointed.

'Your father doesn't have a home at the moment,' said Grace, tight-lipped.

'What do you mean, doesn't have a home? He must be living somewhere?'

'I'm sorry, Louise. I know it's hard for you, but I'm afraid he hasn't got a home so you're not going to be able to visit him. It would be better if you didn't ask questions.'

'Why? Why shouldn't I ask questions? He is my father after all. Why shouldn't I know where he is and what's happening to him?'

Her mother flushed. She was clearly holding something back. She was twisting her hands, pursing her lips, as if she wasn't quite sure what to say.

'He's not well, Louise, that's all I can tell you.'

'Not well? Is he sick? Is he going to die?'

'He's in hospital and he'll probably be there for a few weeks.'

Shock waves washed through her.

'That sounds bad! He must be really ill. What's wrong with him?'

Louise stared at her mother. Grace still had that pained, embarrassed expression on her face. She didn't answer for a time.

'Well?' Louise persisted. 'Aren't you going to tell me?'

'Look Louise, this is difficult,' Grace stammered. 'I... I shouldn't really tell you this, but if you really want to know, the fact is, you father's not well mentally. He drinks far too much and he's had some sort of breakdown recently. He's been detained in a mental hospital in Gloucester.'

Louise stared at her wordlessly, tears of anger and humiliation standing in her eyes. For a while she couldn't speak, didn't know what to say or to ask. But eventually she found her voice,

'But why, Mum?'

'Oh I don't know Louise. I know it's harsh to say, but he's brought a lot of it on himself. He drinks far too much like I said. He's not strong mentally.'

'Why? Why do you say that?'

Grace still wouldn't meet her eye as she went on, 'He was damaged in the war, Louise. That's all I know. He would never talk about it to me, but I'm sure it's at the root of all his problems.'

'Damaged?'

Grace sighed. 'The Japs were brutal to the poor men who built that railway. The stories that have come out... he must have witnessed some dreadful things. I don't know what because he'd never talk about it to me, but it was enough to send him over the edge from time to time.'

'But couldn't you have helped him?'

'I tried, Louise. God knows I tried. But I couldn't reach him. He refused to let me help him. Took refuge in drink instead. That seemed to be his way of coping. It destroyed our marriage and it's destroying him now too.'

'Couldn't I go to see him in hospital?' Louise asked after a pause.

'Not at the moment. He's not well enough to see visitors. Maybe in a few weeks' time.'

But the weeks passed and the subject seemed to have been dropped. Louise went to stay with her grandmother in Harrow again during the summer and when she got back it was time to go back to school. She couldn't help worrying about her father though. What was it like in a mental hospital? Would he be locked up? What would the other patients be like? She worried for him in there; she knew he loved to be out and about, always on the move, meeting different people, doing his painting. How would he cope being confined to a ward?

That was when Louise was fourteen. She only managed to stay with him one more summer whilst she was at school. It was when she was in the sixth form. By that time he had a bedsit in a boarding house in a run-down seaside town in North Wales.

The journey to North Wales took all day and she had to change trains in Birmingham and Shrewsbury. When he met her on the windswept station platform she was shocked at how thin and old he looked, but she ran up to him and hugged him, trying to hide her tears. As he held her at arms' length to examine how much she'd grown, she noticed that his hands were shaking.

His room had a huge bay window that looked out to sea and they would both sit there for hours on windy days watching the breakers crash against the sea wall. He had a job in a local technical college teaching art, and his recent paintings were stacked all around the room. He'd painted the view from his window many times, in sunshine and in rainstorms and in all different lights.

On the way there on the train Louise had thought it would be awkward seeing him after so many years apart, but it wasn't difficult at all; they slipped easily back into their old companionship. She wondered whether to ask him about his time in the mental hospital, but decided against it. He was so obviously making an effort to be positive.

Although he still smoked heavily, he'd stopped drinking and they didn't visit a single pub during her visit. Instead, he took her walking along deserted beaches and climbing in the mountains. They trekked to remote lakes and medieval castles, along sheep paths and quarry tracks, to waterfalls and disused gold mines. They caught a train around the coast to the castle at Harlech where they ate fish and chips in a beach shelter during a rainstorm. In the evenings they would read, play cards, or watch his crackly portable television.

When it was time for her to go home, Louise held him tight.

'Take care of yourself, Dad,' she said looking into his eyes. 'Promise me?'

He winked at her and laughed. 'Oh you needn't worry, it will take a lot to finish old Jack Summers off you know.'

She laughed and kissed him goodbye, but as she leaned out of the carriage to wave, she felt a surge of pity for the frail, solitary figure on the platform, wrapped in a thin charity-shop coat. She wished she could stay longer and look after him properly, shelter him from harm.

But despite Jack's brave words, his resolve didn't last. He soon started drinking again, and before long had lost his job and his home. He was in and out of hostels for the next few years. He stopped writing and it was impossible for Louise to go to see him before she went to university. She never stayed with him again and the next time she saw him was when she was called to his hospital bed.

The truck had been moving through darkness along the rutted roads, up and down hills and round twisting bends for almost two hours. Now, suddenly, the road surface felt smoother. Soon they pulled into an area lit by floodlights and came to a halt. The engine was switched off and there was a moment's silence.

Louise heard the cab door slam up ahead as one of the men got out. She thought she recognised Thuza's voice talking to someone else. Her nerves were taut. This must be the road block they'd told her about. She held her breath and tried to listen, but she could understand nothing of what was being said. Her scalp tingled with fear when she heard movement at the back of the truck.

Thuza was speaking quickly. Was it her imagination or did he sound panicky? She could hear the policeman slapping and punching the fruits at the back of the truck. Surely he'd seen enough by now? Why weren't they moving? Perhaps things hadn't gone to plan and he was going to search the vehicle? Her legs turned to jelly at the thought.

Then she froze in fear. Someone was taking the fruit off the back of the truck. Thuza was speaking even more quickly with a note of desperation. He seemed to be pleading with the other man.

After a few minutes of sitting stock still, paralysed with fear, listening to the fruit being removed from the back of the pile one by one, and Thuza's pleading voice, she heard what she thought must be the rustle of bank notes.

She waited, holding her breath. Would the policeman take the bribe? Would it make matters worse? But after a few seconds she heard the policeman moving away from the truck. Then came the sound of Thuza restacking the fruit that had been removed. He was so close that she could hear his breath on the warm evening air. She wanted to ask him what had happened but didn't dare speak. Soon she heard him move away from the back of the truck and the slam of the door. The engine roared into action and they were on the move once again. Louise sat back against the bank of fruits, weak with relief.

There was only another half hour of rutted roads. She was used to the smell in the truck by now, and to bracing herself against the bumps. Through gaps in the piles of fruit she began to glimpse lights and sensed that they were in a built-up area. Soon the truck pulled off the road, moved slowly up another rutted track and came to an abrupt stop.

Thuza and Mo Chit got out of the front and Louise heard different footsteps on the ground nearby and other voices speaking to them. Then came the sounds of people moving the fruit from the back of the truck and gradually a gap formed in the durian wall. A torch shone directly at her and several faces peered at her through the darkness.

'Don't worry,' Thuza reassured her. 'We've stopped to unload the fruit at the market. This is Lin. He has a stall here and he needs them for the morning opening. Once we've unloaded we'll go to where we will stay the night.'

Soon the durian was unloaded and Thuza helped Louise climb out of the back of the truck. She felt bruised and battered and her limbs ached.

'Are we in Thanbyuzayat?' she asked.

'Of course,' he said, smiling. 'Listen.'

Above the sound of voices she could hear the roll of gentle waves on a beach close by.

'The market is right next to the beach here. Tomorrow you will see it. Now you can ride up in the front of the cab with us. We are only going a short distance.'

She got inside between Thuza and Mo Chit. With a blast of the horn they left the market behind and made their way back down the track to the highway.

'Where are we staying tonight? Are there any hotels here?'

'There is one guesthouse, but if you stayed there you'd have to register your papers and we don't want the police to get interested in you. We are staying with friends.'

She could see little of the town that they drove through. It seemed to be flat with low wooden buildings and tree-lined streets. Soon, they turned off the road again, drove between two high walls and into a courtyard surrounded by two storey wooden buildings. It was lit by lanterns glowing in the trees.

Thuza turned to her smiling as a man with a shaved head, clad in maroon robes came out to greet them.

'It is a monastery. The monks are always willing to help us. They will help you too when they hear your story.'

Soon they were surrounded by young monks who took their bags and guided them into the building. They were shown to a long wooden table in a cavernous hall. The monk who had greeted them said,

'Please sit down. We will bring you food.'

The other monks brought them dish upon dish and soon the table was filled with bowls of curried vegetables, rice, dhal and bread.

Louise ate hungrily. The discomfort of the journey and the stress of the day had given her an appetite. The smiling monk spoke to Thuza for a few minutes and then turned to her,

'I hear you would like to see the place where the POW camp was.'

'Yes. Very much. Would you be able to show me?'

'Of course. One of us will help you tomorrow morning when we return from our alms round.'

'Thank you so much.'

He looked at her, smiling. 'You know, some of the older monks in our order remember what happened back then. They are old enough to have witnessed it first-hand. One of them, Ajaan Kashwin over there, was even in the camp himself when he was a child.'

He inclined his head in the direction of one of the monks who looked up and bowed his head forward, bringing his hands together in a gesture of prayer. He was taller than most of the other monks, darker too.

'He suffered a great deal as a child. He lost the sight in one eye due to disease. He lost both his parents too.'

'How awful,' murmured Louise. 'Do you think he would speak to me about it?'

The monk shook his head slowly.

'Or any of the others?'

'None of them speaks English I'm afraid, and in any case, I'm sure that they would prefer to forget. Their lives are stable now, they are content. But some of them have been very affected by those years.'

She looked around at some of the older monks, they were now clearing the table. Was it possible that some of these men had been here all those years ago, that they too had witnessed what her father had seen?

'Like my father,' she murmured. The monk looked at her inquiringly.

'My father was a prisoner here during the war. He was troubled by it for the rest of his life. When he was dying he told me he'd never managed to get over the things that had happened to him in Burma. I've come to see if I can find out what they were.'

The monk laid a hand on hers.

'You've come a long way, my child. I wish you success in your quest. But remember this. Even if you don't find what you came looking for, you will have made the journey. The journey will always remain with you, it will have taught you much of itself.'

18

Grace
Portsmouth
March 1947

Grace sat on the sofa in front of the flickering gas fire absorbed in the copy of the Portsmouth Evening Post she'd picked up on her way home from the hospital. She'd kicked off her shoes and her legs were tucked underneath her.

Jack sat opposite her at the table drawing. As she read, she was conscious of the quick, expert movement of his hands on the sketch pad, aware of the intense concentration he was pouring into the task. Glancing up from a story about Lady Mountbatten, she caught him looking at her, his head on one side, assessing the angle at which she sat.

'You're not drawing *me* are you?' she asked, her cheeks colouring with pleasure. He'd only just started drawing again in the last few weeks. For months after Grace had lost the baby his sketch pad sat unopened on the shelf. But recently his mood seemed to have improved.

'You don't mind do you, Gracie?' he said, 'You're such a good subject. Such beautiful, clean lines.'

'Of course not,' she said, trying not to show that she was flattered, 'But you'll have to hurry. I need to do the washing up. It's getting late.'

She turned the page of the paper and something caught her eye. She ran eagerly over the text.

'Oh Jack, look at this. They're having an award ceremony for men who served in the Far East during the war. There's a Burma Star for the Malaya campaign. You have to write....' She glanced down at the paper again, reading quickly,

'You'd definitely qualify,' she went her eyes running down the list of criteria. 'You have to have served in Malaya from February 1942. It would be good to go, don't you think?'

She heard the crunch of the pencil on the paper. She looked up at him. The pencil was broken in his clenched fist. He sat staring at her.

'Are you alright?' she asked.

He didn't speak for a time. Then he took a deep breath, a brief shudder went through him, and he smiled.

'Of course. It was a bit of a surprise, that's all, being reminded like that.'

She left the newspaper and went to sit down beside him, slipping her arms around his shoulders.

He stroked her hair.

'You sure you're alright?' she asked again.

'Perfectly. It's nothing, Gracie. Go and sit back down over there. Let me finish the picture.'

He began sketching again. Grace watched his face, relieved to see him absorbed in his work once again.

'It would be nice to go, Jack.,' she went on after a few

moments had passed. 'Perhaps Ernie will be there? You haven't been in touch with him since the wedding.'

'I'm not sure, Grace.'

She put the paper down, disappointed. It would have been good to get out of Portsmouth for a day, put on their best clothes and go up to London for the ceremony. She couldn't help thinking it would do them both good. Looking back on it afterwards though, she was amazed at her own lack of perception. How had she missed the signs?

'It would be lovely to have a day out, though Jack,' she said. 'We've both been very gloomy lately.'

She watched his face. He carried on sketching for a few minutes. Finally he looked up, smiled at her and said,

'You're right. You deserve a trip up to London. We both do. Let's go then shall we? Does it say how to apply?'

The next few weeks flew by. Jack wrote to his regiment and received an embossed invitation to attend a presentation ceremony in Westminster City Hall. On her day off Grace went shopping to the department stores in Commercial Street and bought herself a powder blue dress and coat and a hat to match. When she tried the outfit on at home, Jack put his arms around her and said,

'You look so beautiful, Grace. What have I done to deserve you?'

Things seemed to be turning round at last after their months of grief. Grace started to go about with a spring in her step. The ceremony was in May, and the weather was improving. There were daffodils and primroses on the green at Southsea, and there was a warm breeze on the salty air. Grace bought their train tickets from the station and they both booked the day off work.

But as the day approached, Grace noticed that Jack was getting home later from work than usual each evening. And when he finally did get home, he seemed to be preoccupied. She began to worry that he was slipping back into one of his dark moods.

On the evening before the ceremony, he was late home again. Grace stood watching at the window, praying to see him turn in at the end of the street and walk down the pavement towards the house. When he did finally appear, it was almost dark. He was walking slowly, his head down, trudging as if he were bearing a great burden.

Grace left the window and waited for him at the door of the flat. She heard the main front door slam and watched him come up the stairs. As he got to the top he lifted his face and she saw that his eyes were filled with pain. That old expression she had learned to dread.

'Jack,' she said, 'Are you alright? I was worried about you.'

He didn't reply. Instead, he pushed past her into the flat.

'Wherever have you been?'

He sunk down on the settee, his head in his hands.

'I went to the pier.'

'Why? What's wrong?'

'I needed to think.'

Alarmed, she sat down beside him, put her arms around him.

'Whatever's the matter, Jack? You're shaking all over.'

He didn't answer. She could feel him struggling for breath. After a pause the trembling stopped and he shrugged her arms away.

'Jack, tell me what's wrong. Please,' she was near to tears.

There was a long pause. Then he looked at her and said, 'I'm not going tomorrow Grace.'

'Oh Jack,' she said automatically, disappointment in her voice. 'But we've been so looking forward to it.'

He didn't answer, or even look at her. Instead he got up violently, knocking the chair over and pushing past her as he moved towards the door.

She stumbled after him.

'Where are you going?' she demanded, panic in her voice.

'Out again. I need some air.'

'Can I come with you?' she hated herself for sounding so weak, but this sudden change in him had thrown her off balance.

'Jack please. I'm sorry. Please tell me what's wrong.'

He turned and stared at her. His look sent a shiver right through her. His face was drawn, a picture of suffering, his eyes full of agony.

She stepped back, alarmed.

'Don't you know?' he said.

He wrenched the door open and banged it shut behind him. Trembling with shock Grace tiptoed towards it. Her instinct was to run after him, but she held back. She heard him clatter down the three flights of wooden stairs and then the slam of the front door behind him.

She ran to the window and, parting the curtains, stared out at the street. In the light of the street lamp she saw Jack's head passing under the window and along the pavement. It stung her that he was walking so fast, striding out, his hands jammed in his pockets, as if to get away as quickly as possible from her, from the home they'd made together. Her eyes followed him until he disappeared from view at the end of the road.

She went back to the sofa, sat down and put her face in her hands. There was such a lump in her throat and an ache in her chest she thought she would burst with emotion. She didn't want to cry. She needed to think, to understand; it wasn't the time to panic.

She looked around the tiny flat at their meagre possessions. The wedding photo on the mantelpiece, a couple of Jack's still life watercolours on the walls, the two threadbare armchairs, the second-hand curtains not quite touching the windowsill, the flickering gas fire with the broken pots. Ten minutes ago it had felt cosy. Being with Jack was all that mattered, she never normally noticed the shabby surroundings. But the place felt squalid now, hopeless somehow.

Her mind wandered back to a conversation she'd had with her mother, in the difficult days before her wedding.

'Are you sure you know what you're doing? You hardly know him Grace. You really should give it a bit more time'

'What do you mean, hardly know him? I know him better than I've ever known anyone before.'

Her mother had looked away, avoiding her gaze.

'He's been away all that time in the East. Who knows what might have happened to him out there?'

'I know he had an appalling time. Nearly starved to death.'

'Well, it can alter a man, that sort of thing.'

'Not Jack. You've seen how much he cares for me. How kind and thoughtful he is.'

'Oh, he's charming enough on the surface, I'll grant you that. But that doesn't mean you should rush into marrying him. You always have to be so impulsive Grace. It gets you into trouble but you won't learn. I don't know why you can't be more like your sister.'

'Because I'm not her. That's why, Mum,' she said, exasperated. 'Why should everyone be the same?'

'You're so headstrong, you'll have your way, but don't say I didn't warn you.'

She thought about how she'd been swept up on a tide of passion and romance with Jack, addicted to it almost. It was like a fairground ride that she didn't want to get off. She wanted to spend every minute of every day with Jack and what was wrong with that? Hadn't she spent the last two years nursing wounded men, living on rations, through the Blitz, losing friends and neighbours to the war?

With a heavy heart she went over to the galley kitchen in the corner of the room, filled the sink from the spluttering boiler and began to scrub the greasy pans she'd used to cook their supper.

She didn't feel like eating, so she covered the two plates of stew she'd prepared with a cloth.

All the time she was working she was waiting for the sound of the door opening, of Jack coming back into the flat with a blast of cold air, his arms enveloping her, his lips on her neck. She would turn round to kiss him and everything would be alright again.

But she finished the pans, drying them with a cloth and putting them away in the cupboards. She tidied the tiny living room, emptying the ash trays, straightening the cushions. She sat down with a magazine, but she couldn't concentrate on what she was reading. The hours ticked by and there was no sign of Jack.

At ten o' clock she went through to the bedroom, where her new outfit was hanging ready on the front of the wardrobe. She undressed and slipped into bed. The sheets were so cold she shivered between them for a long time, staring at the pattern made by the street lamps on the ceiling. It was the first time she'd gone to bed alone since they'd been married.

She thought she'd never be able to sleep, but she must have drifted off. The street lights had gone off outside, so it must have been the small hours when she heard the door slam, unsteady footsteps inside the flat, the sound of Jack undressing, cursing under his breath as he bumped into the table. She felt him slide into bed next to her, and she could smell the alcohol on his breath from where she lay. Within seconds he was asleep, breathing heavily. Grace lay wide awake, listening to his rhythmic breathing, her whole being engulfed in emptiness.

THE NEXT MORNING neither of them mentioned the ceremony. Jack got up early. She could hear him tiptoeing around getting dressed.

'What are you doing?' she asked.

'I'm going in to work.'

'But..' she stopped herself saying that he'd got the day off.

'It won't matter,' he said. 'There's plenty of work, and we need the money.'

They never spoke about the ceremony or of the Burma Star again. A week or so later, when Grace got home from the hospital there was a package on the doormat. It bore a postage mark from Jack's regiment. She picked it up and felt it. She knew instinctively that it must be Jack's medal; perhaps they had sent it on as he hadn't turned up at the ceremony. Her heart rate quickened at the thought of Jack seeing it, of how he might react. She knew she couldn't face witnessing his anger and pain again. She took the envelope upstairs to the flat and hid it in one of her hat boxes at the back of the wardrobe.

She never mentioned it to Jack, and it wasn't until after his death that she had the courage to open that envelope, remove the star-shaped medal from the box and hold it in the palm of her hand.

19

Eve
Malaysia, 2015

As the train left Kuala Lumpur and trundled through the northern suburbs on the start of its long journey up the peninsula to Bangkok, Eve watched the rapidly changing scenery and thought about the words of the old man at the No 1 Cathay Hotel. She'd been dimly aware that there had been Asian workers on the railway, but she had been so preoccupied with finding out about what her grandfather might have been through that it hadn't really figured in her thoughts. She wondered if the girl in Jack's picture was one of those people, swept up in the brutality of war along with countless others.

It made her realise that the story of the railway, which she'd only previously thought about in terms of its effect on the Allied prisoners of war, could be told from a different perspective, that the local population too had been torn apart by the crazy Japanese scheme to build a railway through more than 400 kilometres of untamed jungle. As the train made its way up the peninsula through Malaysia and into Thailand, this thought returned to her again and again. She resolved to research the plight of the Asian labourers and find out more about it as soon as she had the opportunity.

In Bangkok they took a taxi for the short distance from Hualamphong Station to the backpacker district; the Khao San road. They wandered down the busy, tree-lined street with their backpacks, scanning the hostels and budget hotels for somewhere to stay the night. Eve caught Louise looking around wistfully.

'This takes me back too,' Louise said. 'You know, I stayed in this road when I came on my trip in the eighties.'

'Really, Mum? Do you remember which hotel?'

Louise shook her head. 'I don't remember the name I'm afraid. I expect it's long gone. But the street looks just the same. A bit more commercialised maybe – more stalls and shops, but it's still got that fabulous, vibrant atmosphere.'

Later, as they relaxed eating Pad Thai and sipping Chang Beer at a street stall, Eve took a deep breath and said;

'I wish you'd tell me more about your trip back then,' she said. 'You've hardly told me anything about it. I'd love to know. Especially now we're going back to Myanmar together.'

Louise put down her fork and looked at her. At first Eve thought she was going to clam up or get angry as she had on previous occasions, but after a few moments, Louise softened her gaze. She took another swig of her beer.

'I suppose you have a right to know about it really. I'm sorry. I found it difficult to talk about for years.'

'Can you tell me why?'

'I suppose because I'm afraid to, in a way.'

'Afraid? What of?'

'Because things have changed so much for me since then. I don't like remembering what might have been. I was free back then, Eve. Free to choose what I did, where I went. It's hard thinking back to those times because it makes me realise what I gave up, what I've missed down the years.'

'Oh Mum. What makes you think like that?'

'Well, I suppose like I was saying yesterday evening. I feel as though I've wasted my life. Made a hash of everything. Squandered all my opportunities.'

'Of course you haven't. No more than me anyway.'

'But at least you finished your education, Eve, qualified as a teacher. Took on a difficult job.'

'Hmm. But look at me now.'

Louise put her fork down.

'We haven't talked much about why you left your job. I'm so sorry Eve, I've been so preoccupied with my own problems.'

'It's fine. I haven't thought about it too much since I left London anyway. Getting away from it has given me some perspective.'

'Do you think you might go back to teaching when you go home?'

'I don't know, Mum. I found it so tough going. It was such a challenge, but on the other hand I suppose it *was* rewarding in the end. I think I'd reached a point in life when I needed to reassess lots of things. Coming on this trip is part of that.'

'Well it's good that you haven't turned your back on it completely. You seemed so happy teaching at first. So well suited to it.'

'I know, Mum. I just need to find something, somewhere that suits me better than my last job, that's all.'

'You're still so young, Eve. You've got your whole life ahead of you. It's different for me. I passed up my education when Dad died, never really stuck at anything. I just trailed around after Jim, looking after him, being around for him.'

'But why do you think that's wasting your life, Mum?'

Louise was silent for a while, watching a group of young men going past, full of energy, laughing, joshing each other. Finally she turned to Eve and said slowly,

'Because if you want the truth he's never been faithful to me. That's why.'

'Mum!'

'I know it must be a shock, but you're old enough to know now. He's been a good father to you, and he's always provided for us both. But fundamentally he's a weak man, Eve.'

Louise's face suddenly crumpled and tears filled her eyes. Eve leaned over and put her arms around her mother's shoulders.

'God knows why I put up with it all this time,' Louise said, making an effort to hold back the tears. 'Twenty seven years! I must be a complete idiot.'

'But Mum... are you sure? Who? When?'

Louise wiped the tears away from her cheeks impatiently.

'Does it matter?' she said. 'It happened a couple of times in London. Once when you were very young. Once much later, when you were a teenager. There were probably others in between that I didn't find out about. When we came out to Singapore I thought it would be a fresh start. He promised it would be. And it was, for a time. We were almost happy. But it started again a few months ago. I can always spot the signs. And I was right.'

'Who was it?'

'Oh, someone at the bank. Someone young and bright and attractive. Everything I'm not of course.'

Eve stared at her mother. She could hardly believe what she was hearing. She wasn't sure she wanted to hear it even. Part of her wanted to change the subject, or put her hands over her ears. It was shocking, having her mother's marriage exposed like this.

'Jim is such a weak man,' Louise repeated, biting her fingernail. 'He's so prone to flattery. He has a fragile ego.'

'What are you going to do?' Eve asked, her own voice tremulous.

She felt as if the foundations of her world were crumbling.

Jim might not have been her blood father, but he'd been good to her. He'd always been around for her when she was little, reading to her at bedtime, teaching her to read, to play chess, taking her out on fishing trips, to the seaside for day trips. It was Louise who'd often been the unreliable one, the one who always seemed to put herself first, who might turn up late to collect her from school, or even forget completely on occasion. Who'd had an unpredictable temper, who sometimes lay in bed all day watching TV, or got drunk quietly by herself, embarrassing Eve in front of her friends.

'I'm not sure yet,' Louise's voice broke into her thoughts. 'But it's good to get away, to get some space so I can think properly.'

'You don't have to make any decisions at the moment, Mum.'

'No. I don't,' Louise said, then, with a forced smile, 'We can concentrate on enjoying the journey and being together.'

The waiter came to take their plates and they ordered two more beers.

'So will you tell me about when you came here before? About what happened to you?' Eve asked as he walked away.

Louise smiled, 'All right. I can try. But you'll have to bear with me if I forget things. It all feels such a long time ago. Like another lifetime.'

THE GUESTHOUSE in Khao San Road where they spent the night organised a minivan to drive them overland from Bangkok, across the land border into Myanmar at Phu Nam Rong and on to Dawei on the southern coast.

They got up before first light the next morning, and although they were on the road just as dawn was breaking, the Bangkok rush hour was already underway. Endless lines of slow-moving traffic coalesced in the baking morning like clots in the city's main arteries.

But after an hour or so of crawling along roads clogged with long suffering Bangkok commuters, they were leaving the city behind, speeding along a straight freeway, through endless straggling suburbs, where despite the speed of the traffic, flimsy homes of wood and corrugated iron bordered the carriageway, people ate at food stalls within feet of the traffic and whole families would cross the carriageway casually, perched four or five to a motorbike.

As they drove, Louise began to tell Eve about her 1988 trip; Eve listened, holding her breath, as her mother spoke. She'd waited a lifetime to hear this and she didn't want to risk putting Louise off by interrupting. As the story unravelled, once again Eve found herself full of admiration for her mother. She found herself comparing the young Louise to how she herself had been at that age. She knew she wouldn't have had the courage to strike out alone like that, let alone take the sort of risks Louise had taken.

Louise told her how she had met Zeya, a young Burmese tour guide through selling her black-market whisky; how he'd agreed to help her to get to Thanbyuzayat in return for taking false identity papers to Moulmein for his associates down there. She told her all about her nail-biting train journey from Rangoon to Moulmein, about meeting Thuza and about how he'd smuggled her in a lorry load of durian fruit as far as the monastery in Thanbyuzayat.

'So you did get to Thanbyuzayat!' Eve said when Louise paused to take a sip of water. 'I'm amazed that you did that, Mum. It must have taken so much courage.'

Louise laughed, a touch of irony in her tone.

'Foolhardy, more like! Until I saw those young Burmese men pulled off the train by the police I had no idea of the sort of danger I could be in if I was caught with those fake ID papers. By that time it was too late. I was trapped on the train and had no choice but to go through with the whole thing.'

She shook her head in disbelief.

'I was so determined to get there and find Dad's diary. Nothing would stop me. I was such an idiot, though, the risks I took! I was so headstrong, and so reckless.'

'So what happened in Thanbyuzayat? Did you get to the camp?'

Louise shook her head with a sigh.

'Not in the end, no. I stayed at the monastery that night. They gave me a separate room all to myself as I was the only female guest. It was bare, with virtually no furniture and I slept on a mat on the floor. Even though it was uncomfortable and I wasn't used to sleeping on the floor, I remember sleeping really well. The monks had been so welcoming and the monastery felt safe and peaceful. It didn't worry me that I was breaking the rules and putting myself and others in danger in going there in the first place.

'I heard the monks getting up very early, before dawn even, and the sound of their chanting as they went out to do their early morning alms rounds. The Abbot had promised me he would take me to the site of the camp when he came back to the monastery later that morning. I went back to sleep for a while, then I felt someone shaking me awake. It was Thuza. I could tell straight away from the look in his eyes that he was afraid.

'He said we had to go back to Moulmein straight away. He'd been told there were soldiers on the streets of Thanbyuzayat going from house to house, searching for dissidents. They must have had wind of the protests and were trying to root out anyone they thought was involved. I didn't even mention about going to the camp to him. I knew straight away it was pointless and that I simply wasn't going to get there. I just got up and followed Thuza out of the monastery.

'There was no time to say goodbye to the monks – they were still out on their rounds. I wanted to leave a note for them, but Thuza said that was too risky – that the police might find it. We had to run through the back streets. The truck was parked on a track right on the edge of town. Mo Chit was waiting with it. They hadn't had time to load up the vegetables they'd planned to take back to Moulmein so there was no cargo to hide in this time. There were just some empty sacks on the floor.

'Shall I hide under them?' I asked, but Thuza shook his head.

'It would look more suspicious that way. You'll have to sit in the front between me and Mo Chit and if we get stopped, we'll just have to hope and pray your disguise works.'

'The journey back to Moulmein was very tense as you can imagine. The two men hardly spoke, just kept their eyes fixed on the road ahead. The most terrifying part was the checkpoints. As we approached them I was shaking so much I thought I would pass out. There were two road blocks where we were stopped and asked for papers. As we approached, the fear in the cab was palpable. Both men had sweat pouring down their faces and none of us spoke or even looked at each other. But each time we were unbelievably lucky; the police on duty just glanced at our papers, peered in the cab at us and nodded us through.

'I've never forgotten Mo Chit and Thuza. Those two men were so brave, taking me back to Moulmein with them. They could have just left me in Thanbyuzayat for the police or army to find, but that wasn't their way. When we got back to Thuza's house, in the late afternoon, I tried to thank him, but he just smiled and waved my thanks away. I didn't have any money with me, or I would have offered him something, but I got the feeling that that wouldn't have been the right thing to do.

'I changed back into my own clothes in the upstairs room and said goodbye to Neema and her children. I wanted to put my arms around her and thank her for her kindness and bravery, but I didn't want to embarrass her.

'Thuza drove me back to the guesthouse. He stopped the truck a nearby side street.

'As I got out he said, 'It would be safest for you if you go back to Rangoon straight away. A group of us is setting off tomorrow morning to be there in time for the march on the 8th. If we get caught with the false identity papers, it would be better if you aren't around. And we don't want people to start asking questions about where you've been for the past 24 hours. The steamboat leaves for Martaban in a couple of hours. It will meet the Rangoon train. It would be best for you if you were on it. I'll let Zeya know you're coming back to the city and he will meet you at the station.'

"There's no need,' I began. 'I can look after myself. I'll just go back to my hotel.

"It would be better if you don't do that,' Thuza said 'The next couple of days could be full of danger. It is best if you stay with us so we can look after you.'

'I smiled at him. There was so much I wanted to say to him. I wanted to thank him for his bravery and for risking so much to help me find Dad's diary. Even though the search was fruitless, that didn't affect how much he'd done for me, a complete stranger, and how grateful I was to him and to Mo Chit. I tried to thank him with stumbling words, but again he just waved my thanks away.

'The old man on the desk in the guesthouse was sitting in exactly the same position as when I had left the day before, wearing the same clothes. It was really weird – like I'd been in a time-warp, almost as if nothing had happened and I hadn't been to Thanbyuzayat at all. I let myself into my room, packed up my gear and checked out. To my relief the old man on the desk showed no sign that anything was unusual about my stay. I got a rickshaw straight down to the docks, bought my ticket to Rangoon and waited there as discreetly as I could amongst the families and traders, waiting for the boat with their piles of possessions, children and the odd chicken, until the boat came in.

'As the ferry pulled away from Moulmein docks I stared back

at the lush greenery and the old buildings, and at the pagodas on the hilltop. I was full of regret that I hadn't been able to get to the camp or find anything out about the place. I knew I hadn't fulfilled the promise I'd made to Dad.But I tried not to be too hard on myself. I knew I had done my best. And at the same time, there was more than a bit of me that was looking forward to seeing Zeya again. I got his card out of my pocket and stared at it, picturing his face as he gave it to me. For some reason I couldn't quite fathom, I found the prospect of him coming to meet me at the station unsettling in a strange way. I was flattered, I think. He'd been a bit of an enigma to me – a strange mixture of fun-loving, passion for his country and cause, and fierce pride.'

20

Grace
Portsmouth, 1947

After the way Jack had reacted to the prospect of the Burma Star ceremony, Grace felt the need to tread more carefully with him. There were times when they recaptured that laughter and rapport they'd first had. But there was so much more that brought them down.

Jack worked long hours, and in his spare time, pursued his art furiously. Grace watched with pride as he produced better and better work. He managed to sell a couple of watercolours through a local gallery. Despite that, random events would tip him over the edge.

One day they'd been to the local market to buy vegetables on a Saturday morning. They were walking home when they saw an Indian family coming towards them down the street. Although it was early autumn, they were bundled up in coats and scarves. The mother wore a pink saree under a thick overcoat. She was shepherding two small children along the pavement. Grace wondered how they could cope in this freezing city when they came from a land of baking sun.

Jack stopped walking and stared at the family as they approached. He moved aside as they passed, but turned and watched them as they walked away. He was frozen to the spot, his face drained of colour.

'What's the matter, Jack?'

Without replying, or even looking at Grace, he set off suddenly in the direction of home. He was striding out, his head down as if he was desperate to get away from something. Grace was almost running to keep pace.

'Let's go to the pub,' he muttered as they reached the end of the street.

'All right,' she said carefully. They hadn't been into a pub together since his drinking bout the night before the Burma Star ceremony. They were both carrying bags of food, but Grace didn't want to anger him by reminding him of that.

There was a pub on the next crossroads. It opened straight onto the pavement and was noisy and smoke-filled, busy with Saturday lunchtime drinkers. Grace's eyes instantly started smarting in the smoky atmosphere. Jack disappeared into the crowd towards the bar and Grace found a table in the corner. She waited, uneasy. As far as she could see she was the only woman in the bar. It was filled with dockers and labourers, spending their pay at the end of a hard week.

When he returned, balancing the glasses in his hands, Grace noticed that he had bought two pints of beer for himself and a glass of lemonade for her. He sat beside her and they sipped in silence, but before Grace had finished her drink, Jack had downed both his pints and was up again, shouldering his way back through the crowd.

Grace heard sudden raised voices at the bar and her heart sank. She craned to see what was going on. As she'd feared, Jack was arguing with another man. The other man was thick set and burly; taller than Jack. He was pushing Jack backwards, his face, red with rage, held close to Jack's.

Grace got up quickly, her heart pounding. She pushed her way through the press of men.

'Let's go, Jack. Please, don't make a scene,' she said, reaching him.

He turned to her, his face red and perspiring. The man, seeing Grace, had now backed away, but she could feel the hostility of the crowd.

'You go if you want to Grace. Get a taxi. I'm staying here.'

'Jack. Please. Come with me.'

He turned on her then. 'You're the one making a scene Grace,' he shouted. 'Just get out of here. Go.'

Humiliated, she went out onto the street carrying the bags of vegetables and began to walk slowly towards home. There were no taxis to be seen, so she walked all the way, the heavy bags making sore grooves in her fingers. But she hardly noticed that; her concern for Jack, mingled with hurt and shame blotted out any physical discomfort.

When he finally blundered home that evening, he was so drunk he could barely speak. There were bruises on his face and his knuckles were covered in blood.

OVER THE NEXT few years Jack's drinking gradually became more frequent and more worrying for Grace. He would often stop off in the pub on his way home from work and stagger home late, wretched, slump in an armchair and fall straight to sleep. Grace worried constantly. She worried that he would lose his job one day, and she worried too about his mental state and increasing isolation. She was aware that he had trouble making friends. He put a wall around himself and seemed to alienate people with his black moods.

Grace knew too, but hardly acknowledged it to herself, that they were gradually becoming strangers. She threw herself into her career, working longer and longer hours on the ward. She made friends amongst the other nurses. One of them, sensing Grace was unhappy, asked tentatively if she'd thought about leaving Jack. Grace was shocked at the suggestion. She was fiercely determined not to give up on him, not to admit she might have made a mistake.

In time, Jack did lose his job. There was one drinking bout too many and after he'd turned up late on several occasions, even missing the whole of some morning shifts, he was told not to come back the next day.

He was waiting for Grace in the flat when she came home from work that day. He'd already downed half a bottle of whisky and was sitting in his coat in the dark.

'What are you going to do?' she asked when he told her he'd been given the sack.

'I need to get away from here, Grace,' he said. His words were slurred, but she knew that it wasn't the drink talking. He meant it. It came as a shock to her, but as something of a relief that he was finally confronting the situation.

'It's not you, Gracie darling. It's me. I can't do this anymore. I need to go away.'

'Where to, Jack?' she asked, tears in her eyes. 'What will you do?'

She knew it was useless to protest and that what he said was true and inevitable.

'I'm not sure yet,' he said. 'I've been thinking. I want to try to make a living from my painting. I can't do that here. And I can't do what I'm doing to you any more, Grace. You don't deserve it. I'm so sorry...'

He wept then and she held him as he buried his face in her

shoulder and sobbed. She wept too, mourning for what might have been, but deep down she knew it was right for him to go.

He left early the next morning, before she set off for the hospital. He carried two suitcases; one containing clothes and the other his paints and equipment. Grace watched from the window with a lump in her throat as he made his way to the end of the street and disappeared from view.

AFTER JACK LEFT, Grace got on with her life. At first he wrote to her every week, telling her about what he was doing and all about the places he'd been. He started out in Hampshire, knocking on the front doors of big country houses, offering to paint them for a fee. Sometimes he sent Grace money for the rent and sometimes he didn't. They never fully acknowledged that they were separated.

If Jack found temporary lodgings, Grace would sometimes go to stay with him for a couple of days. Occasionally too he would return to Portsmouth to visit for a day or so, but he didn't like to stay in one place for long. He would soon be off, roaming the countryside, looking for new places and experiences, new subjects to paint. His paintings were well received, word would spread amongst landowners that he was in a neighbourhood, and he was soon able to make a small living from commissions.

Sometimes things would go quiet for weeks on end and no letters would come. Grace would fret about Jack until she had news of him again, but in time she even got used to these intervals, learning to be patient and to see them through.

One day, several years after Jack had left, Grace was working an early morning shift at the hospital when she was called into the office by the ward sister.

'There's an urgent telephone call for you, Nurse Summers. St

Stephen's Hospital Nottingham.' Sister handed her the phone and left the office, closing the door discreetly.

'Nurse Summers. This is the mental health ward at St Stephens, Nottingham.'

Grace was puzzled. 'I'm afraid I don't understand. You've called the surgical ward at Portsmouth General. Is there some mistake?'

'This isn't a professional call, Nurse. I'm afraid it's about your husband.'

Shock seeped through her as she realised what this must mean.

'I'm afraid he was admitted last night after an episode in the centre of town,' the voice went on. 'It was only this morning that he was able to tell us who he is and where you might be.'

It emerged that Jack had been found wandering around the centre of Nottingham late at night dressed only in his pants. He was drunk of course, but there was something more.

Grace took the next train but it was late afternoon by the time she arrived at the hospital. Jack was in bed and heavily sedated. He barely recognised her.

She found a cheap hotel to stay the night and returned to the hospital the next morning. He was slightly better this time. At least he was aware that she was there.

'I'm so sorry Gracie,' he kept repeating. 'All the trouble I've put you to. I bet you wish you'd never met me.'

'Don't say that Jack. I just want you to get better.'

She didn't ask him what had happened to drive him over the edge like that. He told her, haltingly, that he'd been living in lodgings in Nottingham for a couple of months and that he'd sold a couple of paintings.

'There's some money for you back at my lodgings. For your rent Grace. And the train fares. You've come a long way.'

She shook her head. 'I don't need the money, Jack. You'll need it yourself.'

As she left, he gripped her hand and said, 'Will you come again? On your day off?'

The words struck her as reminiscent of when they'd first got together. But how different things were now from when she'd first got the train from London to see him in Portsmouth on her days off, her heart bursting with pleasure at the thought of spending the day with him. She left the hospital feeling drained and desperately sad.

She did go again, the next weekend, and the weekend after that. Within three weeks he was out of hospital.

'Why don't you come home with me Jack? I could look after you.'

'Could you bear it, Grace?' he asked. 'After everything?'

'Of course.'

So they took the train south and returned to the flat in Southsea together. Jack stayed at home during the daytimes while Grace was out at work. He would spend his days out on the seafront or at the end of the pier painting pictures of seascapes. He would clean the flat and cook for Grace each day. After years of living alone she welcomed the company. She was gratified too to see him get better by the day.

One evening after a few weeks though, she came home from work to a dark, empty flat. There was a letter on the table and a twenty-pound note.

'I'm sorry but I can't handle it here, Grace. I need to be on the road, on the move.'

Grace
Hampshire 1964

GRACE PUT ALL her time and energy into her career and the years passed. She worked hard and soon gained promotion to become a ward sister herself. With the extra salary she moved out of her flat and into a cottage in a village a few miles outside the city.

The sporadic correspondence with Jack resumed. His paintings were selling well again, but he never stayed in one place for very long. Neither of them suggested that he should come to visit again.

But one Saturday morning in the spring of 1964 he appeared on Grace's doorstep. She was astonished to see him standing there when she opened the door. He was thinner than ever, his hair greying at the temples, his face lined now, his skin still sallow and tight from all those years under the Burmese sun.

'I've had a bit of success Grace, and I thought we could celebrate.' He held up a bottle of Champagne.

She invited him in and over coffee he told her that he'd been given a lucrative commission to paint all the racehorses belonging to a noble family. They'd paid him an advance of several hundred pounds.

Seeing him that day brought all Grace's old emotions flooding back. He still had that look in his eyes that had first attracted her to him and he seemed better than she'd seen him in a long time; full of good humour and optimism for the future. Grace had been feeling alone and vulnerable for the first time for years. Her work had been particularly stressful lately; the ward was short-staffed and she'd been working extra shifts. The day before, a patient who had appeared to be recovering well from an operation had died suddenly. It had hit her hard.

They sat at the kitchen table, drinking coffee and chatting. Conversation came easily to both of them, just like when they first met. Grace made them lunch, and in the afternoon they walked out into the countryside together, up onto the South Downs to see the land stretching away beneath them for miles and the sunlight sparkling on the sea, her arm tucked inside his. In the evening they opened the Champagne.

It was natural that she should ask him to stay with her that night, but in the morning she awoke to the sound of him getting up.

'Where are you going?'

'I need to get to Newbury to start work on the commission.'

'I thought you had a couple of weeks before you had to begin?' she asked.

'Oh, I'll need to find somewhere to stay. You know how it is...' He carried on gathering his belongings. She sat propped up on her elbows, watching him.

'I'll write, Gracie,' he said.

'Why don't you come back at the weekend?' she asked.

'I'm not sure,' he said, avoiding her gaze and she knew that he wanted to be off again, that she couldn't ever tie him down.

Grace was shocked to discover that she was pregnant a couple of months later. She kept the news to herself for as long as she could, wondering how to tell Jack, what his reaction would be. She was worried that he might feel compelled to come back to live with her against his wishes.

In the end she made a decision. She would go it alone. She had no wish to tie Jack down and to risk him descending into drink and despair again. In any case, how could she ever subject her child to a life like that? She wrote to tell him and he wrote straight back.

'I'm overjoyed that this has happened Grace. I would gladly come back and live with you and try again, but I know you don't want that. I understand how you must feel. I have let you down so many times and in so many ways that I have no right to insist. I respect your decision, but I hope you will let me help you if you need my help, and that you will allow me to play some part in our child's life.'

~

THE MINIVAN CARRYING Louise and Eve had been travelling through a wide, flat valley, the road bordered by tapioca trees, and long stretches of rubber and banana plantations. They passed through villages where low wooden houses lined the road, temples with their roofs of ornate red and green slates and the occasional school marked out by a row of flags adorning the front fence.

There was very little other traffic on the road except for the occasional farmer on a motor-samlaw pottering along with a huge load of hay or sticks balanced on the side car, or pick-up trucks loaded with workers bound for one of the far-flung towns. For several miles the road ran parallel to a wide straight canal. Mountains could be seen on either side in the far distance. As they got closer to the Myanmar border, they passed fewer and fewer villages. Just the odd house and isolated smallholdings were dotted about here and there. The landscape was wilder, less cultivated here. Untamed bushes and palm trees grew rampant either side of the road. Soon they began to rise into the hills.

'Not long to border now,' the driver said over his shoulder. 'I will leave you there. Myanmar driver will pick you up on the other side. You will need passport and visa for stamping.'

Eve would have liked her mother to carry on with her story. She hoped the hiatus of going through two border checks wasn't going to put Louise off her stride and discourage her from continuing.

Eve got her passport out of her bag and turned to the page stamped with the Myanmar visa. They'd been to the Myanmar embassy in Singapore for the visas. Louise did the same and spent a long time staring down at the visa page in her passport.

'Is everything OK with your passport Mum?'

'Of course. I was just looking at it and thinking how lucky I was to get the visa in Singapore without a hitch.'

Eve looked at her enquiringly.

'You know I was detained by the police when I came here before?'

'Really?'

'I would have been deported if Jim hadn't got me released and helped me to get out of the country.'

'Gran mentioned something about it, but she didn't tell me any details.'

'She doesn't know much about it. I didn't want to worry her by telling her more than she needed to know at the time.'

'Will you tell me?'

'Yes. Of course. When I get to that bit. I'm going to tell you everything, Eve. I promised you that didn't I?'

'Yes, and I really appreciate it. I know it's not easy for you.'

Louise smiled and took Eve's hand. 'It's time you knew about it all Eve. I've kept the truth from you for far too long.'

The Thai border post at Phu Nam Ron consisted of a line of single storey huts with two uniformed Thai officials on duty. There were no other vehicles as they approached. The driver parked up and Louise and Eve got out with their bags.

Louise handed her passport to the official first who studied it for a few minutes. Eve was just starting to wonder if there was something wrong when the official stamped the passport and waved Louise through.

They were met on the other side by their Burmese driver, who drove them the four kilometres through a sort of no-man's-land to the Burmese Immigration checkpoint. This minivan was different; old and battered. The driver was listening to loud Burmese pop music on the radio. He kept turning to smile at them.

At the Myanmar border post, again Louise was the first one to hand her passport over the desk. The uniformed officer took a long time scrutinising it and checking details on a screen in front of him. Eve began to wonder if her mother was still on some computerised list of wanted foreigners. Eve was standing behind

Louise so she couldn't see her face, but she could see the sleeves on her T Shirt trembling.

But after a few agonising minutes the man stamped the passport and waved Louise through.

The road on the Myanmar side was wide but unlike the Thai road was not tarmacked. The surface was made of red earth, hewn straight from the jungle, but that didn't deter the driver from speeding along over the bumps and ruts, his radio blaring, as the jungle closed in around them.

'This road built for deep sea port at Dawei,' he told them, shouting over the roaring of the engine and the relentless music, beaming with his betel stained teeth. 'But construction company pulled out this year. They didn't finish road.'

The evidence was plain to see. They passed several hulks of rusting machinery by the roadside and piles of rubble and earth already beginning to be reclaimed by rampant creepers and jungle plants. The road was sometimes cut through deep rock walls, but there was always that feeling of being a long way from habitation. There were no farms or villages; this was untamed jungle, with huge trees growing right up to the roadside and creepers and vegetation encroaching onto the road. The surface of the track was so rutted and potholed that Eve had to cling to the sides of her seat to stop her head from hitting the roof of the van. Glancing at her mother, she saw that Louise was doing the same. Eve realised there was no possibility of Louise continuing with her story until they got through this stretch of the journey.

The rutted road went on for almost two hours. By the time they were through the jungled hills and emerging onto the coastal plane, the light was fading, but here the road was paved and smooth and the driver picked up speed.

After another hour or two they approached the coastal town of Dawei. The driver took them to a guesthouse on a street of dilapidated buildings. The Diamond Crown Guesthouse, in an old British period villa, with colonnaded balconies. The room was stifling and full of mosquitoes. Eve put on the fan and did her best to swat the insects.

'Shall we see if we can find somewhere to eat?' she asked turning to Louise, but her mother was already sound asleep on the bed, fully clothed.

Eve decided to leave her there and go in search of food herself. She walked a little way down the dark street following the aromas of wood fires and found some food stalls frying fresh fish and rice. No-one here seemed to speak much English, but they were very welcoming. With the aid of smiles and gestures, she managed to buy a couple of cartons of fish risotto and some cans of drink and took them back to the guesthouse.

But she ate hers alone. Louise didn't wake until the alarm went at 5.30, to wake them for their train from Dawei to Thanbyuzayat.

At Thanbyuzayat the stationmaster directed them to the only guesthouse in town. He was full of smiles and was keen to practice his English.

'Normally people not stay in this town,' he said. 'They stay in Mawlmayine and come for day trip to see cemetery.'

There were no taxis in evidence so they carried their backpacks through the darkening, dusty streets in search of the guesthouse the stationmaster had directed them to. They found it eventually. His directions weren't quite accurate, but the town was small, and after going round the same block of streets a couple of times, Eve spotted it next to a building site.

It was really no more than a couple of makeshift wooden huts tacked onto the back of a family house. There were two low beds in the windowless room, an electric fan and a bamboo table.

The owner spoke no English, but wrote down the price of the room on a notepad and handed them the page. Then he beckoned them to follow him and proudly showed them the primitive lavatory and washing facilities in an adjoining shack.

They slept very little that night, and in the morning were woken by the sound of diggers and building works in the next-door plot. They got up, washed in the tub in the open air, and ate their breakfast of chopped pineapple and banana on the little porch outside their room, watched by a group of curious village children.

As they sat at the wooden table, Eve consulted her guidebook. The war cemetery was marked on the map. It was a couple of kilometres from the guesthouse and there was no choice but to walk.

They arrived hot and sweating in the moist heat of the morning and stood at the arched stone gateway, awed by what they saw stretched out in front of them. In the centre of the grave-yard, opposite the entrance, stood a white marble cross. Then fanning out from it, acres and acres of flat slate headstones, symmetrically arranged, as far as the eye could see, with neatly mowed stretches of grass between them and neat hedges surrounding the site.

Exchanging awed looks, they wandered inside and stood together in silence, looking at the first line of headstones.

'Pete Abbot, our beloved son. Died March 1943 in Burma, aged 21. He lives on in our hearts.'

They walked slowly down the lines reading epitaph after epitaph. All were of allied prisoners of war who had died building the Thai-Burma Railway. All were heartbreakingly young and all had died thousands of miles from their homes.

Eve consulted Jack's map and compared it to the one in the guidebook.

'Can you see where the pomelo trees might have been?' asked Louise, shading her eyes and scanning the perimeter.

Eve shook her head. 'It's really difficult to work out. None of the landmarks on Grandad's map seem to be here anymore.'

Eve noticed a group of gardeners working in a far corner of the graveyard, hoeing the grass and watering the flowers on the graves. They wore conical hats, and their faces were shrouded against the sun.

Eve approached them. They stopped working and stood leaning on their tools, watching her shyly.

'Do you speak English?' she asked. After a pause, one of them stepped forward from the group. He gestured with his finger and thumb close together.

'Tiny bit,' he replied.

She showed him Jack's map of the cemetery. She pointed to the trees and the cross he had drawn beside them.

'Do you know where these trees are?' she asked.

The man shook his head, and turned away to confer with the others, speaking rapidly in Burmese. He turned back to Eve after a few minutes and shook his head.

'This not same-same,' he said pointing to Jack's map. 'Other place,' he said, waving an arm towards to the cemetery gates. 'Old camp. In town. You go there.'

He handed the map back to her and carried on pointing to the gate.

'They build museum. In town. You ask there.'

They retraced their steps back into the little town along the dusty road. Eve felt frustration descend on her. How could it be that they had come this far, and this close to where Jack had been a prisoner, but they might end up not being able to find anything after all.

'Why don't we go back to the station?' Louise said suddenly. 'At least the man there could speak a bit of English. He might be able to help us.'

The stationmaster greeted them like old friends and beckoned them into his office where they sat gratefully under the whirring ceiling fan. He brought them black tea in chipped china cups.

Eve asked him where the new museum was being built. He looked back at them with a twinkle in his eye.

'You mean you don't know?'

They shook their heads.

'Behind your guesthouse,' he said laughing. 'You didn't notice the noise? Well that is the site of the prisoner camp during the war. They moved all the graves to the big cemetery some years ago now. They build museum at the old site for visitors. There is a man there. A historian. He works for government. You must ask him to show you where the old cemetery was.'

After saying their goodbyes and thanks to the old stationmaster, they walked as quickly as they could, given the sweltering heat of the afternoon, back towards the guesthouse. They stopped beside the building plot, hovering behind the fence. They saw that a lone digger was clearing soil, and a group of workers were lugging tree roots and rubbish to throw on a bonfire in the corner of the plot. Eve spotted a wooden pre-fab hut in the corner of the plot.

None of the workers looked up as Eve and Louise entered the plot and walked straight across the rutted earth towards the hut.

A man wearing thick, opaque spectacles sat behind a desk inside. He was poring over a collection of rusty metal objects, laboriously making entries in a ledger, his brow furrowed. He looked up in surprise as they entered.

His English was not as good as the stationmaster's, but he seemed to follow Eve's explanation of why they had come.

'Is this the site of the old prisoner of war camp?' She asked. He nodded, a nervous look in his eyes.

'Yes. It is here. This is why we build museum here.'

She spread Jack's map out on the desk.

'We're looking for these trees, she pointed to the pomelo trees with her finger. My grandfather buried something under the roots. His diary. We want to look for it.'

The old man frowned.

'That is impossible, I'm afraid,' he said, shaking his head

slowly. 'All site has been cleared. Trees cut down and burned – for the building work you see.'

'But my grandfather's diary could still be there. It might still be in the ground. If you just could tell us where the trees were?' Eve said.

Again, he shook his head. 'All ground has been dug and cleared. We did find a few artefacts buried, however.'

Eve's heart began to beat faster. 'Do you have them? Where are they?'

'Yes. We have stored them here. They are waiting for me to examine and catalogue them for the museum.'

'Did you find an old tin? With a notebook or diary in it?'

'We haven't checked all the items properly yet. But wait here,' he said, getting up from his chair. They watched as he shuffled to the back of the office where he unlocked a large wooden chest secured by a padlock.

They waited, holding their breath as he rummaged through the chest, muttering in Burmese under his breath. Finally, he lifted something out and brought it to the desk. It was an ancient brown oblong tin, covered in the residue of dusty earth. Rust and dents of varying size scarred its surface. The old man tried to pull the lid off, but it seemed to be welded together. He then produced a hammer and chisel from the drawer of the desk and eventually with much huffing and exclaiming, prised the lid away from the tin.

He tilted it forward to show them the contents. Eve's heart leapt at the sight of it and she could feel Louise gripping her arm, trembling beside her. It was a notebook. Dog eared and damp, with mould obscuring the writing on the cover, but despite that the words leapt out at Eve. She glanced at her mother who was staring at it, her eyes glistening with tears.

21

Jack Summers' Diary
Thanbyuzayat POW Camp, Burma
New Year's Day, 1943

*M*y name is Jack Summers. I'm twenty-five years old and a Private in the Regiment of the Royal Surreys. I have been in this stinking POW camp at the railhead at Thanbyuzayat *for precisely three months and three days. In that time I have suffered sickness and starvation. I've also been subject to and witnessed more beatings from the guards than I can remember, and I've been forced to labour as a slave on a daily basis.*

Today I made a New Year's resolution to write in this diary as often as I can. I know it's risky, but I'm not afraid. What is happening to us POWs in this camp can't be allowed to go unrecorded and un-noticed by the world. If we all die here, killed by the Japs' crazy plan to build their railway through this jungle, perhaps someone will one day find my words and tell others of the injustices and cruelty that they mete out to us here.

I might as well start by describing my day today working on the railway, although I'm dead beat and there's so little light in this flimsy hut that it's not easy.

Today started just like any other day. Roll call at six in the morning. We all drag ourselves out of our huts as soon as we are able. We all know that to be late on parade will mean a beating from the guards. Since our beds are just weevil infested bamboo slats, we have no pillows or blankets, and we only have a tiny space each, most of us hardly sleep despite having been worked to the bone each day. So when we get up we are already exhausted. We move about in a state of near delirium; tiredness and starvation making us dizzy and weak.

We stumble out and assemble on the bare earth clearing in front of the guards' hut. It's known as the 'parade ground'. We stand there to attention under the morning sun in reluctant lines. We hardly look like soldiers any more. We are all thin and unshaven, our ribs standing out in our chests, our faces pale and our bodies wasted. Most of us have stopped dressing properly too. We simply wear ragged shorts or a Jap-Happy – a sort of baggy cloth to cover our loins. Hardly anyone wears a shirt. It's so hot here, we figure that the fewer clothes we put on the better we'll cope with the climate.

Out on the parade ground the Japanese commandant of the camp, or one of his subordinates, will inspect the prisoners. It is a tense time. The Jap officer struts along the lines of desperate men, poking the odd one with a stick if they aren't standing to attention properly. If anyone is faint and falls to the ground guards are sent to beat him.

The reason for roll call is to make sure there are enough workers for the daily shift. Often there won't be, and the commandant will send for back up from the hospital hut. He did it today. And just like every other day, it prompted a fierce exchange between the British doctor and the commandant, resulting in a beating for the doc. He took it bravely, as he does time after time, but it makes no difference. A few poor bastards on their last legs came staggering out of the hospital hut to join the parade. Other men turned their heads away in pity and shame.

When we're dismissed, we line up at the cookhouse for breakfast

which consists of *filthy rice and a cup of weak, black tea. We swill it
down quickly and then set off on our march through the jungle to the
part of the railway where we are to work that day.*

*For the last few days we've been working about four miles down
the line from the camp. To get there we march on the rough track that's
been cleared through the jungle for the railway. My boots finally disin-
tegrated a couple of weeks ago, and my feet are already blistered and
bleeding by the time I reach our place of work each morning.*

*Today we were clearing jungle for the new track. How do I
describe the work? If you could see my bleeding knuckles and torn
palms you might just begin to understand. There are hardly any
tools, just parangs (native knives) and a few blunt axes. With these
hopeless implements we're meant to clear the jungle, so dense that if
you walk a few yards in through the undergrowth no light can
penetrate.*

*So we set to work trying to clear the jungle plants, root up thickets
of bamboo and chop down towering teak trees. It's so hot that as soon
as we begin our bodies are running with sweat but there is no opportunity to rest. If anyone takes so much as a minute's break, one of the
guards will be on him, lashing him with a length of wire, beating him
with sticks.*

*It happened to me today. I was clearing some thick prickly jungle
plant that was a devil to move. I'd been at it for an hour or so and
wasn't making much progress. I stood up and took a look around me.
The man next to me did the same and smiled. He handed me his water
can and I took a sip.*

*I handed it back to him and said, 'I'll give you some of mine later.
I've left it with my pack,' when suddenly one of the guards was rushing
at us screaming. It was the thick-set Korean we've nicknamed 'the
Warthog', known for his evil temper.*

*'You no stop!' he yelled; spit was flying from his mouth. He had a
length of flexible branch from a tree, and he brought it down across my
back with hellish force. I yelled out and fell forwards onto the ground
but he kept on lashing out at me. Then with a curse and a kick with his*

boot in the ribs he left me on the ground, my back stinging with the pain.

The man who had handed me the water rushed over and helped me get up.

'Sorry, mate, didn't mean to get you into trouble,' he muttered, setting back to work on the bushes immediately.

'Don't worry. It wasn't your fault.' I said, beginning work again, the pain in my shoulders intensifying with every movement that I made.

By mid-morning we'd cleared most of the ground cover from a thirty-foot strip along that part of the track. All that remained were the stumps of teak trees that would have to await the elephant gangs to come along behind us to drag them out with chains. We were allowed to sit for twenty minutes beside the track with our packs and eat the rice that we had brought in our mess tins and sip water from our cans.

Normally we try to keep our spirits up with a bit of chat, or by telling bitter stories to ridicule the Japs. But there was no bonhomie in our work party of thirty or so men on that stretch of the line today. Everyone was subdued and didn't dare even look each other in the eye. The Warthog was a known sadist, keen to dish out beatings at every opportunity. He prowled around whilst we were eating, his bayonet tucked under his arm, glaring at us with hate in his eyes, yelling at us to hurry up.

In the afternoon our task was to press forward, to clear the virgin jungle up ahead of us and make first a narrow track through for fifty yards or so, then a corridor of twenty to thirty feet on either side of it.

We stared at the wall of thick undergrowth with sinking spirits. It was just like a living green barrier blocking the way. I stood there imagining the jungle stretching hundreds of miles in front of us, over rocky mountains and through river valleys all the way between where we stood and Thailand. And as it did every day, my heart sank at the thought that we, and thousands of men just like us will continue to be beaten and harried and worked to the bone until the Japanese have their way and the railway is built for the whole length.

The thought of all that suffering and all that cruelty was almost too much to bear.

We moved forward as one and started work on the undergrowth, hacking away at bamboo, hauling out roots and throwing them aside, ripping down branches. I thought of how many years this jungle had been there, of how old some of these bamboo thickets and teak trees were, and how here we were acting like vandals ripping them out unceremoniously in a matter of minutes.

When I looked round, I saw that the Warthog was watching me constantly from wherever he happened to be. In the end he gave up haranguing other prisoners and came to stand over me, watching me with his malevolent piggy eyes, his fat arms folded, his stomach thrust forward.

'You work!' he kept yelling at me. I'd seen him pick on prisoners before, hounding them and bullying them, beating them when they slowed down and a chill went through me at the thought that today it was my turn. He stood over me for the rest of the day and occasionally brought the cane down across my back, pain searing through me making me cry out.

I realised then, with dread in my heart that tonight I would be the one he would select for extra duties. It is his particular pleasure to single out prisoners for more tasks in the evenings, depriving them of rest and sometimes driving them to collapse.

We dragged ourselves back along the line and into camp as the sun was sinking behind the teak trees. We walked slowly and painfully, some of us without shoes, feet filthy and bleeding. Our bodies exhausted and beaten from our twelve-hour shift clearing the jungle.

I stumbled along between my two mates, Robbie and Ernie, my shoulders drooping. My eyes were fixed on the hunched frames of the men ahead of me, sweat trickling down their dirty backs, some running with blood from the beatings from the guards. Some hobbled on crutches, their lower legs eaten away by tropical ulcers, others, too weak from illness or starvation to walk, were supported on either side by their mates. Ernie was limping too, even as he tried to help me. He cut his leg with a rusty parang a couple of days ago and it's already infected and causing him pain.

Exhaustion permeated my whole body. I was ready to crawl onto the bamboo sleeping platform in my hut and close my eyes, but I knew that wasn't going to happen for several hours.

As I stumbled along, I could feel the sharp sting of the raw wounds from the Warthog's beating as the sweat ran into them.

I knew he was right behind me now. I could feel his presence as I walked, and hear his rasping breath. Every few minutes he would jab me with the tip of his bayonet and yell, 'Move! Speedo!'

'Don't let him get to you, mate,' said Robbie between gritted teeth.

We rounded the final bend on the muddy track and the camp came into view in the twilight. The Japanese guardhouse and cookhouse were the only huts lit by oil lamps, so all we could see were the shadowy shapes of the long atap huts where we sleep, built of bamboo and thatched with palm leaves. As we entered the camp, the other men wandered across the parade ground towards their huts. I moved to join them but felt the stab of the bayonet between my shoulders.

'Hey! You stay,' said the Korean.

Robbie and Ernie tried to linger, but the Warthog barked at them to move on. They obeyed grudgingly. As Robbie went past me he whispered, 'Keep your chin up, Jack. We'll save some tucker for you.'

The Warthog turned and grabbed one of the other men at random out of the moving line and made him stand to attention by holding the bayonet to the man's chest.

'More work for you two men tonight,' he said, and in the half-light I could see the evil glint of pleasure in his eyes.

I exchanged a look of dread with the other man. He looked like I felt; beaten and haggard, his face pale under the dirt. In his eyes I recognised the defeat and despair I felt myself.

The Warthog started to propel us across the parade ground. His fingers were digging into my arm, pinching the skin. I tried to shrug him off but it only made him tighten his grip further. Where was he taking us? Normally he makes prisoners do extra tasks in the Japanese guard house or dig the latrines as punishment, but we passed both of those places; the putrefying smell from the latrines rose in the steamy heat of the evening, making me gag.

He forced us to walk between the lines of huts right to the far end of the camp to a gap in the fence. Then, muttering something in Korean he pushed us through the gap and along a narrow muddy path through the undergrowth. My thoughts were racing now. What had he got planned for us? Why was he taking us out into the jungle? Was he going to throw us into a pit and leave us there to starve? Was he going to kill us? He still had his bayonet slung casually across his shoulder.

As we walked along the narrow path, mud from the day's rains oozing between my toes, creepers and undergrowth brushing and tearing my skin, I had a crazy thought that the two of us might be able to overpower the Warthog and escape into the jungle. Chances like this didn't happen every day. I glanced at the other man, but his head was bowed as he trudged along. The thought took root in my mind, though. How could I get him to help me?

But there was no time to act. The next second, we were emerging from the jungle into another clearing filled with row upon row of dilapidated huts. Here the smell of putrefaction and sewage was even worse than in our own camp. Even in the fading light I could see that the huts here were in an even worse state of repair than our own. Some of the roofs were collapsing and a couple of them were held up by fraying guy ropes tied to the surrounding trees.

There were no oil lamps here, but there was a bonfire burning in the middle of the clearing. Around it huddled a crowd of people. In the flickering light from the fire I caught sight of snatches of coloured clothing, people with long hair. I stared in disbelief. For a few minutes my brain couldn't process this information, but my eyes widened as gradually I realised that there were women here. And not just women, children too!

I glanced at my companion.
'I'm Jack,' I said. 'What's your name?'
'Stan,' muttered the other man.

'Do you know what this place is? I asked.

'I reckon it must be the coolie camp.'

'No talk!' barked the Warthog, but as he pushed me forward it became clear that Stan was right.

I've seen the gangs of Asian labourers working on parts of the line as we walk through to begin our own shift each day. (Some call them Romusha which I think means forced labour). If it is possible, they look to be treated even worse than we prisoners of war. Once as we passed a group, I saw a guard beating an Asian labourer unconscious, then kicking his body over an embankment. It shocked me, but I tried to put it to the back of my mind just as I had the numberless other occurrences of cruelty that I'd witnessed over the past few months.

The Korean pushed us forward, past the people huddled around the fire. They stared at us as we passed, fear in their eyes. They were very quiet for such a large group. The only voice we heard was that of a baby crying as its mother rocked it in her arms helplessly.

We reached the opening of a long hut at the far end of the camp. The Korean pushed us into the hut. He then left immediately. I turned in surprise and caught sight of his squat form hurrying back past the fire.

From the smell of rotting flesh, I knew that this must be the camp hospital. There were a couple of oil lamps burning inside this hut. In the flickering light I saw that the bamboo sleeping platforms running the length of the hut on either side were filled with emaciated bodies. Some were covered in gunny sacks, others naked, their limbs skin and bone.

A white man came towards us between the sleeping platforms. He was tall and skinny like most of us, wearing a crumpled khaki shirt and shorts, unusual amongst prisoners of war. I noticed the pips on his shoulder. He saluted and we immediately stood to attention and saluted back.

'I'm Lt Colonel Randall. I'm a Medical Officer and I've been posted here by Japanese command to try to help these wretched people. I have two orderlies with me doing what they can to nurse the sick, but I need your help this evening with some lifting.'

'Yes sir,' we said automatically. It didn't occur to us tell him we were dead beat from our twelve-hour shift hauling earth on the railway, that we hadn't eaten since lunch time and our stomachs were taut with hunger.

'The fact is, two coolies have died today of cholera. We need to get their bodies out of here as quickly as we can and burn them before the disease spreads. It's very contagious I'm afraid and the Japs are terrified of an outbreak.'

Stan's face went pale under the dirt. I felt the same way; a sickly dread in the pit of my stomach.

'I'm sorry, men,' said the colonel, 'it will be a gruesome task and not without risk. You'll need to cover your faces. Make sure you wash your hands as thoroughly as you can afterwards too.'

The colonel showed us two skeletal bodies covered in ragged sacks. They were lying side by side in the middle of the sleeping platform. He then gave us each a piece of cloth to tie round our faces to cover our mouths.

'If you bring the first one out, I'll show you where you can make a fire on the edge of the camp. The best way to do it is for one to take the hands and one the feet and manoeuvre them onto the stretcher.'

We manhandled the first body off the sleeping platform, onto the flimsy bamboo stretcher and carried it out through the middle of the hut. As we moved it there was a nauseating smell. I was astonished at how light the body was. The disease had purged its victim of everything but skin and bone.

As we carried the frail remains through the camp, following the colonel towards the cremation ground at the far end, we passed a small, timid group of people who watched us pass in silence.

One woman clutching a baby to her breast stepped forward as we passed and said something I didn't understand. I looked into her eyes. Tears were streaming down her cheeks, and in the moonlight I could see *that her eyes were wide with fear. She sunk to her knees as we passed and let out a howl that sent chills of horror and pity right through me.*

~

It's thanks to my mate Robbie that I'm able to write anything down at all. He has the cheek of the devil. He managed to wangle himself a job a couple of weeks ago helping out in the Jap cookhouse and he uses his position to full advantage. Each day he manages to scrounge something from one of the cooking pots to bring back to his mates in the hut. Even if it's only a morsel of extra rice, we are all grateful for whatever we can get.

Of course, the Jap soldiers and guards feed themselves a hundred times better than they feed us, even though we are the ones worked to the bone in the fierce tropical heat each day. They regularly have meat and fresh vegetables, rice that isn't swimming with maggots or full of stones, and they get proper portions, not the greasy and inedible filth they expect us to survive on.

He told me recently that he sometimes steals larger items, such as joints of meat and vegetables and sells them to the Burmese villagers who congregate outside the fence to barter and exchange goods. He knows how risky this is; men who've been caught in the past doing such things have been subject to brutal punishment, such as being confined to the punishment cage for weeks without food. One man was even shot for stealing rations from the Japs. But when I warn him, Robbie just laughs and says,

'Those guys weren't careful Jackie old man. I'm cleverer than that. I won't get caught I promise you.'

But I still worry for him. He thinks he's untouchable, but nobody here is beyond reprimand.

When I arrived back at the camp a couple of days ago after a full day's work hauling earth on the embankment, Robbie was there waiting for me in the hut. I was exhausted from the shift and wasn't ready for his banter. I threw myself onto my bunk and tried to ignore him. He'd got one of those smiles on his face that says he's got a secret, or he's got some new plan and he can't wait to tell you all about it.

My heart sank, imagining what he was about to say. Sometimes I wish he'd drop his scheming and plotting and wild escape plans. He must realise it's got him and us precisely nowhere so far. But I would never say that to Robbie himself. Not in a million years. I know that it's what keeps him going in here and I would never take that away from any man.

'I've got something for you, Jackie old man,' he said smiling, 'Call it a late Christmas present if you like.' He tossed this old exercise book onto the bunk.

I snatched it up. It's rare to get paper here. The Japs are paranoid about men writing anything down. With justification, they must be terrified of people recording the truth of what is happening to them, and afraid that if it ever gets out they will be punished.

'I thought you could use it for your sketches,' Robbie said. I looked at it and flicked through the thin pages, with pale grey lines.

'You did some great pictures in Changi,' he went on. 'You've got a real talent.'

I smiled up at him, remembering the few drawings I'd managed to produce in the crowded barracks at the Changi POW camp in Singapore. I'd drawn them on whatever I could find; the inside of dirty cardboard boxes, the back of paper scraps I'd found blowing against the fence. I'd sketched with charcoal from the cooking fire. My pictures had depicted the crowded conditions in the camp, the pitiful state of the men and the beatings I'd witnessed when men had stepped out of line. When our unit had left Changi in September to come up to Burma, I'd left the sketches with one of the officers who was staying behind. He'd said he would try to smuggle them out through his contacts in the resistance. I wonder if he was able to do that; if they'll ever see the light of day.

'I don't think so. I think it would be better to write a diary,' I said.

Robbie raised his eyebrows.

'Good idea. That could be even more risky than just pictures though.'

'Of course. But it would be more effective than sketches don't you think? I've often thought someone should write it all down, as a record for the future.'

'You'll have to find somewhere to hide it. You don't want the Bison finding it during one of his night-time raids.'

I smiled at the nickname Robbie had coined for the Japanese camp commander. He did look uncannily like a large mammal, with his huge squat frame, slightly hunched shoulders, and pugnacious expression.

'Yes, you're right. It would probably be best to bury it. I'll have to find a box or a tin to put it in so it doesn't get wet.'

Robbie rubbed his chin, thinking.

'Where did you get it from anyway?' I asked.

'From the Bison's office of course. I had to take him in a drink. He went out for a moment to shout at one of his underlings. The book had dropped onto the floor so I snatched it up and stuffed it down my shorts.'

I laughed. 'Ever the opportunist!'

Robbie smiled and sat down on the end of my bunk. The spilt bamboo poles squeaked slightly under the strain. He leaned towards me and lowered his voice.

'I've had another idea,' he said. Again my spirits sank, but to humour him I moved closer.

'An escape plan.'

'Another one?'

'This one will work. It's fool-proof.'

'Go on?'

'It's really simple. In fact, it's so simple it's bloody genius. I'm surprised no-one's tried it before.'

'Go on?'

'Well, you know there's a goods yard at the start of the line. All it would involve would be leaving the camp at night, getting to the yard, finding somewhere to hide in one of the goods trains, or on an engine, and just staying on the train until it reaches Moulmein.'

'It sounds easy, but the Japs are sure to search each train before it goes out. Especially if they know there are some prisoners missing.'

'But they wouldn't know there are prisoners missing, would they?'

'Wouldn't they? What about roll call? And anyway, how would you know which train to get on?'

'You? You? Less of the you. You mean 'we' surely?'

'OK, we then. How would we know which train to get on?'

Robbie thought for a moment, then he said. 'They've probably got the schedules somewhere in the Bison's office. I might be able to find them while I'm in there one day.'

He sat in silence for a while, his brow furrowed, trying to work out where the schedules might be found. I felt relieved that it might take him some time to locate them so his plan would not come to fruition for a while.

This was the third escape attempt that Robbie had devised. His first idea was to board the food truck that brought sacks of rice and vegetables into the camp every day. He'd managed to wangle a job unloading the lorry and had tried to bribe the Burmese driver to help him, but the man spoke no English and Robbie couldn't make him understand. I managed to persuade Robbie to drop this plan after I'd seen the driver drinking with the guards on the porch of the guardhouse one evening.

The second plan was simply to disappear into the jungle one Sunday when we had a day off from working on the railway. Robbie figured that we wouldn't be noticed for at least twenty-four hours by which time we could have travelled several miles. We talked about it a great deal. His plan was to make our way down the coast for a few miles, then try to get some friendly villagers to take us by boat to one of the islands that can be seen from the beach at Thanbyuzayat. I'm not sure how he knew that the Japanese weren't occupying the islands, but he was convinced of it. In preparation he'd spent weeks trying to learn Burmese.

But that plan was scotched too when some other men escaped from the camp; a small group of Australians. The whole camp had to stand to attention under the baking sun for hours while the Bison interrogated every man in the escaped men's unit. None of them cracked, but they were all beaten severely, one of them later dying from his wounds in the hospital hut. After ten days the escaped men's bodies were brought back into the camp on the back of a lorry and thrown without ceremony out onto the parade ground. No one knew how they had died; they were not wounded. The assumption was that they had starved, already weak from months of starvation rations in the camp, or died of thirst. It later emerged somehow that some Burmese villagers a few miles away had told the Japanese about the escaped men.

When I got back to the sleeping hut tonight, supper was over long ago. I felt dizzy from hunger and sick from everything I'd seen and done today. Images of the Asian workers' camp kept returning to my mind and I could still taste the putrid smell of the burning corpse in my mouth. Ernie gave me his tin. He'd saved half his rations; some foul overcooked rice with a couple of greasy lumps of indeterminate meat floating in it. But my heart turned over with gratitude that he had saved it for me. He and Robbie sat and watched me eat, their eyes standing out from their hollow cheeks. Robbie produced a pomelo and began to peel it.

'Where did you get that from?'

'Courtesy of the emperor old man,' said Robbie. I shook my head at the risks he was taking, but was happy enough to take my share. The taste of the sweet juicy fruit on my tongue was so wonderful that I was prepared to forget where it came from.

Later, as I lay down on the splintered bamboo slats between my two restless companions, listening to the whoop and screech of the jungle creatures, and the coughing and snoring of other men, my mind went back to what I had witnessed at the Asian camp. I could not get the eyes of that grieving woman out of my mind. They were infinite pools of despair and suffering.

Two of her companions had helped her to her feet; a man and a woman. The woman took the baby from her and they led her away. But I could still hear her anguished cries as we carried the wasted body of her husband to the far side of the camp.

A few glowing cinders were all that remained of the previous fire. The orderlies had left a few sticks lying around. We piled them on top of the cinders as best we could and stirred it to get the fire going. Then we eased the body on top of the flames.

The body began to burn, very slowly. The sticks were wet from the rains and hissed and spluttered as they burned. It seemed to take an age for that body to start burning. My companion, Stan, stood silently, his expression grim in the flickering firelight.

I watched with increasing horror as the flames built, licking and lapping at the body, finally engulfing it. It seemed to take an age. I've never smelt burning flesh before, it was a sweet, sickening smell that rose from the body and filled the air around. I stared as the flames ate away at the flesh and began to devour the glowing bones.

I was suddenly filled with anger as I watched; with a sense of injustice at the way these wretched people were being treated in this camp, and at the needless death of this poor man – a husband and a father. A fresh wave of bitterness overcame me at this evil force that we are all caught up in. And in the heat of the fire I felt tears of pity and frustration course down my cheeks.

22

Jack's Diary
January 2nd 1943

This morning, as we made our way out to roll call on the parade ground, I tried to keep my head down. I didn't want to attract the attention of the Warthog or the Bison after yesterday evening's ordeal in the Asian camp. I had a dreadful feeling that there might be more of the same today. As we lined up to be counted, I tried to position myself so I was standing slightly behind Robbie in the hope that I wouldn't be spotted.

How ironic it was, I thought, that this morning I was longing to be picked for the normal work party for the railway? I thought back over all the days I'd toiled and sweated with the others under the fierce sun, chopping down trees with blunt axes, hauling out bushes by their roots, my arms and torso ripped and bleeding from the thorns and creepers, my feet cut to shreds by the sharp stones. Throughout those long, back-breaking days, I'd longed for a day when I'd be spared the four-mile march to work, the hours of hard labour, the exhaustion of the return *walk to the camp with every muscle and bone in my body screaming out for rest.*

But standing there in that line-up today I'd have done anything not to have to go back into that Asian camp; especially in daylight, to witness the full horror of the place; the women and children with their sunken cheeks and pleading eyes, the men, broken and cowed from months of hard labour and starvation; the broken huts and the sewage-strewn ground, and everywhere that all-pervading stench of putrefaction and death.

I hung my head and studied the earth between my bare toes as the Bison strutted up and down the lines of men.

'He's really going for it today,' remarked Robbie in a hoarse whisper.

There was the usual screaming and yelling at men who weren't standing to attention, the prodding with bayonets, the slapping of faces. Eventually the Bison walked slowly along our part of the line and I stood up straight as he approached, staring ahead, my shoulders back. He paused in front of us and my heart started beating faster, but after a few seconds he moved on down the line. He'd found someone else to pick on, poking them with the end of his bayonet, screaming at the top of his voice for the man to stand to attention.

I breathed more easily when at last the Bison dismissed us and men began to gather in work parties to march to work.

'See you boys later,' said Robbie as he walked off towards the Japanese guardhouse.

I started to move along with Ernie and the others towards the tool hut to collect what was needed for the day. Without warning I felt the dreaded prod of a bayonet between my shoulder blades. I stopped and turned, and there was the Warthog behind me, showing his broken brown teeth in an evil grin.

'You no go to railway today, Private,' he said. 'There is other work for you.'

I didn't protest. Just like yesterday I knew there was no point in that.

'You too!' he said to Ernie who had lingered with me, prodding his chest with a stubby finger. 'You stay too. Job need two men.'

I glanced at Ernie's face that had grown pale under the dirt. Ernie was a plain-speaking farm worker from Norfolk, but even he knew better than to rail against the Warthog.

He must have been thinking about what I told him last night. When I got back to the camp yesterday, Ernie and Robbie had noticed how shaken I was. I wanted to spare them the details of what I'd witnessed, but they kept pressing me. In the end I told them about the Asian camp, about what I had sensed of the conditions there, and of the dreadful suffering of the people. Ernie must know, just as I did, that the work the Warthog had in mind for us today involved the Asian workers' camp again.

'Come. We go now,' said the Warthog. Once again, he led us between the lines of huts to the far end of the camp and through the gap in the fence. I caught Ernie's eye as we ducked through the opening.

'Whatever it is, it's got to be better than a day clearing the jungle, hasn't it mate? Me leg's killing me. I don't know if I could stand another day on the work party.'

I shook my head slowly. 'You might not think that when you get there.'

The sun was already high in the sky as we followed the Warthog along the narrow jungle path. Long before the camp came into view, the smell of it rose to meet us; human sewage mingled with the stench of rotting flesh.

As we finally emerged from the bushes into the dilapidated camp, I saw something that made my blood run cold. A human corpse lay face down on the ground close to the path beneath the undergrowth. I hadn't seen it the night before in the dark and now I wished I hadn't seen it at all. It was crawling with maggots and in an advanced state of decomposition.

'Jesus!' breathed Ernie.

We carried on, past the latrines. They were behind a long fence of rickety bamboo, but the sewage oozed from between the poles in a great *brown pool, alive with flies and maggots. The stench was unbelievable, and it was all I could do to keep myself from gagging as we crossed the clearing in the centre of the camp.*

I could see the sleeping huts more clearly now. As I guessed last night, they were in a poor state of repair, the atap roofs were sagging, and in several places had caved in completely. The thatch on all the huts was old and rotting from months of rain and several of them were secured by ropes tied to the surrounding trees.

But it was the sight of the people that was most shocking; the men must have already gone out to work on the railway for the day. There were only women and children left in the camp now. Some of them were moving around in a desultory fashion, sweeping the ground in front of the huts, cooking over small fires, or hanging out washing that looked like rags. But mainly they were just sitting on the ground in front of the huts doing nothing.

They were all pitifully thin and dressed in rags. They sat motionless and stared at us as we passed. What shocked me most was the look on their faces. There was no spark of curiosity in their eyes. Every single one of them looked as though they had given up the fight, had accepted defeat and were just passing through their days like living shadows.

The children clung to their mothers whining and moaning. It struck me that none of them were out playing like normal kids; they seemed to have no spirit or energy for that.

When we reached the hospital hut the Warthog pushed us inside just like yesterday evening.

'Doctor will give you orders,' he said, and immediately turned and hurried away, as he had done before.

The doctor approached. There were dark circles under his eyes, his face was grey and sweaty and he was stooping with fatigue. We exchanged salutes and he said,

'Thank you for coming here today, men. We've had a few more deaths from cholera in the night I'm afraid. Just like yesterday we need

to get rid of the bodies as soon as we can to minimise the risk of infection. I know it's a dreadful task, but it's an essential one.'

'Yes sir,' Ernie and I said in unison.

'We have three corpses for cremation. And once you've done that, we need to make a start on cleaning up this camp, or everyone here will be dead of cholera within a few days. How the bloody Japs let the place get like this I don't know.' As he said that his fists clenched by his side and his jaw tensed.

'There are various bodies about the camp too. They're not cholera victims I'm relieved to say; they will have died of malaria or dysentery, or from being beaten to death for not working hard enough. They will need to be cremated too; as soon as possible.'

Ernie and I exchanged glances but didn't speak.

'And then there's the latrines,' he went on, 'They're a breeding ground for flies and germs. We will need to dig them over and bury the filth.'

'But sir...' began Ernie. Colonel Randall held up a hand.

'No protests Private. It's a rotten job, but many of us have difficult jobs here. We're in it together. If you look all around you at this camp, I think you'll agree that these people need our help. They're living in hellish conditions; worse even than you POWs and they haven't got any army discipline or skills to help them.'

'Yes sir,' murmured Ernie, looking down in shame.

'Good. Now I've asked the Japs for two men to help here for at least the next week, maybe longer. That will be you two, so you might as well get used to it straight away. Now, I'll show you the corpses for cremation. Prepare yourselves. They're not a pretty sight.'

We followed him down the middle of the long hut, between the rows of sick people, trying not to breathe in the stench of rotting flesh from tropical ulcers, the smell of vomit and faeces from patients with dysentery. And I tried not to look, either, at the patients themselves; harrowing skeletal forms, lying there on their bamboo beds groaning in pain.

The colonel stopped towards the end of the hut.

'Here they are. I'll fetch some gunny sacks to cover them.'

'My God!' said Ernie turning away.

But I couldn't turn away. I stared and stared. There were three bodies lying next to each other. One was the body of a man, naked except for a stained loin cloth, but next to him lay a woman and child. All three bodies, just skin and bone, were contorted, twisted and doubled up, as if they had died in agony. I looked a little closer. The woman was wearing a flowered shawl, filthy now, but I recognised it instantly. She was the wife of the man we had cremated yesterday. The woman with the desperate eyes who had haunted my dreams.

The colonel covered the three bodies with sacks.

'It might be easier if you go out and get the fire going first. That way they will burn more quickly.'

We left the hut and crossed the clearing in a daze.

'Those poor, poor blighters,' said Ernie, in a choked voice.

'What the hell do they bring women and children here for? It's too much for a man to stand, but they don't have a hope in hell of surviving.'

'God knows,' I said. 'Maybe they came because they want to stay together.'

We reached the edge of the camp where the ashes from last night's fire were still smoking. I could see the charred ribs of the man we had burned yesterday, white amongst the embers.

We scouted round for more logs and managed to revive the fire and get it burning properly. Then we returned to the hospital hut and began our gruesome task. We took the body of the man first, carried him to the edge of the camp and put him as gently as we could on top of the fire. As the flames engulfed him, his body seemed to contort in further agony. It was uncanny. I could hardly bear to watch.

I looked at Ernie.

'Shall we get the next one?'

He grunted his assent and we made our way back to the hospital hut in silence. We took the woman first, but instinctively we laid her down beside the fire without saying anything. We both seemed to know that we couldn't put her into the flames without her child.

Watching that mother and child burn on that stinking pyre was one of the worst things I've had to witness in all the dreadful months of hell that I've endured since we were captured by the Japs. I've seen grown men beaten by groups of guards until they fall to the ground howling and begging for mercy. I've watched various forms of torture; from people being thrown in pits without food and water for days, to men being forced to hold a log above their heads out in the full heat of the sun until they've broken. I've seen men die in agony; of malaria, of dysentery and of starvation, and I've gone into the latrine at night and bumped against bodies hanging there when men have just given up the fight. But none of that matched the horror of seeing those two fragile skeletons twist and double up in the flames as if the fire had breathed a brief new life into them.

I turned away from the heat, not able to watch. My face was burning, but despite that my eyes were wet.

Someone was coming towards us. A woman picked her way through the mud and approached the fire. I recognised her as the woman who had helped the grieving widow to her feet yesterday. I watched her now. She was very petite, dressed in a pale blue saree, with a veil on her head. Somehow, amongst all this filth she managed to look clean and fresh.

As she got closer, I saw that she was carrying a bunch of flowers. They were delicate and white with dark green leaves. I recognised them as jasmine which grow in abundance in the jungle. Like me she had tears in her eyes. She glanced quickly at me and Ernie with a hesitant smile. Then she approached the flames and threw the flowers on top of the burning bodies. She then sank to her knees and bent forward, her head on the ground. I realised she was praying. I glanced at Ernie who looked away awkwardly. Neither of us wanted to move away until she had finished.

Finally, she rose to her feet. She looked up at me and pointed at the fire.

'Lady was my friend,' she said. I was surprised that she could speak English.

'I'm very sorry,' I replied. She wiped a tear away.

'We came from Malaya together with husbands.'

'Malaya?' I repeated, not knowing what to say. So, these poor people had come all this way, just like us probably, transported like cattle, to work on this railway. They wouldn't have known what fate awaited them here.

'You speak to my husband later,' she said. 'He speak good English.'

She turned and walked away as silently and unobtrusively as she had arrived.

Ernie and I spent the rest of the day collecting the bodies that were strewn about the camp in varying states of decay and decomposition. As the colonel had warned, it was a gruesome task because those poor wretches had been left to rot where they died. We had to bring sacks to carry some of the remains because they were too degraded to move in one piece. We didn't speak as we worked. Partly out of respect for the dead and partly because there were no words to describe what we were seeing and feeling.

At noon we returned to the hospital hut.

'You can come with me to the cook house. I need some food myself,' said the colonel.

I didn't feel like eating, but knew I had to force myself to take food whenever I could get it. We lined up with the women and children at the long cookhouse in the centre of the camp. The food was dished out onto tin plates by deft Asian women. If it was possible for it to be, it was even worse than the food in our own camp. The rice was grey and full of grit, with a few dark green leaves floating amongst the grains. It might have been spinach, but it might have been weeds. Despite that, and the lingering nausea from the morning's work, we both ate every last morsel and drank the dark brown tea that we were given too.

The colonel came to sit beside us on the ground as we ate. This made us feel slightly awkward. It wasn't usual for officers to mix with men at mealtimes, but he seemed to want to talk.

'How long have you men been in this camp?' he asked.

'Since September last year.'

'Did you come straight from Singapore?'

'Yes, straight to Moulmein by boat, then down here by rail,' I answered.

'We came up to Moulmein from Singapore by boat. It was an old rust bucket, sir,' said Ernie. 'We were packed into the stinking holds like sardines. There were no bunks, men just had to hunker down on the floor. The conditions were filthy on board. Men got sick, but there was nowhere for them to go. We thought we had it bad in the camp in Changi, but that camp was luxury compared to that journey.'

The colonel shook his head.

'Men are being brought up from Singapore by train now to the Thai end of the line. Packed into cattle trucks, thirty to one wagon. Standing room only.'

'Is that how you came?'

He nodded. 'Yep. Came up in December. Two men died in our truck on the journey.'

'The Japs will pay for this one day,' said Ernie.

'You bet they will,' said the colonel. He rubbed the stubble on his chin. His eyes seemed far away.

'I've seen some dreadful things. My first camp was in Kanchanaburi in Thailand. They're building a huge steel bridge across a river there. We started a hospital there near the town. Men were falling sick straight away. They weren't getting enough to eat and the working conditions are appalling. Malaria was rife, and beriberi, dysentery. The lot.'

'How did you get to come up to Burma?'

'I've been posted at several camps along the line. The Japs asked for Medical Officers to help out in the Asian workers' camps. As you can see, the coolies are living in dreadful conditions. They are dying in greater numbers than the POWs. The Japs don't care that they are dying, except it was leaving them short of workers.'

'What are conditions like down in Thailand?' I asked.

'It depends where you are. Some of the bigger camps close to Kanchanaburi are better than those further up the line. Those upcountry camps are the worst I've seen. They've got the Aussies working on a long cutting through a mountain in the middle of the jungle. It's heavy work, cutting through rock. The Japs work them day and night without mercy. They don't care if they drop dead on their shifts. If the men work too slowly, they beat them on the spot.'

Mercifully, the guards had been absent for most of the morning, but we had noticed a guardhouse on the other side of the camp. Now I happened to glance across the clearing and saw two guards approaching. They were carrying shovels. The Colonel got to his feet and bowed as they got close.

'You work!' yelled the first guard, going straight up to the colonel and slapping his face. The other guard lunged towards Ernie and me. We scrambled to our feet.

'Back working!' he shouted, pointing towards the latrines. They threw the shovels on the ground in front of us. We picked them up reluctantly and started towards the latrines.

I won't dwell on our afternoon; suffice it to say it was spent knee deep in human sewage that was heaving with maggots, digging a long pit behind the latrines to bury as much of it as we could. We hardly spoke, each with our own thoughts about the unfortunate souls we'd cremated this morning. After that ordeal, digging the latrines didn't seem so bad.

At twilight, the Asian workers hobbled back into the camp from their day on the railway. We stood and watched them. They looked much like we POWs do when we return into camp after a shift, exhausted and beaten, some men limping, some carried by their mates. The difference here was that the women and children flocked around the group, bringing them water, helping them back to their huts.

I watched the woman in the pale blue saree rush up to one of the men and put an arm around him. He was limping and blood was pouring down his injured leg. It was the man I'd seen support the grieving widow yesterday. We were close enough to see the concern in the woman's eyes. I was struck by the tenderness between them in the midst of all this suffering. She helped him walk slowly along between the sleeping huts until they drew parallel to where Ernie and I were standing, next to the latrines.

She stopped and looked at us.

'This my husband,' she said. 'He speak good English. He want to talk to you.'

The man started to protest, but she silenced him with a sharp look.

'Before you go back to your camp tonight, come to our hut. Behind this one,' she said indicating the place with a nod of her head. 'I will give you tea.'

So later, on our way to return the shovels to the guard house, looking around furtively for any Japanese guards, we took a detour behind the long sleeping hut. There was a line of dilapidated smaller huts built close together, with steep roofs thatched sporadically with atap.

We walked along the line and the woman came out from one of them.

She was carrying two battered tin cups. A meagre cooking fire burned in front of the hut.

'My husband inside,' she said, beckoning us into the hut. She followed with the cups.

We entered, having to stoop to avoid the low ceiling. The hut was lit by a couple of flickering candles set in jars which hung from the bamboo frame. There was nothing inside except a sleeping platform and a string suspended along the ceiling over which some rags were hung. The man lay on the bamboo sleeping platform, on one side of the hut. On the other, a tiny child slept fitfully. As we entered the man levered himself up onto his elbows. The woman put her hands together in a gesture of greeting and said,

'I am Marisa. This my husband, Aadesh.'

'I'm Jack and this is Ernie,' I said and took the proffered tea gratefully.

'Sit down,' said the woman. We sat down as carefully as we could on the sleeping platform next to the child, but even so the whole hut shuddered and shook under our weight.

'What did you want to tell us?' asked Ernie.

The man, Aadesh, sat up, again making the hut wobble on its frame. The baby stirred. I noticed that Aadesh's injured leg was bound up with some coloured cloth.

'We want you to help us,' he said. I was struck by how good his English was. He had only the trace of an accent.

'If we can,' I said. 'What is it you want?'

'Our child is sick. He is covered in sores and has no energy. Doctor Colonel says he won't get better until he has vitamins. There is nothing the doctor can do for him. He is getting weaker every day and we are near despair. We think we might lose him. Could you bring him food when you come again?'

Ernie and I exchanged glances.

'We could try, but it would be difficult,' said Ernie. 'We are living on starvation rations.'

'But you are near Japanese quarters,' the man insisted, 'You could perhaps get some from there.'

I stared at him. 'It's very dangerous to steal from the Japs,' I said. 'They have executed men for less.'

'Fruit and vegetables,' the man went on, as if he hadn't heard what I said. 'That's what he needs most. The doctor said so.'

He wasn't pleading with us, he was stating facts.

'I trust you British,' he went on. 'I worked for British in Malaya. My manager was kind to me.'

'You speak very good English,' I said. He smiled suddenly. A broad smile showing a row of discoloured teeth.

'Whereabouts in Malaya were you?' I asked.

'On a rubber plantation near Kuala Lumpur,' he said. 'I was the overseer. But when the Japanese took over the country, my boss, the British manager and his wife were taken off by the Japanese to an internment camp.

'Then the Japanese took over the plantation. They moved soldiers into the house. We had no work anymore and no money for food. Some of the workers ran away into the jungle, afraid of what would happen to them. We stayed in the workers' village. We started to grow our own food and to catch animals to live on. It was very hard.

'Then one day, some Japanese came to the village with interpreters and said they were looking for workers for a railway to be built through Thailand and Burma. 'Money will be good,' they said, 'conditions good. The work will be easy and regular. You can even bring your family with you.'

'We thought it would be a good opportunity,' he said, glancing at his wife who shook her head and looked down at the bare floor. 'Marisa comes from Kuala Lumpur. She is a city girl. The conditions in the village were getting very harsh. She wasn't used to living like that. She was used to a comfortable life. I thought it would give us the chance to go somewhere different, see another country, and so we could save up for a better life.'

His face was full of anguish as he went on.

'But we were tricked,' he said bitterly. 'It was obvious as soon as we arrived. There is nothing for us here. No facilities, no proper shelter. We are treated far worse than animals. Japanese guards work us to the bone and they don't care if we die working. This is no place for women and children. You have seen the conditions. People are dying every day of disease, hunger, starvation. We would like to run away, but there is no way we can do that. There is nowhere to go and no transport to take us. We can't go home. We can't survive here. We are caught in a trap.'

'It's terrible. Dreadful,' I said shaking my head too. My heart went out to these brave, hardworking people. It was true. They are helpless here in the face of the Japanese war machine. If we soldiers can't escape, are reduced to the status of slaves ourselves, what can these poor people do? They are, alone and helpless, away from their families and their countries, without even any military training or discipline which is a big factor in keeping us soldiers going.

I felt powerless to help them. Even so, I suddenly knew I had to do *everything I could. It would make some sense of this senseless situation, if I could at least ease their pain and suffering.*

'I don't mind for myself,' Aadesh continued. 'I am strong and used to hard work. It was my decision to trust the Japanese and come on this journey so I must take the consequences of that. But I do mind for Marisa and our son. He is only a baby. I cannot stand by and watch them suffer.'

23

Jack's Diary
January 3rd 1943

W hen Ernie and I went back from the Asian workers' camp to our sleeping hut last night, Robbie was still awake. He was trying to read a worn and battered copy of 'Far from the Madding Crowd,' one of the few books in the camp, by the flickering light of a tallow candle.

We told him about Aadesh and Marisa, about their plight and about their desperate plea for fresh food for their son. Robbie didn't hesitate.

'I'll get them what I can from the Jap store tomorrow and you can take it to them the next day. It sounds as though their need is greater than ours. If there are any jackfruits I'll see if I can get hold of a couple. And greens too. Whatever I can lay my hands on, I'll get for them.'

Ernie and I murmured our thanks.

'But you know this won't last long don't you?' he said, suddenly serious, lowering his voice to a whisper. 'We'll be on our way soon. On that goods train on the way up to Moulmein. All three of us. Once I get the plan of that marshalling yard and the train schedules from the Japs.'

Ernie and I exchanged anxious glances. Ernie patted Robbie's back.

'Of course, mate. You're right. Whenever you say the word. We'll be ready.'

I couldn't sleep. I lay awake for hours, listening to the snoring and coughing of the men all around me as the mosquitoes and bed bugs nibbled my skin and the sweat trickled down my face and bathed my body. It was a clear, cloudless night and I could see the stars twinkling through the gaps in the thatch. It made me feel tiny and insignificant – as though our camp was just a speck on the face of the earth, forgotten and isolated in the middle of a vast jungle, and that no-one would ever find us here.

I was thinking of that Indian family too and all the other families like them who were living a miserable waking death, their lifeblood and dreams slowly slipping away from them in that squalid, shameful camp through the fence from ours. I thought of Aadesh's eyes, the desperation in them, the fear he'd expressed for his wife and son and the helplessness he felt. And I thought of Marisa too, her capable, deft hands tending to her family, doing her best for them, trying to make things as bearable as possible in the worst of conditions. I thought of her quiet beauty and the way she had looked at me steadily with sadness in her eyes, which were full of hope and trust.

January 15th 1943

Several days have passed since Ernie and I first went into the Asian workers' camp. The wound on Ernie's leg has become infected. It gets worse by the day. He winces each time he takes a step, but he soldiers on. We go back each morning, and each morning we take (concealed as best we can in our shorts) whatever Robbie has been able to pilfer from the Japanese stores the day before. Aadesh and Marisa had tears in their eyes on the first day, when we gave them the cabbage and mangoes that Robbie had stolen. Marisa immediately set to work chopping it up to cook in a battered pot over their fire.

On the second day, Marisa thanked us for the gift of greens and potatoes. She put half of them inside her hut, then went to her neighbours' huts on either side, whispering to them to keep quiet about the gift, and left a couple of potatoes on the rickety porch of each one.

Each time we go she offers us some tea. It is just boiled water and leaves, but we take it gratefully. Today the baby was awake, lying on his back, following his mother with huge brown eyes. I asked his name.

'Kashwin,' she said, smiling with pride. 'It means star.'

We have carried on clearing the camp and helping the doctor in the hospital hut. There have been no new cases of cholera for two days now. It doesn't mean we don't have to be vigilant the doctor keeps saying, for our own sakes and for others, but he seems quietly hopeful now that the worst is over and the infection has been contained at least for the time being.

January 18th 1943

Tonight, when Ernie and I came back from the Asian workers' camp, we found Robbie pacing up and down outside our sleeping quarters, peering into the darkness looking out for any sign of us. I could tell straightaway that he was bursting with something to tell us.

'You're late. I've been waiting for you,' he hissed, grabbing our elbows and guiding us behind the hut, away from the flickering light of the doorway.

'I've found it. I found it today.'

He was brandishing a thin sheet of paper. In the darkness it was impossible to see what was written on it.

'It's the Japs' timetable. Schedule of movements of goods trains between here and Moulmein.'

'How did you get that?' I asked shivering at the thought of the danger he must have put himself in to get hold of it.

'The Bison was out of the camp all day. No-one was watching his guard room. The guards were all getting drunk and rowdy on arak in their quarters. I just let myself in when no-one was looking. It was right there on his desk.'

'Can you understand what it says?'

'I can understand enough. I've spent all evening deciphering the letters. There's a column for departures. I've worked out what the symbol for Moulmein looks like and there are two trains a week. There's a train leaving for Moulmein next week. Thursday at 6am.'

Ernie's wide eyes gleamed in the half light, as he watched Robbie. I felt the same. The meaning of his words was beginning to sink in. We will be risking everything if we try to leave on that train. Our own lives, the lives of others in the camp too; our mates in our hut and those we work alongside on a daily basis. They could be beaten and tortured just for knowing us or speaking to us.

But it was clear from the expression in Robbie's eyes that he was deadly serious. He'd been building up to this moment all these months he'd been working for the Japs.

'We're going to be on that train,' he said looking from me to Ernie and back again. There was such intensity in his gaze that I wanted to look away.

'Of course, mate,' said Ernie, patting Robbie's back. 'Of course we will be.'

'Good. I'm glad about that,' said Robbie, allowing Ernie to manoeuvre him back towards the entrance to the hut. 'Just for a moment there, I began to think you were having cold feet about the whole thing.'

I lay awake for hours thinking about Robbie's words. It was uncanny how he had sensed our reticence. He must have picked it up from our movements and body language, even though it was dark out there. Maybe he thinks we're cowards, but he definitely sensed that we were having second thoughts about his plan.

But my mind keeps going back to the Romusha family who have come to rely on us; hardworking Aadesh who looks closer to despair every day; the little boy, Kashwin, so weak and helpless, so dependent on the extra food we are now smuggling into them on a daily basis. I can't help wondering how they will cope when we are gone? I can hardly bear to think of them waiting for us, patiently watching that gap in the jungle for a sign of us each morning, sitting on the flimsy porch of that rickety hut, their eyes, larger than normal in their pinched faces, full of hope that we will be bringing them food. And gradually that hope fading from their eyes, to be replaced with that beaten look of fear and desperation. It was the look that I'd seen in the eyes of so many Asian workers since I first arrived in their camp.

I realise now that I am torn. Torn for the first time since we were captured by the Japs back in February '42. Torn between my desire for escape and loyalty to Robbie, and my wish to help that family and the others like them. I still hadn't decided what to do, and I haven't decided now, as I write this this morning.

January 19th 1943

Today when we woke up, I could see straight away from the way he was lying, that Ernie was very sick. When I saw him like that, sweating and delirious on his slatted bunk, my heart gave a jolt of fear. Perhaps he'd succumbed to the cholera after all these days we've both put ourselves at risk, moving the bodies, cleaning up the camp, filthy and infested with the illness.

'You'll be alright, mate,' whispered Robbie, leaning over Ernie, a note of desperation in his voice. 'Give it a day and you'll be right as rain.'

We exchanged a look and I could tell from his eyes that Robbie was thinking about his plan. Before roll call, Lt Cameron, the officer in charge of our unit came to have a look at Ernie.

'There are two things wrong with him. His leg is badly infected, so that could be the cause of the fever. But it looks more like malaria,' he

said, in a matter of fact tone. 'Get him along to the hospital hut, you two men.'

Robbie and I half carried Ernie between us across the parade ground to the makeshift hospital. He was barely conscious, his head lolling forward. The medical officer waved us towards a bare bunk at the far end of the hut. We helped Ernie up onto it. He collapsed back down, exhausted by the effort. He was sweating and shivering, moaning quietly with the pain.

'There'll be no work for this lad for several days,' said the doctor briskly. 'There's not much we can do for him, apart from cleaning out that ulcer on his leg and sponging him down when the fever hits. There's no quinine in this camp. No medicine at all I'm afraid.'

'But he'll get better, right?' asked Robbie. Once again I sensed desperation in his tone. The officer looked at him with a flicker of surprise.

'You must know the prospects, man. Most of us have had a bout of malaria since Singapore. He'll probably recover from that. I'm less optimistic about his leg ulcer to be frank with you. But what he needs now is complete rest.'

Robbie was brooding in silence as we joined the rest of the men for roll call, still fretting about his plan.

'We can always postpone. There'll be another train,' I whispered, trying to lift his spirits.

'The schedule only went to the end of the month,' Robbie muttered, staring down at his bare feet. 'There's one next week. Wednesday I think, but after that I've no idea.'

'You! Quiet! No talk!' yelled the Bison, making his way down the line of ragged, skinny men towards where we stood. We froze, stood to attention and stared ahead as he approached, praying he wasn't going to use this as an excuse for one of his sadistic punishments. But to our relief he strutted past us, his stick under his arm, staring ahead, without further comment.

The Warthog was waiting for me beside the guard house as usual as the other men set off towards the railway for their day's work.

'Where other man?' he barked, as I approached.

'He's sick,' I said and the Warthog exclaimed loudly in Korean.

I half expected him to send me back to work on the railway with the others, but he beckoned me to follow him alone through the trees to the Asian camp. Then, with a malicious glint in his eyes, he put me to work digging the latrines. As usual he stomped away, back to the relative safety of the POW camp.

Although it was filthy work, wading amongst the maggots, gagging at the stench, I felt a strange sense of relief that I was still working in the Asian camp. I realised I had got used to coming here each day, seeing the families, the women and the children, doing whatever I could to help them.

I worked for a couple of hours in the stench and the sweltering heat digging and burying the filth, ankle deep in it. The Warthog had disappeared, but I knew I couldn't relax. He would no doubt be back to check on my work.

After a couple of hours my back was aching and I was getting very thirsty. I put down the shovel and stretched, intending to fetch my water bottle. But when I started towards it, I heard a voice behind me.

'I have brought you tea.'

I turned. It was Marisa. There she was, managing to look clean and fresh in all the filth surrounding her in that godforsaken place. She was very thin, of course, the bones in her cheeks stood out, but the horror of that place hadn't dimmed the look of quiet peace in her eyes.

'Come. Sit with me while you drink. The guard is not here. He is gone to the other camp.'

I followed her to the hut where she gave me a bucket of water to wash my feet. Looking to check no-one else was around, I slipped her the potatoes that Robbie had pilfered the day before that I'd been hiding in my shorts. She thanked me as she usually did, with sincerity in her dark eyes. Then she motioned me to sit down. As I did so, I glanced inside the hut and saw Aadesh lying there asleep next to the young boy.

'His leg is still bad. He cannot work today,' Marisa explained. 'He *will not earn money while he doesn't work.'* A troubled look entered her eyes.

'How is your son?' I asked. She shook her head and looked away.

'Still the same,' she whispered, nodding in the direction of the child. He was lying beside his father on one of Marisa's sarees, grizzling quietly. Both their bodies were glistening with sweat in the stifling heat of the tiny hut. The baby looked thin and weak, mucus streaming from his nose, his little body covered in sores.

'You should take him along to the hospital to see the colonel.'

Her eyes widened in fear. 'There is disease there,' she said. 'Cholera. You know that. He will die if he goes there.'

'The cholera is gone now. The doctor tells me they've had no new cases for several days. You don't need to fear that.'

Still she shook her head, 'They have no medicines anyway,' she said. I couldn't deny that was true.

'Don't worry. I will try to bring more food tomorrow.'

She sat down beside me and as I sipped the tea she gave me, she began to tell me about her life in Kuala Lumpur. She hardly looked at me as she spoke. Instead, she carried on staring down at the ground. It was almost as if she was talking to herself.

I didn't interrupt her. I hardly dared to move or make a sound. I didn't want her to stop. I sensed it was doing her good to speak about it, to recall the good times. It was as if she needed to tell her story, to reaffirm to herself that those things had once happened to her; that it hadn't all been a dream.

'My father and mother came over on a ship from Madras when they were first married, in search of work in Malaya. I am their eldest child. I was born in Kuala Lumpur, and I have never been to India. They both worked so hard. My father worked in mines and on rubber plantations and sent all his money home. My mother also worked. In factories and in warehouses. I don't know all the jobs they had over the years, but they were always busy, working long hours. They saved money and managed to rent a decent house for us to live in.

'I have three brothers and a sister. They sent us all to a good school, *a missionary school where we learnt some English. When father had earned enough to stop working away from home, he opened a small canteen in the Indian Quarter in Kuala Lumpur. When I left school, I used to help him there.'*

She smiled at the memory. 'I was happy back then. Cooking and serving food to workers and shoppers. Helping my father and mother. Working alongside them.'

'Sometimes, when Father was too busy to go himself, I would go over to Chinatown for him to buy vegetables for the canteen. One day I was walking down Petaling Street on my way to the rice wholesaler's. A man came up to me and asked if I spoke Tamil and if I could help him. I saw instantly that he was Indian, like me. He was dressed roughly and was carrying a heavy pack. He looked a little lost. He had such a kind, open face, or I wouldn't have spoken to him. He didn't speak a word of Malay. He told me that he had just arrived in KL. He'd been working for months on a plantation, and he was desperate for good Indian food and needed a place to stay.

'I took him back to my father's canteen. We gave him a meal and that night he came to stay with us as a guest in our family home. It was Aadesh. He was such a sweet man. So gentle and kind. So patient with my younger brothers and sisters. He was the eldest of five children himself, just like me. His father was dead and he'd left his family behind in Madras to find work and to send money home to them. My family felt pity for him and embraced him as one of their own. He and I got on so well right from the start. We seemed to understand each other, straight away without needing to say much, as if we'd known each other all our lives.'

She turned to me and smiled, a flash of happiness in her eyes.

'I often wonder what would have happened if father had gone to Chinatown to buy vegetables that day instead of me. Would I have ever even met Aadesh?'

'When some weeks later the time came for Aadesh to go back to his plantation, he asked me to marry him and to go with him. Father and Mother weren't pleased at first. They had promised my hand to the son

of a business associate of my father. But they wanted my happiness, so after a bit of persuasion they changed their minds and let me go.'

I wanted to tell her that I'd been stationed in Kuala Lumpur before the Japanese invasion, and how Robbie and I used to walk down Petaling street sometimes on our days off, looking for somewhere cheap to eat, or a bar. As she'd been speaking it flashed through my mind that I might have seen her there. What would I have thought? Would I have even noticed her? But I didn't want to interrupt her story.

'We were married quickly, and I went back with Aadesh, to the plantation where he worked. Things were different there. The house was small and bare. No more than a hut really. Aadesh worked long hours, from before dawn until dusk, and I had to look after the house and make my way in the workers' village with the other wives. I missed the bustle of the streets, the companionship of my family and working in the canteen amongst people all day.'

'I lost two babies in those first few months,' she screwed up her face at the pain of the memory and paused for a while. I didn't speak. I didn't know what to say. 'It was so hard, without my family there to help. But my beautiful baby boy was born during the second year. Things were tough for us then, but they got tougher. When the Japanese arrived at the plantation in 1942 with their guns it was a terrifying time. They killed one of the British overseers who tried to stop them coming into the estate. Shot him dead. It was useless to try to stop them. They were soldiers armed with bayonets and guns.

'They took the manager and his family away that day in a lorry. People said they were going to a prison camp. Japanese soldiers moved into the house. There was no work for us workers anymore. They let the plantation go to ruin. Weeds grew between the trees and the jungle took over. We were terrified all the time; scared to go out in case the soldiers took us to a prison camp too. We were hungry all the time too. There was virtually no food for us once we had killed our chickens, and we were living on what we had saved. We tried to grow vegetables behind our hut, but they were washed away by the monsoon. In the end Aadesh and I decided we must go back to Kuala Lumpur to join my *family, but we had no idea how we would get there. It sounds silly now, but we decided the only thing to do was to walk - we were so desperate. Even though it was a very long way.*

'We packed up what we could carry. But, on the morning we were planning to leave, the Japanese soldiers came into the camp with an interpreter and told us there was work for any workers who wanted it. It was a long way away in Siam and Burma, but the Japanese said the transport was free, the pay and conditions would be good and that men could bring their families. Many of the men jumped at the chance. A group of us set off that day from the local station. We were herded into wagons for the long journey. This was a shock. It began to dawn on us, even as we began our journey, that the Japanese promises were empty, but we didn't realise quite how bad things would get.'

She gestured around her helplessly. 'You can see how bad our situation is. Our men work all hours. They are driven, like slaves. If they get sick, there are no medicines. They just die and the Japanese couldn't care less. There is nothing for us here, or for our children. This place is filthy, disease ridden. And sometimes, the guards trouble us women.' She dropped her eyes and looked at me sideways, a flush creeping up her cheeks. 'But there is no escape,' she said.

She shook her head and tears filled her eyes. My heart went out to her. Her story affected me deeply.

As I made my way back to the latrines, I thought about what she had told me. I had an overwhelming feeling of compassion for this brave woman, her plight and that of her family and all those desperate souls trapped in this godforsaken place, caught up in a war that has nothing to do with them.

But I also thought about Robbie and his dogged determination to see his escape plan through. And again I was torn. Just as I had been when I lay awake last night on my bunk, worrying and fretting about it. How can I just leave these people now I know them and their story? What I'm able to do for them each day is not much, I know that, but it is better than nothing, and it is the only help they are getting. I'm not sure if I could just walk away without a word and leave them to their fate.

I know that the Japs could change their minds on a whim and send me back to the railway to work at any moment, or simply ship us all out to another camp altogether. But while it is within my control to help those people, I'm not sure I could leave, despite the chance I might have of getting away from here.

24

Jack's Diary
January 20th 1943

T oday, in the Asian workers' camp, I saw a disturbing sight
which confirmed something Marisa had said when she told
me her story.

The Warthog ordered me to repair the atap roof of the camp
kitchen where the thatch had blown off during a monsoon storm. I had
no tools, so decided the only thing to do was to weave the fallen thatch
straight back onto the roof as best I could. I scouted around amongst the
trees and managed to find some creeper twine from the surrounding
forest. Then I gathered up the fallen thatch and climbed up onto the
roof with it. This was a bit precarious, and I could feel the bamboo
poles bending and swaying beneath me as I climbed and as I began
work on the roof. I had to work slowly to avoid slipping off the brittle
rafters and falling through into the hut.

From my vantage point up there on the roof I could see over into
the family quarters. I watched the women sitting on their porches list-

lessly, the children playing in the mud. They play with sticks and stones. They have no toys.

At one point, when I'd only been working for half an hour or so, I looked up. What I saw made me pause and watch. A Japanese guard had wandered into the area in front of the huts. I've not seen that before. Normally the women and children are left alone to get along as best they can in their squalor and hunger. At first I thought he was going to give them something or to help them in some way, but I could see that he wasn't carrying any food or supplies. And his manner was very odd too. He looked unsteady on his feet, swaying from side to side. I quickly realised he must be drunk.

He went up to one of the women and said something to her. She held her veil across her face and shook her head. Then he started pawing at her. He ripped her veil away from her face and pulled her towards him. He was trying to kiss her. I watched horrified, transfixed, hardly believing my eyes. The woman pushed him away frantically, but he then grabbed her with both arms and began to manhandle her away from the line of huts. She lost her footing and stumbled. He then lifted her bodily with both arms around her waist and started to drag her through the mud. She was yelling and screaming by now, pleading with the guard. The other women, Marisa amongst them, must have seen what was happening. They surrounded the guard, pulling at his clothes, hitting him, screaming at him.

I jumped down from the roof and ran towards them, yelling at the guard to stop. The guard looked across at me and put the woman down. As he began to slink away I felt someone grab me from behind by both elbows. I was pulled to the ground with a thump, which sent all the wind out of my lungs.

I found myself lying on my back, staring up at the Warthog. He eyed me for a few seconds. I could see the contempt in his black eyes. Then he drew his bayonet and shoved the sharp end in my stomach.

'You work. Not bother Japanese soldier.'

'Look what he's doing to that woman. He must be stopped. You should stop him,' I yelled, but the Warthog stared at me with blank eyes.

'He go away now. Not your business.'

I squirmed under his bayonet, each time I tried to get up he prodded the blade deeper into my skin. I tried to raise my head to check that the guard had really gone. From the sound of the women's voices I realised that the crowd was dispersing.

After several minutes, the Warthog snatched the bayonet away and clicked his fingers at me.

'You get up. You work now,' he motioned towards the roof.

I got to my feet and the Warthog shoved the bayonet between my shoulder blades and pushed me forward with a prod that almost sent me sprawling to the ground again.

As I reached the hut he nodded for me to climb back on the roof. He then drew his rifle and pointed it at me. He stood there for the rest of the afternoon, pointing the rifle at me as I did my best to rethatch the roof.

Just before sunset the Warthog told me to get off the roof. Then he forced me to walk, still at gunpoint, through the undergrowth and the gap in the fence and back to our camp. As I went, I tried to look round to see if Marisa was in front of her hut, but I was too far away to see anything.

I got back to our quarters and lay on my bunk for a while, staring up at the palm thatch, my mind filled with images of what I'd seen. I was so angry that my fists kept clenching involuntarily. White hot rage rose inside me. Rage with those ignorant, vicious guards, rage that those poor, helpless women are at their mercy day in, day out.

I lay like that for a while, wrestling with my fury and my shame, when suddenly I sat up. I'd remembered Ernie, and that he was lying there sick in the hospital hut. Perhaps he was waiting for me, watching the gap in the wall for any sign of me or Robbie. How could I have forgotten him?

When I got to Ernie's bedside, Robbie was already there. He was sponging Ernie's forehead with a dirty wet cloth. Ernie was semi-conscious and covered in a thin film of sweat, his face deathly pale, his eyes glazed and unseeing.

'He's going to get better, Jack,' Robbie said, looking up, his voice full of optimism. 'I'm sure of it. He'll be better for next Wednesday. And he'll be coming with us.'

I didn't tell Robbie my qualms during supper. I was finding it hard to broach the subject, worried that he would think I was letting him down, or bottling out of his escape plans. After all we've been mates since we first signed up; we fought side by side, we were together when we were captured by the Japs at Singapore, all through those long, hard months at Changi. I owe him my loyalty many times over.

It was really hard to find the words to tell him what I was thinking, but when we sat smoking afterwards, a little apart from the others, I managed to tell him what I'd witnessed today in the camp. Then I told him Aadesh and Marisa's story, about how they had been tricked by the Japs into coming here to work. I told him about Aadesh being injured and how their little boy was still lying sick in their hut beside his father. He listened in silence, his head bowed forward so I couldn't see his face, but when he looked up I could see from his eyes that he understood how I felt.

'You don't want to come with me, do you?' he said slowly. 'You want to stay and do what you can for them here.'

When I didn't reply he said, 'I don't blame you, Jack. I don't blame you at all. I think you're right to want to help those people. We can't go anyway until Ernie's recovered, but how about this for an idea? I'll step up my efforts to get food from the Japs. I'm sure I could get more than I've managed so far. You can smuggle it through to them and when the little boy is on the mend we'll be able to go.'

'Are you sure? I know your heart was set on going in the next few days.'

'Quite sure. We've lasted this long in this hell-hole. We can last a bit longer. I'll have to find a way of getting more details of trains to Moulmein, but I'll probably be able to if the Bison goes out again. It wasn't too difficult last time.'

January 28th 1943

I can barely hold the pen to write today. I'm having to force myself to put it all down. But I must get it down on paper. It will be difficult to find the words to describe what has happened, but I know I must. For Robbie's sake and for all of ours.

Over the last few days Robbie has managed (I've no idea quite how) to get more food from the Japs' kitchen, and I've been giving it to Marisa. Yesterday I took in a slice of buffalo meat that Robbie had pilfered from right under the nose of the Jap cooks. With the extra food, the baby has been showing signs of improvement, and yesterday Aadesh's leg was well enough for him to go back to work on the railway.

Ernie was also looking a lot better this morning too. He was sitting up on his bunk in the hospital hut and eating some of the filthy brown water that passes for soup around here. He even smiled when he saw us coming.

We chatted to Ernie for a while, gave him some bananas that Robbie had pilfered.

As we left the hospital hut Robbie said, 'Ernie'll be up and about by Wednesday after all. And your friends in the Asian camp are getting better too. It's all coming together, mate. This could be our last few days in this godforsaken place. In a few days we'll be on that train and bound for freedom.'

He left with a spring in his step and the last I saw of him was when he turned round and winked at me as he headed off to the guard house.

I did my usual shift in the Asian workers' camp. I managed to slip through to see Marisa and the baby when the Warthog had gone off to the guardhouse to drink toddy with the other guards.

She gave me a cup of tea as usual and I sat beside her for a few minutes on the rickety porch. Her mood seemed lighter today. The little boy appeared to be a little better too. He was playing listlessly with the other children on the bare earth between the huts, but at least he was up and about and not lying whimpering inside the hut.

When the time seemed right, I asked Marisa about the incident with the guard. She lowered her eyes to the ground.

'I told you. Sometimes Japanese soldiers bother us.'

'That's terrible,' I said. 'It shouldn't be happening. I will tell our captain about it. He will complain to the Japanese commandant if he can.'

But she shook her head, and looked at me with wide, terrified eyes.

'Please, please don't do that,' she said, 'I don't want to make trouble.'

She said it again and again when I pressed her. She seemed so terrified of what might happen if I spoke out that in the end I dropped the subject.

I thought about telling her about Robbie's plans. I wanted to let her know that any day now I could be gone. I might never see her again.

But I couldn't bring myself to do that. I've probably still got a few days yet and I don't want to spoil any shred of relief she might be experiencing with Aadesh and the little boy recovering, or bring yet more worry into her life. So I said nothing.

When I came back into the POW camp at the end of the shift, I knew straight away that something was very wrong.

As soon as we emerged back through the fence and into the camp perimeter, the Warthog drew his bayonet and I felt the sharp, cold prod of it between my shoulder blades just as I had the other day. Normally at this time there would be a lot of noise and activity; the bustle of men going to the cookhouse, the murmur of them talking, smoking, relaxing after their day's work. Tonight, the camp was eerily silent.

The Warthog forced me to walk forward. As I stumbled along in front of him my mind was full of dread at what might be happening. As we came between the huts and onto the parade ground, what I saw chilled me to the core.

It wasn't time for roll call, but the entire camp was assembled on the parade ground, standing to attention in motionless rows. There was a deathly silence over the assembled lines. Men stood with their heads bowed.

My eyes were drawn to the front of the parade ground. I stopped and stared. I nearly cried out at what I saw.

It was Robbie. Those brutes had lashed his wrists and ankles by rope to a couple of thick bamboo poles they'd driven into the ground. He was spread-eagled, stretched out between them, naked except for his Jap-Happy, his head lolling forward. As I got closer, I could see his face was bruised and puffy, his eyes swollen and his nose streaming with blood.

The Warthog kept prodding me forward until we were parallel with the front line of men. Then he forced me to turn and walk along in front of the line right up to the place where Robbie was tied up. Then he made me stand a few yards in front of him. I could hardly bear to look at Robbie, but I made myself. His eyes were swollen and closed. I prayed he was unconscious because the pain must have been excruciating.

'You missed the beating,' whispered a man in the line behind me. 'We were all made to watch. Brutal it was. Never seen anything like it.'

I kept my eyes to the ground. 'Why? What has he done?'

'Stealing from the Jap kitchens,' came the reply. 'They caught him with a bag of dried fish.'

Shock washed over me. Shock, mingled with shame. He'd done it for me. Because I'd insisted on helping Aadesh and Marisa. I hadn't been content with the few vegetables he'd been able to pilfer to smuggle to them. I'd insisted on more. It was my fault that he'd been caught.

We carried on standing there in silence, contemplating Robbie's broken body as the sun went down and darkness descended on the camp. The night sounds of the jungle started up; the whoops of monkeys, cries of night birds, the whine and buzz of insects.

After what felt like a lifetime of standing in the open, being eaten alive by mosquitoes, the Bison strode out of his guardhouse accompanied by a couple of guards. He had his stick under his arm as usual and he walked with a swagger. He walked up to Robbie, kicked his feet aside casually, then nodded to the guards who untied him and let him drop to the ground with a sickly thud.

Then the Bison turned to face the camp and said in his barking, broken English;

'This man very, very bad man. He commit crime. He steal good food from Imperial Japanese Army. This is the food for our soldiers. Let this man and his crime be an example to you prisoners. If anyone else steals, punishment will be worse. Even death. This man is lucky. Today we are generous and merciful.'

He stood there for a moment, swaying back and forth in front of Robbie's prone body.

'Camp dismissed,' he said and strutted away.

I dashed to Robbie as the lines broke up and other men began to drift away murmuring to each other in shocked, subdued voices.

'Robbie, mate. You're going to be alright,' I said desperately, shaking him, slapping his cheeks, trying to get some response. 'It's OK now. We're all going to help you.'

With the help of a couple of other men from our hut, I managed to get Robbie up into a sitting position, but he was still unconscious, his head flopping forwards. We then got him upright, hoisted him onto our shoulders and half carried and half dragged him between the three of us across the parade ground. He felt like a dead weight; he had no strength in his body.

Other men surrounded us, trying to help, expressing their sympathy and their disgust at the brutal punishment. That walk across the parade ground to the hospital hut seemed to take forever.

The doctor was waiting for us at the door.

'Bring him in here,' he said sharply. I saw consternation in his face. 'Lie him out on this bench,' he said, motioning to an empty sleeping platform.

He asked one of the orderlies to hold a lantern up over Robbie, then he set to work, sponging him down, examining his cuts and bruises, holding a tiny torch up to his eyes. He slapped Robbie's cheeks, trying to get a response from him. I watched helplessly, my heart filled with anger and fear.

When the doctor had finished, he turned to me and said.

'He's not responding to any stimulus. He's deeply concussed, I'm afraid. I watched what they did to him myself. They were kicking him all over. There were several blows to his head.'

'He's going to recover, isn't he?' I asked. The doctor put a hand on my shoulder.

'I hope so, Private. I really hope so. He's relatively strong compared to lots of the men in this camp. He was as healthy as he could have been. We'll have to hope and pray.'

'But isn't there anything you can do for him?'

He shook his head. 'I'm sorry. There's very little we can do. Just wait and pray, like I said. We don't have any medicines here. And even if we did, there's not much we could do with the injuries he has.'

'I'll stay with him,' I muttered.

The doctor, pressed and overworked as always, returned to his other patients, and the men who'd helped me bring Robbie into the hut drifted off to go to the cookhouse with apologies and good wishes.

But I had no appetite at all. I just sat on a makeshift bamboo stool beside his sleeping platform and watched Robbie by the light of a kerosene lamp. I talked to him all the while, trying to remember some of the stories he'd told us about his family and to repeat them back to him, of some of the things that have happened to us since we were captured, of our friendship and our loyalty to one another.

'I'm going to make sure you get better mate,' I said leaning forward and whispering into his bloodied ear. I realised, even as I spoke that it was as much to try to convince myself as for Robbie. 'Then we're going to do what we decided to do. Don't give up hope.' I didn't dare say more about it, afraid that one of the orderlies or other patients would hear me and that word would get out.

Sometimes through that long night I reached out and held his hand, hoping he would return the grip, but he never did. All the time I watched the rise and fall of his chest, worried that if I stopped watching, he would stop breathing.

A couple of times one of the orderlies came to our end of the ward and peered at Robbie's face. 'No change?' they asked me and I shook my head helplessly.

As the ward settled down for the night, there was still the sound of men thrashing about and shouting out in feverish delirium, the soothing voices of the orderlies as they went about their work and the snores and night time sounds of others. The stench of putrefaction from the men whose flesh was being eaten away by tropical ulcers permeated the hot night. On occasions, entering the hospital hut I'd gagged from the sweet sickliness of it, but tonight I hardly noticed it. So focused was I on willing Robbie to open his eyes, to sit up, to wink at me and to say. 'Jackie, old mate, it's all going to be alright. We'll be on that train to Moulmein in no time.'

But as the night wore on, and the night time sounds of the jungle enveloped the hut; the whoops of monkeys, the cries of nightjars and the buzz and whine of a billion insects, I must have drifted off to sleep. When I awoke, my forehead was resting on Robbie's bunk and the first weak rays of morning light were seeping through the holes in the atap thatch and the bamboo walls.

But I knew then, without even looking that the body in front of me was completely still and that while I'd been sleeping the life had drained away from my friend.

January 29th 1943

I left the hospital hut in the early hours of the morning and stumbled across the parade ground towards the sleeping quarters I'd shared with Robbie and Ernie since we arrived here. My vision was blurred with tears and I felt as if a dead weight was blocking my throat and pressing down on my chest. I was dimly aware that it was getting light; that milky light of dawn, the coolest part of the day before the sun gets high in the sky and red hot. In a sudden flurry of noise and colour a flock of green parakeets flew overhead flapping and cawing. It made me look up despite my turmoil.

The slim moon was setting behind the jungle and above it, a sprin-

kling of distant stars. There was one single bright star hovering above the moon, bravely giving its last display of light before being blotted out by the fierce fire of the sun. I thought of Robbie then. About his star that had burned so brightly and lit up our dismal days in captivity, giving them love and hope and laughter.

For some reason the sight of that star, still burning valiantly in that Burmese morning sky gave me a glimmer of hope. I stood there in the middle of the parade ground, squared my drooping shoulders and lifted my head. Then I saluted it for a long moment.

'So long Robbie old friend,' I said.

25

Jack's Diary
January 30th 1943

We buried Robbie at first light this morning. The camp padre, Father Stone led the sombre procession up to the cemetery on the little hill behind the camp. It's a place which is so familiar to me. It's where I go every day to bury this little book in its biscuit tin under the pomelo tree.

It was like all the other funerals of men who we've lost to disease or to starvation over the past months in this place, and those who've just given up the will to live. Only there were more men than usual to say goodbye to Robbie. They must have been inspired to come to show solidarity against the Japs and support in the light of Robbie's brutal murder. And it was testament too to Robbie's character; his constant good humour and his optimism; his open, generous nature. Many of the men who trooped up single file behind Robbie's coffin were men he'd given up some of his rations for when he'd seen them dead beat on a shift on the railway, or who he'd given some extra baccy to when we'd been sitting round the campfire in the evenings.

We stood around the freshly dug grave, our heads bowed while Father Stone said prayers thanking the Lord for Robbie's life and for the lives of all the men we've lost. I couldn't really take in what he was saying. I've never been one for religion and that sort of preaching leaves me cold. But there was something else stopping me too. I didn't want to acknowledge that Robbie is gone from us. I just want to remember him as he was; bursting into our sleeping hut late at night with some new plan or idea, keeping our spirits up with his jokes. I'd like to think that he's just gone off somewhere for a short while; that he will be back amongst us before too long.

March 1st 1943

I HAVEN'T WRITTEN in this little book for a while because I've been feeling so low. After Robbie's death everything seemed pointless. I've been dragging myself through each day, the only thing keeping me going being Marisa and Aadesh and the little boy, and their neighbours who smile at me and welcome the scraps of food I manage to smuggle them. Of course, now Robbie is gone I can't bring them very much, but I have found a way of creeping up to the Jap kitchen store in the dead of night to pilfer a few potatoes or cabbage leaves that have been discarded at the back of the hut before the rats get to it.

I've been helping Doctor Randall in the Asian workers' hospital each day once I've dug the latrines or mended broken huts or done whatever jobs the Warthog gives me in the mornings. The doc has taught me to clean wounds and bandage them, to cleanse his blunt surgical instruments by passing them through a flame, and to assist him by holding the kerosene lamp or passing instruments when he performs minor surgery.

When I get back into our camp each evening, I go to see Ernie in the POW hospital. It's much bigger and better organised than Doctor Randall's outfit, but with no more medicines or supplies than he has.

Two days ago, Ernie had the operation that he has been dreading and anticipating in equal measure for months. The tropical ulcer that has been plaguing him has grown to such an extent that it has begun to eat away at the bone in his leg. The doctors decided that the only thing to do to save his life was to amputate the bottom of his leg.

I asked Ernie if he wanted me to be there for the operation, but he laughed and shook his head.

'I don't want you to see me yelling like a baby, mate,' he said. 'The doc tells me they don't have any anaesthetic. I'll just have to bite down on a filthy bit of cloth and think of England.'

When the leg had been removed, I went to see him. He looked drained and exhausted, but he was in good spirits considering what he'd just been through.

'It feels better already,' he said smiling. 'Now that filthy sore's been cut away. They're going to fit me up with a wooden leg made of bamboo and I should be able to walk again before too long. You know what Jack. Perhaps we'll be on that Moulmein train one day soon after all.'

I smiled back at him, but I think we both know that's going to be a big challenge and that just talking about it is probably all we're going to do for a long time. It was good to see him being so brave and positive, though, after the dreadful pain and trauma he's been suffering for months. I write this tonight with my spirits lifting a little for the very first time since Robbie's death.

March 15th 1943

ONCE AGAIN, my hand is shaking so much with anger and frustration that I can hardly write. I thought I had been to the depths when Robbie was killed, and his death still haunts me every waking hour, but today there's been a fresh blow; it has torn me apart, such that I feel I will never be whole again.

What do I or my feelings matter anyway? That's not what I'm troubled about. I'm truly afraid now. It is a new, visceral sort of fear. It's not for my own safety or even my life. I'm afraid for humanity. Today I've had a glimpse into hell. Into the truly evil and depraved side of human nature that this war and this situation has fed and nurtured.

I went into the Asian workers' camp this morning as usual and straight away I knew something was wrong. I mean even more wrong than the everyday picture of disease, squalor, suffering and starvation that it normally presents. The first thing I noticed when I emerged into the camp through the undergrowth was that everything around me was quiet and still. A sudden chill went through me because in a split second I was back there walking across the silent parade ground the day that Robbie had been beaten and brutalised. The tension that hovered in the silence and the smell of fear on the air was exactly the same.

The Warthog was right behind me with his bayonet at my back so I couldn't stop and look around, but as soon as I began walking past the huts, I knew I wasn't imagining things.

Most mornings the women sit out on their porches. Their children play in the dirt in front of the huts. They usually watch me and some smile shyly at me as I pass. But today no one was sitting out. Not a single soul was visible in the whole length of the row of dilapidated huts. I could sense though, from the odd sound and glimpse of movement that they were actually all there, cowering inside their huts. It felt to me as if they were sheltering from something or somebody.

With the Warthog prodding at my back I had no choice but to walk on past, the feeling of unease mounting as I walked down the line of dilapidated homes towards the hospital hut.

But when I drew parallel to Aadesh and Marisa's hut I stopped dead and stared at it, stunned at what I was looking at.

Something or someone had virtually destroyed the whole construction. The front panel of woven rattan was completely caved in and the platform where Marisa normally sat out had collapsed, the woven bamboo walls splintered and shredded.

The Warthog's bayonet dug sharply into my spine and I lurched forward. But I kept looking back at the hut over my shoulder. As I passed it I strained to get a glimpse inside. There were a few scraps of torn rags on the floor; bright blue, orange, green. I recognised them instantly as bits of Marisa's colourful sarees. Fresh fear sliced through me.

The Warthog prodded me on past the latrines and across the bare earth of the camp to the hospital hut. With every step I took my mind was racing; wondering, frantic to know what had happened to the little family whom I now count as my friends.

Colonel Randall was waiting for me at the doorway to the hospital hut. He normally smiled his welcome, but this morning his expression was grim. He took my arm as soon as the Warthog had scuttled off.

'What happened?' I asked.

'I'm so sorry, Summers,' he said. 'I know how fond you are of the family. Something awful happened last night.'

I looked at him. His eyes were grave. I had a sudden urge to cry but I fought it back.

'Sit down, man,' he said, guiding me to a sleeping platform. I sank down on it, feeling my limbs quivering, a sick feeling in the pit of my stomach.

'I'll have to tell you straight,' he said. 'The man, Aadesh, is dead. His wife and baby are here in the hospital.'

I stared at him. I had no words. Nausea rose in my throat.

'One of the guards has been pestering the women on and off for a while. I know you've seen that before.'

My scalp prickled with shock and with the dread of what he was about to say. I felt my fists clenching.

'Last night that evil bastard got drunk on arak with some of the other guards. I don't know where their officers had got to. They went along to the coolies' quarters, making a hell of a racket. Yelling and laughing as they went. I heard the shouting myself and went out to *see what was happening. There were a few of them. Not just one man.'*

'No!' I said, my fists clenching.

'Aadesh and Marisa were outside their hut. Sitting on the porch. It happened so quickly. One of the brutes grabbed Marisa. Aadesh tried to stop him of course. The other Japs surrounded him. They threw Aadesh down onto the ground. He kept struggling up, trying to fight them. In the end they all set on him. They beat him and kicked him, and one of them drove a bayonet through his stomach. I saw him drop to the ground writhing and screaming in pain. Then they went for Marisa, battering down the porch and the front of the hut.*

'I ran over, yelling at them to stop, but they pushed me back with their bayonets. One of them held his rifle to my chest. I could smell the whisky on his breath. They dragged Marisa away. She was screaming and crying out, pleading with them. It was pitiful to hear.'

He passed his hand over his sweating face and paused. It was a minute or two before he could go on. 'The drunk with the rifle held me there with it until the others had dragged her out of sight. They must have taken her to their quarters the other side of the trees.*

'When he let me go and ran off after the others, I ran over to where Aadesh lay. He was still alive. I did what I could for him, but he'd already lost a lot of blood. Two of the workers helped me get him back to the hospital hut, but he was dead by the time we got him here.'

I couldn't look at Doctor Randall. I had to look away to hide the tears that I could no longer hold back.

'I went back for the little boy,' he said. 'One of the women was looking after him in her own hut, but he had screamed so much and was so traumatised, his temperature was already soaring. He's gone down with a high fever now.'

'And Marisa?' I asked. 'Where is she?'

'She's asleep now. I stood outside the hut and waited for her until dawn. Eventually she came stumbling back through the trees. She was crawling on her hands and knees. I could see, even from a distance, that she was battered and bruised and covered in blood, her clothes ripped to shreds. I helped her in here and cleaned up her injuries. She couldn't speak. All she could do was sob.'

I sat there, my head in my hands. The anger and hurt and frustration were overwhelming.

'Can I go and see her?' I asked at last.

He nodded and beckoned me through the hut, between the two long rows of sleeping platforms, between the sick and desperately thin patients, who lay there either semi-conscious or moaning in pain and distress.

She was lying right at the end of the hut, the tiny child by her side. Her dear face was bruised and swollen almost beyond recognition. There was a bloody wound on the side of her head where she must have been struck. Her eyes were so swollen it was hard to tell if she was asleep or awake but her regular breathing showed she wasn't conscious.

The little boy slept fitfully on the platform beside her. He was lying on his side, his knees drawn up in the foetal position, snuggled up to his mothers' side. A film of perspiration covered him in the stifling heat of the hut, his black hair was plastered to his head.

I spotted a rag in a bucket of water on the ground beside them. I squeezed it out and as gently as I could I bathed the baby's face, in an effort to cool him down. Then I took Marisa's hand, limp as it was, and just stood there, helplessly, watching her, praying for her to come round, to open her eyes, to at least show some sign that she was going to live. But I realised then that if she lives, she is never going to recover from what happened to her last night, from the physical and mental scars and from the horror and shame those brutes have inflicted on her.

I just stood there, holding her cold hand for what seemed an age, whispering stories to her; nonsense, anything I could think of, just letting her know I was there. I carried on until one of the orderlies came and told me the Warthog had been looking for me.

He was there at the door to the hospital hut. He never comes in because he's too afraid of catching some disease. I was so angry I couldn't look at him, but he barked his orders at me as usual.

I spent the rest of the day doing the Warthog's bidding; digging the latrines, repairing holes in the wall of the guardhouse. The sadness and despair I felt affected me physically. I dragged through my tasks with such a heaviness in my heart that I couldn't focus on what I was doing. I could hardly even move my limbs

At midday the Warthog came back to check on my progress. After he'd looked at the work I'd done, he ordered me to dig a grave on the edge of the camp. I knew where he meant. It was with the other graves where Asian workers who've died have been thrown, some of them heaped together, those who weren't cremated on the funeral pyre. When the Warthog handed me the spade today, though, I knew it was for Aadesh.

It took me all afternoon to dig that grave. So drained and weakened was I with the shock of what had happened. All the time I shovelled that heavy, red earth I was thinking about Aadesh. How his beaten body would be thrown into it, wrapped in a rice sack from the hospital, or completely naked as they often were.

I knew that the Japs wouldn't allow proper funeral for him. They don't allow the Asian workers that dignity. To the Japs they are a disposable commodity. They don't value their lives or have any respect for their customs or beliefs.

I finished the pit as the sun went down. The Warthog came back and strutted around the pit, assessing it, fixing me with his narrow gaze.

Then he stopped.

'Fetch body. Coolie man,' he ordered, pointing to hospital hut. I threw down the shovel. I had no choice but to obey him. All the time I was walking back I was thinking that at least if it was me burying Aadesh, I could give him some respect.

The doctor showed me where Aadesh was lying. The bayonet wound in his stomach had been covered with a rice sack as I'd predicted, but the blood had seeped through and dried making a black spreading sticky stain on the hessian. A sickening stench arose from the wound and I had to concentrate hard not to gag. Aadesh's eyes were closed. There were bruises on his face and head, but astonishingly, his expression was full of peace.

I said a quick prayer for him under my breath, regretting that I didn't know any of Aadesh's own Hindu prayers to say for him. Then Doctor Randall nodded to me with a grim look. He lifted Aadesh by the shoulders, and I took the body by the feet. As carefully and gently as we could, we carried him out through the hut, down the central platform and out into the darkening evening.

A few of Aadesh's neighbours were standing; watching silently as we carried him across the clearing to the pit I'd dug on the edge of the camp. They knew from bitter experience that if they tried to follow us, they would be beaten back, reprimanded severely by the guards. So, they stayed where they were.

We lowered Aadesh's body into the pit as gently as we could. Then I shovelled the soft freshly dug soil over him while Doctor Randall watched and waited, his head bowed, his hands clasped in front of him. I could hear him muttering the Lord's prayer as I tipped the last clods of earth over Aadesh and his face gradually disappeared from view for the last time.

The colonel and I walked back to the hospital hut in silence. Words were beyond us. All I could think of was of the senseless loss of a loving, hardworking family man, cut down in his prime by the brutality and depravity of others.

When we reached the hut I was about to go in to see if Marisa had woken. But the Warthog stood barring the doorway. With a sideways jerk of his head he indicated in the direction of the POW camp and I knew what he meant. I had to go back without going inside the hospital hut.

Now I lie on my bunk writing this. All I can think of is Marisa's smile, of her kindness towards me. Of all the times she asked me to sit with her and offered me food and drink that she couldn't really spare. I can't help going over and over the story she told me, about the way she and Aadesh met in Petaling Street in Kuala Lumpur. I think of her as he must have first caught sight of her, emerging from the shop with her graceful movements, her long hair falling around her shoulders, her dark eyes clear and bright. He must have been so struck by her presence and her beauty that even though he was alone and poor, and badly dressed, he knew he had to seize the moment, take his chances there and then and open up a conversation with her.

As I lie here, I can imagine him going up to her and speaking to her for the first time, and for her to turn her gaze on him, to smile and laugh and respond to what he is saying. I can't help feeling how that moment was pivotal in both their lives. How desperately tragic that the happiness they found together ended in such appalling circumstances here in the Burmese jungle.

I remember too, though I try to stop myself thinking these thoughts, how I would walk along Petaling Street on my occasional evenings off when we were stationed in Kuala Lumpur in November 1941, and how I might have seen either or both of them. Would I have even noticed them back then? I'm almost sure I would have noticed Marisa if she had been there then. But I know that in those days I wouldn't have noticed the local people as I do now. They would have just blended into the background for me as people with whom I had nothing in common, and no points of reference. How wrong I was. How deluded. It is ironic how much I've learned from my enforced weeks here in the camp, helping these desperate people, being amongst them and seeing their daily struggles. Witnessing their bravery and dignity in the midst of the most desperate situation and feeling privileged to count them as my friends.

March 1943

The days wear on. The lads in my sleeping hut who have been working on the track, tell me that this section of the railway is almost finished. There is a jumpy feeling amongst the guards. They are quick to clamp down on the most minor transgression at roll call, or failure to bow. We're all wondering what will happen to us then. Will they get rid of us somehow? Or will they take us down the line to another camp?

I am still going through each day into the Asian workers' camp. I help Dr Randall in the hospital, or I do the tasks the Warthog sets for me. I try to bring whatever food I can pilfer to smuggle to Marisa and the baby. It has been two weeks now and although her bruises have healed, she hasn't spoken a word. When she is not sleeping, she stares blankly ahead. She doesn't seem to recognise her surroundings or to respond to what anyone says to her.

The baby has developed a fever and an eye infection. It is so severe that the doctor is worried that he might lose the sight in his right eye. I fear for his life. The orderlies do what they can for him, but there is no medicine at all and very little food. I bring him what I can, but he doesn't want to eat. He lies listlessly beside his mother and grizzles, a thin weedy cry. I worry that he is pining for his parents and that without their love and attention he will just waste away, like so many others.

I cannot bear to think what will happen to the two of them if we are sent away. I know the doctor would do his best, but he has others to care for, and they are just two out of so many.

March 30ᵗʰ 1943

I haven't been able to write in this book for several days. Each evening when the camp settles down, I've tried to, but I've been overcome with exhaustion that I've dropped to sleep on my bunk straight after the evening meal.

Three days ago, when I went to report to the Warthog after roll call, he waved me away with an impatient gesture.

'You no go coolie camp,' he said. 'You work on railway now.'

I stood in front of him for a second and opened my mouth to protest. I saw the anger rise in his eyes.

'You go!' he snapped pointing in the direction of the other men who were collecting tools to take on their long march to the railbed.

Someone handed me a shovel, and I joined one of the work parties who were just setting off into the jungle.

I fell in with a group of men from my unit. As we walked, they explained that the Japs are having a final push to finish this stretch of track. The track bed is built and flattened, chippings have been put down too and now sleepers are being laid. They have been brought by wagon to the end of the line. Each one is so heavy that three men are needed to carry it on their shoulders. They have to be carried to the right place on the line, where the Japanese engineers are waiting to give orders as to the precise place it must be laid.

When we reached the place where work had finished yesterday, we were set to work straight away. After carrying just one sleeper, my shoulders were raw, and bleeding, and I was feeling weak with the effort.

I've worked alongside two men from my hut; Fred and Joey. All day every day they've ribbed me for being weak and soft and not being able to work as quickly as they can.

'You're out of condition, man,' said Fred, laughing, displaying teeth knocked out by an altercation with one of the guards a few months ago.

The ribbing was fair enough and I took it in good part. I didn't want to tell them about the work I'd had to do in the Asian camp. About the horrors of the cholera epidemic, about carrying the bodies to the funeral pyre and watching their final contortions as they burned. I didn't want to speak about the women who sit listlessly in their shabby little huts, starving and helpless. About the brutality and the depravity of the guards. I just keep my silence and work on.

But all the time I think about Marisa and the little boy. I picture her lying there, her eyes empty, the will to live ebbing away from her. I wonder whether she will survive, and whether the baby will recover. I know I must find a way of getting back there and taking them some food. Tomorrow I will try to slip out of the camp and through the undergrowth without the guards noticing. I'll take some of the food I will get from the cookhouse for my own supper.

April 3rd 1943

For the last three nights I've tried to get through into the Asian workers' camp and failed. On the first evening I managed to persuade the men in the cookhouse to give me some leftover slivers of fish. I hid them in my Jap Happy and when the hut had settled down for the night I crept out and made my way to the latrines. From there it is a short walk to the edge of the camp and the path that leads to the Asian camp. But as I neared the perimeter fence, I caught sight of the red glow of a cigarette and I realised that the path was barred by a guard. I stopped dead; my heart beating fast. I prayed that he wouldn't have spotted me.

At the same time I wondered why on earth would they have put a guard there? I retraced my steps to the sleeping hut, frustrated and anxious that once again I couldn't get the food to the baby, that he would pass another night without the extra rations that could help him.

April 4th 1943

We finished laying the sleepers on the last bit of our stretch of track today. Tomorrow a mobile work party will go through on a flatbed rail trolley and lay the rails. This part of the track will be complete. As we walked into camp there was a palpable feeling of relief amongst the men. They had worked together all these months on this stretch of track, from clearing the jungle to flattening the railbed, building embankments and chipping out rock for cuttings. They'd endured beatings, starvation, illness and the loss of many of their mates. But they were relieved it was over, despite the knowledge that this would bring the Japs closer to their aim of completing the railway and being able to supply their war effort in Burma, there was a sense of finality, of achievement almost. I also sensed a feeling of trepidation. We were all wondering what the Japs had in store for us next.

'They'll probably take us back to Changi, or to work on another bit of this god-awful track,' said Fred.

'They need to get us out of here quickly,' said Joey. 'There's another outbreak of cholera in the coolie camp.'

'How do you know that?' I asked sharply.

'They've put guards on the entrance. They're not letting anyone go in or out. Jap or prisoner.'

I was silent for a while as we trudged on through the jungle path, following the bare backs of other men.

'The doctor managed to bring the last outbreak under control,' I said.

'You mean Doc Randall? The Japs have ordered him out of there. He came through yesterday. Didn't you know? They've told him he's needed in the hospital in the POW camp.'

'Why would they do that?' I said, my scalp prickling with alarm. 'If there's cholera surely they need a doctor more than ever in that camp.'

Joey shrugged. 'They're probably cutting their losses. They don't give a damn about the Asian workers, or their families, the poor blighters. The Japs probably think now that the railway's finished here, what does it matter if they all die.'

I trudged on in silence. I knew he was right, but having it spelled out in such brutal terms was hard to take.

I went to find Doctor Randall this evening after my visit to Ernie in the hospital hut. I was desperate for news of Marisa and the baby.

He was cleaning out a tropical ulcer when I approached him. The smell of putrefying flesh was unbearable, the man whose leg he was working on with a metal spoon was writhing in pain, his body bathed in sweat, but Doctor Randall just carried on digging away at the rotting flesh calmly and carefully. I asked him what was happening in the Asian camp. He shook his head.

'It's dreadful. We lost twenty people overnight a couple of nights ago.'

'Why did you come out?'

He put the tool he was working with down.

'I had no choice, Summers. They brought me out at gunpoint.'

'How is Marisa? The baby?'

Again he shook his head.

'I'm sorry, Private. Marisa died two nights ago.'

'Cholera?' There was a huge lump forming in my throat.

'No. Thank God. She was spared that. She just closed her eyes and drifted off. Gave up the fight to live.'

I was silent, fighting back the tears. If only I'd been able to get back to see her.

'What will happen to the child?'

'I left him in charge of a couple of the natives who were doing their best to care for the patients. He was getting better gradually. The eye infection has gone, although as I feared he will never regain the sight in his right eye. I'm sure he'll pull through, though, Private. He's a strong little lad.'

'But what if he gets cholera? Surely the hospital hut is the worst place for him.' I knew he had no answers. But I couldn't help badgering him anyway.

'There's nothing we can do, Summers. We've done what we can.'

I can't help thinking there's still a way of helping the boy. There must be a way through into the camp to take him some food and check how he's doing. All the sadness and grief I'm feeling for Marisa is channelled into thinking about how I can help the boy.

April 5th 1943

THERE WAS NO WORK TODAY. We were given a rest day after roll call, as a reward for completing the track. Most men lay on their bunks, glad of the opportunity to rest away from the baking sun. Others smoked and played cards or chess in the shade of the hut walls or read the few dog-eared books that circulate around the camp.

I wandered along the perimeter of the camp, trying to find a place to get through into the Asian workers' camp. I had to try and make it look as if I was just going for a casual stroll. The barbed wire fence only covered a corner where there was no undergrowth. The rest of the boundary was marked by dense jungle. I managed to pick out a couple of gaps between the great clumps of bamboo where it might be possible to get through.

Before supper I went along to the cookhouse and pilfered some more bits of fatty meat from the cooks. They know me as Robbie's mate, and will often give me some scraps.

I waited until it got dark, when most men were snoring on their bunks, then I crept out of the sleeping hut. There was one guard stationed on the gap in the fence. I crouched under cover of the hut wall and waited for an opportunity to slip across the open ground. Occasionally he left his post and walked the 20 yards or so of the fence and back again.

I waited until his back was turned, then I darted across the open ground to the cover of the bamboo on the perimeter. I had to wait a while there amongst the bamboo until he repeated his short march up and down the fence. I had miscalculated and overshot the gap. I had to come out of my hiding place and feel my way to the opening. Then I took my chances and plunged into the thicket. It took me some time to push my way through to the other side. As I went, I thought I caught the smell of smoke on the air, but it was tough going and I had to concentrate. The bamboo was thick and strong, creepers with thorns were clinging to it and they ripped my bare skin. By the time I crawled out on the other side my arms and legs were scratched and bleeding.

I straightened up, and it was a moment or two before I registered what I was seeing. The stench of kerosene was all around. The huts were on fire; all of them, including the hospital hut. It was burning strongly, and chunks of the roof and walls were dropping down inside, sending showers of sparks out in all directions. The bamboo skeleton of the hut was visible through the flames, and as the walls dropped away, the sleeping platform inside was exposed. I stood rooted in horror. On the sleeping platform were the unmistakable shapes of human bodies. I watched, horrified as the flames licked around them and engulfed them just as they had on the countless funeral pyres Ernie and I had built for the cholera victims. And like those bodies, these too contorted grotesquely as the heat of the fire engulfed them.

Forgetting myself I ran towards the burning hut, a roar of anger and grief escaping my lungs, drowned out by the roar of the flames.

April 6th 1943

There was still a curl of smoke in the sky above the jungle this morning as we trudged out of our huts and lined up for roll call. Images of the burning camp scarred the back of my mind. I was dazed, shocked to the core at what I'd seen. I stared up at the smoke as the Bison strutted along the lines of men, prodding at one here, hitting some with his stick, yelling at others.

'You OK, mate,' the man next to me muttered. 'You look to be in a bad way.'

I had tried to wash the smoke from my body, but I was still streaked and blackened all over, and the cuts and scratches from crawling through the undergrowth were livid and raw in the heat of the morning.

'I saw what they did through there,' I said, nodding in the direction of the smoke. 'They torched the place.' I trailed off. I couldn't find words to describe what I'd seen.

'The Japs are terrified of the cholera,' he muttered. 'I was in a camp down the line where they did the same thing. Burned the victims in their beds. They have no mercy.'

I couldn't answer him. I was thinking of little Kashwin. What had happened to him? Had he succumbed to cholera and been left to die, wretched and alone and in agony, or burned alive by those murderers? How will I even know what happened to him?

April 10th 1943

Tomorrow we leave this camp. The Bison addressed everyone at roll call this morning. We have finished our job here, he said. We should be proud of the work we have done for the Emperor. Having surrendered as we did, instead of fighting to the death as a soldier of honour would have done, we should be proud that we have at least done something of service to the Japanese war effort. I heard men grunting and sniffing in disapproval and discomfort at his words, but we were all avoiding each others' eyes. Shame coursed through me at the thought that we had contributed to the Japs' war effort. And from the look in the Bison's eye as he delivered the speech, he knew exactly how it would make us feel.

They are taking us by train up to Moulmein. We have no idea where they intend to take us after that. If we survive the journey, that is. I leave this book here at Thanbyuzayat. Buried in its usual place under the pomelo tree, near the graves of my dear friends, where so many suffered and died, watched over by Robbie's star. I cannot take it with me. There is no place to hide it in my belongings as we will all be searched before we leave the camp we have been told. I will have to hope that one day, after this mad war has ended, someone, some day will find it and read it and understand the dreadful events that happened here.

26

Louise
Myanmar, 2015

Louise put Jack's diary down and glanced out of the open window as the train limped through the outskirts of Yangon at the end of a journey that had started late and got later and later as the day progressed.

Dusk was now gathering rapidly, and she leaned out of the glassless window to look up at the sky. She was hoping to catch a glimpse of the star her father had been inspired by seventy odd years before. But tonight the weather was brooding and overcast, the sky filled with rainclouds blotting out the moon and the stars.

She sighed and looked across at Eve who was asleep, lolling in the corner of the opposite seat beside the window. Louise smiled. How peaceful her daughter looked and how wonderful that they had made this journey together at last.

When they'd found Jack's diary in Thanbyuzayat, the curator had reluctantly allowed them to take it with them the next day once he'd photocopied it in its entirety. Louise and Eve had agreed to read it simultaneously with Louise reading a few entries before passing it to Eve. But that first evening, they had sat at the bamboo table outside their hut by the light of a paraffin lamp and read the first few extracts out loud to each other. They had both cried as they read, as the light faded, and progress had been slow. They had read long into the night.

This morning she and Eve had boarded the train in Moulmein after spending two days there. Louise had tried to find the Government Guest House where she had stayed in 1988, but although they walked the length of Strand Road with its mixture of modern buildings and crumbling facades, she couldn't for the life of her remember which building it had been housed in. They had visited the 'Old Moulmein Pagoda', and the markets, and interspersed with this they had carried on reading Jack's diary.

It had distracted them from that other story that Louise had been trying to tell Eve; the story of her 1988 journey. Louise had tried to tell Eve as much as she could on the way from Singapore to Thanbyuzayat, but she hadn't told her the most important part yet; the part she knew Eve was aching to know, and she hadn't been able to find the words to tell throughout Eve's twenty-six years of life. But as the train moved further and deeper into the heart of the city, Louise knew that the time and the place had come for her to let Eve know the truth and to face up to it herself.

~

LATER, she sat beside Eve on the back seat of a taxi as it crawled through the gridlocked streets of Yangon. Ahead loomed the glowing stupa of the Schwedagon Pagoda, impossibly immense, lighting up the fading afternoon sky , casting a golden glow over the streets below. Burmese pop music blared from the tinny radio on the dashboard, and the driver puffed absent-mindedly on a cheroot between shifting the gears and grinding the car forward a few feet.

'We should have walked, Mum,' said Eve. 'It's not that far. Why don't we walk now?'

Louise smiled at Eve. It was their first outing in Yangon. They'd arrived first thing this morning on the night train from Moulmein after a sleepless night sitting upright on wooden benches, fending off the insects that flooded through the open windows, drawn in by the neon lights in the carriage. They had checked into the Strand Hotel and fallen straight to sleep after the exhausting train journey.

The lack of sleep had exacerbated Louise's feeling of dreamy detachment, arriving back in the city where so much had happened to her. It had felt odd walking through the crumbling streets of the capital again, carrying a backpack, after so many years away and after so much had changed in her life. She'd thought that she would remember everything about the city, but she was surprised to find that her memory had been selective. She held no memory at all of some of the streets between the railway station and Strand Road.

She'd promised Eve that she would treat them both to a stay in the Strand Hotel, and they had already booked a room, calling ahead from the train. The hotel was expensive now, so Louise had known that it must have been refurbished since she'd stayed there all those years before, but she wasn't prepared for the beauty of the newly restored building. As they entered through the covered portico, she stared around her at the muted décor, at the sumptuous armchairs and gleaming tiled floor. It was a far cry from the shabby, gloomy interior she remembered: the utilitarian reception area, the pillars with their peeling paint.

As they crossed the entrance hall her heart beat faster as she saw the spot where she had met Zeya for the first time. Of course, it wasn't quite the first time, she reminded herself, but the time she'd seen the back of his head in the old Cadillac didn't really count. She stared across the reception hall to the spot where he'd stood that afternoon, tapping his foot, waiting for her impatiently beside the staircase. She'd had to check herself; she was half expecting him to be there, waiting for her still.

The porter showed them up to a beautiful, spacious room on the second floor, overlooking the Yangon river.

Once they'd showered and changed, Louise said;

'Come on. I'll take you down to the bar. It's where I first met Jim.'

'Really, Mum? You didn't tell me that!'

'I know. I should have done. There's quite a bit I still need to tell you Eve.'

Eve smiled at her. She'd seemed to understand that Louise would tell her the rest of her story when the time was right. Jack's diary had eclipsed everything else for both of them for the last few days. They'd been so preoccupied reading about his experiences, passing the diary between them, discussing everything he'd written, ensuring they digested every page to the full. Sometimes what they read had overwhelmed both of them into stunned and contemplative silence. Louise's own story had seemed less important somehow in the face of that. It had to wait its turn.

Eve had suggested they visit the Sule Pagoda, but Louise wasn't ready for that. She needed to acclimatise to the city, feel her feet again, before venturing anywhere near the street where those things had happened to change her life that fateful day in August 1988. And she needed to talk to Eve too, to finish telling her about the past; the story she'd started to tell on the mini-bus to Dawei but hadn't been able to finish. She knew that Eve was waiting for her to continue, and she got the sense that Eve was holding herself back from asking. Waiting for Louise herself to volunteer the rest of the story. Maybe now was the time?

'Let's walk then. Why not?' she said, reaching for the door handle.'

Eve paid the driver, who accepted the loss of his passengers with quiet resignation and they made their way through the stationery traffic to the far pavement.

They started walking along the uneven pavement towards the pagoda, and as they walked Louise got the sense that others were walking too in the same direction. Of course. The Pagoda was a well-known attraction both for tourists and locals alike.

'Was it the same when you were here before?' asked Eve. She must have sensed too, that Louise was ready to speak about it. How perceptive she was.

'The buildings haven't changed much. If anything, it's even more shabby. There are more tourists around. There were hardly any when I was here.'

'Will you tell me about it, Mum?' Eve's voice was tentative, but Louise took her hand.

'Of course. We can talk as we walk up to the Pagoda. There's a lot to tell.'

27

Louise
Moulmein, August 7th 1988

The sun hadn't yet risen as her rickshaw made its way through the dark, silent streets to the quayside. The ferry from Moulmein to the railhead at Martaban was full to bursting, even busier than the one she'd arrived on. Was it really only two days ago? She was swept on board by the swarming crowd in the half-light of dawn. There was excitement in the air, a sense of anticipation that was different from anything she'd experienced on the way down from Rangoon. It was almost a carnival atmosphere. As she looked around her, she realised that the people on board were different from those on the way down too. There were groups of young people instead of families; young men especially, talking feverishly amongst themselves. She thought of Zeya's words;

'People will be coming from all over Burma for our march. You'll see.'

As the steamer drew away from the Moulmein quay and cast out into the current, the waterfront, with its line of semi-derelict colonial buildings gradually melted into the morning mists. Louise leant on the rail and looked back at the town as it shrunk away, receding into the vapour. Soon all she could see was a tree covered peninsula with the spires of temples dotted along its spine.

The train was waiting for the ferry in the station at Martaban. Once again, people scrambled from the ferry and hurried up to the station for the places on the dilapidated carriages. It was even more packed than the one she'd come down on from Rangoon. Louise managed to fight her way onto a third-class carriage, but the seats were already occupied, some with more than one passenger. She spent the first part of the journey perched on her backpack, rocking precariously back and forth in the lobby between carriages, trying to dampen down the nausea she felt, catching the smell of the 'hole in the floor' lavatory on the feotid air. The door had no latch and blew open with every jolt and rattle of the train.

A couple of hours into the journey a family got down with their assorted baggage and children at a village station, and the other passengers, with smiles and gestures, motioned to Louise to take up a spare seat in the corner of the carriage.

She sat on the wooden bench beside the open window as the train rattled through the countryside, watching the rocky hills with temples perched like shimmering eagles' nests on top, and the rice paddies roll by as the dust blew in and dried her mouth and filled her hair. She found herself thinking of Zeya. She had protested to Thuza that there was no need for Zeya to meet her at the station, but in spite of that, she realised that she was looking forward to seeing him. She was slightly surprised at the feeling that grew inside her as the train got closer to Rangoon. She even began to fret that he might not be there after all. The thought of returning alone to the Strand Hotel and leaving the country without ever seeing him again filled her with emptiness.

She got out her passport and examined the stamp on her visa. She only had two more nights left before the seven days were up. The airline ticket to Bangkok was in her money belt. She got that out too and stared at it, trying to imagine being back there in Bangkok on the Khao San road, swapping travellers' tales with other young backpackers. There were no words to convey what she'd experienced over the past few days here in Burma and she knew she wouldn't be speaking about what she'd seen and done; not to anyone.

She closed her eyes and thought back over everything that had happened since she'd stepped off that flight five days ago. From trading her whisky in the old Cadillac to spending time with Zeya and meeting his friends in the teashop, agreeing to smuggle the papers down to Moulmein in return for his help; riding in the back of the truck hidden in durian fruits down to Thanbyuzayat; sleeping in the monastery, and the gentle kindness of the monks there, of the kind bravery of Thuza, of Neema, who had given her her ID papers, of Mo Chit and of everyone she had met here. The pleasure and warmth she felt was tinged with regret though, at not having found Jack's diary. But she would be back. She promised herself that. One day she would be back and somehow she would find a way of getting to the camp and finding it if it was still there.

Zeya was waiting on the platform as the train creaked and groaned into the station. She saw him before he caught sight of her and her heart swelled with relief. He was dressed in a white shirt and a blue checked longyi, scanning the carriages with his eyes shaded against the flickering neon lights on the platform. Louise smiled inwardly. He had that impatient look about him again, shifting around, tapping his foot, just as he had done that day he came to meet her in the Strand. Was it really only a few days ago?

'Come quickly,' he said, taking her arm as soon as she got down. 'Let me take your pack.'

He was unsmiling, his face tense.

'Why? What's the hurry?'

'Police will be boarding that train, searching passengers. You don't want to get caught up in it.'

Sure enough, as he took her by the elbow and ushered her off the platform, a group of policemen in black uniforms bearing batons and guns pushed them out of the way, making for the train. Zeya hurried her across the concourse, barging through the crowds of passengers ambling for trains in the opposite direction. She could feel his tense fingers gripping her arm all the way, the urgent press of his body behind her.

Outside on the pavement he stopped, let go of her arm, and adjusted the backpack as the crowd thronged around them. His face relaxed for a moment and he smiled down at her; that broad smile that lit up his whole face, displaying his white teeth. Looking up into his eyes, Louise couldn't help smiling back. It was almost a reflex response to his smile; impossible not to.

'That was close,' he said. 'The police know that supporters of our movement have arrived on that train. Come. Come this way. You will be safe with me.'

He shouldered her backpack and began striding in the direction of the river.

'I could always go back to the hotel,' she began, hurrying after him. It reminded her of the first day he had guided her around the city.

He shook his head. 'It is too risky. The authorities will probably have checked up on your movements. They might even know you went to Thanbyuzayat. If you surface today, when security is at its height, they could take you in for questioning.'

Shock washed through her at his words. Was that true? How could anyone have found out about where she'd been? Her mind flew to the old man on the reception at the Government Guest house in Moulmein. Surely he wouldn't have reported that she'd been missing for a night?

'Are you sure? How do you know?'

He shot a look at her, the smile gone. 'Believe me. I know what happens in this country. I've seen tourists arrested for far less. You must stay with us until the march is over, then tomorrow evening, you must go straight to the airport. That way you might escape notice.'

She hadn't bargained on this. Suddenly her return to Rangoon had become complicated and fraught. Her body ached from the long journey. She felt wobbly from lack of sleep; she certainly didn't feel ready for more danger. She suddenly realised how naive she must have been, to have looked forward to collapsing into a bed at the Strand Hotel and sleeping for hours. She glanced up at Zeya as they walked, side by side now. Could she really trust him?

'You go back to the Strand if you like,' he said, as if he could read her thoughts. 'But it would be better to stay with me. Believe me.'

She looked away, shamefaced, in two minds. Surely there could be no danger if she just went back to the Strand and checked in quietly? She glanced up at him again. He was still waiting for her to answer. There was something in his look that told her to trust him.

'OK. I'll come,' she said after they'd walked a few more steps. 'Where are we going?'

'To my place. Down near the river, off Merchant Street. It's only small, but you can stay there and rest. Tomorrow morning, I will be going on the march. I think it better you stay away and afterwards make your own way to the airport. OK?'

'But ... couldn't I come with you? On the march? I'd like to be part of it. We talked about it before. Remember?'

He shrugged. 'Now I don't think that would a good idea.

Things are more dangerous than I thought. You would be noticed. You could be arrested.'

'Seriously? But surely there'll be so many people they wouldn't notice me?'

He didn't answer, just carried on walking, striding out silently. She followed him through the maze of streets where shopkeepers were opening their shutters and vendors were setting up food stalls for the day. Delicious smells of frying meat, of herbs and spices, floated on the air, but there was something else too. There were more people around than she'd noticed at this hour before. Several of them nodded to Zeya, looking at him with a sideways look before flicking their eyes away.

They turned off Merchant Street and walked down a narrow street flanked with tall terraced townhouses. Zeya stopped halfway along.

'Here it is.'

She looked up at the house. It was shabby, like all its neighbours, with crumbling façade, greenery sprouting from the walls and rusting iron balconies on the top floors. He pushed open the front door and beckoned her into the dark interior. The bare wooden staircase wound straight up in front of them. Zeya bounded up the stairs, two at a time.

'Come,' he said, looking back over his shoulder. 'Second floor.'

She followed him up the bare wooden staircase into the stifling gloom. He unlocked a battered door on the second-floor landing and beckoned her to follow him.

She went inside and looked around. He was standing in the middle of a small room, an expectant look on his face.

'It is not much, but it is my home,' he said, spreading his arms out in a gesture of welcome.

There were some brightly coloured floor cushions along one wall, and a low table in the middle of the room. Patterned curtains hung at the windows, which overlooked the street, and scarlet bougainvillea burst through the bars of the balcony. In one corner of the room was a tiny camping stove and a kettle. The back wall was covered with books, stacked on shelves, floor to ceiling. Through an open door she glimpsed a bedroom, with a low bed, covered with an embroidered cover. She was surprised at how tidy and ordered the place was; how neatly and sparsely Zeya must live in these two tiny rooms.

'Sit down, sit down, please.' He flicked a switch and a ceiling fan began whirring overhead.

'It's very nice,' she said, sitting on the cushions, while he busied himself in the corner putting a kettle on the stove. Louise stretched her legs out, exhaustion seeping through her bones and muscles.

'I will make some tea,' Zeya said, smiling down at her. 'You must be thirsty after your journey.'

He sat down beside her and they sipped the clear jasmine tea that he poured from a metal teapot into tiny china cups. He wanted to hear all about what had happened to her during the past two days, beginning with her trip down to Moulmein with the false ID papers. She told him about the tense train journey when the youths were pulled off the train and beaten by the police on that remote village platform. Zeya shook his head, his eyes narrowed, filled with pain and anger. She told him about meeting Thuza and handing over the papers, about Neema who had lent her clothes and her ID; about hiding in the back of the truck amongst the durian fruits (this elicited wide smiles and laughter from Zeya). She talked about the terror of the road-blocks, and finally about the peace and tranquility of the monastery.

All the time she was speaking he listened intently, sitting motionless beside her, his eyes fixed on her face. Sometimes he exclaimed, sometimes he laughed, sometimes he clicked his tongue in disapproval and shook his head. When she finished, there was silence in the small room. Down in the street the buzz of a scooter echoed between the buildings, the distant sound of horns on the main road. Voices of children playing floated up through the window.

His eyes held her gaze for a moment. Then he said.

'You are very brave, Louise. Very brave indeed.'

It was the first time he had called her by her name.

She was wondering how to reply, when Zeya sprang to his feet and busied himself gathering the cups, taking them through into the bedroom where she could hear his sluicing them under a tap.

'My friends will come later,' he said. 'When they have finished their studies for the day. We will have a meal together and plan for the march tomorrow. But first, perhaps you'd like to take a shower and rest for a while?'

He handed her a threadbare towel and directed her to a tiled washroom along the landing, where there was a plastic hose attached to a tap and a couple of tin buckets. She peeled off her clothes, damp with the sweat and grime of the journey and sluiced herself down. The water felt deliciously cool on her skin, but she was careful not to use too much, conscious that it was probably scarce and expensive.

When she'd dried herself and dressed in a fresh T shirt and some drawstring trousers she'd bought in Bangkok, she felt revived.

'Why don't you rest for a while?' said Zeya when she was back in his room. 'You can take my bed. I need to go out for an hour or two. There are some people I need to see about tomorrow, and I must go to the market and get some food for this evening.'

She hesitated. What was she doing? Alone in a flat with a young Burmese man, about to accept an offer to go into his bedroom, lie down on his bed. Was that stepping over an invisible line? Grace's voice was suddenly in her head.

You must be careful, Louise, in those far off countries. They don't know our customs and we don't know theirs. You need to keep your

*wits about you. You sometimes give the wrong impression. You know
that don't you?*

Was she giving the wrong impression now?

Zeya was looking at her, waiting, an embarrassed frown on
his face, wondering no doubt why she hadn't replied.

'It's alright,' she said, feeling the colour rush into her cheeks. 'I
can just lie down on these cushions here.'

'You don't need to worry,' he said. 'I will sleep on those cushions tonight. I put new sheets on the bed for you. It is your home
for tonight. Please…'

'That's very kind of you, but…' her cheeks were burning now.

'No please. I insist. You must be very tired. You must not
worry about it. There is no problem.'

Wanting to spare him further embarrassment, she stepped
inside the room and smiled up at him. 'Alright. Thank you. You're
being too generous. There was no need…'

'It is just our Burmese way. Hospitality is very important in
our country. Now please. Rest and be comfortable here. I will be
back in an hour or so.'

He shut the door behind her and she looked round the room.
It was sparsely furnished apart from the bed, a low table with a
lamp beside it, and a desk under the window, stacked with books
and papers. Glancing at them, she saw a page of equations and
diagrams. She quickly realised they were the books from his engineering course; that this was where he must sit to study.

She lay on the bed and began to read her book, but her eyes
skated across the page, not taking in any of the words. They kept
wandering to Zeya's desk. She imagined him sitting down there
in the evenings, after a day guiding tourists around the city in the
sapping heat, poring over his textbooks as the light faded outside.
She thought of his dogged determination to get his degree, and
that of all his friends, and compared it, once again, to her own
lack of direction. How could she have just walked away from her
studies like that? She'd been telling everyone, and even herself

that it was because of her father's illness, but deep down she knew it wasn't really that.

She sat up, feeling her cheeks heat up with embarrassment, even now, several months after she'd left, at the humiliation she'd suffered; the real reason that she'd run away from her studies. She thought of the English Literature tutor she'd become infatuated with; how she'd hung around after tutorials just to get to speak to him alone, not realising that everyone else on the course had noticed and were laughing at her behind her back. She recalled how he'd asked her to stay behind after the others one day for a drink and she'd ended up in his bed. For her it had meant everything, but he'd made it clear in the morning that it was a one off; that she meant nothing to him and that if she made a fuss, he would ensure that she failed the course.

She'd struggled on for a few weeks, enduring comments and ridicule from other students. When she'd received the call from the hospital that Jack was ill, it had seemed the perfect opportunity to walk away from the university and focus on her father instead. She sighed now, thinking back over it, angry with herself for her own weakness and naivety.

Soon her eyes became heavy. She lay back and drifted off to the sounds of the restless city, the children playing in the street and the car horns and boat sirens from the docks on the Strand Road.

When she awoke it felt as though hours had passed. The bedroom door had been closed and she could hear Zeya moving about in the other room. She got up hastily, yawning and stretching.

'You slept a long time,' he said as she came through. 'Please, sit down. I've just made some more tea. My friends will arrive soon.'

The low table was loaded with dishes of food; curries, pickles, spices and flat breads.

'Did you make all this?'

He laughed. 'No. There is not much room for cooking here. I bought it from my friend who runs the food-stall at the end of the road. It is cheap. And good. Help yourself.'

'Oh no. I'll wait until your guests arrive.'

Soon there were voices on the stairs. Zeya opened the door to the five friends Louise had met in the teashop on the first day he'd guided her around the city. No-one showed any surprise at her being there. They greeted her as if she was an old friend.

Louise struggled to remember their names, and only three of them came to mind. The two young women, Myat Noe and Yupar, were probably younger than herself, but they seemed to have so much more self-possession and poise as they entered the room, greeting her with warm smiles and handshakes. She also remembered Nakaji, the slight young man with the serious face who had spoken with such passion about the shocking events of March 12th. The two others followed, and Zeya introduced them as Denpa and Htut.

'They are brothers,' Zeya explained with his broadest smile, and Louise then noticed the resemblance between the two.

Everyone sat on the cushions or cross –legged on the floor and Zeya handed out plates and cups of tea.

'I hear you have been down to Thanbyuzayat,' said Myat Noe to Louise, as she delicately rolled some pickles into a flat bread. 'Zeya mentioned that you were taking something to Thuza for our movement.'

Louise nodded.

'We're very grateful to you for doing that,' said Nakajii, leaning forward, speaking in his quiet way. 'Before you came, we couldn't think of a way of getting those things to Thuza. He and others down there might not have been able to come for tomorrow.'

'It was nothing,' Louise said, feeling self-conscious that the eyes of everyone in the room were on her.

'You will come on our march tomorrow?' it was Yupa's voice. Louise glanced at Zeya who was frowning.

'No,' he shook his head. 'It's not a good idea. It will be too dangerous. She could get arrested.'

Yupa laughed. 'There is no need to be so protective, Zeya,' she said. 'Louise can take care of herself. She's come all the way from England by herself after all, she got down to Thanbyuzayat and back without too much of a problem.'

Louise glanced up at Zeya. She noticed spots of colour on his high cheek bones and she looked away.

'Well?' demanded Yupa. 'what do you say, Myat Noe?'

Myat Noe put down her plate and smiled up at Zeya. 'She should come, brother. What is the problem? There is no more danger for her than for any of us. And if you think about it, it is good that foreigners will be there to see what happens. Perhaps Louise will take the story back to her country, spread the word about how we students in Burma are fighting for democracy.'

'Of course,' Louise found herself saying, caught up in Myat Noe's enthusiasm. 'I will come. I want to come with you. I'm not afraid.'

Zeya was shaking his head still.

'Oh come on!' said Yupa.

Zeya held up his hands. 'OK, OK,' he said. 'I can't stop you. You are welcome to march with us, but if you do get arrested, we won't be able to help you. We will be powerless.'

Louise felt chills running through her body at his words. What on earth was she letting herself in for? Again, she heard her mother's voice in her head, *You're so impulsive, Louise. Just like your father. When are you going to learn?*

The others had fallen silent, waiting for her to speak.

'I'm not afraid,' she said. 'If you are all going. I should come with you too.'

They clapped enthusiastically; all except Zeya, who got up suddenly and began collecting up dishes and cups. Myat Noe and

Yupa exchanged glances but said nothing and the conversation moved on. They spoke of their hopes for the next day; how it could be the beginning of the end of the military regime. Louise sensed the excitement in the room, the pent-up energy suppressed during the years of oppressive rule.

They talked for hours, until it grew dark outside. Then the friends drifted away from Zeya's apartment in ones and twos, taking leave of each other with emotional embraces, their faces full of apprehension for what the next day would bring.

When the last guest had gone, Louise got up from the cushions and stretched her aching limbs. She helped Zeya wash the dishes and cups, clear up the food scraps. He spoke little as they worked, his gaze turned away from her. In the end she said,

'If you don't want me to go tomorrow, I won't.'

'It's fine,' he said. 'I'm sorry. It is good that you want to join us. I shouldn't have tried to stop you.'

'It's kind of you to be concerned. But I'll be fine.'

They were standing side by side next to the washbasin in the tiny bedroom. He turned to look at her, his eyes serious.

'You have no idea about this country,' he said suddenly, a bitter edge to his tone. 'This is just a game to you, isn't it? Something to tell your friends when you're back home? Something daring you got caught up in.'

'No, not at all!' she said, stung by his words.

'You don't know what we've all been through down the years. What we'll still be going through once tomorrow is over. We have to carry on whatever happens. We can't just get on a plane and fly back somewhere safe.'

She hung her head. 'I'm sorry,' she whispered.

'You Westerners are all the same. You dip into it for a week. You think you are experiencing the real Burma. You know nothing about us or this country really.'

'Well why don't you tell me?' she said, finding her voice again. 'Tell me about your life. How can I know if you don't tell me?'

She forced herself to look straight back at him. He was staring at her, his eyes blazing, full of pent up frustration. The intensity of his gaze made her want to look away, but her instinct told her that it would be a cowardly thing to do; that it would reinforce everything he'd just said.

Neither of them spoke for several minutes. It seemed like a lifetime. The tension hovered between them and Louise realized how little she did know him. His change of mood had unnerved her. Again she thought of Grace; of what she might say.

'All right. I'm sorry,' he said finally, 'That was wrong of me.'

'I'm serious. I want to know. Please tell me.'

He didn't reply. He just carried on looking at her. Still she couldn't make out the expression in his eyes, but she knew it would be a bad move to release his gaze.

'I won't know if you don't tell me, will I?' she asked again gently.

'All right. I will tell you,' he said finally, reluctance in his voice. He released her gaze and motioned her to sit down on the cushions.

She sat down beside him and he began to speak. Slowly and quietly, his head bowed forward, his fringe flopping in front of his face so she couldn't see his eyes.

'I was born in a small town just outside the city,' he began, almost in a whisper. 'My parents were not rich, but they were educated. My father had studied English at the university here you see. He was a schoolteacher. In his spare time at weekends, he ran a second-hand bookstall at the local market. He was determined for people to read, and that literature and reading was the best way to keep a sense of independence during the worst of the military rule. He had grown up under British rule and didn't have any time for the British, but he did realise that their literature... that is, your literature, speaks to us all.

'Some of the books he sold were banned. He kept them hidden in the house at home and he had some secret contacts who would supply them. He would pass them on to people he knew he could trust to keep his secrets. Only one day someone must have informed the authorities of what he was doing. The police came to the house, arrested him and took him away.'

Louise gasped. 'How dreadful for you.'

'That was when I was ten years old. I am twenty-five now and he is still in Rangoon jail, in a cell with four other men. He hasn't been out once since that day. He is fifty-five years old now, but he looks like an old man. His sight is failing but they have not given him glasses. He was in jail for two years before he came to trial. The trial was a farce. The judge was biased- he must have been bribed. He didn't listen to my father's lawyer. He'd already made up his mind. My father was convicted and sentenced to twenty-five years in jail.'

'How awful,' Louise murmured, shocked, not knowing what to say. Her words sounded so inadequate. 'Do you ever see him?'

'I only get to see him once or twice a year. My mother too. It has destroyed her life. She too has grown old prematurely. She barely goes outside the house and hardly eats. She is so afraid. She can no longer work. She depends on me and my cousins for money to live. That is why I work with my cousins. You know, they operate on the black market.'

She thought of the old Cadillac, the covert transaction with the whisky that first day.

'What do your cousins do exactly?' she asked.

'Oh, you know. Currency deals. Smuggling. Nothing big, but it's risky all the same.'

'So, you see now,' he said, leaning forward and looking at her intently once again, 'You understand the reasons why I hate the regime; why tomorrow's march is so important to me.'

His eyes were no longer blazing with anger and indignation. Instead, they were full of pain, and to her surprise, they were shining with tears in the half light. Zeya didn't blink, but a drop escaped and rolled down his cheek. Still he didn't move.

Almost as a reflex action, Louise lifted her hand and wiped the tear away with her finger. As she drew away, he took her hand in his.

'I'm sorry,' she said. He shook his head.

'It's fine.'

'I mean I'm sorry for everything you've told me. About what happened to your father.'

Still holding her hand, he lifted it to his lips and kissed it gently. The sudden feel of his lips on her fingers sent shivers through her.

'I'm sorry too,' he said, 'For what I said just then. I'm not angry with you... Just with being in this situation - with the world, I suppose.'

'I understand,' she said, but she didn't take her hand away. It felt quite natural to leave it in his. They sat there, side by side on the cushions, holding hands in silence, enveloped by the sounds of the street floating up through the window, and the distant buzz and hum of the city.

Louise wondered what she could say about her own life that was remotely comparable. Zeya was right. Westerners had no idea what it was to suffer in poverty under a harsh, unjust regime. She thought with shame, as she had before, about how she'd squandered her own chances at university, and of the ultimate humiliation she'd suffered. She closed her eyes. She couldn't think about that now.

Then, she felt Zeya move closer to her, and suddenly his soft lips were on her eyelids, covering them with kisses, then on her face, and then he was kissing her lips and she was kissing him back. She slid her arms around his neck, pulling him to her, kissing him urgently. Then she was running her hands inside his shirt, feeling his smooth cool skin against hers. She was pulling him closer and closer until he was moving on top of her and she could feel the strength and energy of him pressing against her, melding with her movements. She drew him into her deeper and deeper, quicker and quicker until she opened her eyes and he was staring deeply into them as they moved together in the darkness.

Afterwards they lay side by side on the cushions in the dark apartment. The only light was from a flickering street lamp outside the window. They spoke in whispers, even though they were alone. He told her about his childhood in the village, about his friends at the small school there and about the strength and love of his parents. In turn, Louise told him about Grace; about her courage and support and she told him about Jack too, and of the promise she'd made to him as he lay dying.

'I feel as though I've failed him this week,' she said softly. 'Not being able to get to the camp to look for his diary like I promised.'

Zeya shifted beside her and she felt him prop himself up on his elbow.

'Perhaps I could find it for you?' he said. She opened her eyes. She could see his face close to her, his eyes glinting in the half-light.

'Do you think you could?' she asked, holding her breath. He sat up, drawing his knees up.

'Of course. It is possible. After tomorrow, when things have settled down, I will go down to Thanbyuzayat for you. I will find a way. But before you go tomorrow, you must tell me where this diary is buried, and I will go there. If it is there, I will find it for you.'

'Would you really? Wouldn't it be dangerous?' she asked, stroking his hair. He'd already given voice to the words that she'd been dreading. A reminder that she must leave the country the next day. How could she bear to do that, after what had happened between them? She already knew she wanted to stay with him, to be close to him, to hear his voice, talk to him endlessly, to feel his touch, to know everything about him.

'I will find a way,' he said, taking her face in his hands, turning it towards his and kissing her again.

28

Louise
Yangon, 2015

Louise and Eve had reached the platform of the great Shwedagon Pagoda. They hadn't taken the lift, preferring instead to climb the long flights of covered stairs between the stalls loaded with incense, and lotus flowers for temple offerings, as well as jewellery and tourist bric-a-brac. Louise had talked as they climbed, telling Eve all about how she'd met Zeya, and about that fateful night, more than twenty-seven years ago. Finally, as they emerged onto the platform of the great temple they were engulfed in bright sunlight. Eve stopped and stared up at the spectacle of the shimmering stupa that towered above them, at the endless golden shrines and elaborate statues crowded around its base.

'It's stunning isn't it?' said Louise, remembering how Zeya had guided her around the base of the stupa that first day he'd shown her around the city. She recalled how all the time they'd walked, he spoke in a formal, stilted voice, explaining the history of the pagoda, the significance of the various shrines and statues, an anxious frown on his face, keen that he should tell her everything; that nothing should be missed out of her tour.

Eve remained silent, lost in thought. They began to wander clockwise around the platform. But they hadn't gone far when Eve stopped beside one of the shrines. There were a couple of tiled benches beside some marble steps.

'Let's sit here, Mum, while you finish telling me. I can't concentrate on sightseeing. I need to know everything before we can go on.'

They sat down, side by side.

'Zeya is my father, isn't he?' Eve said, her eyes searching Louise's face, an anxious frown on her face.

Louise nodded. Unbidden tears welling in her eyes.

'You've got to tell me everything now, Mum,' said Eve. 'Why did you lose touch with him? Why keep it a secret all those years? Why ever didn't you tell me about him before?'

Louise swallowed hard brushing a tear from her cheek impatiently. She didn't want to cry now. She needed to be strong, so she could find the right words. She must tell Eve everything. She owed it to her.

She took a deep breath.

'You were conceived that night, Eve. August 7th 1988. It was our only night together.' She paused, pursing her mouth, working hard to swallow her tears, to find the right words.

'I lost Zeya the next day.'

There was a pause. She could feel Eve's eyes on her face, incredulous, accusing.

'Lost him? Whatever do you mean? How?'

'The next day we went on the march. The 8888 march that Zeya and his friends had all been so keyed up about. It was supposed to be a peaceful protest. And it was at first. There was a wonderful atmosphere. People marching seemed full of hope and joy. Singing, chanting. But when everyone had gathered at the Sule Pagoda, the soldiers suddenly appeared. They had orders to stamp out any protest, however peaceful. They came with their tanks and guns and started beating people, shooting randomly. I was arrested and Zeya was dragged away by the soldiers.'

'What happened to him?' Eve was staring at her now, her face full of anguish.

Louise hesitated. There was no easy way to deliver the news.

'He was shot, Eve. Shot by a firing squad. I heard it happen.'

Eve gasped and Louise felt her body stiffen beside her on the bench. Then she felt Eve's hand taking hers and squeezing it.

'Why? Why did they shoot him?'

Louise shook her head, she could hardly form the words, but she knew she must go on.

'He was a member of a banned group. Anti-government protesters. The military leaders decided to crack down on them. They couldn't brook any protest; any challenge to their regime. Zeya was rounded up with a lot of other young men. They were shoved into an alleyway, lined up against a wall and mowed down with machine guns.'

She glanced at Eve, whose eyes were filled with tears.

'How awful,' Eve whispered at last.

They sat in silence for a while, watching a procession of monks clad in maroon robes walk past them holding offerings of incense and lotus blossom, moving sedately in single file towards one of the shrines.

At last Eve said, 'But I still don't understand. Why didn't you tell me about him Mum? Why keep it a secret all these years?'

'I'm so sorry, Eve. I've felt so guilty about keeping it from you. It was selfish of me I know. It's hard to explain why. I just tried to blot it all out. I didn't want to think about it. It was just far too painful. And I wasn't myself after what happened that day. I was in shock for a long time; years, perhaps. I hardly knew what was going on some of the time. I wasn't in my right mind.'

'What happened to you, Mum?'

'I was arrested during the march too. It was total chaos. I was terrified when the soldiers turned up with their tanks and their guns. A couple of them dragged me off to a truck and took me to a police station. I was in total shock. I couldn't believe what I'd just seen. I was reeling from what had happened to Zeya and the others.

'They put me in a cell in the police station. There were lots of other women in a great big cage in there who'd been arrested on the march. Some of them were screaming and shouting, some had been beaten and were covered in blood. The police put me in a separate cell. I was in a dreadful state. I just lay on the hard bed, crying my heart out, not knowing what to do. After a while they took me into another room and asked me a lot of questions about who I'd been with, why I'd been on the march. I didn't give anything away. I was in shock about Zeya and petrified for his friends. The police weren't violent towards me but the whole thing was so intimidating. I thought I would never get out, Eve. I'd been there for three days and nights when they told me there was someone to see me.'

Eve looked at her expectantly. 'Jim?'

'Of course. It was Jim. Was I glad to see him! He took charge of everything. He spent a long time speaking to the police chief. Eventually he managed to convince them that I knew nothing. That I hadn't been with anyone on the march, that I'd just been out sightseeing and got caught up in it by chance.

'It took him several hours, but finally they agreed to let me go. Then he went back to the embassy and organized some temporary papers for me to get me out of the country. By this time my visa had expired of course. Jim was so kind, Eve. I had no idea what would have happened if he hadn't come along.'

'How did he know you were there?'

'They searched my pockets and I still had his card on me. The one he'd given me on my first day in Burma. The police must have phoned him at the British Embassy and told them I'd been arrested. I don't think they wanted any trouble with foreigners. They didn't know what to do with me. When I was released, Jim told me that the embassy had booked me on a flight to Bangkok that was leaving the next day. He said that he was going to Bangkok on the same flight.'

'Why was that?'

'It was his last day in the job and he was going to spend a week in Thailand before flying back to the UK. So I went with him. I stayed in the Strand Hotel again that last night. I didn't have any of my stuff – it was all at Zeya's. Jim got me a few essentials, organised a taxi to the airport, and we sat together on the flight. When we got to Bangkok, he asked me where I was going to stay. I hadn't got a clue. I'd hardly thought about it. When I vaguely mentioned the Khao San Road, he laughed his head off.'

"Come on Louise. Have a bit more style, for God's sake,' he said. 'You can come and stay with me in the Oriental. It's a beautiful old building and it's right on the river. The best place to stay in Bangkok. I'll show you around.'

'I was too numb to resist, Eve. I let him take control. Sort everything out.'

And so it had started. The next chapter in her life. Louise fell silent. She remembered how she'd let Jim distract her, take her out and about. He knew the city well and showed her a different side to Bangkok than the one she'd experienced as a backpacker. He took her to hidden temples at dawn to listen to the morning chanting of the monks, to markets in backstreets selling amulets and antiques that only the locals knew, to obscure food stalls down buried alleyways where Jim spoke to the owners in fluent Thai and where they sampled the most delicious, authentic food imaginable. After a couple of days, the resistance movement, Zeya, everything that had happened to her in Burma had seemed like a dream. But she watched the news reports showing Aung San Suu Kyi, with her charismatic charm becoming the unexpected leader of the protest movement, with tears in her eyes. If only Zeya could have been part of that renewal of hope.

They flew back to England together and Jim offered to put her up in the spare room in his flat in Chelsea. She drifted along with his suggestions, still too shocked to think properly, to make decisions for herself. Jim started his new job in the City and Louise found bar work in a pub in the King's Road. After a few weeks, to her astonishment, she discovered that she was pregnant. She remembered telling Jim.

'I'll take care of you Louise. You don't need to worry.'

And so he had. She couldn't recall at this distance in time precisely how it happened that she had moved from the spare room into Jim's own, and that within a couple of months they were married; a quiet ceremony in Chelsea town hall. Grace had been there, a couple of Louise's friends from university and a handful of Jim's friends and colleagues. Afterwards, they'd celebrated in the pub where Louise worked. Louise had gone through the whole thing like a sleepwalker. She'd hardly cared what happened to her. But at any time of the day or night something might happen to transport her back to that alleyway in Rangoon, the sound of tanks and guns ringing in her ears, watching in horror as Zeya was dragged away, the shock of those shots that had ended it all.

'Will you take me there?' Eve's voice broke into her thoughts.

'Where?'

'Everywhere. Everywhere that you went with him? The Sule Pagoda? The apartment? The places he showed you?'

Louise hesitated. How could she go back there? To the place where everything had happened. Would that alleyway still be there? A chill went through her at the thought of going there again. She glanced at Eve's expectant face, her dark eyes searching her face. The eyes that so reminded her of his? How could she deny her anything at this moment? After keeping her in the dark all these years?

'Of course,' she said, forcing a smile. 'Come on. Let's go back down the steps and find a taxi.'

~

THE SULE PAGODA was just as Louise remembered it; rising up in all its golden splendour in the middle of a traffic roundabout, partly hidden by unsightly modern buildings. The last time she'd been here it had been surrounded by a moving sea of protesters who'd filled the roads and pavements. Now those same roads were filled with slow-moving traffic, belting out smoke fumes and engine noise in the heat.

Louise paused on the pavement opposite the temple, Eve beside her, staring up at the ancient stupa. A chill went through her at the thought that this temple had not changed since that fateful day in August 1988. It had stood on the same spot for hundreds of years. It struck her as odd that the buildings looked just as they had that day, bearing silent witness to everything that had happened around them then and since.

She took Eve's arm and they dodged through the lines of vehicles. Then they walked between the shops through one of the covered entrances and mounted the steep steps to the temple platform. A group of guides hung about chatting near the entrance. One of them detached himself from the group and approached them. He was short, slight, with an intelligent face behind thick black-rimmed spectacles.

'May I show you ladies around the temple?' he asked in perfect English. They agreed a modest price and he told them his name was Kywe.

He walked them slowly around the temple platform, pointing out the various shrines and symbols, telling them the history of the building. He was eloquent, and his stories of the Buddha and of the history of the temple caught Louise's imagination.

'Is this your first time in Myanmar?' he asked as they had

almost completed a full circuit around the base of the pagoda. Louise shook her head.

'I was here when I was in my twenties. In 1988 actually.'

His eyebrows shot up and he stopped walking and turned to look at her.

'A turbulent year for our country,' he said shaking his head gravely. 'Many people died or were imprisoned in the riots.'

'Do you remember it yourself?'

'Oh yes,' he said, lowering his voice, subtly drawing them into the shadows of a doorway to one of the shrines. 'I lost an uncle in the crackdown in August that year. None of us will ever forget what those young men and women sacrificed for us. But we never give up. That year, our Lady, Aung San Suu Kyi came to us. And because of her, there is hope for our country now.'

Louise glanced at Eve, who had been silent and reflective in the taxi from the Shwedagon. She had hardly spoken as they'd followed Kywe around the Sule Pagoda. It worried Louise that Eve was so silent. What was going through her mind, now that she knew the truth? She watched her daughter anxiously, trying to read her expressions, her movements. She hoped fervently that Eve would understand the reasons for Louise's own silence; and that if Eve *was* angry with her, that she wouldn't be angry for long. The two of them had been closer on this trip than they had been for years. Reading Jack's diary had created a new, stronger bond, repairing some of the past misunderstandings that had put distance between them.

Finally, they completed their tour around the base of the pagoda. Kywe showed them to the exit.

'Would you like me to accompany you to visit some other places in Yangon?' he asked. 'The old colonial buildings are very interesting, you know. Some of the former headquarters of the trading companies and banks. The High Court building... or if you prefer some local colour, I could show you to one of our traditional tea shops.'

Louise's scalp prickled at the words. The tea-shop. Of course.

'I went to a tea shop when I was here before,' she said. 'I wonder if it's still there?'

Kywe inclined his body forward and smiled. 'It could well be. Some of our Yangon tea shops have been in the same place for centuries. Do you remember where it was exactly? There are very many of them to choose from, I'm afraid.'

Louise fell silent, racking her brains for some memory; something about the teashop that would set it apart from the others. She was aware of the chanting of the monks and the temple gongs, of the horns and engines on the road outside. Kywe was waiting, watching her patiently, his head tilted sideways in expectation.

'I can't remember very much about it,' she said, frowning, but then it came to her. 'There was a young shoe-shine boy working outside. People would leave their shoes with him to be cleaned while they went inside for a cup of tea.'

Kywe's eyes lit up behind the thick glasses.

'Ah yes... I remember that one well,' he said with a broad smile. 'It was in Pansodan Street,' but then his face fell. 'But I'm afraid I must disappoint you, Madam. That particular tea shop was closed down during the troubles that year I'm afraid...'

Louise's heart sank. He didn't need to say more. He must know that the teashop had been a place where pro-democracy activists had gathered. She shuddered, not wanting to imagine what might have happened there when the soldiers came to shut the place down.

'But don't worry,' the guide went on, recovering his smile. 'There is another one nearby. A few doors along from it in fact. It isn't quite the same, but I can take you there. I often take foreign visitors as part of a tour of the city.'

Louise hesitated, wondering if the place he was suggesting was full of tourists just like them.

'Let's go there, Mum,' said Eve, speaking for the first time since they had left the Shwedagon Pagoda. 'I'm sure we could both do with a sit down and a cup of tea.'

The teashop opened on to the street and you had to step down from the pavement to get inside. Louise and Eve had to duck their heads as the ceiling was so low. They sat at low tables on wooden chairs overlooking the street, and Kywe ordered tea from the young boy who came to serve.

It came in a battered metal teapot, just as Louise remembered, and Kywe poured it into the tiny china cups. It was sweet and cloying, tasting of cardamom and cinnamon. Kywe began to explain to Eve how important tea shops were to Yangon people; a place where everyone came to meet, to pass the time of day, to gossip or discuss current events. Louise's mind wandered as they spoke, relieved that Eve's mood seemed to have lifted. She looked around the other tables. To her relief there wasn't another tourist in sight. A few businessmen sat in one corner, a mother and two children at another table, some students at another.

As she watched, the sky darkened and there was a sudden opening of the clouds; a typical tropical downpour. Passers-by, hardly pausing, put umbrellas up or donned plastic macs and carried on walking; others huddled together in doorways or sheltered under the awnings of shops or food stalls. The serving boys from the teashop scurried outside and began unfurling a plastic curtain over the entrance, to shield the customers. As they worked, two middle-aged women appeared with bright patterned umbrellas and ducked under the plastic sheet. They were laughing at being caught in the downpour; the sound was so spontaneous and full of joy that everyone in the teashop looked up and smiled; there was a moment of shared pleasure.

The two women shook out their umbrellas and sat down at the next table. Louise watched them. Something stirred inside her as she listened to their voices. They were speaking in rapid Burmese, exchanging news and gossip. One of them had her back to Louise, but she could see the face of the other woman plainly.

The woman was about her own age, good-looking and elegantly dressed. As Louise watched, she gradually realised that she recognised those high cheekbones and perfect features. Although the woman's hair was streaked with grey and her features had altered with age, her face seemed familiar. Louise's heart began to beat fast as she realised who she was reminded of. Myat Noe, the young girl with the beautiful face, the gentle smile and such warmth. It was she who had persuaded Zeya to take Louise on the march that day.

Louise was about to get up and cross to the table when her nerves failed her and she was immediately thrown into a dilemma. What if it wasn't Myat Noe after all? Just someone who looked a bit like her? And if it was her, what if she didn't want to be reminded of that day, of what had happened to her friends? It might bring back bad memories. It might be dangerous for her to be recognised, even now.

So instead of acting on her impulse, Louise stayed where she was, pondering these thoughts, sipping her tea and wondering, while Kywe and Eve chatted together. He was explaining some more of the history of the city. Eve seemed to be back to her normal self now, chatting in a relaxed way, asking a hundred and one questions. She has a connection here, Louise thought. She wants to find out as much as she can about the city her father grew up in and where he lived his short life.

As she watched, the woman looked up and caught her eye. She smiled at Louise and her gaze lingered and she frowned, as if puzzled. Then she turned back to her companion and carried on with her conversation.

'Mum,' Eve was saying. She turned to smile at her daughter. 'Shall we go now? Kywe's just been telling me all about Bogyoke market. It's amazing apparently. Full of authentic Burmese antiques and jewellery. If we go now, we'll get there before it packs up for the day.'

'Of course,' Louise said quickly, getting up. Glancing back at the woman again. Perhaps it wasn't Myat Noe after all. She sighed. 'Come on then. Let's go shall we?'

The rain had stopped, but the pavements were still wet, steam rising from them in the heat as they headed towards the market.

'Are you OK Mum?' asked Eve. 'You seemed very quiet in the teashop.'

'I'm fine. A little tired, that's all.'

'Do you want to go back to the hotel and have a rest?'

'I thought you wanted to see the market?'

'Well I did, but we could go tomorrow.'

'I don't want to spoil your day. Why don't you go on with Kywe?'

'Are you sure?'

'Of course. I probably could do with a lie down. You go on. I'll walk back in the direction of the hotel and if I see a taxi I'll flag it down.'

'Well, if you don't mind...' said Eve. Her face was lit up in a smile now and Louise felt a surge of relief. Eve stepped towards her and put her arms around her.

'Thank you for telling me everything today, Mum. I know it wasn't easy.'

Louise hugged Eve to her and held her for a long moment, 'Thank you for being so understanding,' she whispered.

'Let's talk about it later, back at the hotel shall we?'

Louise stood and watched Eve and Kywe disappear into the crowd in the direction of the market, relieved that Eve, in her typical way, had put aside her sadness and embraced her surroundings, keen to make the most of where she was. She watched their backs for a few moments, then she turned and began to walk back in the direction of the teashop. She couldn't leave without finding out, but she sensed that it would be far better to be alone when she did. She walked quickly, hoping against hope that the two women would still be there, fearing that their table might be empty, the tea boy clearing the cups away, wiping down the surface.

But as she approached the shop, her heart skipped a beat. The two women *were* still there, sitting at the table in the entrance, still deep in conversation.

She hesitated for a moment, watching them, then taking a deep breath, and still not sure what to say, she walked up to the table, her nerves taut. The two women stopped speaking and looked up at her, surprise in their eyes.

'Do you speak English?' Louise asked.

'We do! Are you English? Do you need some help? Please – sit down,' the other woman beckoned to her.

'This is going to sound very strange,' she said, sitting down on the chair between them and addressing the one she had recognised, 'but you look so much like someone I met many years ago. I came here when I was young, you see,' she began. She lowered her voice. 'The person I knew was called Myat Noe.'

Both women smiled instantly, astonishment in their eyes.

'Yes. It's me! I am Myat Noe. You know, when you were at that table a few minutes ago, I was wondering whether I'd seen you before. But now I do remember you. You were here that day, weren't you?' she leaned forward and whispered. 'The day of the march in August '88.'

'Yes. I was. It was me. I'm Louise.'

'Louise! Yes, of course. I remember you now. And this is my friend Yupar. She was also with us that day. Do you remember her?'

Louise looked at Myat Noe's companion.

'Of course. Yes I do,'

As the other woman turned and shook her hand she looked into her eyes and remembered Yupar as she'd first seen her all those years ago; a young student, with bright eyes full of hope and passion.

'It is all coming back to me now,' said Myat Noe. 'You were with Zeya, weren't you?'

Louise's heart gave a sickening beat at the sound of his name. She nodded slowly and dropped her gaze, looking down at the table, the pain of loss coming back to her afresh.

'Have you been in touch with him?' asked Yupar gently.

Louise stared at her, not comprehending her words. 'In touch with him?' she repeated.

'Yes,' Myat Noe chipped in. 'He could do with visitors. I try to drop in to see him each day. It will take time for him to adjust. It's early days yet of course.'

Louise could feel the blood draining from her face. Her surroundings became an unfocused blur, as if everything solid around her was melting away, even the ground beneath her chair. She gripped the edge of the table and stared at the two women. No words would come to her. All she could do was shake her head. Yupar was waiting for her to speak, a sympathetic but puzzled frown on her face.

'Are you alright, Louise? Is it the heat in here? It's very close after the rainstorm.'

'No, no, I'm alright. I'm fine. It's just that I thought...' she swallowed. Her mind and emotions were scrambling. Surely there must be some mistake. They must be thinking of someone else. They were still watching her, waiting for her to go on.

'I thought that Zeya had been... that he was dead.'

Yupar reached across the table and took her hand.

'No. No,' she said, leaning forward, speaking in a whisper. 'Zeya is not dead. He was taken away by the soldiers and put in prison on the day of the march. He's been there almost ever since. All these years. Twenty-seven years we campaigned for his release. We did what we could for him and for others like him. They finally let him out about six months ago. It was some sort of... what do you say... amnesty?'

Louise stared at the faces of the two women, looking from one to the other. None of them spoke for several minutes.

'I can hardly believe it,' she said finally, shaking her head slowly. 'I mean...all these years, I've thought...' she stopped herself.

She was going to tell them that she'd seen a group of men shot in the alleyway, Zeya amongst them, but she realised now, for the first time, that it might not have been what she'd seen. She'd seen what she'd assumed to be Zeya's sandals and the bottom of his longyi as she'd been dragged through that alleyway. She hadn't even had the courage to lift her face to look into his eyes. If only she'd turned round and watched what happened, perhaps she would have seen that he'd survived the firing squad... perhaps he wasn't even in that alleyway after all, perhaps it was someone else, she'd mistaken for him in the terror and panic of the moment?

'Is he... is he alright?' she finally asked.

Yupar dropped her gaze and frowned. She leaned forward and once again whispered.

'He is as well as could be expected. He wasn't treated well all the time. The food wasn't good. He has suffered much illness...'

'Poor, poor Zeya,' she pictured his face as they'd set off for the march, his anxiety for her safety, the way he'd touched her cheek.

'You should go and see him,' Yupa repeated. 'As I said, he needs to have visitors.'

'I will,' Louise found herself saying. 'Is he here in the city? Where can I find him?'

Yupar produced a small diary and pencil from her handbag, scribbled an address and tore out the page.

'It is not far from the street where he lived before. Do you have a tourist map of the city?'

Louise nodded and pulled her map from her bag. Myat Noe and Yupar leaned over the map, conferring briefly in Burmese.

Then Yupar marked a cross on the map with her pencil and pointed the street out to Louise.

'It's here. A few streets back from the High Court building. His room is on the ground floor. He has a little yard at the back where he's started a small garden. If he doesn't answer the door, just open it and go through. That's where he'll probably be.'

Louise stared at the address. '35, Seikkantha Street, off Merchant Street, Yangon.'

'Do you think it would be alright to go there without contacting him first?' she asked, 'Perhaps I should try to call him?' her nerves were jangling at the thought of seeing Zeya face to face after all these years.

'Of course!' said Yupar, smiling encouragement. 'He doesn't have a cell-phone or a computer. The world has changed a lot while he was locked away.'

As we said,' said Myat Noe, 'It's good for him to have visitors.'

LOUISE MADE her way along Seikkantha Street, counting the numbers on the doors as she walked. The street was lined with tall terraced houses, just like that other street that was etched on her memory.

When she reached number 35, she stood on the step, in front of the bare wooden door staring at it for a long time. Her stomach was churning, and her heart was beating unnaturally fast. Her mouth was so dry that she wondered if she'd actually be able to form any words if she tried to speak. She was aware that her face was red from walking in the heat, strands of hair were plastered to her forehead and her shirt was sticking to her body. The sultry heat of the late afternoon was at its intense height. Should she go back to the hotel and come back tomorrow? Perhaps it would have been better to give herself time to get used to this momentous news before acting on it?

With these thoughts still swirling around in her head she peered at the bells to the flats in the building. There were ten of them, the writing beside each was Burmese. Panic seized her. How would she know which bell was his?

She was still pondering this when she heard footsteps behind her and a voice said,

'Can I help you?'

She straightened up and whipped around.

It was a Burmese man. About her own age and taller than average. He was dressed in a crisp white shirt and a cotton longyi, but from the way his clothes hung on his body she could tell that he was pitifully thin. His shoulders were stooping slightly, and his grey hair flopped untidily over his forehead. His face was gaunt and sallow skinned and there were deep lines around his eyes and mouth. She looked at him for a second. He frowned and peered back at her, then suddenly his face cleared, and he smiled; a huge wide smile that lit up his whole face. It was impossible for Louise not to respond. She found herself smiling back automatically, even as the tears began to fall.

EPILOGUE

Grace stood at her front door waving as the taxi taking Eve and Louise away from her and back to the train station in Totnes pulled away from the house, passed through the open gateway and out into the lane. Then it disappeared from her line of sight, but she stayed where she was for several minutes, listening to the sound of the engine accelerating up the lane, round the bend and up the hill out of the valley.

She gripped the door frame, temporarily rooted to the spot by the wave of emptiness that washed through her at the knowledge that they'd both gone away again, after their love and laughter had filled the house for the past five days.

It wouldn't be for long, she told herself. Eve would be back in a couple of months, and when she returned, they would be preparing for a journey together. Grace had agreed to go back with Eve to Myanmar later that year.

'I must be mad!' she told herself now, but inwardly she couldn't suppress the excitement the thought of flying out there to South East Asia stirred in her. The outrageousness of it. At her age, and after all these years. She would finally get to see where Jack had suffered during the war.

She'd been reluctant at first.

'But you must come, Eve had insisted, 'I want you to meet Apay Zeya. And he wants to meet you too, Gran.'

How could she refuse her granddaughter that request? When the girl had waited a lifetime to find her real father? Eve had seemed so full of enthusiasm too for her new venture. Zeya had persuaded her to find a job teaching English in a school in one of the poorest parts of Yangon, so they could spend some time together, getting to know one another. She was flying back to start her new job the following week.

'I'm so looking forward to it,' Eve had said to Grace. 'I'll be doing what I love again, in a way that I'm hoping will make a real difference.'

Grace smiled at the thought of Eve's face, radiating hope and enthusiasm.

Louise too had been changed by her journey. She'd hinted that things were about to change in her life too, but she'd stopped short of explaining exactly how or why. Grace had had the impression that Louise was shielding her from something. She sighed and shook her head. Louise would tell her in her own time, she was sure of that. The two of them had got on better over the past few days than they had for years. Grace was even prepared to admit that she might have been unfair and judgmental about her daughter in the past.

She closed the front door, went through to the dining room and sat down at the table. Pulling the manila envelope to her, she eased its contents out. Louise had handed it to her the evening she'd arrived. Her scalp had tingled at the thought of what it contained.

Louise and Eve had tried to persuade her to begin reading it while they were there, but she'd stood firm.

'I've waited all these years. I can wait another few days,' she'd said sharply, and they had known not to push it. Grace needed to be on her own before she could begin.

Now she pulled it towards her and eased the battered note-book out of the envelope. It was falling apart, the pages bulging from the disintegrating cover, soft with age and impregnated with mould and earth from the Burmese jungle.

She sat staring at the front cover for a long time. Just the words on it, 'Jack Summers' Diary' brought tears to her eyes. It was the thought of what this little book must contain, the secrets it harboured that had wrought so much destruction to both their lives. Taking a deep breath Grace steeled herself, opened the notebook and began to read.

ACKNOWLEDGMENTS

Special thanks go to my friend and writing buddy Siobhan Daiko for her constant support and encouragement over the past decade, and for all her help with the formatting and design of the *A Daughter's Promise*; to Trenda Lundin for her inspiring content editing; to Rafa and Xavier at Cover Kitchen for their wonderful cover design; to Jane Addison for her patient proof-reading, to Helen Judd and Mary Clunes for reading and commenting on early drafts; and to everyone who's supported me down the years by reading my books.

ABOUT THE AUTHOR

Ann Bennett was born in Pury End, a small village in Northamptonshire, UK. She read Law at Cambridge and qualified as a solicitor. She started to write in earnest during a career break to have children.

Her first book, *Bamboo Heart: A Daughter's Quest,* was inspired by researching her father's experience as a prisoner of war on the Thai-Burma railway. It won the 2015 Asian Books Blog award for fiction published in Asia. *Bamboo Island: The Planter's Wife, Bamboo Road: The Homecoming, The Tea Planter's Club* and *The Amulet,* are all about WW2 in South East Asia.

She has also written *The Lake Pavilion,* set in British India in the 1930s, *The Lake Palace,* set in India during the Burma Campaign of WWII, *The Lake Pagoda* and *The Lake Villa,* both set in Indochina during WWII.

Ann's other books, *The Runaway Sisters,* bestselling *The Orphan House, The Child Without a Home* and *The Forgotten Children* are published by Bookouture.

Ann is married with three sons and a granddaughter, lives in Surrey and works as a lawyer.

OTHER BOOKS BY ANN BENNETT